# *Satan's Fist*

# Satan's Fist

*Book 1 of Operation Clean Slate*

Mark Kennedy

Satan's Fist

Book 1 of Operation Clean Slate



Published by MKK Publishing

First Edition, 2026

ISBN 979-8-9949731-4-1 (Paperback)

*To my parents, Bob and Peg. I hope that where you are now, you are proud of your son.*

# Contents

# Prologue

It was Mother's Day, May 9th, 2049 when the object – it didn't have any of its colorful names yet – arrived in our solar system. It slipped through the heliopause, the boundary which delineates our sun's influence, unnoticed. Slipped, if you can call traveling at roughly 50 kilometers per second slipping. It would remain unnoticed for nearly ten more Mother's Days. Looming, like an undiagnosed cancer.

On Earth and on Mars, life moved on, unaware. They lived, loved, fought, hated, killed as they had for thousands of years before. As they would, for a while longer, until the uninvited visitor made its presence known.

# CHAPTER 1

## *The Discovery*

*October 20th, 2058.*
*Object distance ~20 AU, Speed unknown.*
*Earth ↔ Mars: ~2.5 AU, Communications: ~21 min one-way.*

• • •

The broadcast had been running for twenty minutes and Robert Hamner had absorbed almost none of it.

He was in the control room at Cerro Paranal, halfway through the handoff between the evening shift and his own, sorting the small administrative debris that accumulated between observations. Equipment logs to sign. A calibration note from Santiago about a detector artifact in the southern array — intermittent, probably thermal, would need monitoring. The automated pipeline had processed the previous night's survey data while the mountain slept, and the results sat in queue, waiting for human eyes. His eyes. He'd get to them in a few minutes.

The control room was a long, low space carved into the shoulder of the mountain — windowless by design, kept at a constant eighteen degrees regardless of what the desert was doing outside. Banks of curved displays lined three walls, most of them running instrument telemetry in the muted blues and grays of the observatory's standard interface. The lighting was dim, tuned to the warm amber that preserved dark adaptation for anyone stepping out to the dome floor. It made the room feel like the inside of a submarine. Hamner had worked this mountain for six years and had stopped noticing.

The Atacama night was clear and still outside the dome. It usually was. That was why they'd built here — one of the driest places on Earth, air so thin and stable that the seeing conditions rivaled space-based platforms. Hamner still noticed the stillness when he stepped outside between shifts — the absolute silence of a place where nothing lived and nothing grew, just rock and sky. Tonight he hadn't stepped outside. The handoff had been routine and the calibration note wanted attention.

On the wallscreen, a woman named Ashford was interviewing Haldane. The chyron identified her as a "journalist" — investigative, by the look of the questions — and him as, well, him. Charles Haldane, the executive director of the Haldane Foundation and God only knew how much more. She was asking about fellowship placements. Where the money went. Which programs, which sectors, what the criteria were for selection.

Haldane was good. Better than good — he was preemptively thorough, the kind of interview subject who answered the follow-up before it was asked. Mid-sixties, silver-haired, with a boardroom tan that had never seen actual sunlight. He sat with the relaxed posture of a man who had never been surprised by a question in his life. The foundation had placed fellows in policy institutes, media organizations, academic research programs. Ashford pressed: the placements spanned an unusual range of sectors. Haldane had numbers. Acceptance rates, completion rates, career outcomes five years post-placement. The data was clean. The answers were specific.

Then Haldane broadened. The fellowship program, he said, was only a portion of what his foundation did. He listed the rest with the practiced ease of a man who had given this speech before: clean water infrastructure in southeast Asia, agricultural development across sub-Saharan Africa, disaster preparedness programs in the Caribbean, educational grants spanning thirty countries and four continents. Maternal health initiatives. Climate-resilient housing. A recently funded study on antibiotic resistance in developing nations. The fellowship program was one line in a portfolio that stretched across every continent and most of the causes that mattered.

Ashford wrapped the segment professionally. Thanked him. No tension in the handoff. Nothing to write about.

Hamner pulled up the calibration note from Santiago and read it twice. The artifact was in the right quadrant of the southern detector — a warm pixel cluster that appeared intermittently during long exposures. Probably a bonding issue in the focal plane. He flagged it for the engineering team and moved on.

"Next up," the anchor said, "our conversation with Alexis Dren."

There was a brief disclosure — the kind that had become standard practice in broadcast journalism over the past decade. Due to the communication delay between Earth and Mars, this interview had been pre-recorded and the delays removed. No content had been edited. The audience absorbed this the way they absorbed all such disclosures: as furniture. Mars was twenty-one light-minutes away at current opposition geometry. Interviews were pre-recorded. This was how things worked now.

Hamner set the calibration note aside and queued the pipeline results. The broadcast continued behind him.

The anchor's tone shifted. It was subtle — a half-degree of hardness, a lean into the questions that hadn't been there with Haldane. Dren was introduced through his holdings: belt mining contracts that supplied raw materials to half the inner system's manufacturing base. Mars-side production facilities that had grown from a single fabrication plant to the largest off-world industrial operation. Launch infrastructure, orbital assets, supply chains that stretched from the asteroid belt to Martian surface depots to spaceports on Earth. The graphic on screen showed the scale of it —

shipping routes traced in blue arcs from the belt to Mars, red lines from Mars to Earth orbit. An empire drawn in logistics.

The anchor pressed: accountability. Who governed an industrial operation that spanned three gravitational wells and operated beyond any single Earth jurisdiction? What oversight existed for a man whose manufacturing capacity exceeded most nations? The stated topic was quarterly industrial output reporting. The actual topic was power.

Dren began to answer. Even in a pre-recorded, delay-scrubbed format, his presence came through — a voice that was sharp and unhurried, a cadence that suggested a man who had heard every version of this question and found them all slightly amusing. He talked about regulatory frameworks that had been written for a world with one inhabited planet and hadn't adapted to a world with two. He talked about Earth's dependence on belt-sourced rare earth elements and deuterium, and how the logistics of that dependence meant that the real leverage in the relationship wasn't where the anchor thought it was. He was charismatic in the way that polarizing figures often were — you either admired the directness or distrusted it, and he didn't seem to care which.

Hamner caught fragments. Mars politics were background noise to him, the way all politics were — something that happened on screens while he worked. He knew the broad outlines. Everyone did. Mars had industrial capacity. Earth had population and institutions. The belt had resources. The three-body problem of twenty-first-century geopolitics played out in trade disputes and regulatory hearings and the occasional Congressional spectacle, and Hamner followed none of it unless someone in the break room had it on.

The control room was quiet. It usually was at this hour — the gap between shifts when the daytime staff had gone home and the night crew had settled into their routines. Mercer was working in the adjacent bay, his screen visible through the glass partition — running calibration checks on tomorrow's observation queue, from the look of it. He was a big man, broad-shouldered, with hands that looked like they belonged on a rock hammer rather than a keyboard. He'd come to observational astronomy late, after a first career in planetary geology, and he still carried himself like someone more comfortable in the field than in front of a terminal. The hum of the cooling systems was the only sound that competed with the broadcast, and it was winning.

The AI pipeline results had loaded. The screen in front of him was far more interesting than the screen on the wall.

It always was. Hamner had been an observer for twenty-three years — fourteen at various facilities, six here at Paranal — and in all that time he had never lost the specific anticipation that came with a fresh night's data. It wasn't excitement, exactly. It was closer to the feeling a chess player had when the board was set up and the clock started: everything was possible, most of it was routine, but the possibility of something that wasn't routine was enough. The pipeline might have found nothing. The pipeline might have found everything. You didn't know until you looked.

He scrolled through the summary queue. The pipeline had done its work overnight — extract sources, match them against the catalogs, flag anything that moved, fit an orbit. Hamner knew its outputs the way a mechanic knew engine sounds. The routine flags that meant nothing. Detector artifacts. Satellite trails. Cosmic ray ghosts. He scrolled past them without reading.

Then he stopped.

An unmatched object. No catalog entry within the positional uncertainty. The orbit fit had been attempted and the result was tagged with a classification he didn't see often. Hyperbolic.

Hamner stared at the flag for ten seconds. His hand had stopped on the scroll surface and he didn't move it. Something in his chest had gone very still — the feeling he'd had exactly once before, twenty years ago at Siding Spring, when an object that shouldn't have been there was there. The amber light of the control room caught the gray at his temples and the reading glasses he'd pushed up onto his forehead an hour ago and forgotten about. He was fifty-four, lean in the way that men who forget to eat lunch tend to be, with deep lines around his eyes from years of squinting at screens in dim rooms. He didn't look like a man having a significant moment. He looked like a man who had stopped scrolling.

For a moment he didn't do anything. The cooling system hummed its indifferent hum and nothing in the room had changed except the screen in front of him and everything the screen implied. Twenty-three years. Twenty-three years of careful, quiet survey work, and the pipeline had just handed him something that might be real. He realized his mouth was dry. He realized he was holding his breath. He let it out slowly, and for one more second he sat with it alone — this thing, this flag on a screen, this possibility that was still his and nobody else's — before he did what he was supposed to do.

Then he leaned back and looked through the glass partition.

"Mercer."

Brian Mercer looked up from his calibration checks. Hamner didn't call people over often. The tone was enough.

"What've you got?"

"Come look at this."

Mercer came through the partition door and pulled a chair up to Hamner's station. He moved the way large men in small spaces learn to move — carefully, aware of the equipment. He read the summary data in silence for a moment — position, brightness, preliminary orbital elements, the hyperbolic tag.

"That's not a marginal eccentricity," Mercer said. "That's well above one."

"I know."

"And detectable at roughly two billion miles out — that's about twenty AU. That's a lot of reflected light for that distance. Pipeline's saying no catalog match?"

"Nothing within the positional uncertainty. I've checked the cross-match twice."

"So either the pipeline's hallucinating, or we've got a seventh."

Hamner nodded. A hyperbolic orbit meant the object was gravitationally unbound — not in a closed ellipse around the sun, not a member of the solar system's permanent inventory. Passing through. An object on a hyperbolic trajectory had come from somewhere else and was going back there. If the orbit fit was correct.

"When was the last confirmed?" Mercer asked.

"6I/Jenkins. Seven years ago. Caught outbound, observed for a few weeks, faded. Before that, 5I/Nakamura in forty-four, 4I/Okonkwo in thirty-eight, 3I/ATLAS in twenty-five. Six confirmed in four decades."

"Right, and none of them were caught this far out."

"No. Oumuamua was post-perihelion. Borisov was inside Mars. ATLAS was outbound. If this is real, it's the first one we've caught early."

Mercer suddenly burst with energy. He clapped Hamner on the shoulder and started to shake him.

"Do you know what this means if it's real Oh, baby, we have *got* to check this out and make sure you've got what it sure looks like you've got!"

Hamner had never seen Mercer this energized. But his excitement was contagious. Hamner felt it growing in him as well.

• • •

They went to the raw data together.

Hamner pulled the previous night's imaging — four exposures of the same field, separated by intervals calibrated for motion detection. The technique was old — fundamentally the same blink comparison that Clyde Tombaugh had used to find Pluto in 1930, updated with digital frames and software alignment but still, at its core, two human beings looking at images and asking: did something move?

He blinked between them. Frame one. Frame two. Frame three. Frame four.

“There!“ Mercer said, pointing. A point source shifting against the fixed stellar background. Consistent rate of motion. Consistent direction.

“Not a cosmic ray,” Hamner said. “Those show up in one frame and vanish.”

“Not a detector artifact — those stay fixed while the stars drift. And the catalog cross-match would have caught any known asteroid,” he continued.

“So it’s real. Something’s moving out there. Something the pipeline says is hyperbolic,” Mercer added, rubbing his hands like a child waiting for candy.

“The pipeline says a lot of things. I know the pipeline’s the pipeline. But to trust it to something this big? No, let’s check the old fashioned way,” Hamner decided.

Mercer paused at that. “You’re sure? You doubt the pipeline?” he asked, genuinely confused.

“It’s my way, it won’t take me that long,” Hamner assured him.

Hamner reran the orbit fit independently — his own constraints, a different minimization algorithm than the pipeline’s default. He tightened the error bounds, excluded the noisiest position measurements, and forced the fit to explore both bound and unbound solutions. Mercer watched the computation converge. He was gripping the edge of the console and moving impatiently. Hamner didn’t think Mercer knew he was doing it.

“Same answer!“ Mercer said confidently. “See? I told you. Same answer. Hyperbolic. Inbound.“

Hamner agreed. He checked the residuals — the difference between the fitted orbit and the actual measured positions. “Residuals are small. Consistent. No systematic trend. The fit’s clean.”

“What about a second source? Can we cross-check?” Mercer asked. He was already pulling his chair closer.

"Already looking." Hamner pulled up the belt-based infrared survey archive — one of the distributed observatories that had been seeded through the asteroid belt over the past fifteen years. The same region of sky, covered several days earlier. "Here! The Japanese belt telescope flagged it too. Unmatched, anomalous, low confidence score because they only had two exposures."

"But now we've got four, plus their two!" Mercer said, going in for a high five.

"And we've got parallax." Hamner's voice changed — not louder, but tighter, the way a voice gets when the chest muscles contract around it. The angular offset between the belt telescope's position and their position on Earth meant they were looking at the same object from two points separated by billions of kilometers. The geometry was simple. The distance fell out directly.

"Twenty AU," Mercer said, reading the result. "Consistent with the pipeline's estimate, but now it's measured, not inferred." He slapped the console. Once, flat-handed, the way a man slaps a table when the hand needs somewhere to go. Then he caught himself and went still again.

"And with distance pinned down, the angular motion converts to a physical speed."

"How fast?" Mercer asked.

"High. Significantly higher than anything in a bound solar orbit at that distance."

They sat with that for a moment. Two independent instruments, two independent methods, converging on the same answer. The belt parallax had turned a preliminary flag into a confirmed detection. Hamner's pulse was doing something it hadn't done in a control room in twenty years. He could feel it in his throat.

"All right," Mercer said. His voice was steady again, but his knee was bouncing under the console. "What else does the characterization tell us?"

Hamner pulled up the photometric data. "Size: large. Larger than any previous interstellar detection, based on the parallax-calibrated brightness. Spectral data's limited at this range — the object's faint despite its size — but what we have doesn't match standard cometary profiles cleanly."

"How so?" Mercer asked.

"Spectral slope's steeper than expected. Colors are off. Not drastically — but enough to note."

Hamner frowned at the display. The excitement that had been building in his chest shifted, not disappearing but changing shape — the way a clear signal develops static. Something about the spectral profile wasn't sitting right. He wasn't ready to say what.

"Interstellar composition," Mercer said. Not a question. An explanation, offered before Hamner had finished frowning. "Different formation environment. Different stellar metallicity in the home system. You'd expect the colors to be off."

"Maybe," Hamner said. He was still looking at the profile.

"And there's this." He pointed to the photometric data. "Look at the light curve."

Mercer looked. "There isn't one."

"Exactly. Flat line. Four exposures across several hours, and the brightness doesn't vary at all. No rotational signature."

Hamner sat back. The spectral anomaly was one thing — explainable, marginal, the kind of oddity that showed up in interstellar objects because they formed somewhere else. But flat photometry at this size was different. Most bodies this size tumbled. You should see something — a period, an amplitude, a wobble. A flat light curve meant the object was either oriented pole-on, or nearly spherical, or spinning so slowly that four hours couldn't resolve it. None of those were impossible. But together with the spectral slope, together with the size, together with the velocity — he was aware of a pattern forming at the edge of his thinking that he didn't want to look at directly. Not yet. Not with this little data.

"Pole-on orientation," Mercer said immediately. "Statistically unlikely but not remarkable. Or a long rotation period — spinning so slowly that four hours can't resolve it. That's the easiest one to test with follow-up." He was talking faster than usual. Hamner noticed it the way you notice a change in engine pitch — not alarming, but noted. Mercer was filling the silence where the questions would go.

"Note it and move on?" Mercer asked.

Hamner hesitated. The hesitation lasted less than a second. Then he nodded and typed it into the characterization section: *No detected rotational variability. Flat photometry across observation window. Possible pole-on geometry, high symmetry, or long rotation period. Follow-up photometric monitoring recommended.*

One line among dozens. They moved on.

But the frown stayed. Not on Hamner's face — he'd smoothed that out before Mercer could read it. In his chest, where the excitement had been, something else was settling in. Not alarm. Not suspicion. A question he couldn't quite form, sitting underneath the data like a shape under ice.

• • •

The trajectory computation was Hamner's work — Mercer danced back to his bay to start drafting the notification template while Hamner ran the numbers.

An orbit told you the shape of the path. A trajectory told you where the object was going and what it would pass on the way. Hamner ran it against Earth, Mars, Venus, Mercury, and Jupiter, propagating the motion forward through the gravitational field of the solar system with the standard N-body integrator.

"Mercer."

Mercer came back to the partition door. "What?"

"Miss. Several million miles. Not a threat."

"That's good. Though, it would have been more exciting," Mercer laughed.

"I don't need exciting. I'm just glad it's below the threshold for even a preliminary notification to planetary defense."

“So your great find is scientifically extraordinary and existentially boring,” Mercer concluded, dropping his voice an octave for effect. His knee had stopped bouncing. The energy that had been building in him all night —had drained out somewhere between “not a threat” and “planetary defense.” He was still smiling, but the smile had settled into something closer to professional satisfaction, which was a lesser thing, and they both knew it.

“That’s a way to put it.” Hamner pulled up the trajectory plot on the main screen. “Closest approach is comfortable by any standard. I perturbed the initial conditions — nudged the position and velocity within uncertainty bounds — and every realization produces a clear miss. The uncertainty cloud’s wide, but it’s entirely on the safe side.”

“What about inclination?” Mercer inquired.

Hamner paused. He hadn’t mentioned it yet, but it was there in the trajectory summary. “Low. 2.3 degrees to the ecliptic.”

Mercer raised an eyebrow. “That’s flat. Interstellar objects should come in from random directions.”

“One in ten random trajectories would fall within that range. It’s a coincidence. Interesting for the population statistics,” Hamner said confidently.

“And not interesting for anything else?” Mercer asked, the playfulness returning to his voice.

“Not interesting for anything else.”

Mercer nodded slowly. “You’re going to note it in the report.”

“One line. No emphasis,” Hamner said.

“Good. That’s the right call. Let’s get this baby written up,“ Mercer concluded.

• • •

The notification followed a format that hadn’t changed much in decades, despite everything else that had.

The form was standardized. The fields were specific. The language was deliberately flat — designed to convey information without interpretation, to let the data speak and the reader decide. Hamner appreciated this. He'd read discovery announcements that tried to be exciting and found them embarrassing. The data was either interesting or it wasn't. Adjectives didn't help.

He and Mercer worked through it together. Object designation: pending formal assignment, but he'd propose 7I/Hamner. The I-number for interstellar, following the convention established after 'Oumuamua. The seventh. Discovery circumstances: Cerro Paranal, ESO VLT Survey Telescope, pipeline version 4.7.2, human verification by the discoverer. Astrometric positions and times for all four exposures, plus the belt telescope parallax data. Preliminary orbital elements with formal uncertainties. Estimated absolute magnitude, calibrated against the parallax distance. The flat photometry, noted without interpretation. The ecliptic coincidence, listed as a statistical property of the trajectory. The hyperbolic excess velocity, now firmly established by the combined dataset. The recommendation for immediate follow-up observations across all available platforms.

Hamner sent it at 03:47 local time. Mercer was standing behind him, coffee in hand.

The first response arrived in eleven minutes — a confirming redirect from an automated telescope in Chile that had slewed to the coordinates and acquired the target within its survey queue.

"And so it begins," Mercer said, his voice artificially deep.

Hamner didn't answer. He knew what he meant. What would begin once you put a discovery into the system. But Hamner had heard something else in the words, or felt it — the moment when the thing on his screen stopped being his and became everyone's. The first response had taken eleven minutes. The next would take less. By morning the object would belong to a hundred telescopes and a thousand inboxes and none of them would remember what the control room had felt like at three in the morning when it was just two men and a flag on a screen.

Then a scheduling request from the European Southern Observatory's Mars orbital platform. The object was in its observable sky and the platform had the sensitivity to do spectroscopy that ground-based instruments couldn't match at this distance. The request was flagged urgent — someone on the Mars-side scheduling team was awake and paying attention.

Then a burst. Three responses in ninety seconds: two additional telescope redirects — one from the Canary Islands, one from the South African Large Telescope — and a terse message from a senior astronomer at the Harvard-Smithsonian Center for Astrophysics. No pleasantries. No congratulations. No commentary on the significance of a seventh interstellar detection. Just five words: Send positions. Including belt parallax.

"Friendly," Mercer said.

"That's Vasquez's group. They don't do friendly. They do fast," Hamner said.

Hamner sent the positions.

The community had the scent now. Within an hour, telescope scheduling queues on three continents and two planets were being reshuffled to accommodate 7I/Hamner. Priority overrides were being filed. Director's discretionary time was being claimed. Graduate students were being woken up.

The pipeline at the Pan-STARRS facility in Hawaii independently recovered the object in archival data — a faint trace in exposures taken three weeks earlier, too dim to trigger automated flagging at the time but visible in retrospect now that someone knew where to look. The additional positions stretched the observational arc from days to weeks. The orbital solution tightened. The eccentricity firmed up. The hyperbolic classification was no longer preliminary. Everything the pipeline had computed, and everything Hamner and Mercer had verified by hand, held under the weight of additional data.

The name would stick. 7I/Hamner. It would appear in the circulars and the databases and the scheduling queues and eventually the press releases. Not his choice of legacy — he'd spent his career doing careful, quiet survey work, the kind that produced catalog entries, not headlines — but the designation rules were clear. He'd found it, verified it, and proposed the name — and nobody would challenge it.

The wallscreen was still running. Neither of them had looked at it in over an hour. The broadcast had moved on from Dren to something else — weather, or markets, or one of the small catastrophes that filled the spaces between the interviews that mattered.

Hamner's terminal chimed. A new message, flagged priority, from a name he recognized — deputy director of the Solar System Dynamics group at the Jet Propulsion Laboratory. The subject line was three words: Regarding your object.

Mercer read it over his shoulder. "JPL. Fast."

"Yea, they would be."

The machinery had taken over. The discovery was in the system now, moving through channels that Hamner could observe but no longer control. The telescopes would track it. The orbit would refine. The papers would be written, the press releases drafted, the allocation committees convened, the conference sessions scheduled.

The object was twenty astronomical units away and closing, and the entire apparatus of planetary science was beginning to turn toward it with the slow, grinding thoroughness of a machine that had been built for exactly this purpose.

Outside, the Atacama was doing what it always did — nothing. Hamner could feel the mountain under him the way you felt a building's hum when you'd been inside it long enough — the thermal regulation, the dome mechanisms cycling, the deep vibration of a place designed to be still. His coffee had gone cold hours ago. He picked it up and drank it anyway, the way he always did, because the taste was familiar and the night was not.

Hamner opened the message from JPL and began to read.

# CHAPTER 2

*The Anomaly*

*December 15th, 2058.*
*Object at ~18 AU, ~50 km/s. 557 days to orbital intersect.*
*Earth ↔ Mars: ~2.3 AU, Communications: ~19 min one-way.*

• • •

Two months after the discovery, Robert Hamner's life had become unrecognizable.

Not dramatically — he still worked the same shifts at Paranal, still signed the same equipment logs, still drank the same bad coffee from the same machine in the break room that nobody had fixed since before he'd arrived. But the margins of his days had filled with something new: other people's urgency.

His apartment in Antofagasta smelled like a place nobody lived in. He'd noticed it last Tuesday, coming back after three consecutive nights on the mountain — the stale air, the dishes he'd left in the sink, the bed made with the mechanical precision of a man who hadn't slept in it long enough to disturb the covers. He'd stood in the doorway for a moment, keys in hand, and thought: this is what happens when the work eats the rest of it. Then he'd dropped his bag and gone to sleep, and the thought had gone wherever thoughts go when you're too tired to hold them.

The discovery of 7I/Hamner had done what interstellar objects always did to the planetary science community — it had set the machinery to maximum speed and pointed every available instrument at a single dot of light. Telescopes worldwide had been redirected. The venerable Webb, thirty-seven years into a mission that had been designed for ten, had been allocated observation time over the protests of three competing programs. The ESO Mars orbital platform was running continuous spectroscopic monitoring. Belt-based survey telescopes had adjusted their scheduling queues. The Americans, the Europeans, and the Chinese had all filed competing observation campaigns, each arguing that their instruments were uniquely suited to the task and that the other proposals were redundant.

Hamner was at the center of it. Not by choice — by convention. The discoverer was the point of contact. The person whose inbox absorbed the scheduling conflicts, the data-sharing requests, the interview inquiries. He had become a coordinator, an administrator, a switchboard.

The observatory had assigned him a postdoc — Lena Soares, a Brazilian-born data analyst who had been finishing a fellowship in astrometric calibration when the discovery redirected her career along with everything else. She was short, dark-haired, and moved through the control room like she'd been there for years rather than weeks — already knowing which terminals had the sticky keyboards and which chairs had broken lumbar support. Sharp, organized, and utterly unimpressed by the significance of the object she was helping to track. This made her useful. She managed the data flow, wrangled the scheduling conflicts, and translated Hamner's terse directives into the diplomatic language that multi-institutional collaborations required. Hamner had worked with postdocs who needed managing. Soares managed herself.

"The Japanese consortium wants to know if we'll share raw tracking data before the first paper," Soares said, dropping a tablet on his desk one afternoon. "And the Mars platform is requesting an extension through February. Again."

Mercer leaned through the doorframe before Hamner could answer. "Tell them yes and yes. We've been over this."

"I'm not telling them anything until Hamner tells me to tell them," Soares said, without looking up.

"Yes to the extension, conditional on the data release," Hamner said. "We share everything. That's the deal."

"That's going to make the Europeans nervous," Mercer observed.

"The Europeans are always nervous. Send it," Hamner said.

Soares typed something on her tablet and disappeared. Mercer lingered.

"Characterization meeting at three," Mercer said. "Kimura's joining from the Mars platform — nineteen-minute delay, so it'll be the usual awkward pauses. And Vasquez's group at Harvard sent their spectral analysis overnight. You've read it?"

"I've read it," Hamner said flatly.

"And?"

"Three o'clock, Mercer," Hamner sighed.

• • •

The interview requests had started within hours of the discovery announcement and hadn't stopped. Hamner had done six in the first week — two print, two broadcast, two for outlets he'd never heard of — and then told Soares to decline everything that came in after that. She'd been declining them ever since, with a form response that cited ongoing observation commitments and directed inquiries to the ESO press office.

Jessica Saunders got through anyway, because she didn't go through Soares.

She'd contacted Kimura on the Mars platform, who'd told her Hamner was the person to talk to. Vasquez at Harvard had said the same thing. The ESO press office had offered a fifteen-minute phone call. She'd said she didn't want a phone call — she wanted two days at Paranal. The press office had said no. She'd sent them a list of her previous work and said she'd wait.

The press office called Hamner directly, which they never did.

"She's persistent," the press liaison said, with the tone of someone who had tried and failed to make a problem go away.

"They're all persistent."

"She's not like the others. She's the senior science correspondent for the Meridian Science Monitor. She has a doctorate in planetary geology from Caltech that she never uses but never hides. She's the one they call when they want coverage that doesn't make them cringe."

Hamner sighed. "Two days."

"Two days. And Robert — she asked specifically about the phase curve data. Not the size, not the trajectory. The phase curve."

That was unusual. Hamner filed it and went back to work.

She arrived on a Wednesday afternoon, driving up from Antofagasta in a rented SUV that she parked in the visitor lot like she'd been there before. She had — twice, covering instrument upgrades for the VLT, which she mentioned in passing and didn't dwell on. Mid-thirties, maybe. Dark hair pulled back. Dressed like someone who'd packed for a mountain in the desert, not a television studio. She carried a messenger bag with a tablet, a voice recorder, and a notebook — actual paper, bound, unlined — which Hamner noticed because nobody used paper anymore. The people who did usually had a reason, and hers was obvious enough once he thought about it: paper had no metadata, no sync history, no remote access. You couldn't subpoena it from a server or wipe it without touching it. For an investigative journalist, a paper notebook wasn't a relic. It was tradecraft.

They met in the break room because everywhere else was either occupied or too cold. Hamner poured coffee for both of them without asking. She accepted it without comment.

"Dr. Hamner. Thank you for the time. I know you've been buried."

"I've been declining interviews for two months."

"I know. I read the form response." She opened the notebook — not the tablet — and clicked a pen. "I've read the discovery circular, the preliminary characterization summary, the working group's first two data releases, and Vasquez's spectral analysis that went up last week. I want to talk about the things the press releases aren't covering."

Hamner studied her. Most journalists opened with the question that would make the best headline: Is it a threat? Could it hit Earth? Is it alien? The ones who'd done their homework opened with size or speed, because those were the numbers that translated to television graphics. Nobody opened with what the press releases weren't covering, because that required knowing what the press releases contained.

"Such as?"

"The albedo." She said it the way a person says a word they've been using professionally for years — no emphasis, no self-consciousness. "Your characterization summary reports an albedo lower than typical cometary nuclei. Dark object, dark surface, consistent with irradiated organic crust. That's the standard template for interstellar objects with anomalous spectral profiles. Fine."

She looked up from the notebook. "But the phase curve is flat. No opposition surge, no rolloff. And the polarimetry shows no variation with phase angle. If the surface is rough enough to produce that kind of isotropic backscatter — which is the explanation that flattens the phase curve — then the albedo should show microvariation as the object rotates. Rough surfaces scatter light differently at different rotational aspects. You'd see it in the photometry as low-amplitude periodicity. And you're not seeing it." She paused. "Which means either the surface is perfectly uniform at every scale the photometry can resolve, or the object isn't rotating.

And a body that size, with that density, that isn't rotating — that's not in your press release."

The break room was quiet. The coffee machine gurgled to itself in the corner.

Hamner set his mug down. "Where did you study?"

"Caltech. Planetary surfaces. I wrote my thesis on regolith scattering models for C-type asteroids."

"And then you became a journalist."

"And then I realized I was better at explaining science than doing it. Different skill." She clicked the pen again — a habit, not a nervous tic. "Dr. Hamner, I'm not here to write a headline about alien spacecraft. My readers are educated, curious, and they'll know if I'm faking it. I want to write about what this object actually is, what we actually know, and what the data is telling you that you haven't said publicly yet. Not because you're hiding it — because it's too early and you're being careful. I understand careful. I'm asking you to let me watch the process."

Hamner drank his coffee. He thought about the flat phase curve, and the low albedo, and the ecliptic coincidence, and the density that didn't match any cometary template. He thought about his private log — the accumulating file of things that were individually meaningless and collectively nothing. Not yet. And he thought about the fact that it had been two months since anyone had walked into his control room and immediately seen the shape of what was bothering him.

He thought about every other journalist who'd contacted him in the past two months. None of them had connected the albedo to the phase curve to the rotation question. None of them had even known there was a rotation question.

"The characterization meeting is at three," he said. "You can sit in. You don't record, you don't quote anyone without clearance, and anything you write gets reviewed by the press office before it goes out."

"Understood."

“And Saunders — if you write the phrase ‘alien spacecraft’ in any context other than debunking it, you’re off the mountain.”

She almost smiled. “Understood.”

• • •

The conference room at Paranal was small, functional, and perpetually too cold — an artifact of the cooling systems that kept the instruments at operating temperature and the humans as an afterthought. The shared display along the back wall still showed annotations from the previous meeting — orbital parameters in blue, scheduling conflicts in red, someone’s coffee order in black that nobody had bothered to clear. Hamner sat at the head of the table because nobody else would sit there. Mercer was to his left, laptop open, his big frame making the ergonomic chair look undersized. Soares was across from him, managing the remote connections on the wallscreen. Dr. Asha Patel, a spectroscopist from the ESO science team who had been seconded to the observation campaign in November, had taken the chair nearest the door, which she always did and which Hamner suspected was a commentary on meeting length. She was a compact woman in her forties with reading glasses on a chain and an expression that suggested she had somewhere better to be, which she probably did.

On the wallscreen, Dr. Kimura’s face appeared from the Mars orbital platform — frozen for a moment in the lag, then animated, then frozen again. The nineteen-minute delay made real-time discussion impossible, so Kimura had pre-recorded his updates and would respond to questions in the next cycle. It was clumsy but functional. Everyone was used to it.

“Let’s start with size and albedo,” Hamner said. “Lena, where are we?”

Soares pulled up the consolidated dataset on the wallscreen, overlaying it next to Kimura’s frozen face. “Size estimates have crept upward since October. The parallax distance is firm, the brightness calibrations are consistent across instruments, and the albedo is low — lower than typical cometary nuclei. It's darker than we thought, which means it's physically larger than the brightness alone suggested."

"How much larger?" Patel asked.

"Current best fit puts it comfortably beyond any previously observed cometary nucleus," Soares said. "We're in new territory for this class of object."

Mercer leaned back in his chair. "Which raises questions about internal structure. Something this big with cometary composition should be fragile — a rubble pile, loosely bound. Tidal stress from the sun should be a concern at perihelion."

"That depends on the density," Hamner said. "Kimura?"

He pressed play on Kimura's pre-recorded segment. Kimura's voice was calm and precise, the cadence of a researcher accustomed to composing his thoughts for delayed transmission: "Thermal observations from the platform, combined with the refined size estimates, allow a rough density calculation. The shape is still uncertain at this distance, and density depends on volume, which depends on shape. But even with generous assumptions about elongation and porosity, the number is high."

Kimura paused in the recording — a pause he'd left for effect, or perhaps just for breath. "Not impossibly high. There are metallic asteroids with comparable bulk densities. But for a body of presumed cometary origin — interstellar or otherwise — the thermal profile suggests something more consolidated than we'd expect. Comets are loose aggregations of ice and dust. This object's signature is more consistent with competent rock, or a mix of rock and metal with minimal porosity."

The recording ended. Nineteen minutes until he'd hear their response.

"So it's dense," Patel said flatly. "Dense and dark. That doesn't match any standard cometary template."

"It doesn't have to," Mercer said. "It's interstellar. Different formation environment, different stellar metallicity, different ice ratios, different everything. We're applying solar system templates to an object that didn't form in the solar system."

"I know that," Patel said, somewhat shortly. "I'm the one who wrote the spectral analysis. Which brings us to the next problem." She turned to Hamner. "You've read Vasquez's team's work?"

"Yes, I've read it," Hamner responded, a little annoyed by the question.

"Then you know the surface doesn't match anything clean. Spectral slope is steeper than expected. The absorption features for common ices — water, CO2, methane — are either weak or absent. It's dark and spectrally bland." Patel brought up a comparison chart on her section of the wallscreen. "This is 7I against the standard templates. Carbonaceous asteroid — partial match on albedo, wrong spectral slope. D-type asteroid — closer on slope, wrong albedo. Cometary nucleus — wrong on both. Irradiated organic surface — best match, but even that has problems."

"Irradiated organic crust is the explanation that's going to stick," Mercer said. "The 'Oumuamua template."

"It's the 'Oumuamua hand-wave," Patel said. "We keep applying the same patch to the same hole."

Hamner let the exchange settle. Patel wasn't wrong. The irradiated organic crust model was a catchall — it explained any dark, spectrally red surface by invoking a process that was physically plausible and practically unfalsifiable. You couldn't prove it wrong because you couldn't measure the interstellar radiation history of a specific object. It was the explanation of last resort, and it had become the explanation of first resort.

"Note it in the characterization summary," Hamner said. "Best-fit model is irradiated organic surface, with caveats about the template limitations. We flag the discrepancies and recommend follow-up spectroscopy at closer range."

He pulled up his own notes on the wallscreen. "One more thing before trajectory."

He put the phase curve plot on the screen. For any rough-surfaced sphere, the brightness should follow a predictable pattern as the viewing geometry changed — a surge when you looked almost straight down the sun line, where shadows disappeared and every grain of surface scattered light back at you, then a smooth falloff as the angle widened. The polarization of scattered light should vary too, in ways that depended on surface texture and curvature. Every well-characterized solar system body showed these signatures. Astronomers called the brightness spike the opposition surge. It was one of the most reliable diagnostics in photometry.

"We're not seeing it," Hamner said. "The curve is flat. No surge, no rolloff. And the polarimetry shows no variation with phase angle."

Patel looked at the data. "That's unusual."

A flat phase curve with no polarimetric variation meant either the surface had unusual reflective properties or the geometry wasn't what they assumed.

"Could be a surface effect," Mercer said. "Highly porous regolith, deep surface roughness — you'd get isotropic backscatter that flattens the phase curve. Washes out the opposition surge. We've seen it on some Kuiper Belt objects."

"At this albedo?" Hamner said.

"Low albedo doesn't rule out isotropic scattering. A dark, rough surface can still flatten a phase curve. The models aren't well constrained for interstellar objects because we've had exactly one before this, and we barely had photometry on that." Mercer shrugged. "It's interesting, but it's within the noise of what we don't know about these surfaces."

Hamner looked at the phase curve data a moment longer. He added it to the characterization notes, flagged it as anomalous, and moved on.

"Trajectory," he said.

Soares brought up the orbital solution. "Two months of continuous tracking plus the archival recovery data. The uncertainty has collapsed. Miss distance is now 3.9 million miles, plus or minus a hundred thousand. Hazard assessment: negligible."

"And the inclination?" Hamner asked.

"Still low. 2.1 degrees to the ecliptic, tight uncertainties."

Mercer glanced at the number. "7I's really threading the needle on that ecliptic. Weird coincidence."

"One in ten," Hamner said. "Coincidences happen."

"Sure they do," Patel said, already closing her laptop. "Are we done?"

They were done. The characterization campaign had produced its results, the working group had processed them, and the consensus had formed around the table without friction. Fascinating interstellar visitor. Unusually large. Unusually dense. Unusual composition. Clear miss. No threat. Schedule observations through perihelion. Publish early results.

The conference room was cold. It was always cold, but now it was cold and empty and the arc was still on the screen and the chairs were pushed back at the angles people had left them and nobody was here to fill the silence with explanations. He put his hands flat on the table. They were steady. He looked at them as if checking, and then he looked at the trajectory plot one more time, and the 2.1-degree inclination, and the flat phase curve data still minimized in the corner of the display, and he felt the shape of something he couldn't name pressing against the underside of his thinking like water under ice.

He closed the display and went back to work.

Saunders was waiting in the corridor. She'd sat through the entire meeting in a chair against the back wall, notebook open, pen moving occasionally, saying nothing. Hamner had almost forgotten she was there, which he suspected was the point.

"Dr. Hamner. Do you have five minutes?"

He didn't, but he stopped.

She flipped back a few pages in the notebook. "I want to make sure I understood what just happened in there. For my readers, not for the journal."

"Go ahead."

"The object is bigger than you originally thought, because it's darker than you originally thought. Darker surface means it reflects less light, which means the amount of light you're seeing represents a bigger object than you'd assumed. And it's denser than a comet should be — more like solid rock than a dirty snowball."

"That's correct so far."

"And the surface doesn't match anything in your catalog. You're using a model — irradiated organic crust — that's basically a catchall for 'we don't know what this surface is, but cosmic radiation could plausibly produce it.' And you used the same model for the last interstellar object because nothing better fit then either."

The corner of Hamner's mouth twitched. "You're making Dr. Patel's argument."

"Dr. Patel was making a good argument." Saunders clicked the pen. "So here's what I'd write for my readers. You've found something that's too big, too dense, and too dark to be a normal comet. It doesn't match anything in our solar system. And the best explanation for its surface is 'billions of years of radiation damage,' which you can't test because you can't replay billions of years of radiation. It's the explanation that works because it can't be proven wrong."

"That's — yes, that's essentially what we're saying."

"But here's the part I want to check." She looked up from the notebook. "The phase curve. You said the brightness doesn't change the way it should as your viewing angle changes. And in the break room, I pointed out that connects to the rotation question — if it's not showing brightness variation, either the surface is perfectly uniform or it's not spinning. But in the meeting, Dr. Mercer offered another explanation. Rough surface, isotropic backscatter. So my question is: could it just be that the surface is so rough that it scatters light equally in all directions, like a dark sponge?"

"That's one possibility."

"So it's a dark, dense, non-comet-like rock that's either not rotating — which would be very strange for something that's been traveling through interstellar space — or has a surface so uniformly rough that it looks the same from every angle. And your team is treating both of those as 'interesting but not alarming.'"

Hamner considered the summary. It was accurate. It was clear. And it was missing one thing.

"You left out the third option," he said.

She waited.

"The surface could be geometrically simple. A shape with minimal curvature variation would produce a flat phase curve regardless of rotation. A sphere would do it, but so would —" He paused. He was about to say a cylinder, and the word felt wrong in his mouth for reasons he couldn't articulate. "So would other regular geometries. We can't resolve the shape at this distance. We're inferring surface properties from photometry, but the photometry is degenerate — multiple shapes and surfaces can produce the same brightness profile."

Saunders was watching him from the back wall. He could feel it without looking — the specific attention of someone who had just seen a person almost say something and then not say it. He kept his eyes on the display and his voice on the technical explanation, and after a moment the feeling passed. But the shape of the unsaid word sat in his chest like a stone he'd swallowed.

"So you can't tell the difference between 'weird surface' and 'weird shape' from this far away," she said.

"Not until it's closer, or until we get better data."

Saunders wrote something in the notebook. "That's what I'll lead with. Not 'mysterious object baffles scientists' — that's every headline already. What I want to write is: here's what the data actually looks like, here's what it tells us, and here's what we honestly can't determine yet. The ambiguity is the story."

Her pen had stopped moving. She was looking at what she'd written with an expression Hamner couldn't quite read — not satisfaction or confusion. Something closer to the look a person gets when they realize the story they came to write isn't the story that's here. The pen hovered over the page for a moment, and then she closed the notebook on it, marking the place, and looked up.

"That," Hamner said, "is the first time a journalist has said something to me that I didn't want to argue with."

She almost smiled. "Can I sit in on the next update? When new data comes in?"

"When new data comes in," Hamner said, and left it at that.

He walked back to the control room. The corridor was empty and cold and lit by the emergency strips that ran along the baseboards at ankle height. His footsteps echoed. Somewhere below him, the mountain's cooling systems cycled through their thermal regulation sequence, keeping the instruments at the temperature they needed to see clearly. The instruments didn't have stomachs. They didn't tighten when the data looked wrong. They just measured, and the measurements sat in the pipeline, and the pipeline waited for human eyes. His eyes. He sat down at his terminal and pulled up the private log — the file that wasn't part of any data release, the one where he wrote the things that weren't ready to be sentences yet — and added one line. Then he closed it and went back to work.

# CHAPTER 3

## *Directions*

*December 15th, 2058.*

*Object at ~18 AU, ~50 km/s. 557 days to orbital intersect.*

*Earth ↔ Mars: ~2.3 AU, Communications: ~19 min one-way.*

• • •

Chloe Ashford was brushing her teeth in her DC apartment when she decided to tell Greg about the Haldane connection.

She could hear him in the bedroom — the creak of the mattress, the click of his phone being set on the nightstand. He'd gotten in from Cleveland around seven, dropped his garment bag in the hallway, and eaten leftover pad thai standing at the kitchen counter while she finished a database query. They'd managed about forty minutes of overlapping consciousness before the day caught up with both of them. This was the relationship: two schedules that intersected when the geometry allowed, and the rest of the time they were somewhere else being someone else's problem.

"So I found something today," she said, around the toothbrush.

From the bedroom: "Yeah?"

She spat, rinsed, checked her face in the mirror — forty-one and it was starting to show around the eyes, though that might have been the bathroom lighting — and walked out past the bedroom door toward the office. The spare bedroom across the hall, or what had been a spare bedroom before she'd converted it. Greg was propped against the headboard with the lamp on his side still lit. He was a pleasant-looking man — square jaw, kept himself in reasonable shape, the kind of face you'd cast as "supportive husband" in a pharmaceutical ad. He sold surgical robotics systems for a company based in Research Triangle, which meant he spent three weeks out of four in hospitals and hotel rooms across the eastern seaboard. When people asked how the relationship worked, Ashford usually said they were both too busy to get on each other's nerves. It was meant as a joke. It was also the truth.

"You know the influence mapping thing I've been doing?" she called from the office. "The fellowship placements?"

"The foundations. Yeah."

She stood in front of the investigation display, scanning the connections she'd mapped there. Funding charts and organizational trees layered three deep on the air-gapped screen. Her laptop sat open on the desk, running the database she'd built herself because the bureau's tools weren't granular enough. The room told the story of four months of work that refused to become a story.

"So the original lead — the one from the Department of War source, the mid-level administrator who noticed all those fellowship recipients ending up in policy positions —" She pulled a pin, moved a card, replaced the pin. Stood back. Moved it again.

"Career positions. Not appointed. Right, you told me," Greg said. He'd raised his voice slightly to carry across the hall.

"Right. No Senate confirmation, no media attention. Just people quietly ending up in policy-adjacent roles across multiple agencies. She mentioned it as a curiosity over drinks. I heard it as a pattern." Ashford pulled her hair back and started working it into a loose braid — the absentminded kind she did when she was processing, not the deliberate kind she did for the camera. "So I've been widening the net for four months, and three weeks ago I hit a new node. Fresh Start Foundation."

She walked back through the bedroom toward the bathroom, braiding as she went. Greg's eyes tracked her across the room.

"Don't know it," he said.

"You wouldn't." "They're mid-tier — not big enough for regular scrutiny, not small enough to be invisible. But they have a specific ideological angle that makes them more interesting than the generic civic-engagement shops. Their position is that automation and material abundance are eroding human purpose. That people are meant to work, to struggle, to solve problems that matter. And when survival is guaranteed, communities atrophy."

"That's not crazy," Greg said from the bedroom.

"No, it's not. They fund programs that match the philosophy — skills training, local food production, off-grid energy systems, civic service initiatives." "It's post-industrial nostalgia sharpened into policy. Things were better when people had to earn their lives, and the current course is making humanity fragile."

"Sounds like half my clients in the Rust Belt."

She walked back to the office.

"Their front man is a guy named William Novak. Background in community organizing, migrated into philanthropic administration. He gives good interviews. Polished origin story — grew up in a town that automation gutted, watched his neighbors lose not just jobs but purpose, decided to build something that gave it back." She was looking at the investigation display again, tracing a connection with her finger. "I've heard a dozen versions of that story from foundation heads. Novak's version has an edge the others don't — a quiet conviction that the comfortable world is the broken one." "Sounds like a true believer," Greg offered, from what sounded like deeper in the pillows. "He is. And he looks the part. Tall — really tall — built like someone who does actual physical work, not gym work. Square jaw, intense eyes. The kind of presence that rearranged a room just by entering it." She tapped a node on the display to check the linked records, then closed it. "He's fond of a version of that quote — 'Hard times breed real men, real men breed good times, good times breed weak men, weak men breed hard times.' It's clear he considers himself in the first category and most of the political and business class in the last."

"You seem to have studied his appearance pretty carefully," Greg said.

"I study everyone's appearance. It's called research." She walked back to the bedroom doorway and leaned against the frame, arms crossed. "But here's what caught my attention. It's not Novak — it's the fellowship placements." They're broader than a foundation that size should produce. Policy institutes in Washington and Brussels. Media organizations — not the big names, but the second-tier outlets that shape coverage without drawing attention. Academic programs with advisory connections to government agencies. There's even a science communication fellowship that places graduates in public affairs roles at research institutions."

"So they're ambitious."

"They're connected." She pushed off the doorframe and crossed to the bathroom again, picking up the hairbrush she'd left on the counter. "The chart on my investigation display went from one node to fourteen organizations across four sectors in three weeks. Funding flows, personnel overlaps, board memberships, fellowship alumni in current positions. And every single connection, looked at individually, is completely legitimate. Foundations fund things. Fellows take jobs. Board members serve on multiple boards." She pulled the braid out, brushed through it, started over. "It looks exactly like what you'd find if you mapped any moderately successful philanthropic organization."

"So what's the problem?" Greg said. She could hear in his voice that he was asking out of courtesy rather than curiosity, but she needed to say it out loud. Sometimes the shape of a thing only became visible when you put it into words.

"The problem is I can't tell if it's a structure or a coincidence. And today I found something that made it worse." She finished the braid and tied it off, then came back into the bedroom and sat on her side of the bed, facing the open office door and the display beyond it. "I was going through their organizational materials — professionally done, by the way, with this distinctive logo. Kind of two arrowhead shapes, one nested inside the other, pointing up. And below that, two flat sort of — trapezoid things? With a little diamond shape in the middle. It's on everything they put out."

"Okay," Greg said. He'd settled deeper into the covers. His eyes were open but his body had made its decision.

"Three layers deep in the funding trail — through a fiscal sponsorship arrangement and a donor-advised fund — I found the name Haldane." She turned to look at him. "Not Charles Haldane specifically. The Haldane Foundation. They're one of eleven donors to a fund that supports a program that grants money to Fresh Start's fellowship initiative. Five-figure contribution, unremarkable for a foundation that size."

That got a flicker. "Haldane. The guy from the interview last month? With the fellowships?"

"Same foundation. And the connection is real, traceable, and completely ordinary. Big foundations donate to smaller ones through intermediary vehicles all the time. Tax-efficient, administratively routine, nearly invisible unless someone's specifically looking."

"And you were specifically looking."

"And I was specifically looking. And I found it. And it either means nothing or it means everything, and four months of work hasn't told me which." She stared through the doorway at the display, at the web of dotted lines and solid lines and names that connected to other names through channels that were perfectly legal and perfectly opaque. "I logged it as a peripheral node. Three steps removed. Dotted lines through the intermediaries."

Greg didn't answer right away. Then: "Come to bed, Chloe."

She looked at him. He had the expression he wore when he'd given a presentation the amount of attention it was going to get and was ready to move on to the next agenda item. It wasn't dismissive

— Greg was never dismissive, it wasn't in his operating system — but it was finite.

"Yeah." She got up, crossed the hall, and closed the laptop. The display stayed where it was, the connections mapped in place, the Haldane Foundation sitting at the periphery where she'd put it. Three steps removed. Dotted lines.

She turned off the office light and came to bed. The object that was dominating every science headline in the world had not crossed her attention once. She had no reason for it to.

Greg was already breathing the slow, even rhythm of a man who could fall asleep in hotel rooms and airport lounges and any horizontal surface that held still long enough. She lay on her back and looked at the ceiling and listened to him breathe and thought about the look on his face when he'd said Come to bed, Chloe. He'd meant it kindly. He always meant it kindly. But kindly and interested were different things, and she'd stopped being able to tell which one she wanted from him.

• • •

Twelve thousand kilometers away, on a mountaintop in Chile, the anomaly arrived. It was on Christmas Eve, and it was a gift, if more attention was on your list.

Most of the staff had gone home or down to the residencia for the evening. The skeleton crew that remained was running automated observations — the telescope tracking its queue without human intervention, the pipeline processing data as it came in. Hamner was on shift because he'd volunteered for it. Christmas meant nothing to his schedule and everything to the people who had families in Santiago or São Paulo or further. Hamner had none, near or far. Mercer had stayed too, for reasons he hadn't explained and Hamner hadn't asked about.

The mountain was quieter than usual. Not the instruments — those ran at the same pitch regardless of the calendar. The human sounds were gone. No footsteps in the corridor. No break room conversation bleeding through the walls. No one calling across the control room about a scheduling conflict or a coffee run. Just the cooling systems and the terminal fans and the faint, almost subliminal vibration of a facility designed to hold very still while the universe moved overhead. Hamner had eaten Christmas dinner from a foil tray in the break room at seven-thirty. He'd thrown the tray away and come back to his terminal and the tray was the only evidence that the evening had been different from any other.

They were in the control room together, the way they'd been on the night of the discovery. The amber lighting cast the same long shadows across the terminal banks. Hamner reviewing the weekly tracking update, Mercer running calibration checks three terminals away. Outside, the Atacama was doing what it did on every night that wasn't this one — being empty and dark and still.

For two months, the deviations had been zero. The object had followed its computed trajectory with the mechanical precision of a body responding to nothing but gravity. Each weekly update had confirmed the orbital solution within measurement uncertainty. The trajectory was clean. Boring, from a dynamical standpoint.

"Mercer," Hamner said.

The tone was enough. Mercer rolled his chair over.

"Look at this." Hamner pointed to the consolidated tracking data on his screen. "The nightly update. Positional offset."

Mercer scanned the numbers. "How big?"

"Fractions of an arcsecond. Small enough to be calibration noise."

"But?"

"But it's persistent. Look — multiple instruments, multiple nights, spread across the whole week. Paranal, La Silla, South Africa, Mars platform. Four facilities, two continents and a planet, and they all agree."

Mercer pulled up a chair and sat down properly. "They agree on the offset direction?"

“Same displacement. Same magnitude within measurement uncertainty. The instruments disagree on everything else — calibration, sensitivity, noise characteristics — but they all say the object isn’t quite where the model predicts.”

“Could be the Mars platform’s attitude control,” Mercer said. “You know it introduces a systematic when it’s in that drift-correction mode.”

“Checked it. The platform was in nominal mode all week. And even if it wasn’t, that doesn’t explain La Silla and South Africa showing the same thing.”

Mercer leaned in, reading the data more carefully.

“So the offset is real,“ Mercer said.

“The offset is real,” Hamner confirmed.

They sat with that.

“Non-gravitational acceleration,” Mercer said. Not a question.

“That’s what it looks like. Something changed the object’s velocity in a way that gravity doesn’t explain.”

Mercer leaned back. “Outgassing. It’s at eighteen AU, it’s getting more solar flux than it was at twenty. If there are volatiles under that irradiated crust, they’re starting to cook off. We should have expected this.”

“We should have.”

“So it’s good news. It means there are volatiles, despite the spectral profile. The crust model holds — dark surface, active interior. Sublimation jets pushing through vents or fractures.”

“That’s the obvious interpretation,” Hamner agreed.

Mercer heard the tone. “But?”

Hamner pulled up the deep imaging data. “If it’s outgassing at a rate sufficient to produce this acceleration, where’s the coma?”

Mercer looked at the images. Point source. Sharp. No diffuse envelope, no asymmetric brightness, no tail. Just a dot.

“Same problem as ‘Oumuamua,” Mercer said slowly.

"Same problem. Same explanations available. Narrow subsurface jets, transparent volatiles, below the coma detection threshold but above the acceleration detection threshold."

"All plausible," Mercer said.

"All plausible. All the same explanations we used last time, which were never resolved to everyone's satisfaction," Hamner added, though his voice contained hints which said he was less than satisfied.

Mercer looked at him. "You're noting this in the file."

"I note everything in the file."

"Right." Mercer rolled back to his terminal. "I'll draft the working group circular. Non-gravitational acceleration, consistent with outgassing, updated orbit fit, no change in hazard assessment. Standard language."

"Standard language," Hamner confirmed.

"You know what the press and public are going to say, right?" Mercer asked.

"Yes," Hamner sighed. "And every UFO kook and doomsday cult are going to crawl out of their holes and start up with their nonsense. Great Christmas present, huh?"

Mercer nodded. "That is what history tells us will likely happen. Hope your schedule's free for the tabloids!"

Hamner put his head in his hands. Just what he needed.

• • •

Saunders had gone back to São Paulo for the holidays, but she'd left Hamner her direct contact with a standing request: if anything changes, call me before you call the press office. He hadn't agreed to that. But when the non-gravitational acceleration appeared in the Christmas Eve data, she was the second person he thought of after Mercer. Not because he wanted to talk to a journalist. Because she'd ask the right questions, and hearing himself answer them would help him think.

He called her on December 26th.

"It moved," he said.

A pause. He could hear what sounded like a family gathering in the background — voices, music, a child laughing. Then a door closing and silence.

"Moved how?"

"The tracking data shows the object isn't where the model predicted. Small offset, but persistent across four facilities over a week. The most likely explanation is non-gravitational acceleration. Outgassing — volatiles under the crust heating up as it gets closer to the sun, venting through fractures, pushing the object off its predicted path."

"Like a jet on a spacecraft," Saunders said. "Except it's gas, not a rocket, and it's not controlled."

"That's —" He stopped. It was close enough for a first pass, but not quite right. "Not exactly. A jet on a spacecraft is directed. It pushes in one direction because the engine points in one direction. Outgassing is messier. The vents are wherever the fractures happen to be. The direction depends on which part of the surface is facing the sun, how the object is oriented, whether the jets are steady or episodic. It's stochastic — random pulses in semi-random directions that add up to a net push."

"So it's not like a rocket. It's like a balloon you inflate and let go — it shoots around the room, but you can't predict which direction."

"Better. Except the room is the solar system and the balloon is the size of a city."

"My readers will like that." He heard the pen click. "So the object is venting gas, and the venting is pushing it off course. How far off?"

"The miss distance changed from 3.9 million miles to about 3.5 million."

"Is that significant?"

"No. It's well within the original uncertainty bounds. The object was always going to pass somewhere in that range. This just refined where."

"But there's something else."

Hamner paused. "Why do you say that?"

"Because you called me on December 26th. You wouldn't call me to report a routine refinement of a number that was already safe."

He rubbed the bridge of his nose. She was right, and he wasn't sure he wanted to examine why.

"There's no coma," he said. "If the object is venting enough gas to change its trajectory, you'd expect to see a cloud of material around it — a coma, like a comet's halo. We're not seeing one. It's still a sharp point of light in every image."

"So something is pushing it, but you can't see what."

"The explanations exist. Narrow jets, transparent volatiles, below the visible threshold. It's the same situation we had with 'Oumuamua — acceleration without visible outgassing."

"And 'Oumuamua was never explained."

"'Oumuamua was explained," Hamner corrected. "Multiple plausible mechanisms were proposed. None were confirmed, because the object left the solar system before we could collect enough data. That's different from unexplained. It's unresolved."

The distinction mattered. *Unexplained* invited speculation. *Unresolved* invited patience. The difference between the two was the difference between a headline and a research program.

"Unresolved," Saunders repeated. He could hear her writing. "I can work with that. Invisible force, known candidates, insufficient data to choose between them. That's honest."

"That's where we are."

The background noise had returned — she'd opened the door. The family was still there. Christmas was still happening in someone's world.

"Dr. Hamner. Thank you. I'll have a draft to the press office by the 28th. You'll see it before it goes out."

"Saunders."

"Yes?"

"When you write it — the object moved closer. Not farther away. Don't bury that."

A pause. "I won't."

She hung up. Hamner sat in the control room and looked at the tracking data on his screen. He hadn't told her about the direction — Earthward, in the ecliptic plane. He'd told her the miss distance decreased, which was the same information stated differently. The fact without the frame. She'd report that the object moved closer, which was accurate. She wouldn't report that it moved toward Earth specifically, because he hadn't said that, and she wouldn't infer what he hadn't implied.

He went back to the data.

• • •

The working group call happened two days after Christmas. Eight researchers on a shared screen — Hamner and Mercer at Paranal, Patel from ESO headquarters in Munich, Vasquez's team at Harvard, two groups in Japan, and Kimura's pre-recorded segment from Mars.

Mercer presented the finding efficiently. "7I's venting. Non-gravitational acceleration detected in the weekly tracking data. Persistent offset across four facilities over seven days. Magnitude consistent with cometary outgassing triggered by increasing solar flux. Updated orbit fit converges cleanly. Miss distance revised slightly. Still negligible."

"How much did the miss distance change?" one of the Japanese researchers asked.

"Revised to approximately 3.5 million miles," Soares confirmed. "Well within the original uncertainty bounds."

The call moved on to scheduling — adjustments to the monitoring cadence, allocation of additional telescope time to track the outgassing activity, a discussion about whether to trigger a formal alert to the planetary defense coordination office. The consensus was no. The hazard assessment hadn't changed. Outgassing that reduced the miss distance by four hundred thousand miles was a scientific observation, not a safety concern.

Hamner agreed with the assessment. The data supported it. The physics supported it. The precedent supported it. There was no reason to think it was anything other than what it appeared to be. The press, and the public — that had been a different story. Right on cue the non-gravitational acceleration had brought out the UFO crowd. Alien spacecraft. Invasion from Mars, before we actually invaded Mars. Hamner's predicted headaches were genuine.

The call ended. Soares closed the connections and collected her notes. Patel signed off with a wave. The Japanese groups dropped simultaneously. Vasquez lingered on screen for a moment, looking at something off-camera, then disconnected without a goodbye.

Mercer closed his laptop. "Merry Christmas, 7I."

"Go home, Mercer."

"Going." He paused at the door. "You're staying?"

"For a while."

Mercer looked at him for a moment, then nodded and left.

The door closed behind him. Hamner heard his footsteps recede down the corridor — heavy, deliberate, the footsteps of a big man trying to be quiet in an empty building — and then nothing. He sat at his terminal and the data was still on his screen and he became aware, with a specificity that surprised him, of how much air was in the room. All of it unoccupied. All of it his. The control room was very large for one person on Christmas Eve.

• • •

His tablet chimed twenty minutes later. Saunders. A text, not a call: *Draft filed with press office. Covered the acceleration, the missing coma, the revised miss distance. Kept it clean. One question when you have a minute.*

He typed back: *Go ahead.*

The response came quickly: *The outgassing pushed it closer. Random venting should push it in any direction — closer, farther, above the orbital plane, below it. Was the acceleration in a preferred orientation?*

Hamner stared at the screen. Something in his chest tightened — the feeling of being seen. It was a better question than anyone on the working group call had asked. Not because the scientists hadn't thought of it — they had, and dismissed it, because at a margin of 3.5 million miles the vector decomposition was academically interesting and operationally meaningless. The hazard assessment didn't change based on which component of the acceleration dominated. At that distance, the direction of the push was a footnote.

But she'd found the footnote. Because a journalist who'd written a thesis on surface scattering models understood that outgassing was a three-dimensional process, and a change in miss distance was a one-dimensional summary. She wanted the other two dimensions.

He typed: *Lateral. In the ecliptic plane. Toward Earth's orbital position at closest approach.* He paused, then added: *One data point. Consistent with random outgassing. No preferred orientation implied.*

Her response took longer this time. Nearly a minute.

*Understood. Not in the article. But that's a very specific direction for a random event.*

He set the tablet down.

• • •

Alone with the data, Hamner ran the vector.

Not the magnitude of the acceleration — that had been computed, published, and discussed. The direction. The net displacement. Where the outgassing, if that's what it was, had pushed the object relative to its previous trajectory.

He'd done this computation a thousand times for other objects — comets with well-documented non-gravitational accelerations, asteroids with Yarkovsky drift, even 'Oumuamua's anomalous acceleration, which he'd reanalyzed as a graduate student exercise years after the debates had cooled. The math was simple. Decompose the acceleration vector into radial, transverse, and normal components. Compute the resulting change in the orbital elements. Propagate the revised trajectory forward and compare the new closest approach to the old one.

The answer was clean and, on its own, meaningless. The correction had nudged the object's closest approach to Earth slightly inward. Closer. Not by much — the miss distance had decreased from 3.9 million miles to approximately 3.5 million miles. A change that didn't register on any hazard scale. A rounding error in planetary defense terms. The object was still passing safely. The margin was still enormous.

But the direction was Earthward. And the correction remained in the ecliptic plane. The non-gravitational acceleration hadn't pushed the object out of the plane — hadn't nudged it north or south in a way that would be random and unremarkable. It had moved the object laterally, within the plane, toward Earth's position at the time of closest approach. The miss was still in the plane of Earth's orbit. It had been in the plane before the correction. It was in the plane after. The plane hadn't changed. Only the distance.

One data point. One direction. One correction among the billions of stochastic events that shaped cometary trajectories across the solar system every year. The probability that a random outgassing event would push an object toward Earth rather than away from it was roughly fifty percent — the geometry was more complex than a coin flip, but the intuition was right. There was no statistical significance in a single Earthward nudge. None.

Hamner knew this. He'd written papers on the statistics of non-gravitational accelerations. He knew how easy it was to see patterns in noise, how the human brain imposed directionality on random data, how a single data point in a preferred direction meant exactly nothing in a universe of stochastic processes. He knew all of this and it didn't quite stop the thought from forming.

He logged the direction. He logged the updated miss distance. He flagged the observation cadence for a modest increase — more frequent tracking passes, tighter monitoring of any further non-gravitational accelerations. Standard practice for an object showing activity. The request went through without comment. Nobody would question an increase in monitoring cadence for an active interstellar object. It was the obviously correct thing to do regardless of the direction of the acceleration.

He did not raise the Earthward direction with the working group. There was nothing to raise, and the nuts out there didn't need any more fuel. A single data point in a single direction meant nothing. Raising it would turn careful science into speculation, speculation into headlines, and headlines into noise that made it harder to do the actual work. He'd seen it happen to colleagues who'd floated preliminary results too early — the media cycle had chewed them up and the retraction never got the same coverage as the claim. He wasn't going to be that astronomer.

He noted the direction in his private log. One line. The same notation he'd used for every anomaly before this one. The accumulating file of things that were individually meaningless and collectively nothing.

The file was getting longer. It had started as a handful of lines — observations without conclusions, data points without interpretations, the kind of notes a careful scientist kept because you never knew what would matter later. Now it filled two screens. He scrolled through it sometimes, reading the entries in order, watching the pattern that wasn't a pattern yet assemble itself one line at a time. The flat photometry. The absent coma. The ecliptic coincidence. The Earthward correction. Each one explicable. Each one filed. Each one sitting in the document like a weight on a shelf, and the shelf was starting to bow.

Not yet.

# CHAPTER 4

## *40%*

*March 18th, 2059.*

*Object at ~15 AU, ~50 km/s. 464 days to orbital intersect.*

*Earth ↔ Mars: ~1.7 AU, Communications: ~15 min one-way.*

• • •

The second event arrived three months after the first, and it arrived in the same direction.

Soares found it. She was running the weekly tracking consolidation — a task she'd taken over from Hamner in January, when the coordination burden had grown past what one person could manage alongside actual science — and the pipeline flag stopped her mid-scroll.

"Hamner," she said, not looking up from her screen. "We've got another one."

Hamner crossed the control room and looked over her shoulder.

"Same signature as December?" he asked.

"Same signature as December. Persistent offset, five facilities. They all agree."

"Pipeline's calling it non-gravitational acceleration. Again."

Hamner pulled a chair over and sat down next to her. He studied the residuals in silence for a full minute. The pattern was identical to the Christmas Eve detection: a small, persistent displacement between observed and predicted position, visible across every instrument in the network. Real.

"Run the updated orbit fit," Hamner said. "I want to see the revised miss distance before we circulate anything."

Soares ran it. The computation took less than a minute with the current dataset — five months of tracking data made the orbital solution robust enough that small perturbations converged quickly.

"Miss distance revised from 3.45 million miles to approximately 2.83 million miles," she reported. "Hazard assessment unchanged. Negligible."

Hamner nodded slowly. He didn't say anything for a moment.

"Do you want me to draft the circular?" Soares asked.

"Let Mercer do it. He's got the template from December."

Soares gave him a look that he couldn't quite read — curiosity, maybe, or the beginning of a question she decided not to ask — and went to find Mercer.

• • •

The community processed the second event the way it had processed the first. Outgassing. The object was approaching the sun — fifteen AU now, inside Uranus's orbit, receiving more solar flux than it had in December. Increased sublimation. Increased thrust. Comets didn't outgas once and stop. A second non-gravitational acceleration three months after the first was exactly what the models predicted.

Mercer updated the working group within a day, his summary efficient and familiar: "7I's venting again. Stronger event this time — consistent with increased solar heating. Updated orbit fit converges. Miss distance revised. Still negligible."

• • •

Saunders called that evening. She'd been monitoring the working group's public data releases since December — Hamner had given her access to the non-embargoed feeds as part of their arrangement, and she'd been filing regular pieces for the Monitor that were, by Hamner's grudging assessment, accurate.

"Second outgassing event," she said. "Stronger than December, consistent with increased solar heating, miss distance revised inward. I can write that in my sleep. What's the part you're not saying?"

Hamner leaned back in his chair and stared at the ceiling. He was in the control room, alone, the door closed. Soares had gone home. Mercer was at the residencia.

"The miss distance decreased again," he said.

"I saw. From 3.45 to 2.83 million miles. Still enormous."

"Still enormous."

"And the direction of the push?"

He'd known she would ask. She'd asked it in December, by text, and he'd given her the answer then. This time she was asking by phone, and the pause before he answered carried more weight than he intended.

"Same as before. Lateral. In the ecliptic plane. Toward Earth's position at closest approach."

Silence on her end. Then: "Both of them."

"Both of them."

"Dr. Hamner, I want to ask you something, and I want you to answer it the way you'd answer it in a seminar, not the way you'd answer it in a press release." The pen clicked. He could hear it through the phone. "The object is traveling almost exactly in the plane of the planets. Two degrees off. And now it's made two course changes, and both of them were also in the plane, both toward Earth. If this were random outgassing — gas venting from fractures in random directions — why would the net push stay in the ecliptic? Why wouldn't at least one of them kick it north or south, out of the plane?"

It was the inclination question. The one he'd been carrying since October and nobody had pushed him on. The 2.1-degree ecliptic alignment that everyone had filed as "one in ten" and moved past.

"Because the geometry favors it," Hamner said carefully. "The object is already in the plane. Its velocity vector is nearly in the plane. If you decompose a random acceleration into components, the in-plane component is larger than the out-of-plane component for an object with this orbital geometry. The plane isn't special. It's just where the object already is."

"So the object happens to be in the plane, and the pushes happen to stay in the plane, and both happen to point toward Earth. And individually, each of those is unremarkable."

"Individually, yes."

"What about collectively?"

Hamner closed his eyes. "Collectively, it's a forty-percent result. I ran the Monte Carlo this afternoon. Ten thousand random two-event sequences with the correct orbital geometry. Forty percent of them produce two consecutive reductions in miss distance."

"Forty percent," Saunders repeated. "So six times out of ten, random chance would have pushed it farther away or out of the plane. And four times out of ten, you'd get exactly what you're seeing."

"That's correct."

"That's not a comfortable number."

"It's not a significant number. In statistical terms, forty percent is well within chance. You'd need to be below five percent before most scientists would consider it worth formal discussion."

"But you're discussing it with me."

Another pause. Longer than the first. "You asked."

"I did." Click of the pen. "I won't write the forty percent. Not yet. But I want you to know that I'm keeping my own file."

"I know you are," Hamner said, and he meant it in a way that surprised him — not as an accusation, but as recognition. She was doing what he was doing. Collecting things that were individually nothing. Waiting for the weight to become undeniable or to dissolve.

"If there's a third event," she said, "call me before the circular."

He didn't agree to that. But he didn't say no.

• • •

Hamner didn't move on. Not immediately. Not this time.

That evening, after the working group call had ended and Mercer had gone to the residencia for dinner, Hamner sat alone with the data and ran the vector analysis. The direction of the second deviation was not identical to the first — the geometry had changed as the object moved inward and the relative positions of Earth, the sun, and the object had shifted. But the net effect was the same. The deviation had nudged the trajectory closer to Earth. Again.

Two events. Two path movements. Both Earthward. Both in the ecliptic plane.

He ran the probability.

This was not a casual exercise. Hamner had spent his career thinking about statistical significance, about the difference between patterns and noise, about the human tendency to see intention in randomness. He knew the traps. He knew about the look-elsewhere effect — the statistical inflation that occurred when you tested multiple hypotheses and reported only the interesting ones. He knew that "two Earthward movements" was not the same question as "what is the probability that two random movements would both be Earthward," because he hadn't decided in advance to test that specific hypothesis. He'd looked at the direction because it was there, and now he was computing a probability that was contaminated by the very act of noticing.

He ran it anyway, carefully, accounting for every bias he could identify.

The geometry was not a simple coin flip. The probability that a single random non-gravitational acceleration would reduce the miss distance to Earth depended on the object's trajectory, the relative positions of all the bodies in the system, and the direction of the acceleration vector in three dimensions. He modeled it properly — a Monte Carlo simulation, ten thousand random acceleration vectors applied at the December epoch and again at the March epoch, propagated forward to compute the resulting miss distances. The question was simple: what fraction of random two-deviation sequences would produce two consecutive reductions in the miss distance?

The answer was not fifty percent squared. The geometry introduced correlations. The object was on an inbound trajectory that passed near Earth's orbital plane, which meant that certain acceleration directions were more likely to reduce the miss distance than others. The null hypothesis — random outgassing — predicted that roughly forty percent of two-deviation sequences would show two consecutive reductions.

That meant the observed outcome — two Earthward nudges — was consistent with random outgassing at the forty-percent level. Not even a one-in-ten result. A result that would occur four times out of ten by chance alone.

It was not conclusive. It was not alarming.

It was uncomfortable.

Forty percent was not a reason to sound an alarm. It was not a reason to publish a paper. It was not a reason to go on the record with a concern that could end a career if it turned out to be nothing. But it was low enough that Hamner's private file — the accumulating list of individually meaningless observations — had acquired a weight that he could no longer quite ignore.

Flat photometry. Ecliptic alignment. Unusual density. Absent coma. Earthward deviation. Earthward deviation again.

He closed the simulation and stared at the screen for a long time.

Forty percent. He said it to the empty room, quietly, the way you'd say a diagnosis you'd been expecting. It should have been a relief. Forty percent meant the outgassing model held. It meant the consensus was intact. It meant he could close the simulation, file the result, and go back to being the careful astronomer who'd found the seventh interstellar object and tracked it with appropriate rigor. But it also meant sixty. Sixty percent of random sequences wouldn't produce this. And the number sat in him the wrong way — not in his head, where probabilities lived, but lower, in the part of his gut that had been tightening since October and hadn't stopped.

• • •

The next morning, Hamner raised the statistical concern.

Not publicly. Not in a paper, not in a circular, not in a press statement. He raised it in an email to the working group's principal investigators — seven senior astronomers who had been coordinating the 7I/Hamner observation campaign since October. The email was measured, technical, and carefully framed. He presented the Monte Carlo results. He noted the forty-percent probability. He noted that while this was not statistically significant by any conventional threshold, the cumulative pattern of anomalies — the flat photometry, the ecliptic alignment, the absent coma, and now two consecutive Earthward deviations — warranted at minimum a formal discussion about whether the standard outgassing model was sufficient to explain the observed behavior.

He wrote the email three times before sending it. The first draft was too tentative — it read like an apology for asking the question. The second was too assertive — it implied a conclusion he hadn't reached. The third struck the balance he wanted: a professional raising a professional concern, supported by data, without advocacy for any particular interpretation.

He did not use the word "artificial." He did not suggest an alternative hypothesis. He simply asked whether the working group should consider expanding the range of models being tested against the tracking data.

The responses arrived over two days. Three of the seven didn't reply at all. Two replied with brief, technical pushbacks: the probability was well within chance, the flat photometry had multiple natural explanations, and the ecliptic alignment was a one-in-ten coincidence that had already been discussed and dismissed. One replied with a longer note that acknowledged the cumulative weight of the anomalies but concluded that no individual datum was strong enough to justify a formal model revision. The working group's resources were finite. Model revisions consumed time and attention that could be spent on the observation campaign itself.

The seventh reply came from Mercer. Not in an email — in a private conversation.

Mercer had started calling him "7I" in November. Hamner had never decided whether it was affectionate or reductive. Both, probably. The name of his discovery becoming the name of the man who'd made it — the object swallowing the astronomer.

"7I, I heard you sent an email expressing some concerns about the outgassing," Mercer started. "I really wish you had discussed this with me before sticking your neck out like this — and ours with you."

"How did you know about the email?" Hamner asked.

"7I, come on, it's a small community. I'm not the only one worried about how this might impact you. I won't say who, but a copy of the email was sent to me, asking me to talk to you about the implications of what you're implying."

"You found this object," he continued. "Your name is on it. If you push this — if you go on the record saying the deviations look directional — you know what happens."

Hamner knew what happened. He'd watched it happen to others. He'd watched a colleague at the European Southern Observatory float a preliminary claim about biosignatures in a Venusian atmosphere and then spend two years walking it back while the media cycle shredded his credibility. He'd watched a postdoc at MIT suggest that 'Oumuamua's acceleration profile was inconsistent with outgassing and get quietly shut out of the follow-up observation campaign. The scientific community didn't punish dissent with formal sanctions. It punished dissent with gravity — the slow, invisible weight of professional skepticism that accumulated around anyone who got ahead of the evidence.

"I'm not saying it's directional," Hamner said. "I'm saying the cumulative pattern is worth discussing."

"I know what you're saying," Mercer replied. "I'm telling you what other people will hear. They'll hear: the discoverer thinks his object is special. They'll hear: he's found a statistical anomaly and he's overinterpreting it. They'll hear: he wants attention." A pause. "You found the biggest interstellar object in history. Don't become the guy who cried alien."

The advice was protective. Hamner recognized that, even as it landed with a weight that felt less like protection and more like a door closing. Mercer wasn't dismissing the data. He was describing the system — the professional ecosystem in which careers were built on careful, conservative science and destroyed by premature claims. The cost of being wrong was asymmetric: a retracted alarm did more damage than a missed signal. The incentive structure was clear, and Mercer was simply stating it out loud, as a friend, because nobody else would.

"I hear you," Hamner said. The words came out steady, but something behind his ribs had gone tight — the specific weight of being professionally alone for the first time in his career.

He sat at his terminal after Mercer left and put his hands on the keyboard and didn't type anything. The cursor blinked on the draft of a follow-up email he'd been composing before the conversation. He read it back. It was reasonable. It was well-supported. It was the kind of email that would, if he sent it, confirm everything Mercer had just warned him about. He deleted it one line at a time, watching the words disappear, and when the screen was blank he sat with the blankness for a while.

"The data will keep coming," Mercer said. "If there's a third event, and it's Earthward, then the statistics change. At three out of three, you're below ten percent on the Monte Carlo. That's a paper. That's a real conversation. Until then, you're at forty percent. That's not a story. That's a coin flip that came up heads twice."

"I know."

"Good. We're in agreement. Keep monitoring. Keep the cadence high. And keep the Monte Carlo to yourself until you have something that can't be explained away."

Hamner thanked him and Mercer went back to his workstation. The conversation had lasted four minutes. It had been collegial, respectful, and entirely correct by the standards of the system in which both men operated. Mercer had told him, in effect: the system requires three data points before it will listen. You have two. Wait.

He added nothing to his private file that night. The file didn't need updating. The data hadn't changed. Only his relationship to the community had shifted — slightly, invisibly, in a direction that nobody would notice and everybody would deny. He had asked a question and received an answer, and the answer was: not yet.

• • •

Alexis Dren read the second event report fifteen minutes after it was published.

Not on a screen. The data arrived the way all data arrived for Dren — routed through the cortical interface behind his left ear, the feed landing in his memory as cleanly as if he'd read it on paper and remembered every word. Which, functionally, was what happened. The implant didn't think. It didn't analyze, didn't summarize, didn't suggest. It stored, and it retrieved, and it never forgot. It also transmitted — encrypted, direct, thought-mediated communication that looked like silence to anyone watching and left no record that anyone could audit. Nine years he'd had it — one of the first commercial-grade units manufactured on Mars — and what it had given him was not intelligence but capacity. Perfect recall of every document, every dataset, every conversation. Seamless communication with anyone on the same network, without speaking, without typing, without moving. His brain did the rest. It always had.

He was sitting in his office in Ares City — a room that said exactly as much about its occupant as he intended, which was very little. Clean desk, dark composite surface, nothing on it except a water glass and a stylus he never used but kept because it had been his father's. The walls were the same pressed-regolith panels as every other room in the complex, insulated against the Martian cold, sealed against the Martian atmosphere. One window, floor to ceiling, triple-paned against the pressure differential. No art. No photographs. No plants — those were for the residential habs, where people needed reminders of the world they'd left. Dren didn't need reminding. He knew exactly where he was.

He was fifty-four, slight, clean-shaven, with dark hair trimmed precisely short — the same length every two weeks, because he saw no reason for it to be otherwise. His clothes were simple and immaculate: fitted, well-pressed in a place where nobody pressed anything, the muted colors that Mars-side manufacturing produced because the first fabrication plants hadn't prioritized dye variety and nobody had revisited the decision. He sat still when he thought, hands flat on the desk, posture exact. People who met him for the first time often noticed the neatness before they noticed the man — everything aligned, everything controlled, not a crease or a thread out of place. It read as vanity until you realized it was the same principle he applied to everything else: eliminate variables, reduce friction, keep the system clean. The neatness wasn't about appearance. It was about discipline.

He'd pulled the 7I/Hamner working group data automatically — one of several hundred filtered streams he maintained in the interface's storage, covering commodity prices, regulatory filings, orbital mechanics for belt transit scheduling, political developments on Earth that might reshape his trade agreements. The report had arrived, he'd absorbed it — every number, every table, every footnote — and now his mind was doing what the implant couldn't: connecting it to everything else he knew.

Two Earthward events.

He didn't need Hamner's Monte Carlo to understand the implication. Dren didn't think in p-values. He thought in risk profiles

— the framework that had guided every significant decision he'd made since arriving on Mars twenty-two years ago with a fabrication plant, a mining contract, and a tolerance for discomfort that most people mistook for recklessness. It wasn't recklessness. It was the recognition that certainty was a luxury, and that waiting for certainty was itself a decision with consequences.

The scientific community's forty-percent comfort meant sixty percent of the risk was unpriced. He wasn't computing a probability. He was computing a cost. And the downside of that unpriced sixty percent — if the deviations continued, if the course converged, if the thing at fifteen AU was not a comet — was an impact event that would make every other problem in human history irrelevant.

Expected value. That was the calculation the scientific community wasn't running, because their framework wasn't designed to run it. They were asking: "Is the null hypothesis rejected?" The answer was no. Dren was asking a different question: "What's the expected cost of being wrong?" The answer was: everything.

He opened a channel to Sato. Not a call — nothing so crude. He thought her name with the specific intention the interface recognized as a connection request, and the link established: encrypted, Mars-side relay, no Earth-facing mirrors. To anyone watching, nothing changed. Dren sat at his desk, hands flat on the surface, expression neutral. The conversation happened entirely behind his eyes.

***I need you to model something,*** **Dren began.** ***Interceptors. Kinetic, nuclear, whatever the payload. How fast could we ramp production — not one, a fleet. Dozens. Using existing manufacturing lines, existing supply chains, belt-sourced materials.***

Sato considered. He could feel her thinking — not hesitating, but running her own rapid assessment, sorting constraints from assumptions, bottlenecks from throughput.

***You're talking about Hamner,*** she said. Not a question.

***I'm talking about a production capacity study,* Dren replied. *Stress-testing the lines for surge scenarios. I want timelines, bottlenecks, material constraints. How fast, how many, what breaks first.***

***Alexis.*** Her tone was careful, even through the interface — the system preserved inflection, cadence, the micro-signals that made a thought-voice distinguishable from text. ***The working group says it's outgassing. The hazard assessment is negligible.***

***The working group says a lot of things,*** Dren told her. ***The hazard assessment is based on two data points and a model that assumes the object is a comet. I'm not asking you to agree with me. I'm asking you to model it. Quietly. Don't tell anyone what it's for.***

***And the propulsion team?*** Sato asked. She'd been with him long enough to know that production questions were never isolated from propulsion questions.

***Shift ten percent of the development budget toward high-thrust mission profiles,* Dren said. *Maximize delta-v per unit mass. Deprioritize fuel efficiency in favor of raw acceleration.***

***That's going to set the belt transit optimization back by months,*** Sato warned.

***I know what it costs,*** Dren said. ***Model it.***

***I'll have a preliminary by end of week,* she said.**

***End of day would be better,*** Dren replied, ***but I trust you'll handle it.***

He closed the channel — a thought, and the connection was gone. The conversation had taken ninety seconds. Sato didn't need things explained twice and Dren didn't explain things twice.

He sat with his hands flat on the desk. The stylus was where it always was. The water glass was where it always was. Nothing in the room had moved. He had just told Sato to begin modeling interceptors — the word he hadn't used but they both understood — based on a footnote in a technical report that seven astronomers had tried to suppress. If he was wrong, he'd spent resources and attention on a contingency that would never materialize. If he was right, he'd started ninety seconds too late. The asymmetry was the only calculation that mattered, and he'd made it the way he made all of them: alone, in silence, with his hands flat on the desk.

Dren's companies had been developing pulsed fusion engines for three years, originally as a way to cut belt transit times. The physics was straightforward: detonate a series of small fusion charges behind a pusher plate, ride the shockwaves outward. The engineering was not straightforward — charge containment, plate erosion, structural fatigue from repeated detonations, the thermal management nightmare of running sustained pulses in vacuum. But the engines worked. They were inefficient by theoretical standards, expensive to operate, and brutal on the spacecraft structure, but they produced thrust levels that chemical rockets couldn't match and specific impulses that made deep-space maneuvers feasible on timescales that mattered for commerce.

The commercial application was belt transit. Faster shipping. Shorter supply chains. The competitive advantage that came from getting materials to market before anyone else could. That was the application his investors understood, the one his engineers were optimizing for, the one that justified the R&D budget.

The secondary application — the one that existed in the private partition of his memory where the interface's feeds didn't reach, where no audit trail recorded what he was thinking — was intercept. A pulsed fusion engine could accelerate a payload to velocities that no existing chemical or ion propulsion system could achieve in the required timeframe. The delta-v budget for an intercept mission depended on the trajectory, the timing, and the mass of the payload, but the numbers were already assembling themselves — orbital parameters he'd absorbed from the report, trajectory math he'd done a thousand times for commercial route planning, the same calculations repurposed for a very different kind of mission. The engines he was already building could, with modifications to the thrust profile and the structural margins, do the job.

He looked out the window of his office at the Martian landscape. Rust-colored regolith stretching to a horizon that was closer than Earth's, under a sky that was the wrong color and had been the wrong color for twenty-two years and would be the wrong color for as long as anyone alive would see it. Late afternoon — the light thin and amber, never quite sunlight even after two decades. Ares City spread below and to the left: hab modules, fabrication buildings, the landing pads where cargo shuttles came and went on schedules his logistics systems managed without his attention. Thirty-eight thousand people. Most of them worked for him, directly or through the supply chains his operations sustained. He had come to Mars with a plan. He had built something that mattered. He had not come to Mars to watch it —- or the planet it stood on, or the planet that planet depended on —- become a variable he had failed to price. The Martian gravity pulled at him differently than Earth's had, even after twenty-two years — a looseness in the joints, a lightness in the chest that never quite became natural.

He didn't know yet whether Hamner's object was a threat. He didn't need to know. He needed to be ready if it was.

• • •

Chloe Ashford had expanded the map.

Three months of additional work — patient, systematic, the kind of investigative labor that produced no headlines and no breakthroughs — had widened the Fresh Start Foundation's connection web from fourteen organizations to twenty-three. The pattern hadn't changed. Funding flows through intermediary vehicles. Fellowship placements across policy, media, and academic sectors. Personnel overlaps at the board level. Each new connection was individually legitimate and collectively… present.

The academic fellowship program was the newest thread. She'd found it in February, buried in Fresh Start's tax filings — a grant to a consortium that administered fellowships in science communication and public policy. The program had been running for eight years and had placed forty-seven fellows across research institutions, government advisory boards, and science media outlets. The placement rate was high. The career outcomes were strong. The program was, by every available metric, successful.

What caught Ashford's attention was a single name in the fellowship alumni list. Dr. Reyes. A science communication fellow who had completed the program four years ago and was now serving on the public affairs team at the International Astronomical Union — the organization coordinating the global response to 7I/Hamner. Ashford had found the name while cross-referencing Fresh Start's fellowship alumni against current institutional directories. It was a routine check, the kind she ran on every fellowship program she mapped: where did the graduates end up?

Dr. Reyes had ended up at the center of the biggest science story in decades.

One person. One fellowship. One position. It meant nothing. The IAU employed hundreds of people. Public affairs was a normal career path for a science communication graduate. The connection between Fresh Start's fellowship program and the IAU's public affairs team was a coincidence that populated every network map — the inevitable result of mapping enough nodes across enough sectors. If you traced any fellowship program's alumni far enough, you'd find someone adjacent to something significant. That was how networks worked.

Ashford logged the connection. She noted the path: Fresh Start → fellowship consortium → Dr. Reyes → IAU public affairs. She added it to the investigation map, a new line connecting the educational cluster to a node she hadn't mapped before — the scientific community's response to the interstellar object.

She didn't know what to make of it. She didn't try. Trying to make something of insufficient data was how journalists fabricated stories, and Ashford didn't fabricate stories. She collected connections. She documented paths. She waited for the pattern to declare itself or to dissolve into the noise of normal institutional life.

The pattern had not declared itself. Three months of work, and she still couldn't tell whether she was looking at something or nothing. The Haldane Foundation was still a peripheral node, three layers deep. William Novak was still a charismatic front man with a coherent ideology and a clean record. The Fresh Start emblem was still a logo on a brochure.

She saved her files and moved on to other work. The fellowship connection would sit in her database, one line among hundreds, waiting for a context that hadn't arrived yet.

• • •

The second event was published in the April issue of the working group's data release.

The report was technical, comprehensive, and entirely consistent with the community's existing framework. Non-gravitational acceleration detected in the March tracking data. Magnitude consistent with increased cometary activity at reduced heliocentric distance. Updated orbit fit converges within nominal uncertainties. Miss distance revised from 3.45 million miles to 2.83 million miles. Hazard assessment unchanged: negligible.

Hamner had insisted on a footnote. The cumulative statistical properties of the two events: both had reduced the miss distance, and a Monte Carlo analysis showed this outcome was consistent with random outgassing at the forty-percent confidence level. Technically precise. Carefully worded. No conclusions. No alternative hypotheses. Just the probability and the simulation parameters.

The footnote nearly died in review. Soares brought him the feedback from the steering committee, reading from her tablet in the doorway of his office.

“Two of three reviewers flagged it,” she said. “Quote: ‘may be misinterpreted by non-specialist audiences.’ The third approved without comment.”

“What does the committee say?” Hamner asked.

“They debated it for three days. The vote was to include it — suppressing a factual observation is worse than the risk of misinterpretation. But it was close.” She looked up from the tablet. “They also want you to know that the discussion was noted in the committee minutes.”

“Noted how?” he asked.

“As a ‘difference of opinion regarding appropriate scope of the data release.’ Diplomatic language.”

“Diplomatic language for what?” he asked guardedly.

Soares hesitated. “For: the discoverer is pushing a narrative that the data doesn’t support, and we accommodated him to preserve working group cohesion.”

Hamner absorbed that. “The footnote stays?”

“The footnote stays,” Soares confirmed.

It stayed. But the debate had cost something. Not goodwill, exactly — the working group remained collegial and functional — but something more subtle. Hamner had pushed for an observation to be included in a report, and the push itself had become a data point in the community’s assessment of Hamner. He was the discoverer who was asking questions about direction. He was the PI who had circulated a Monte Carlo that concluded nothing but implied something. He was, in the specific taxonomy of academic reputations, developing a lean.

The report circulated. The media coverage was minimal — a few science outlets noted the updated course, and one ran a brief article with the headline *Interstellar Visitor Adjusts Course — Scientists Say No Cause for Alarm.* The article quoted the working group’s hazard assessment. It did not mention the footnote.

Mercer read the published report the day it went out. When he reached the footnote, he looked up from his screen and held

Hamner's gaze for a beat longer than usual. Then he went back to his screen. He didn't say anything. He didn't need to.

Hamner's email to the PIs — the one where he'd raised the cumulative pattern — was not referenced in the published report. It existed in the private correspondence of seven astronomers, none of whom considered it significant enough to discuss further. Two of them had already forgotten about it.

The consensus held. It held because the threshold for overturning it had not been met. It held because two data points did not constitute evidence of anything except the ordinary variability of cometary physics. It held because the people maintaining it were competent, rigorous, and operating within a framework that had served planetary science well for decades.

Hamner did not disagree with any of this. That was the difficult part. The system wasn't broken. The system was working exactly as designed. The question he couldn't answer — the question that kept his private file open on his screen later than it should have been — was whether a system designed to process natural phenomena was capable of recognizing something that wasn't natural. If it couldn't, what would that look like? It would look exactly like this. A well-functioning system producing correct assessments of data that it was fundamentally misframing.

• • •

Saunders mentioned the footnote three days after the report went public. Not in a call — in a short, precise email that read like she'd written it in one draft.

*Dr. Hamner — I read the April data release. The trajectory update, the outgassing characterization, the revised miss distance. Standard coverage, standard framing. I also read footnote 14. It's buried on page 31 of a 34-page technical report, in eight-point type, after the acknowledgments section.*

*Two questions. First: whose idea was it to include it? Second: whose idea was it to put it after the acknowledgments?*

Hamner read the email twice. He didn't reply for two days. When he did, he kept it short:

*The footnote was my request. The placement was the steering committee's compromise. The content is factual and I stand behind it.*

Her response came in an hour:

*Understood. For what it's worth — I've covered enough institutional science to know what a footnote after the acknowledgments means. It means someone fought to include it and someone else fought to make sure nobody would read it. That's not a scientific judgment. That's a political one. I'm not writing about this. But I noticed.*

She was building the same file he was. Not of deviations and probabilities — of institutional responses. What got published and where. What got discussed and what got suppressed. What the system did when someone asked a question it wasn't designed to answer.

Hamner saved the email in a folder he hadn't labeled.

• • •

On Mars, Dren read the published April data release the same way he'd read the March circular — absorbed in full, instantly, through the interface. Every number. Every table. Every footnote.

He read footnote 14 twice. Not because the interface had failed to store it the first time — it never failed — but because his mind wanted to sit with it. Someone inside the working group had run a Monte Carlo on the deviation directions. Someone had fought to include it in the report, and someone else had fought to bury it after the acknowledgments in type small enough to miss.

Dren didn't know who. The footnote didn't carry a name — it was attributed to the working group collectively, the way all content in the release was. But the act of computing the probability, of framing the question as a cumulative statistical pattern rather than two isolated events, told him something about the person who'd done it. They were thinking the same way he was. They were asking the question the system didn't want asked. And they'd been permitted to ask it exactly once, in a format designed to ensure nobody heard.

He filed the observation in the private partition. Not the footnote itself — the interface already had that. The inference. Someone on the inside was watching the same pattern and being managed for it.

It didn't change anything operationally. Sato's preliminary production model had arrived — faster than end of day, because Sato was Sato — and the numbers were what he'd expected: aggressive but feasible. The manufacturing lines could be repurposed. The supply chains could be redirected. The timeline was tight but not impossible, if the decision came soon enough.

The decision, for now, was to continue modeling. Not to build. Not yet. The forty percent wasn't enough to justify the cost, the secrecy, or the political exposure of a unilateral interceptor program launched by a private citizen on Mars. But it was enough to justify being ready to justify it.

Dren closed the feed and went back to the commodity reports. Tungsten futures were up. Rhenium supply from the belt was stable. Hafnium was tight, as always. The materials he'd need for interceptor hulls, if it came to that, were the same materials he used for industrial fabrication. Nobody would notice the procurement. Nobody would ask.

He looked out the window again. The Martian sky was darkening — the thin amber fading to something that wasn't quite dusk and wasn't quite night, the transitional light that had no name because nobody had bothered to name it. Ares City was switching to interior lighting. The fabrication buildings glowed.

Thirty-eight thousand people. His.

He went back to work.

• • •

Hamner worked late that night. Not on the object — on routine survey data, the kind of patient, solitary observation that had defined his career before October 2058. The pipeline flagged nothing. The stars were where they were supposed to be. Everything in the sky was behaving exactly as the models predicted, except for one thing at fifteen AU that was behaving almost exactly as the models predicted.

He locked his workstation and stood in the doorway of the control room. The corridor beyond was empty, lit by the low amber strips that ran along the baseboards — energy-saving mode, the mountain conserving power for the instruments. The building didn't know what it was tracking. The building just tracked.

He stood in the doorway and pressed his palm against the frame. The metal was cold. His back ached from the chair — eight hours in the same position, the posture of a man leaning toward a screen that wouldn't tell him what he needed to hear. He could feel the mountain underneath the building, the mass of it, the indifference of rock that had been here for sixty million years and would be here after the instruments were dismantled and the control room was empty and nobody remembered what a pipeline flag had looked like on a night in October.

He turned off the light and closed the door.

# CHAPTER 5

## *Enemy Action*

*June 1st, 2059*

*Object at ~13 AU, ~50 km/s. 389 days to orbital intersect.*

*Earth ↔ Mars: ~0.9 AU, Communications: ~8 min one-way.*

• • •

The third event arrived in June, and it arrived in the same direction.

Soares didn't call him over this time. She sent a one-line message to his terminal: *Pipeline flag. Same signature. You should look at this.*

Hamner looked at it. The display was familiar now — observed versus predicted, residuals plotted, the automated flag. Persistent offset. Multiple instruments. Multiple nights. The same displacement that had appeared in December and again in March. A non-gravitational acceleration, the third in seven months, and the pipeline didn't care about the significance of that number. It flagged the deviation the way it flagged everything: mechanically, without interpretation.

He ran the vector before he ran anything else. Before the orbit fit, before the miss distance update, before the working group circular. He ran the direction first because the direction was the only thing that mattered to him now.

Earthward. In the ecliptic plane. Again.

Three events. Three Earthward movements. Three for three.

He ran the Monte Carlo. The same simulation he'd built in March, updated with the June epoch — ten thousand random three-event sequences, propagated forward, testing the null hypothesis that random outgassing would produce three consecutive reductions in miss distance. The geometry was different now. The object was closer, the relative positions had shifted, the acceleration vectors sampled a different part of the probability space. But the question was the same: what fraction of random sequences would look like this?

The answer came back and Hamner stared at it for a long time.

Six percent.

Not forty. Not twenty. Six. The probability that three consecutive random outgassing events would all reduce the miss distance to Earth, given the trajectory geometry and the observed magnitudes, was six percent. One in seventeen. Below ten percent — the threshold Mercer had named in March as the point where it became "a real conversation."

He sat alone in the control room and let the number settle.

Six percent was not zero. It was not proof. It was not even, by the strictest conventions of statistical hypothesis testing, significant — the standard threshold was five percent, and he was above it. A statistician could look at six percent and say: insufficient to reject the null hypothesis. A reasonable person could look at six percent and say: probably coincidence.

But six percent was the answer to one question — the direction question, isolated from everything else. It didn't account for the flat photometry, which had its own probability. It didn't account for the ecliptic alignment, or the anomalous density, or the absent coma. Each of those had been assessed independently, dismissed independently, filed under "interesting but explicable." Hamner had never combined them because combining independent anomalies into a joint probability was exactly the kind of exercise that looked like motivated reasoning. You could make anything look improbable if you multiplied enough small numbers together.

But he'd done it anyway, late one night in March, as a private exercise he hadn't shared with anyone. The joint probability — assuming independence, which was generous to the null hypothesis — of an interstellar object showing all of these properties simultaneously was small. Much smaller than six percent. Small enough that the number itself felt like an argument, which was exactly why he hadn't published it. A number that felt like an argument was a number that had left the domain of science and entered the domain of advocacy.

He kept it in the file. He kept everything in the file.

Soares appeared in the doorway. "The orbit fit is done," she said. "Miss distance revised to approximately 1.2 million miles. Hazard assessment…" She paused.

"Still negligible?" Hamner asked.

"Still negligible. Technically. The automated system doesn't flag anything above a million miles." Another pause. "But 1.2 is a lot closer than 2.83."

"I know."

"Hamner." Soares stepped into the room. Her voice had changed — not louder, but more deliberate. "I've been running the consolidations for seven months. I process the data every week. I see the residuals." She stopped, as if deciding how far to go. "Three events. All in the same direction. I'm not a dynamicist, but I can count."

It was the first time she'd said anything that wasn't strictly professional. Hamner looked at her for a moment.

"Run the circular," he said. "Standard language. Let Mercer review it before it goes out."

"Standard language," she repeated. The look she gave him said everything the words didn't. She left.

Hamner sat with the number for a while longer. Then he opened his private file and added the six-percent result, and the joint probability estimate he hadn't shown anyone, and the updated miss distance. The file was no longer a list of curiosities. It was becoming something else — a document that, if anyone ever read it, would show that the pattern had been visible from the beginning, and that one person had been tracking it, and that the system had processed it and produced the only answer the system was designed to produce.

Insufficient data. Continue monitoring.

• • •

Saunders called within the hour. He'd expected that. In March, she'd said: *If there's a third event, call me before the circular.* He hadn't called her. She'd called him. The difference was cosmetic and they both knew it.

"Three for three," she said. No preamble. No pleasantries. The pen was already clicking.

"Three for three," Hamner confirmed.

"What's the Monte Carlo?"

"Six percent."

Silence. Longer than any pause she'd given him before. He could hear her breathing, and the absence of the pen.

"Six," she said finally. "That's below Mercer's threshold."

He was surprised she remembered that. He'd never told her Mercer's threshold — Mercer had told him, in a private conversation in March. But she'd been covering this for seven months, and she was building her own model of how the people around the data were behaving. She'd inferred the threshold from the institutional dynamics, or someone had told her, or she'd simply arrived at the same number independently because ten percent was the obvious line.

"It's below ten. It's above five," Hamner said. "The null hypothesis technically holds."

"The null hypothesis technically holds," Saunders repeated. "And the miss distance?"

"1.2 million miles."

The pen clicked once. "That's a third of what it was three months ago."

"It's still a million miles. It's still negligible by any formal hazard standard."

"Dr. Hamner." Her voice had changed. Not louder. Quieter. "I've been covering this for seven months. I've watched the miss distance go from 3.9 to 3.5 to 2.83 to 1.2. I've watched every deviation push the object closer, in the same plane, toward the same planet. I've watched you put a footnote in a report and get buried for it. I've watched the community process each event individually and decline to look at the pattern. And I've been writing careful, accurate, responsible pieces for the Monitor that say exactly what the press office approves and nothing more." A pause. "I'm running out of room to do that honestly."

Hamner closed his eyes. She was telling him something. Not that she was going to break the arrangement — she was too professional for that, and too smart. She was telling him that the gap between what she knew and what she was allowed to write was becoming a professional problem. A journalist who sits on a story isn't doing journalism. She was doing it anyway, because the alternative was to publish half the picture and call it the whole thing.

"What do you want to write?" he asked.

"I want to write about the pattern. The direction. The cumulative statistics. The fact that every anomaly gets explained one at a time and nobody puts them next to each other." Her voice was tight — not rehearsed, not polished. Frustrated. "I want to write that the system isn't failing. It's *succeeding*. And that's what scares me."

"You can't write that."

"I know I can't write that. I'm telling you what I'd write if I could. So you know where I am." A pause. Then, quieter: "You've got your file. I've got mine. Neither of us can use them."

Another pause. Then: "The circular will go out today. Standard language. You'll see it."

"I'll see it," she said. "And I'll write the standard piece. Accurate. Responsible. Approved."

She hung up. Hamner sat with the phone in his hand for a moment. She'd never pushed him like that before. In December, she'd been curious. In March, she'd been careful. Now she was frustrated — not with him, but with the architecture of the situation. She could see the pattern. She'd been seeing it as long as he had. And the rules of her profession, like the rules of his, required her to wait for a threshold that the system controlled.

He set the phone on the console and pressed his thumb against the bridge of his nose. The gesture had become a habit — a physical placeholder for the thought he kept having and couldn't finish. She was three months behind him on the same road. She'd arrive at the place he was standing now, and when she got there she'd find the same thing he'd found: that knowing the truth and being unable to say it was a weight the body carried whether the mind acknowledged it or not. He couldn't protect her from that. He couldn't even protect himself.

• • •

The broadcast segment aired three days later, and it changed everything.

Hamner was in the break room when it happened — half-watching the midday panel on the wallscreen while he ate a sandwich he'd forgotten to eat at lunch. A segment that filled airtime between the stories that mattered: a planetary scientist from JPL, a science journalist, and a retired military analyst discussing the third event and the updated trajectory. Routine coverage. The planetary scientist — young, polished, good on camera — explained outgassing with practiced clarity. Solar heating, volatile sublimation, measurable thrust. Standard physics. The journalist asked whether the public should be concerned. The planetary scientist said no. The miss distance was 1.2 million miles. Still enormous. Still safe.

Then the third panelist spoke, and Hamner set down his sandwich.

Colonel Richard Adler, retired, formerly of the United States Space Command's orbital analysis division. He was a big man — tall, heavy through the shoulders and chest, with a broad, weathered face that looked like it had spent decades outdoors before spending decades in briefing rooms. Close-cropped gray hair. No smile. He sat in his chair the way men of that size sat when they weren't trying to make anyone comfortable — square, taking up space, arms on the armrests like he owned them. He'd been quiet through the planetary scientist's explanation, watching her with the flat patience of a man who had sat through a thousand briefings and could tell within the first sentence whether the briefer was giving him the real picture or the approved one.

"I've spent thirty years analyzing orbital trajectories," Adler said. His voice was blunt and unhurried — not loud, but the kind of voice that filled a room without trying because the man behind it had never seen the point of hedging. "Military satellites, debris tracking, collision avoidance. I know what random perturbations look like. I know what stochastic acceleration profiles look like. And I know what directed course adjustments look like." He didn't pause for effect. He paused because he was done with one sentence and was starting the next, and the gap between them was his business, not theirs. "There's an old intelligence maxim: once is happenstance, twice is coincidence, three times is enemy action. We've had three events. All three reduced the miss distance. All three stayed in the ecliptic plane. At some point we have to stop assuming this is a comet and start asking what else it could be."

Hamner stared at the screen. Someone had just said it. On television, to a national audience, a man with thirty years of orbital analysis credentials had looked into the camera and said the thing that Hamner had been writing in a private file for six months.

The reaction was immediate.

The planetary scientist pushed back in real time — the outgassing model was well-supported, the statistics were not conclusive, the phrase "enemy action" was inflammatory and irresponsible in a public broadcast. "You're not a planetary scientist," she said. "You're applying a military heuristic to a natural phenomenon."

Adler didn't flinch. He didn't lean forward or raise his voice or do any of the things that people did on television when they felt the ground shifting. He looked at her the way he'd been looking at her the entire segment — straight on, unhurried, the way a man looked at you when he'd already said what he meant and wasn't going to say it differently because you didn't like it — and said: "I'm applying pattern recognition to a dataset. The methodology doesn't care about my job title."

The science journalist tried to moderate. The segment ran four minutes over its allocated slot. The producers cut to commercial.

Hamner sat in the break room for a long time after it ended. His sandwich was still where he'd set it down.

His hands were shaking. He noticed it the way you noticed a change in air pressure — not through any single sense but through the body's aggregate awareness that something had shifted. A man he'd never met had just said, on national television, with his name and his credentials attached, the thing that Hamner had been writing in a password-protected file on a personal device for eight months. And the man was going to be destroyed for it. Hamner knew this with the certainty of someone who understood the system, because the system was his system, and he knew exactly what it did to people who said things it wasn't ready to hear. He picked up the sandwich. He put it down again. He wasn't hungry anymore.

The aftermath lasted weeks.

"Outgassing denier" appeared on social media within hours. Hamner first saw it in a comment thread under a science news article about the third event — someone dismissing Adler's analysis as "outgassing denial, same as climate denial, same playbook." The phrase spread with the velocity that only weaponized labels achieved online. By the end of the week it had its own hashtag. By the end of the month it had migrated from social media into opinion columns, into podcast discussions, into the casual vocabulary of people who wanted to signal that they trusted science and distrusted alarmists.

But the mainstream consensus was not the only consensus. Adler's segment, killed in the prestige press, found a second life in the alternative media ecosystem — independent podcasts, subscriber-funded news platforms, the distributed network of commentators and analysts who had built audiences precisely by questioning institutional narratives. Within days, the full unedited segment had been clipped, reposted, and viewed tens of millions of times. Adler himself appeared on three long-form interview programs in the following week, each running over two hours, each giving him the space to lay out the trajectory data, the Monte Carlo statistics, and the pattern recognition argument that the four-minute broadcast segment had compressed into a soundbite. The interviews were calm, technical, and detailed. They reached audiences that the midday news panel never would have.

An opinion poll published in mid-July crystallized the divide. Thirty-six percent of respondents believed that scientists were not being fully transparent about the potential danger posed by the interstellar object. The number cut across demographic lines — it wasn't concentrated in any single political faction or education level. It was simply the fraction of the public that looked at three consecutive Earthward events and didn't find "outgassing" to be a satisfying explanation. The scientific community dismissed the poll as evidence of public scientific illiteracy. The alternative media cited it as evidence that a third of the population could count to three.

• • •

Saunders watched the Adler aftermath from the peculiar position of a journalist who knew more than she could publish.

She'd covered Adler's broadcast in the Monitor — a straight report, factually precise, quoting both the planetary scientist's pushback and Adler's statistical claims without editorializing. The piece included the miss distance update, the outgassing model, and a single line noting that a Monte Carlo analysis in the April data release had found the cumulative deviation pattern consistent with random outgassing at the forty-percent level. She reported what was public.

The press office approved the piece without changes. It was the last time they would.

Her follow-up — a longer analysis piece examining the institutional response to Adler, the speed of the "outgassing denier" label, and the structural question of how scientific consensus handles directional anomalies — came back from the ESO press office with four paragraphs redacted and a note: *Content may be interpreted as lending credibility to non-scientific speculation. Please revise to focus on the observational data and the working group's published assessment.*

She'd read the note twice, then called Hamner.

"They killed the analysis," she said. "Not the data — the framing. I wrote about how the institutional response is shaping which questions are permissible to ask. They said it could be interpreted as supporting speculation."

Hamner was quiet.

"I'm not calling to complain," she continued. "I agreed to the arrangement. Everything I write goes through review. I'm calling because you should know what the review process looks like from this side. The data pieces go through clean. The moment I write about how the data is being *handled* — who decides what's significant, who decides what gets published where, how the language of denial is being used to foreclose legitimate statistical questions — that's when the red pen comes out."

"What are you going to do?" Hamner asked.

"Revise and resubmit. Remove the institutional analysis. Keep the data. File the piece the press office wants." A pause. "And keep the original draft in my own file. The one that says what I actually think."

"You're keeping a file," Hamner said. It wasn't a question.

"I've been keeping a file since December. You know that."

He did. He'd known it since the text exchange about the vector orientation, when she'd said *Not in the article. But I noticed.* She'd been building a parallel record — the story she could publish alongside the story she couldn't. When the gap between them became wide enough, one of two things would happen: either the public record would catch up to her private one, or she'd have to decide what her obligation was to the truth she was sitting on.

"Be careful," he said. It was inadequate and he knew it.

"I'm always careful," she replied. "That's becoming the problem."

• • •

The scientific community's response was swift and unified — and, Hamner suspected, partly a reaction to the poll numbers. Three separate statements from professional organizations — the IAU, the American Astronomical Society, and the European Planetary Science Congress — reaffirmed the outgassing consensus. The working group issued a special communication noting that the third event was "entirely consistent with the expected outgassing profile for a volatile-bearing interstellar body at this heliocentric distance." Hamner's name was on it. He'd been asked to sign, and he'd signed, because the statement was technically correct. The third event *was* consistent with outgassing. Everything was consistent with outgassing if you didn't look at the direction.

Patel called him from Munich the day the IAU statement went out.

"You signed it," she said.

"It's factually accurate," Hamner replied.

"It's factually accurate and strategically convenient. There's a difference."

"I know there's a difference."

"Do you?" Patel's voice was sharp but not hostile. "Because right now, anyone who questions the outgassing model gets called an outgassing denier and compared to conspiracy theorists. And you just put your name on the statement that enables that."

"What would you have me do, Asha?" Hamner asked. "Refuse to sign and become the face of the fringe?"

"I don't know what I'd have you do," Patel said. "I'm just noting that you signed."

Hamner didn't respond. Patel let the silence hold for a moment, then disconnected.

• • •

The quiet minority found him over the following weeks.

Not publicly. Not in working group emails or conference sessions or published correspondence. They found him in private channels — encrypted messages, personal emails sent from non-institutional accounts, phone calls made from personal devices. The operational security was instinctive, not coordinated. Nobody had organized a resistance. Nobody had drafted a manifesto. People had simply run the same numbers Hamner had run and arrived at the same uncomfortable place.

The first was a dynamicist at the Tokyo consortium — one of the groups that had been contributing belt telescope data since October. His message was brief: *I've seen your Monte Carlo footnote in the April release. I ran my own simulation independently. My numbers agree with yours. Six percent on three events. I am not comfortable with the current consensus position, but I am not in a position to say so formally.*

The second was a postdoc at the Harvard-Smithsonian Center, working under Vasquez. She called on a weekend, from what sounded like a coffee shop. "I can't say this in any official capacity," she told Hamner. "But the direction pattern concerns me. Three for three in the ecliptic plane. The coma absence concerns me. The density anomaly concerns me. I've raised these points with my supervisor and been told to focus on the spectral analysis."

"What did Vasquez say specifically?" Hamner asked.

"He said the data is interesting but insufficient," she replied carefully. "And he said I should publish the spectral work and build my CV, not chase statistical ghosts."

"That sounds like Vasquez," Hamner said.

"It does. And he's not wrong — the spectral work is good, and my career needs publications, not speculation. But I wanted you to know that your Monte Carlo is not an outlier. Other people are running the same simulation and getting the same answer."

The third was Patel, who had already made her position clear on the phone after the IAU statement. She followed up with a longer conversation a week later — encrypted voice, her initiative — with specific technical objections to the outgassing model that went beyond the direction statistics. The acceleration profile was too clean, she argued. Real outgassing was messy — jets fired from random surface locations, the thrust vector wobbled as the body rotated, the net acceleration showed the kind of noise that came from a fundamentally stochastic process. These events were noisy on the surface but suspiciously coherent in their net effect.

"The timing bothers me too," Patel said. "Three events in seven months. The spacing is almost regular. Outgassing doesn't work on a schedule — it depends on surface geometry, subsurface volatile distribution, thermal lag. This looks more like a system executing a sequence than a body venting randomly."

"You're seeing a pattern that could be coincidence," Hamner cautioned.

"I am. So are you. That's why neither of us is publishing it."

"How many of us are there?" Hamner asked.

"More than you think," Patel said. "People reach out to me too. They don't reach out to each other. Everyone's running the simulation independently, getting the same answer, and assuming they're the only one who's concerned."

"So we're a minority that doesn't know its own size."

"That's about right," Patel confirmed. "And none of us will say it publicly because of what happens when you do."

Hamner didn't need to answer that. They both knew what happened. Colonel Adler was finding out in real time — welcomed in the alternative media, destroyed in the mainstream. His thirty-year career in orbital analysis reduced to a punchline in the prestige press, his professional reputation reframed as "outgassing denier" by editorial boards and institutional spokespeople who couldn't compute an orbit fit. That his long-form interviews were reaching larger audiences than the outlets that had dismissed him didn't matter. Credibility flowed from institutions, not view counts. The mainstream had spoken, and the mainstream was where careers lived or died.

• • •

Mercer found him in the break room a few days later. The conversation was brief — two minutes, maybe less — and it began with the sound of coffee being poured.

"You hear what they're calling people now?" Mercer asked, settling into the chair across from Hamner. "Outgassing deniers." He said it with a sympathetic wince, the way you'd report bad news about a mutual friend. "That military guy on the news really stepped in it. Now anyone who questions the model gets lumped in with the conspiracy crowd."

"I saw," Hamner said.

"It's ugly," Mercer continued, shaking his head. "The guy had a real point buried in there somewhere — three events in the same direction is worth discussing. But the way he said it? 'Enemy action'? On television? He handed them the ammunition to dismiss everything."

"He wasn't wrong about the statistics."

"No, he wasn't wrong about the statistics," Mercer agreed. "But being right about the statistics and being wrong about the delivery is worse than being wrong about both. Now nobody can raise the direction question without being called a denier. The conversation is poisoned." He took a sip of his coffee. "Just make sure you stay on the right side of that line, 7I. You've got the footnote in the April release. That's on the record. That's enough for now."

Hamner looked at him. "Is it?"

"It is until the data says otherwise," Mercer said. "And the data hasn't said otherwise yet. Six percent is below ten, sure. But it's above five. The null hypothesis holds. The process works."

"The process works," Hamner repeated.

"It does." Mercer stood up, coffee in hand. "Look, I know this is frustrating. But you're doing the right thing — monitoring, logging, keeping the cadence high. When the evidence is strong enough, the system will respond. That's what it's designed to do."

He left. Hamner sat with his coffee and thought about what Mercer had just done. He'd acknowledged the statistics. He'd sympathized with Hamner's frustration. He'd validated the footnote. And he'd drawn a line — gently, collegially, with a sympathetic wince — between responsible skepticism and outgassing denial. The line was clear: Hamner was on the right side of it. For now. As long as he stayed quiet.

Hamner sat with his coffee and listened to Mercer's footsteps fade down the corridor. The coffee was still warm. Nothing about the conversation had been threatening or confrontational or even tense. It had been kind. That was the part that stayed with him — the kindness. Mercer had warned him the way a friend warns a friend, and the warning had been accurate, and the accuracy made it worse, because it meant the system didn't need to be hostile to work. It just needed to be right about the cost.

• • •

The Monitor published Saunders's revised piece two days later. It covered the third event, the updated trajectory, the miss distance revision, and the outgassing model. It quoted the IAU statement and the working group's special communication. It was accurate, balanced, and indistinguishable from the coverage in every other reputable science outlet. The institutional analysis was gone. The pattern was absent.

Hamner read it on his tablet in the control room. It was a good piece. It was the piece the system wanted written about itself, by a journalist smart enough to know it wasn't the whole story.

He thought about the draft she'd described — the one the press office had killed. The one about how the language of denial was being used to foreclose legitimate questions. The one about institutional response shaping the boundary of permissible inquiry. Something in his chest ached for it — the specific frustration of watching someone else be constrained by the same architecture constraining him. It existed somewhere in her files, alongside the vector orientation she'd noticed in December and the footnote placement she'd caught in April and every number he'd given her on the phone.

The object was at thirteen AU and closing.

• • •

Alexis Dren absorbed the Adler broadcast in his office on Mars, eight minutes after it aired on Earth.

Not watched — absorbed. The feed ran through his interface the way all media did, the audio and video encoded into memory as cleanly as if he'd been in the studio. He could replay any frame, any inflection, any micro-expression on the planetary scientist's face when Adler said "enemy action." He didn't need to. He'd caught everything the first time.

The delay was shorter now — Earth and Mars were approaching opposition, the closest point in their orbital dance, and the communication lag had dropped from nineteen minutes in October to eight. Dren noticed these things. The geometry of the solar system was not abstract to him. It was the operating environment of his business, and changes in light-speed delay meant changes in how fast information moved, which meant changes in competitive advantage.

He sat at his desk, still as always, hands flat on the dark composite surface. The Martian afternoon light came through the window at a low angle, casting a faint amber wash across the room that made the pressed-regolith walls look almost warm. They weren't. Nothing on Mars was warm without engineering.

He watched Adler say "enemy action" and watched the planetary scientist's face tighten. He liked Adler. Not the delivery — the delivery was a tactical error that had handed the institutional response exactly the weapon it needed. But the analysis was clean. The man had looked at the same data everyone else was looking at, ignored the social pressure to look away from it, and said what it showed. That he'd been destroyed for it was predictable. That he'd said it anyway was interesting. Dren filed the name.

He watched the aftermath unfold over the following days — the label, the statements, the consensus hardening. He watched the system do what systems did when threatened: close ranks.

Three events. All Earthward. Six percent on the Monte Carlo, if the astronomers were computing it honestly. Dren didn't care about the exact number. He cared about the trend. The trajectory was converging. Each event brought the object closer to Earth. The outgassing model explained each event individually. It did not explain the pattern.

He thought Sato's name, and the channel opened.

***The production study you ran in March,* Dren said. *Activate it. Begin the ramp.***

Sato didn't hesitate. ***Full authorization?***

***Full authorization,*** Dren confirmed. ***Retool Lines 3 through 7 for interceptor platforms. Activate the belt supply chain for surge-rate delivery. I want the first hull in fabrication within sixty days.***

***That's going to create noise,*** Sato warned. ***Shipping schedules will shift. Equipment allocations will conflict with existing contracts. The Ceres consortium is expecting their next delivery in August, and if I pull fabrication capacity—***

***Delay the Ceres delivery,*** Dren cut in. ***Blame a supply bottleneck. There was a conveyance failure at Vesta last month — use that as cover. The timeline's close enough.***

***And when they push back?*** she asked.

***They'll push back,*** Dren said. ***Offer a ten percent discount on the delayed shipment and an accelerated schedule for Q4. They'll take it. They always take it.***

Sato was quiet for a moment. ***And the propulsion program?***

***Full commitment,*** Dren told her. ***The prototype gets adapted for intercept. I want mission profiles — delta-v budgets, payload mass constraints, launch windows — for a range of intercept trajectories against the current orbital solution for Hamner.***

***Alexis, that's a specific ship for a specific mission,* Sato said. *If anyone looks closely at the engineering requirements, they'll see that this isn't a belt transit vehicle. The thrust-to-mass ratio alone—***

***Then make sure nobody looks closely,*** Dren interrupted. ***The paperwork says high-thrust belt transit stress test. The engineering team gets the mission parameters, not the context. Compartmentalize.***

***You're asking me to build a weapons platform and hide it in the shipping manifests,* she said.**

***I'm asking you to build an interceptor and file it under R&D,*** Dren corrected.

***The line you're walking is thinner than you think There's a difference. One is illegal. The other is creative accounting,*** Sato said.

***I know exactly how thin it is,*** Dren replied. ***Start building.***

Sato's response came after a beat — not hesitation, but the specific delay of someone rewriting a number in their head. ***I'll have a revised production timeline by end of day,*** **she said.** ***And Alexis — if this turns out to be a comet, we will have burned through forty million in fabrication costs for nothing.***

***If it turns out to be a comet,*** Dren said, ***I'll write it off as the most expensive insurance policy in history. If it's not a comet, forty million will be the best money I've ever spent.***

A pause. Then: ***And that other thing we discussed,*** Dren added. ***Proceed.***

Sato was quiet for longer than usual. ***Are you certain?***

***Proceed,*** Dren repeated.

The channel closed. Dren hadn't moved. His hands were still flat on the desk, his posture still exact. The conversation had taken three minutes, and to anyone who might have walked past the open door of his office, he'd been sitting in perfect silence the entire time, looking out at the Martian afternoon.

Dren had made two decisions in those three minutes. The first — begin interceptor production — was a bet against the consensus. The second — commit the pulsed fusion prototype to intercept adaptation — was a bet on himself. Whether the object hit or missed, he intended to get to it. If it was a comet, he'd have wasted money and embarrassed his engineering team. If it was something else, he'd have the only ship in the solar system capable of reaching it.

The belt supply chains would shift. Shipping schedules would adjust. The Ceres consortium would receive an apologetic message about a Vesta conveyance failure and a generous discount offer. Equipment allocations would create minor friction — a delay here, a reassignment there, the industrial noise that happened every quarter in an operation of this scale. Nobody would look twice. Not yet.

On Earth, the scientific establishment was closing ranks around outgassing. On Mars, Dren was building.

The object was thirteen AU away and closing, and for the first time in eight months of watching it, Hamner was not the only person who thought something was wrong.

He was just the only one whose name was on it.

# CHAPTER 6

## *The Ambush*

*September 2059.*
*Object at ~10 AU, ~52 km/s. 288 days to orbital intersect.*
*Earth ↔ Mars: ~0.5 AU, Communications: ~4 min one-way.*

• • •

The summons arrived on a Tuesday, routed through the standard diplomatic channel that Earth's legislative bodies used for official communications with Mars-based entities. Sato flagged it before Dren saw it — she flagged everything that came through diplomatic channels, because diplomatic channels were where surprises hid.

Her voice arrived through the interface, clean and immediate. ***Congressional oversight committee,*** Sato reported. ***Hearing scheduled for October 3rd. Stated topic: routine review of off-world industrial operations and compliance with Earth-Mars trade framework provisions.***

***Which committee?*** Dren asked.

***Commerce and Industrial Oversight,*** she said. ***Chaired by Beckett.***

***Beckett.*** Dren was at his desk, hands flat on the dark composite surface, the Martian mid-morning light casting its thin amber wash through the window. He didn't move when the name landed, but the interface was already pulling — Beckett's voting record, committee history, donor filings, public statements on Mars trade policy, all of it surfacing in his memory as fast as he could think the queries. Senator James Beckett, Virginia, second-term, chair of the committee that technically had jurisdiction over Earth-Mars commercial operations. Young for a committee chair — mid-forties, sharp-featured, with a résumé that read like a machine-generated career path: law review, Justice Department, state attorney general, Senate at thirty-eight. A politician who understood supply chains well enough to ask questions that other politicians couldn't follow. Not hostile to Mars interests, historically. Not friendly, either. Transactional.

***When did they schedule it?*** Dren asked.

***Two weeks ago,*** Sato said. ***The notice was held in the diplomatic queue — standard processing delay.***

***Two weeks.*** Dren looked at the calendar on his wall display. October 3rd was twelve days away. Earth and Mars were approaching opposition — the closest point in their orbits, when the light-speed delay dropped to its minimum. Right now, the delay was about four minutes each way. Close enough to something resembling a conversation. In six weeks it would be eight minutes and climbing. In three months it would be over fifteen.

The hearing had been scheduled for the one window in the orbital cycle where a near-real-time exchange was possible. That could be coincidence — committees scheduled hearings when communication was practical. Or it could be something else.

***Standard prep,*** Dren told her. ***Pull the trade compliance files, the quarterly production reports, the belt sourcing documentation. Whatever they'd want for a routine review.***

***And the non-routine material?*** Sato asked.

***What non-routine material?*** Dren said.

Sato didn't answer immediately. When her voice came back through the interface, the tone had shifted — careful, deliberate, the way she sounded when she was saying something she knew he didn't want to hear. ***Alexis.***

***Standard prep,*** he repeated.

• • •

The hearing convened at 14:00 UTC on October 3rd, 2059. Dren appeared on the committee's wallscreen from his office in Ares City — a feed that crossed half a billion kilometers at the speed of light and arrived four minutes and eleven seconds later. The delay made normal conversation impossible but permitted something close to it: a question asked, a pause, an answer received, another question. Awkward but functional. The committee members had been briefed on the protocol. The viewing public had been warned about the delay. Everyone understood the constraints.

On his end, Dren sat in the same posture he always sat in — still, upright, hands resting on the desk just below the camera's frame. His office was deliberately neutral behind him: the pressed-regolith wall, the window showing Martian sky, nothing personal, nothing that gave a commentator anything to work with. He'd considered and rejected the idea of a more staged backdrop. The room said what he wanted it to say: I'm on Mars. I built this. I'm not performing for you.

On the committee's end — visible to Dren through the return feed, four minutes delayed — the hearing room was the standard Congressional theater: dark wood paneling, raised dais, microphones on articulated arms, the committee members arrayed in a semicircle with their staff seated behind them. Beckett occupied the center chair. He was younger than most committee chairs — lean, dark-haired, with the sharp, clean-cut features of a man who had looked like a senator before he was one. He sat with the coiled stillness of someone athletic who had learned to hold himself motionless for cameras, and his expression was the carefully calibrated neutral that certain politicians wore like a second face — attentive, pleasant, giving nothing away. Dren recognized the type immediately: not the old-guard senators who telegraphed their punches with theatrical gravity, but the newer model — the kind who smiled while they set the trap and never raised their voice when it closed.

The first forty minutes were routine. Trade volumes. Shipping schedules. Belt sourcing contracts and their compliance with the Earth-Mars Materials Framework. A question about deuterium pricing that Dren answered with numbers the interface had loaded before the hearing started. A question about employment practices at the Ares City fabrication complex that his team had anticipated and prepared documentation for. A question about environmental impact assessments for belt mining operations that he answered with barely concealed impatience — the belt had no environment to impact, and the senator who asked it knew that. His legal team, monitoring from an adjacent room in Ares City, flagged nothing. Sato, watching from her office, flagged nothing. The questions matched the stated agenda. Dren began to suspect he'd been called across half a billion kilometers to participate in a compliance exercise that could have been handled by a filing clerk.

Then Beckett leaned forward. It was a small movement — an inch, maybe two — but it changed the geometry of the room. The other senators had asked their questions from the posture of men and women reading prepared notes. Beckett moved toward the microphone the way a man leaned toward a conversation he'd been waiting to have.

"Mr. Dren, I'd like to shift to a related matter." His voice was measured, conversational — the tone of a man asking about quarterly shipping figures, not the tone of a man detonating an ambush. The disconnect was deliberate, and Dren saw it four minutes too late to do anything about it. "We've received intelligence — and I want to be precise here — indicating that your Mars-based manufacturing facilities have, over the past several months, retooled multiple production lines for the fabrication of what appear to be nuclear-armed interceptor platforms. Can you confirm or deny that your facilities are currently engaged in the production of weapons systems without authorization from any Earth government or international regulatory body?"

The question crossed half a billion kilometers.

In the hearing room on Earth, the four minutes and eleven seconds that followed were not silence. They were the most consequential dead air in the history of Congressional testimony. The committee members reacted — some with rehearsed gravity, others with what appeared to be genuine surprise. The gallery stirred. Staff members leaned toward screens. Beckett sat back — the lean was over, the device delivered — and folded his hands with the patience of a man who had asked exactly the question he intended to ask and was content to let the silence do its work. The cameras caught every face in the room — and every face told a story before Dren could tell his. Commentators filled the gap. The phrase "nuclear-armed interceptor platforms" was repeated, analyzed, and contextualized in the four minutes and eleven seconds before the man who built them could say a single word in response. The feeds began transmitting. The chyrons began writing themselves.

On Mars, Dren heard the question four minutes and eleven seconds after it was asked. He absorbed it in approximately two seconds. The remaining delay had already been filled on Earth by people who had never built anything.

He did not look at Sato, who he knew was watching from her office. He did not look at his legal team, who he knew were already drafting objections. He looked into the camera and composed his answer. His pulse had spiked — he could feel it in his throat, the one system the interface couldn't govern. To anyone watching the Mars-side feed, he was a slight, immaculate man sitting perfectly still at a clean desk, and the only thing that changed was a barely perceptible narrowing of his eyes.

Four minutes. On Earth, the silence was filling with other people's voices. On Mars, the silence was his. He sat in it the way he sat in everything — still, contained, the pulse in his throat the only evidence that the question had reached the man inside the posture.

He had four minutes to compose an answer that would be heard after the world had already decided what it thought. So he used the time the way he used all time: precisely. He thought about the trajectory. He thought about the interceptors in fabrication bays three levels below his office, half-built, their existence now public, their purpose about to be reframed by people who had never computed an orbit. Then he thought about what to say, and he said it.

"Senator, I can confirm that my facilities have been engaged in the production of spacecraft platforms capable of high-velocity intercept missions. These platforms are being developed as a contingency measure in response to the ongoing trajectory corrections of the interstellar object designated 7I/Hamner, which has now undergone three consecutive non-gravitational acceleration events, all of which have reduced its miss distance to Earth. The current miss distance is 1.2 million miles — down from 3.9 million at discovery. The production was initiated on my authority as the operator of the facilities in question. I did not seek authorization from Earth governments because no authorization framework exists for this category of activity, and because the timeline for the object's approach does not permit the luxury of waiting for one to be written."

His answer crossed half a billion kilometers.

It arrived four minutes and eleven seconds after the question had already reshaped the room. By then, the hearing had moved on. Other committee members had spoken. Beckett had made a follow-up statement about "unilateral military action by private actors operating beyond Earth jurisdiction" — still in that same measured voice, still with that same expression of calibrated concern, as if the revelation had surprised him rather than served him. The media feeds had their headline. The chyrons were already running: MARS INDUSTRIALIST BUILDING WEAPONS IN SECRET — CONGRESSIONAL HEARING REVEALS UNAUTHORIZED INTERCEPTOR PROGRAM.

Dren's response, when it arrived, was carried live on the same feeds. It was composed, factual, and unapologetic. It cited the trajectory data. It cited the miss distance — 1.2 million miles and shrinking. It cited the absence of any governmental interceptor program. It made the case that someone had to build a defense, and that the someone with the manufacturing capacity and the propulsion technology was him.

It didn't matter. The narrative had formed in the eight-minute gap between the question and the answer. The gap was the weapon. Whether Beckett had understood that when he scheduled the hearing during the one month of the orbital cycle where the delay was short enough to create this exact dynamic — short enough for near-conversation, long enough for the story to crystallize before the response arrived — was a question that would never be answered. Dren noticed it. Sato, who messaged him within thirty seconds of the question, noticed it. Nobody in the hearing room seemed to.

• • •

The firestorm consumed the news cycle for weeks.

Every screen, every feed, every platform ran the same core story: a private industrialist on Mars, operating beyond the reach of Earth's regulatory framework, had been secretly building nuclear-armed interceptor platforms without authorization, oversight, or accountability. The framing was consistent across outlets — mainstream and alternative alike, for once united in the same direction. Dren's power. Dren's judgment. Dren's motives.

Not 7I/Hamner. 7I/Hamner was background. The course corrections, the shrinking miss distance, the six-percent Monte Carlo — all of it was subordinated to the more immediate, more human, more politically useful story of a man with too much power doing what he wanted with it.

A few voices tried to refocus the conversation. Adler, from his new perch in the alternative media ecosystem, pointed out that the hearing had not addressed the object's trajectory at all — that a Congressional committee had spent four hours discussing Mars manufacturing capacity and zero minutes discussing the reason the manufacturing had begun. His observation was noted, shared, and drowned.

The talking heads found a more compelling angle. Mars, they observed, was not in the object's path. If the interstellar object struck Earth, Mars would survive — damaged economically, severed from its largest trading partner, but physically intact. So why would Dren, a Mars-based industrialist whose empire depended on Earth-Mars trade, want to stop an impact? The rebuttal — that Mars depended on Earth for population, institutional support, and the economic foundation of its entire industrial base — was offered by Dren's spokespeople and by several Mars-based economists. It failed to gain traction. The conspiracy was simpler and more satisfying: Dren was building weapons because Dren wanted power, and the object was his excuse.

Hamner watched the coverage from the break room at Paranal The object's course — the actual data, the actual pattern — had disappeared from public discourse entirely. The story was about Mars. The story was about Dren. The story was about power and accountability and the question of who had the right to build weapons in space. 7I/Hamner itself had become a prop in someone else's argument.

He was sitting in the chair nearest the door, and his hands were wrapped around a coffee mug that had gone cold. On the screen, people who had never looked at a tracking residual were explaining why the tracking residuals didn't matter. His jaw ached. He'd been clenching it without realizing.

Mercer, passing through on his way to the coffee machine, caught the broadcast running on the wallscreen.

"They're not even talking about the course," Hamner said.

"Why would they?" Mercer replied, filling his mug without looking at the screen. "The course is boring. Mars building nukes is exciting. That's how news works, 7I."

"The course is the reason the nukes exist."

"Maybe. But nobody's going to run a headline about Monte Carlo simulations when they can run one about unauthorized weapons programs." Mercer shrugged. "Dren handed them the story they wanted. They're going to run with it."

Hamner turned off the broadcast.

• • •

Over the following weeks, things started going wrong in Dren's operation.

The first incident was a manufacturing equipment failure — a high-precision fabrication unit on Line 4 that seized during a retooling cycle. The unit had been running at accelerated capacity for three months, pushed past its rated duty cycle to meet Dren's sixty-day hull deadline. The failure was consistent with mechanical fatigue from overuse. The engineering team diagnosed it, ordered replacement components from the belt supply chain, and estimated a two-week repair timeline.

The second was a shipping delay. A belt freighter carrying structural alloys from the Vesta processing facility was rerouted due to a navigation dispute — a competing mining operation had filed a priority claim on the transit corridor, citing an orbital mechanics conflict that required the freighter to hold position for seventy-two hours. The claim was procedurally valid. The delay cascaded through the production schedule.

The third was a quality control flag. A component supplier — one of the smaller belt operations that fed raw materials into Dren's manufacturing lines — reported that a batch of reactor shielding had failed inspection. Metallurgical analysis showed contamination — trace elements in the alloy that shouldn't have been there. The supplier attributed it to a feedstock problem at the refinery. Dren's quality team quarantined the batch and ordered replacements.

Sato compiled the incidents in a weekly report and brought it to Dren's office. She stood in front of his desk — Sato never sat unless invited, and Dren never invited, and neither of them had ever commented on this — holding her tablet at her side rather than reading from it.

"Three disruptions in three weeks," she said. "The fabrication failure is fatigue — that's on us. We pushed the equipment too hard. The shipping delay is procedurally legitimate. The contamination could be anything."

"Could be," Dren agreed. He was still at his desk, still in the same posture, but his eyes were on Sato in a way she recognized — the look he got when he was running scenarios faster than he could voice them.

"But three in three weeks, all hitting the interceptor lines, all at different points in the supply chain." Sato set the report down on his desk. "If someone wanted to slow us down without leaving fingerprints, this is what it would look like."

"It's also what normal operational friction looks like when you're running a crash production program on retooled lines with surge-rate supply chains," Dren said. "But I'm not going to bet the program on which one it is."

"What's the net impact on the timeline?"

"Four to six weeks of delay across the program. The first hull is still in fabrication, but the second and third are pushed back. The propulsion prototype is unaffected — different supply chain, different facility."

"Here's what I want," Dren said. He stood up — one of the few times Sato had seen him move from his desk during a meeting — and moved to the wall display. "Split the supply chains. The alloy sourcing — I don't want a single supplier feeding more than thirty percent of any critical component. Diversify across at least three belt sources for shielding, structural, and reactor materials. If one gets disrupted, the other two keep the line moving."

"That's more expensive," Sato said.

"I know what it costs. Second — the shipping corridors. From now on, every belt freighter carrying interceptor materials runs under a commercial manifest. Different routing each time. No pattern. If someone's targeting our logistics, make them guess."

"And the fabrication lines?"

"Compartmentalize. Line 4 team doesn't know what Line 5 is building. The integration team sees the full picture. Nobody else does. If we have a leak — and after that hearing, we have to assume we might — I want to limit what any single person can compromise."

"Alexis, that's going to slow us down almost as much as the disruptions did."

"No. The disruptions cost us four to six weeks. Compartmentalization costs us one, maybe two. I'll take the trade." He sat back down. "And keep the records. Every disruption — dates, causes, who had access, who benefits from the delay. If this is friction, the pattern won't repeat. If it's something else, it will."

"I'm already keeping records," Sato said.

"I know you are. That's why you're the one I'm having this conversation with."

• • •

Chloe Ashford and Greg were eating Chinese takeout in front of the television when the Dren hearing replay came on.

They were on the couch in the DC apartment — Greg at one end with his feet on the coffee table, Ashford cross-legged at the other with a container of lo mein balanced on her knee and her laptop open beside her. Greg had been home for four days, which was long for him. A canceled client meeting in Philadelphia had given them an unexpected overlap, and they'd settled into the easy routine of two people who liked each other and didn't need to fill every silence. The TV had been on all evening — background noise, the way it usually was when Greg was home and Ashford was half-working.

The hearing footage had been running on every channel for two days. Ashford had already watched the full four hours twice, once live and once at double speed with a notepad. This was the condensed version — the money shot, the eight-minute gap, Beckett's question and the long silence and then Dren's answer arriving from Mars. The anchors were treating it like a procedural thriller.

"You have to admit," Greg said, pointing at the screen with a chopstick, "the guy's got nerve. Building nuclear interceptors in secret and then just — confirming it. On camera. To a Senate committee."

"He didn't have a choice. They had the intelligence. Denying it would have been worse."

"Still. Most people would have lawyered up and stalled. He just sat there and said yes."

"That's because he thinks he's right," Ashford said. She set the lo mein on the coffee table and pulled her laptop closer. "Which isn't what interests me."

"What interests you?"

"The reaction. The coordinated push afterward." She was already pulling up her database, the connection chart that had outgrown a single display months ago. "Watch — within forty-eight hours of the hearing, you had three op-eds in major outlets calling for sanctions on Mars manufacturing. A letter signed by forty academics demanding 'responsible governance of off-world military capabilities.' A policy brief from a DC think tank proposing an international regulatory framework. All aligned. All on message. All within the same week."

"So? Big story, lots of opinions. That's how it works."

"It is how it works. But I ran the names." She turned the laptop so he could see, though she knew he wouldn't read it. "The policy analyst who wrote two of the op-eds? Former fellow of a program funded by the same consortium that administers Fresh Start's fellowship initiative. The communications strategist who organized the academics' letter? Advisory board member of an organization that shares two board members with Fresh Start. And this one took me a while —" She tapped the screen. "A congressional staffer who prepared Beckett's briefing materials. It was buried in a LinkedIn history that had been partially scrubbed, but she completed a Fresh Start policy fellowship six years ago."

Greg looked at her. "So three people who went through the same fellowship program ended up on the same side of a political fight. Isn't that just — networking?"

"Yes. That's exactly what it is. That's also exactly what it looks like if a fellowship program is designed to place people in positions where they'll naturally align on specific policy questions when the moment comes." She closed the laptop. "Each connection is normal. Think tanks employ fellows. Strategists organize letters. Staffers have backgrounds. Finding three from the same network in one fight in one week is not evidence of coordination."

"But?"

"But my chart went from twenty-three organizations to thirty-one this week. And for the first time, I have a visible event where the network's alumni are active, in public, simultaneously, on the same side." She picked up her lo mein again. "It's still not a story. But it's the closest thing to one I've had in eleven months."

Greg chewed slowly, watching the hearing replay cycle back to Beckett's question. "So you think someone's pulling strings behind the Dren thing?"

"I don't think anything yet. I'm documenting connections." She took a bite. "But I'll tell you this — the speed of that response wasn't organic. Forty academics don't sign a letter in forty-eight hours unless someone had the letter ready before the hearing happened."

Greg looked at her with an expression she hadn't seen from him before — not the pleasant half-attention of a man waiting for her to finish, but something sharper. "That's a hell of a thing to say without proof."

"Which is why I'm not saying it. I'm documenting it." She pointed at the screen with her chopsticks, where Dren's face was frozen in the four-minute delay. "But someone knew what Beckett was going to ask before he asked it. And someone had the response infrastructure ready before the answer arrived."

She saved her files. She didn't file a story. She wasn't ready. But for the first time in eleven months of work, she thought she might eventually be.

• • •

The fourth event arrived while Earth was still arguing about Mars.

Soares found it in the weekly tracking consolidation — the familiar pipeline, the familiar flag. But the flag was different this time. Larger. The offset between observed and predicted position was not the fractional arcsecond deviation of the previous three events. It was bigger. Measurably, unmistakably bigger.

She didn't send a message to Hamner's terminal. She walked to his office and stood in the doorway — a small woman framed against the amber light of the corridor, hands at her sides, tablet nowhere in sight — until he looked up.

"How big?" Hamner asked. Her face was enough.

"Big," Soares said. "Larger than the previous three combined. And the profile is different."

Hamner followed her to the control room. The data was on her screen — the residuals plot showing the deviation, the acceleration profile spread across the observation window. He studied it in silence, one hand on the back of her chair, reading glasses on his face for once instead of forgotten on his forehead.

The previous events had been small, noisy, stochastic — consistent with the messy, irregular signature of cometary outgassing. This one was not. The acceleration was sustained over a longer period — days, not hours — and the direction was more coherent, the thrust vector holding steady instead of wobbling with the randomness of surface jets. The net delta-v was approximately seventy-five meters per second. The previous three events, combined, had totaled roughly the same. This single event had matched all of them.

And they were at ten AU. Ten astronomical units from the sun — out past Saturn's orbit, where solar flux was one percent of what it was at Earth. Outgassing at this distance required the most volatile ices — carbon monoxide, molecular nitrogen — and even those sublimated weakly this far from the sun. To produce seventy-five meters per second of delta-v through gas ejection, the object would need to be venting mass on a scale that was no longer physically ambiguous. Hamner ran the numbers in his head — exhaust velocity for sublimating volatiles, the object's estimated mass, the rocket equation. The mass flow rate required was staggering. Millions of tons per second, sustained over days.

That would produce a coma visible to amateur telescopes. It would produce a tail. It would produce the most spectacular cometary display since Hale-Bopp, visible across every observatory in the network and half the backyards on Earth.

There was no coma. There was no tail. The object's photometric signature was unchanged — the same flat, featureless light curve it had shown since discovery. Whatever was pushing it, it wasn't gas.

Hamner stared at the screen. For eleven months, he had maintained the professional discipline of a scientist working within the system — noting anomalies, computing probabilities, filing observations, accepting that the data was insufficient to overturn the consensus. The data was no longer insufficient.

"Run the orbit fit," he said. Soares ran it. The computation took longer this time — the perturbation was large enough to shift the orbital solution significantly, and the minimization algorithm needed more iterations to converge.

It converged.

Soares read the result. Then she read it again. Her hand went to the edge of the desk and stayed there.

"Hamner," she said. She'd never said his name like that before — stripped of its professional briskness, just the word.

"Tell me."

"Miss distance is gone. The updated trajectory — the best fit to all available data — passes through Earth's position at the time of closest approach. Within the uncertainty ellipse."

Hamner looked at the number on the screen. The number that had been shrinking with every event — from millions of miles to 1.2 in June.

It was zero. His hands were shaking. He put them flat on the desk and held them there until they stopped.

Not precisely zero — the uncertainty ellipse still spanned hundreds of thousands of miles, and the formal probability of impact depended on the size of that ellipse relative to Earth's cross-section. But the nominal trajectory — the best-fit solution, the center of the ellipse — no longer missed. The center of the ellipse was on Earth.

And they were at ten AU. That was the detail that would end the debate. At twenty AU, small trajectory uncertainties propagated into enormous positional errors by the time the object reached Earth's orbit — which was why the early miss distances had been stated with large error bars and the hazard assessments had been labeled "preliminary." But at ten AU, with eleven months of tracking data from six facilities on two planets, the orbital solution was precise. The uncertainty ellipse was shrinking with every week of additional observations, and the center of that ellipse was not drifting back toward a miss. It was sitting on Earth.

The system was going to flag this. The automated hazard assessment that had scored every previous report "negligible" was going to see a nominal impact trajectory with a probability above its threshold, and it was going to do what it had been designed to do — escalate. There would be no committee vote, no steering group debate, no three-day discussion about whether to include a footnote. The algorithm would run, the flag would trigger, and every planetary defense protocol on Earth would activate simultaneously.

"Run it again," Hamner said.

"I've run it twice."

"Run it with different initial conditions. Perturb the inputs. I want to see the uncertainty cloud."

Soares ran it. The cloud of possible trajectories, generated by varying the input parameters within their measurement uncertainties, was wide. Many of the realizations still missed — barely, by margins that would have been called "comfortable" six months ago. But a significant fraction did not miss. The probability of impact, formally computed from the Monte Carlo distribution of possible trajectories, was no longer negligible.

It was not certain. The uncertainty was real and large. The formal probability was a number that the automated hazard system would flag — would have to flag — and the flag would trigger a cascade of institutional responses that had been designed for exactly this scenario and never used.

Hamner stared at the screen. The control room was quiet. Soares stood beside him, not speaking, waiting for him to say what they both already knew.

"Get Mercer," Hamner said. "And get me the planetary defense coordination office. Direct line."

He paused.

"And pull my private file. All of it. Every entry since October. They're going to want to see it."

Soares left. Hamner sat alone with the trajectory plot — the hyperbolic arc that had been curving through the inner solar system for eleven months, tracked by every major observatory on two planets and in the belt, explained by outgassing, dismissed by consensus, ignored by the public, built against in secret by one man on Mars.

The arc now passed through Earth.

Four events. Four Earthward movements. The system had required three data points before it would listen. It had gotten four. And the fourth had ended the conversation.

The object was ten astronomical units away, closing at fifty-two kilometers per second. In two hundred and eighty-eight days, give or take the uncertainties that no longer mattered as much as they used to, it would arrive.

The miss was over.

# CHAPTER 7

*Zero*

*November 2059.*

*Object at ~9 AU, ~52 km/s. 236 days to impact.*

*Earth ↔ Mars: ~0.6 AU, Communications: ~5 min one-way.*

• • •

The outgassing model died in seventy-two hours.

It didn't die in a paper. It didn't die in a working group circular or a steering committee vote or a carefully worded press release. It died in the data pipelines of six independent tracking facilities on two planets, each running the same orbit fit against the same observations, each converging on one result: the fourth non-gravitational acceleration event was too large, too sustained, and too directionally coherent to be produced by cometary volatiles at nine astronomical units from the sun.

The math was not subtle. A hundred and sixty-eight meters per second of delta-v, applied over days, at a heliocentric distance where solar flux was one percent of Earth's. That was more than the previous three corrections combined — three point seven times larger than the third event alone. The mass ejection rate required to produce that acceleration through outgassing would have generated a coma visible to backyard telescopes across the Northern Hemisphere. There was no coma. There was no tail. The photometric signature was unchanged — the same flat, featureless light curve the object had shown since discovery. Whatever was producing the acceleration, it was not sublimating ice.

The European Southern Observatory published first — a terse, two-paragraph alert noting that the fourth event was "inconsistent with any known cometary outgassing mechanism at this heliocentric distance." The Japanese belt telescope consortium followed within hours. The Harvard-Smithsonian group, Vasquez's team, published by end of day. The working group that had maintained the outgassing consensus for eleven months issued a revised assessment forty-eight hours after the event was confirmed: "The non-gravitational acceleration profile of 7I/Hamner is no longer adequately described by cometary outgassing models. Alternative mechanisms are under active investigation."

No one used the word "artificial." Not yet. The revised assessment was careful to frame the failure as a modeling problem — the outgassing model was inadequate, not necessarily wrong in principle, and the community was exploring alternatives. But the alternatives that remained — radiation pressure, magnetic interactions with the solar wind, tidal effects from planetary encounters — were individually insufficient by orders of magnitude. The community knew this. The public, reading between the lines, knew this too.

The "outgassing denier" label disappeared. Not retracted. Not apologized for. Just abandoned — the way a crowd abandons a position it never formally held, leaving behind no fingerprints and no accountability. The hashtag stopped trending. The opinion columns that had deployed the phrase moved on to new vocabulary. The scientists who had signed the consensus statements did not issue corrections. They issued new statements, with new language, describing a new situation — as though the previous eleven months of institutional certainty had been a preliminary assessment rather than a verdict.

Hamner watched this happen from Paranal with a bone-deep exhaustion that left no room for vindication. He had been right. The pattern had been real. The corrections had been directional. The outgassing model had been wrong. And none of that mattered now, because being right had never been the point. Being heard in time had been the point, and the time that had been lost — the eleven months of institutional resistance, the suppressed footnotes, the "outgassing denier" label, the quiet minority afraid to speak — could not be recovered.

• • •

Saunders called him one last time. Not from São Paulo, not from the Monitor's offices. From Paranal. She'd driven up the mountain without telling the press office, parked in the visitor lot the way she had eight months ago, and found him in the control room where he'd been living for three days.

She stood in the doorway. She looked tired — not the polished fatigue of a journalist on deadline, but the real kind, the kind that settled behind the eyes and didn't leave. She was holding the notebook. The paper one. It was thicker than it had been in December. Eight months of notes in a hand that Hamner had never read but knew was precise.

"I came to give you something," she said.

She set the notebook on the desk beside his keyboard. Next to it, she placed a data token.

"That's everything," she said. "Every draft. The approved versions and the originals — the ones the press office killed. The institutional analysis they redacted after Adler. The six-percent piece I never filed. My notes from every conversation we've had since December, dated and sourced." She paused. "And my file. The one I told you about. The parallel record."

Hamner looked at the notebook and the drive. He didn't pick them up.

"Why?" he asked.

"Because somebody should have the complete record. Both sides of the architecture. Your file shows what the science said and when. Mine shows what the public was allowed to know and when. Together they're the story of how a system that was working correctly almost got us all killed." She clicked the pen — the same pen, the same habit — and put it on the desk next to the notebook. "I can't publish it. Not now. The story isn't the suppression anymore. The story is the object. Everything I've been sitting on for eight months is yesterday's news, and yesterday's news doesn't run when the world is ending."

"It's not yesterday's news," Hamner said.

"It is today. It will matter later — if there is a later." She said it without melodrama, the way she'd said everything for eight months: factually, precisely, with the flat affect of someone who had trained herself to report what was true regardless of how it felt. "When the inquiries come — and they will come — your file and mine together tell the story that neither of us could tell alone. Keep them together."

Hamner picked up the notebook. It was heavier than he'd expected. Eight months of a journalist watching the same pattern he'd watched, from the other side of the information wall. The drafts the press office had approved. The drafts they'd killed. The gap between them, documented page by page.

"Saunders," he said. "Jessica."

It was the first time he'd used her first name. She noticed. He could tell she noticed because her expression shifted — not much, not dramatically, just the faintest movement around the eyes, the way a person's face changed when a professional boundary became something else. Not warmth. Recognition. Eight months of shared vigilance, ending in a control room on a mountain in Chile because the thing they'd both been watching had turned out to be exactly what they'd feared.

"Write the story," he said. "When it's time. Write the real one."

"That's the plan," she said. "Assuming there's someone left to read it."

She didn't say goodbye. She picked up her messenger bag — the same bag, the tablet, the voice recorder, the space where the notebook had been — and walked out of the control room. He heard her footsteps in the corridor, then the exterior door, then the sound of the SUV starting in the visitor lot.

Hamner sat with the notebook and the drive and the pen she'd left on his desk. The pen was still warm.

He put all three in a secure case with his private file. When the military transport came for him twelve hours later, he carried them to Washington together — his record and hers, side by side, the complete account of thirteen months of watching a system work exactly as designed while something that wasn't natural fell toward Earth.

• • •

The press found a name for it within days. Not a scientific designation — a tabloid headline that stuck because it was short and brutal and accurate: Hamner's Hammer.

Hamner heard it first from Soares, who found him at his desk in the control room — where he had been for most of the past seventy-two hours, eating when someone put food in front of him, sleeping in the chair when his body demanded it — and held up her tablet with an expression that was somewhere between sympathy and dark amusement.

"I didn't name it that," he said.

"Nobody names these things," Soares replied. "They name themselves."

It spread the way these things spread — faster than the science, faster than the official statements, faster than the institutional machinery could produce a preferred alternative. Within a week, every news outlet, every feed, every conversation about the interstellar object used the name. Hamner's Hammer. The object he had discovered, tracked, flagged, and been ignored about now carried his name twice — once in the formal designation, once in the phrase that described what it was going to do.

• • •

The quiet minority — the scientists who had privately shared Hamner's concerns through encrypted messages and weekend phone calls and coffee-shop conversations — were now the people everyone was calling. The Tokyo dynamicist. The Harvard-Smithsonian postdoc. Patel. They had run the numbers months ago. They had seen the pattern. They had the head start. And the head start gave them nothing except a longer acquaintance with the dread that was now settling over everyone else.

Patel called Hamner the day the impact energy was published. He was at his desk at Paranal — the same desk, the same view of the Atacama through the window that he'd stopped seeing weeks ago. He picked up because it was Patel, and Patel was one of the six people in the world who had earned the right to call him without warning.

"They're calling us for comment," she said. "Asking what we knew and when we knew it."

"What are you telling them?" Hamner asked.

"I'm telling them I ran a Monte Carlo in June and got six percent and kept my mouth shut because of what happens to people who don't. They don't like that answer."

"No. They wouldn't," Hamner said flatly.

"Some of them are asking why we didn't push harder. Why we didn't go public. Why we let the consensus hold when we knew it was wrong."

"We didn't know it was wrong," Hamner said. "We knew it was uncomfortable. There's a difference."

“Is there?” Patel’s voice was sharp. “Because from where I’m sitting right now, the difference between ‘uncomfortable’ and ‘wrong’ is two hundred and forty days.”

Hamner didn’t have an answer for that. He sat with the phone against his ear and looked out at the Atacama — the brown nothing of the desert stretching to the horizon under a sky that was, for once, exactly the right color — and said nothing, because there was nothing to say.

• • •

The assessment was held in a secure conference facility outside Washington — a windowless room three stories underground, designed for conversations that could not leave the room. Fluorescent light, dropped ceiling, long table with microphones at every seat, screens on three walls. The kind of room where the furniture was chosen for function and the air tasted like it had been recycled since the Cold War.

The other attendees included the national security advisor, the secretary of war, representatives from NORAD, the European Space Agency, the newly activated Planetary Defense Coordination Office, the joint chiefs’ strategic planning division, and a small number of scientists who had been cleared for the briefing. Hamner was one of them. He had been flown from Chile on a military transport that had landed at Andrews at four in the morning. He hadn’t slept on the flight. He was wearing the same clothes he’d been wearing at Paranal and carrying a secure case that contained his private file — every entry since October — compiled, indexed, and complete.

President Whitfield was already seated when Hamner entered. She sat at the head of the table — a small woman, compact, precise in the way she held herself, with close-cropped silver hair and dark eyes that moved across the room the way a camera tracked a scene, taking in everything and signaling nothing. She wore a dark blazer over a white blouse, no jewelry except a watch, and she had the particular stillness of a person who had learned that the most powerful thing in a room full of powerful people was silence. She did not take notes. She did not fidget. She listened with the focused attention of someone who intended to make a decision and wanted to make sure she had everything she needed before she made it.

The briefing began with the trajectory. The impact probability was now formally above the automated threshold — the number that the system had been designed to flag. The flag had triggered. The cascade of institutional responses was underway. Everything that Hamner had wanted the system to do for eleven months was now happening, rapidly and simultaneously, because the system had finally been given data that its own machinery could not ignore.

"Walk me through the impact scenario," Whitfield said. "Assume I've read the summary. Tell me what the summary doesn't say."

The colonel who delivered the assessment was a NORAD officer named Reeves — tall, narrow-shouldered, with the clipped diction of a man who had spent his career briefing people who didn't have time for adjectives. He stood at the front of the room with a pointer and no notes.

"The nominal trajectory is a central Pacific ocean strike," Reeves said. "Velocity at impact: approximately sixty-five kilometers per second. That's faster than any natural impactor in the historical record. The object isn't bound to the solar system — it's on a hyperbolic trajectory, falling in from interstellar space, picking up speed from the sun's gravity as it comes. By the time it reaches us, it's carrying the velocity of the galaxy."

"How bad?" Whitfield asked.

"We don't know the mass," Reeves said. "From a head-on view, all we can measure is the cross-section — roughly four and a half kilometers across. Whether that's a sphere, a disk, or something else, we can't tell from this angle. Without mass, I can't give you an energy number." He paused. "What I can tell you is that a solid object of that cross-section, at sixty-five kilometers per second, delivers energy in the range of Chicxulub. The impact that ended the Cretaceous. If it's denser or larger than we think, it's worse. Mega-tsunamis across the Pacific. Coastal destruction on every Pacific Rim nation. Multi-year dust veil. Agricultural collapse. Billions dead." He paused. "Planet killer is not a metaphor, ma'am. It's a job description."

"When?"

"Strike day: June 24th, 2060. Two hundred and forty days."

Whitfield's expression didn't change. She looked at the trajectory plot on the wall screen — the hyperbolic arc sweeping in from beyond Saturn, curving toward the inner solar system, the projected impact point marked with a red circle in the empty blue of the central Pacific — and her face showed exactly what it had shown since she sat down: nothing. The calculation was happening behind it. The reaction would come later, or not at all.

"Defense options," she said.

Reeves moved to the next slide. "Our planetary defense fleet — deployed and maintained by Space Force — was designed for asteroid deflection. Kilometer-scale rocks on predictable orbits, detected years in advance. Kinetic impactors, gravity tractors, standoff nuclear detonation. The infrastructure is real. It works. It was built for a specific class of threat."

He paused.

"This is not that class of threat. The object is faster than anything in the historical record. It's more massive than our baseline scenarios. And it is —" He chose the word carefully. "— maneuvering. Four corrections, each one larger than the last, each one directional. Toward us. This is not a ballistic path. The hammer is being guided."

The room absorbed the word. Hamner, sitting in the third row, watched it land on each face — the flinch that wasn't quite a flinch, the recalculation happening behind the eyes, the moment when "guided" stopped being an adjective and became a fact.

“The fleet wasn’t designed for a maneuvering target,” Reeves continued. “If the hammer corrects after a deflection attempt, we’re in a scenario we’ve never modeled.”

“We don’t need to have modeled it.” The voice came from the second row — General Vickers, Department of War, who had overseen the planetary defense procurement program for six years. He was a thick, broad-shouldered man with a shaved head and the unhurried bearing of someone who had spent three decades in rooms where the wrong sentence could start a war and had learned to make every word carry its weight. He had been listening with the patience of someone who had heard threat briefings overshoot the data before.

“The fleet was designed with margin,” Vickers said. “That’s what margin is for — the things you haven’t modeled. The warheads are five hundred megatons each. Ten platforms. We have the throw weight. The intercept geometry is favorable. The question of whether the hammer can correct afterward is a question, but it’s not a reason to doubt the first intercept.”

He paused, then continued. “And if — and I say if — it maneuvers after we hit it, we hit it again. As many times as is necessary.”

Reeves looked at him. “The intercept assumes a passive target.”

“The intercept assumes physics,” Vickers said. His voice didn’t rise, but it filled the space between them the way a stone fills a glass — completely. “We detonate, we transfer momentum, the object moves. It doesn’t get a vote on that. Whether it corrects afterward is a second-order problem. And as I said, if it does then we hit it again.”

It was a reasonable thing to say. Calm. Professional. Several heads nodded.

The implications of that word — guided — settled over the room like a change in air pressure. If the hammer was capable of course correction, then any deflection attempt faced a problem that no planetary defense scenario had ever modeled: the target could adjust. A kinetic impactor that shifted the trajectory by ten thousand kilometers could be countered by a fifth correction that shifted it back. The defense was not a one-time intervention. It was the opening move in a contest against an adversary whose capabilities, intentions, and response time were unknown.

"How much can we move it?" Whitfield asked. "In plain numbers. How far does it shift if we hit it with everything we have?"

"Against the current mass estimate — assuming roughly spherical, four-point-four kilometers in diameter — we can deliver close to six hundred thousand kilometers of deflection at the earliest feasible intercept point," Reeves said. "We need six thousand."

The room exhaled. Not just margin. Massive margin. Nearly a hundred times what they needed.

"So we have enough," Whitfield said.

"Against a passive target," Reeves said. He let the qualifier settle. "And against our current mass estimate. Both of those assumptions are doing heavy lifting."

Whitfield studied him — the look she gave everyone who delivered bad news with a caveat, patient, attentive, waiting for the part he hadn't said yet. "The mass estimate. How confident are we?"

"Moderately, ma'am. We know the size from brightness and albedo — roughly four and a half kilometers across. We have thermal data that gives us a density range. The mass follows from size and density. The uncertainty is in the composition. If it's cometary — porous ice and rock — the mass is at the low end and we have even more margin. If it's denser — consolidated rock, metal content — the mass goes up and the margin comes down."

"What does the thermal data say?"

"The thermal signature suggests something more consolidated than a typical comet. Higher density. More consistent with rock or a rock-metal mix." Reeves pulled up the comparison chart on the wall screen. "At the high end of the density range, the mass is roughly three times our baseline estimate. That would reduce our margin from a factor of ninety to a factor of thirty. Still comfortable."

"And at the high end, what are we actually hitting?" Whitfield asked. "What's this thing made of?"

"We don't know," Reeves said. "The spectral data is ambiguous. Dark surface, low albedo, doesn't match any clean template. The best-fit model is irradiated organic crust, but that's a surface description, not a composition. We don't know what's underneath."

The room was quiet.

"Is there any way to get a closer look at this hammer?" Whitfield asked.

The question landed in a brief silence. Then the NASA representative — a deputy director who had been brought in for the planetary defense component, a tall woman in a navy suit who had been taking notes steadily for the past hour — leaned forward.

"We have the Cassini III probe," she said. "Titan orbiter, operational, in the Saturn system. Saturn is currently offset from the Earth-object line by about sixty degrees. The probe can't resolve the object at this distance — it's a planetary orbiter, not a deep-space telescope. But it can observe from a substantially different viewing angle. If the object looks the same from sixty degrees off-axis as it does from Earth, it's a sphere. If it doesn't, we learn something."

"How long?" Whitfield asked.

"Retasking takes hours. The observation and downlink — maybe a day, depending on orientation and scheduling."

"Do it," Whitfield said. Two words, no inflection, and the NASA representative was already reaching for her phone.

The order went out before the briefing broke for lunch.

• • •

The Cassini III data arrived forty-one hours later. The briefing reconvened in the same room, most of the same faces — though some had not left the building in the intervening time, and it showed.

It was the NASA representative who presented. She stood where Reeves had stood, pointer in hand, the Cassini downlink on the wall screen behind her.

"The probe couldn't resolve the object's shape," she began. "At several AU, it's a single pixel — a point source indistinguishable from a star. But we don't need shape to learn something. We need brightness."

She pulled up the photometric comparison. "From Earth, the object has shown a consistent apparent magnitude — consistent with our size and albedo estimates over thirteen months of observation. From Cassini III's viewing angle, sixty degrees off-axis —" She tapped the screen. "— the object is significantly brighter. Not subtly. The difference is unmistakable."

"Meaning what?" Whitfield asked.

"Meaning it's not a sphere," the NASA representative said. "A sphere looks the same from every direction. This doesn't. It's presenting a larger reflecting area to Saturn than to Earth. The shape that fits the data is an elongated body, long axis aligned with its direction of travel, aimed at Earth end-on."

"We've been seeing the small face," Whitfield said.

"Yes, ma'am. Head-on. Cassini is seeing the flank." She pulled up the aspect ratio constraints. "The brightness difference tells us the long axis is at least six to eight times the short axis. We can't determine the exact shape from this — a prolate spheroid, a cylinder, a cigar, all produce the same brightness asymmetry."

Whitfield looked at the screen for a long moment. "So for thirteen months, we've been estimating the mass of this thing based on a cross-section that's six to eight times smaller than its actual profile."

"Yes, ma'am."

"And the mass estimate we've been using for deflection calculations —"

"Is based on a sphere," Reeves said from his seat. He was already running numbers on his tablet. "Which it isn't."

Whitfield turned to him. "How bad?"

"We need the actual dimensions before I can give you a number," Reeves said. "Six-to-one and eight-to-one are very different answers."

"Then get me the actual dimensions," Whitfield said. "Who can resolve this?"

The answer came from the back of the room — one of the ESA scientists, who had been in contact with the Japanese belt telescope consortium throughout the briefing. "Kimura's array," he said. "Long-baseline interferometry. Four optical telescopes on separate asteroids, baselines measured in millions of kilometers. They've been tracking the hammer continuously. The Cassini photometry tells them exactly how to optimize — maximum resolution along the flight axis, looking for the elongation."

"How long?"

"Thirty-six hours for the integration. Maybe less if they prioritize."

"Tell them to prioritize," Whitfield said.

• • •

The Kimura reconstruction arrived on schedule. The interferometric image went up on the wall screen for a group of people who had spent the previous thirty-six hours sleeping in offices, eating from vending machines, and running scenarios they hoped the data would render irrelevant.

The image was not a photograph — it was a reconstruction built from the interference patterns of light waves collected across millions of kilometers of baseline, processed through algorithms that extracted shape from the fringes. It was grainy, pixelated, more suggestion than portrait. But the shape was unambiguous.

A cylinder. Or something close to one. Long axis roughly eight to nine times the short axis. The dimensions, reconstructed from the fringe pattern and the known distance: approximately four thousand four hundred meters in diameter and thirty-seven thousand meters in length.

"Thirty-seven kilometers long," Whitfield said quietly. It was the first time her voice had changed — not louder or softer, but different. The tone of someone who had been processing numbers and had just been handed a shape. Behind the composure, something cold had settled in her chest — the weight of a number that meant everyone she was responsible for.

Her hands were under the table. Nobody could see them. She pressed her thumbs against the pads of her fingers, one at a time, left hand then right — a habit from her first campaign, when she'd learned that the body needed somewhere to put the things the face couldn't show. Thirty-seven kilometers. She thought of the length of Manhattan. She pressed her thumbs harder and stopped.

Reeves was already at the front of the room. He had run the mass recalculation before the image finished rendering — the dimensions were all he needed, and the first numbers had come through before the full reconstruction was complete.

"The shape changes everything," Reeves said. "A cylinder thirty-seven kilometers long and four and a half wide. We don't know the internal structure — it could be solid, hollow, anything in between. Without density, I can't give you an impact energy."

He put the dimensions on the screen. The cylinder hung there, annotated with the probe's error bars.

"What I can tell you is that nothing this size has entered the inner solar system since Theia." He let that land. "The impact that formed the Moon. Four and a half billion years ago. Whatever this thing is made of — rock, metal, something we don't have a word for — the energy at sixty-five kilometers per second is beyond any comparison in human experience."

The room did not exhale this time.

"Does that mean what I fear it means?" Whitfield asked.

"It means the previous estimate was wrong," Reeves said. He said it flatly, the way he said everything — because the scale said it for him. “We were modeling a four-kilometer sphere. This is a thirty-seven-kilometer cylinder. The mass could be ten times higher, fifty times higher — we don’t know. What we know is that the damage profile just moved past anything we’ve modeled.”

Whitfield held his gaze for three seconds. Then: “And the deflection math.”

“The fleet that offered six hundred thousand kilometers of margin against a sphere offers fifty thousand against the cylinder,” Reeves said. “We need six thousand. So we still have margin — roughly eight to one. But it’s not ninety-eight to one anymore.“

“Eight to one,” Whitfield repeated. “If everything works.”

“If everything works. Yes, ma’am.”

The wall had become a fence.

“There’s a targeting constraint,” Reeves said. He picked up a pen from the table and laid it flat, pointing away from him. “The hammer is a cylinder, thirty-seven kilometers long, traveling at sixty-five kilometers per second.” He pushed the tip of the pen with his finger. The pen rotated on the table, swinging sideways. Its center barely moved.

“If we hit the nose — head-on, or near the front — we apply torque. The object rotates. It may tumble. But the center of mass continues on essentially the same trajectory. We’ve changed its orientation, not its direction.” He reset the pen. Then he pressed his finger against the middle and pushed sideways. The pen slid across the table without rotating. “We have to hit broadside. Dead center of the long axis. That’s a lateral push on the center of mass. That’s deflection.”

He let the pen sit. “Against a sphere, you hit it anywhere and the geometry works. Against a cylinder, you have to come in perpendicular to the long axis and hit the midpoint. Off-center and you waste energy in rotation. That constrains the intercept geometry significantly.”

“How significantly?” Whitfield asked.

"Our platforms approach head-on. For a broadside detonation, they need to arrive perpendicular to the cylinder's length. At a hundred and fifty kilometers per second closing velocity, the entire length of the object passes any fixed point in a quarter of a second. The detonation window for a centered broadside hit is measured in milliseconds."

The room was quiet.

"Still enough," Reeves said. "Against a passive target, with all ten platforms performing nominally and the targeting packages updated for the cylinder geometry."

"Walk me through what happens when they don't all perform nominally," Whitfield said.

Reeves did. Lose one platform to launch failure — which had happened on two of the last six deep-space missions — and the margin dropped to seven-to-one. Lose a second to guidance error or intercept timing and it was six-to-one. Add the cylinder targeting constraint — millisecond precision on a broadside detonation at a hundred and fifty kilometers per second — and the probability of optimal energy coupling dropped. Each platform that detonated off-center, or at the wrong angle, delivered less deflection than the model predicted. Three platforms lost and degraded coupling could bring the margin to three-to-one. And three-to-one assumed the object held still.

"What's the minimum?" Whitfield asked. "How many platforms do we need if everything else works?"

"Two," Reeves said. "Two platforms, optimal detonation, full energy coupling. That's our floor. Anything less and the deflection falls short."

"And if it corrects after we hit it?"

"Then we need a second wave, and we don't have one."

The fence, under examination, had gaps.

• • •

The briefing continued. Contingency plans. Evacuation scenarios. Communication protocols. The question of when and how to inform the public — a question that generated more debate than any technical issue, because the technical issues had numbers and the communication question had politics.

Someone — Hamner didn't see who — raised the question that had been forming in the silence.

"What about Mars?"

The room shifted. Mars. Dren. The interceptor program that had dominated the news cycle for two months. The unauthorized weapons production that had triggered Congressional hearings and international sanctions debates and editorial condemnations. The man who had started building before anyone else believed there was something to build against.

"What do we know about Mars's actual capacity?" Whitfield asked.

The intelligence briefer — a civilian analyst from the national security apparatus, compact and precise, reading from a tablet he held close to his chest — pulled up a slide. The estimates were based on satellite imagery of the Ares City industrial complex, trade flow analysis, and the testimony Dren had given at the Beckett hearing. Manufacturing lines retooled. Hull fabrication in progress. Propulsion development ongoing. The numbers were uncertain.

"Our best estimate is three to five interceptor platforms in various stages of completion," the analyst said. "Pulsed fusion propulsion — higher specific impulse than anything in our fleet. If operational, they could add to the deflection budget. But the real value would be redundancy — additional platforms on different trajectories, arriving at different times. If the object corrects after the first intercept, follow-on waves improve our odds."

"How much?" Whitfield asked.

"Unknown. We don't have reliable data on the propulsion system's actual performance, and we can't verify the number of operational vehicles. Three to five is our best estimate. It could be fewer."

The room's estimate was drastically low. Three to five platforms. The reality — which Dren had not shared and which the intelligence community had not detected — was different. But nobody in the room knew that yet.

• • •

Mercer was there. He had been included in the briefing as a member of the working group's core team — a logical selection, given his proximity to the discovery and his role in coordinating the observation campaign. He sat in the second row, three seats ahead of Hamner and one row in front, close enough that Hamner could see his profile when he turned to speak to the person beside him. He had been taking notes on a tablet, his expression the same controlled attentiveness he brought to every professional setting.

When the Kimura reconstruction had appeared on the screen — when the room had watched the sphere assumption die and the margin collapse from ninety-eight to eight — Mercer's face had shown what a genuinely shocked scientist's face would show: the recalculation happening behind the eyes, the magnitude of the error settling in. He had set his pen down and said, quietly, to the person next to him: "We should have looked sooner."

It was exactly the right thing to say. Appropriate. Shaken. Human. The kind of remark that drew a nod from the person beside him and then disappeared into the ambient noise of a room full of people confronting the same reality.

Hamner heard it from two rows back. He didn't react. There was nothing to react to. Mercer had said what anyone would say in that moment — what anyone should say, looking at a margin that had just lost two orders of magnitude because nobody had thought to point a different camera at the thing.

• • •

Hamner sat through all of it. The object he had found and named. The corrections he had flagged. The pattern he had tracked. He had been right, and it didn't matter. Being right had never been the goal. Being heard in time had been the goal, and the time was gone.

He thought about the private file — the document he had maintained since October 2058, now sitting in the classified briefing materials, every entry timestamped, every observation logged. Thirteen months of anomalies that had been assessed individually and dismissed individually. It showed that one person had seen the pattern and that the system had processed his observations and produced the only answer it was designed to produce: insufficient data, continue monitoring.

The file was evidence now. Evidence of what had been known and when. Evidence of what had been suppressed — not by conspiracy, but by the ordinary operation of a system optimized for caution. The footnote. The Monte Carlo. The committee minutes. The email responses — three silence, two pushback, one acknowledgment, and Mercer.

The file would be studied, eventually. There would be inquiries. There would be committees. There would be questions about who knew what and when and why the system had failed to escalate. The answers would be unsatisfying, because the system hadn't failed. It had worked exactly as designed. The failure was in the design.

None of that mattered now. What mattered was the number on the screen — a cylinder eight times heavier than they'd thought, an energy eight times larger, a margin eight times thinner — and the fence that only held if the target cooperated.

Hamner's hands were in his lap. He was aware of them the way you became aware of your heartbeat in a quiet room — the fact of his own body, sitting in a chair, in a basement in Washington, listening to people discuss the end of the world in the language of megaton yields and deflection margins. The object on the screen was his. He had found it. He had named it. He remembered his and Mercer's excitement. And now thirteen months later he was sitting in a room where a colonel was explaining how many people would die if the thing he'd found couldn't be stopped. He found himself wishing the object he had been so excited to find never existed.

• • •

The communication from Mars arrived while Whitfield was reviewing the evacuation timeline for the Pacific Rim.

An aide entered the room — a young man in a dark suit who moved with the careful urgency of someone who knew that every person at the table outranked him by a distance he couldn't calculate — crossed to Whitfield's position, and handed her a printed message. Routed through the secure Mars-Earth relay. Classified. Addressed to her by name. She read it, read it again, and set it on the table.

"We have a communication from Alexis Dren," she said. The room went still. "He's requesting a direct, secure channel." She looked down at the message one more time, and something shifted in her expression — not a smile, not surprise, but the faintest recalibration, the look of a woman who had spent three days receiving bad news and had just been handed something that might not be. "The message reads: 'I have some information I think you'll want to hear.'"

The timestamp on the message showed that Dren had sent it after the Cassini photometry and the Kimura reconstruction had been released — after the shape had been confirmed, after the mass had been recalculated, after the margin had collapsed from absurd to thin. He had seen the same data from Mars, run the same mass calculation, computed the same deflection arithmetic against the cylinder, and reached the same conclusion the room had reached an hour ago: the numbers still worked, but the margin was gone.

And he had something the room did not have. Something he had been building while the room was still arguing about outgassing.

Whitfield looked around the table. "I think we take that call," she said.

No one disagreed.

# CHAPTER 8

*27*

*November 2nd, 2059.*
*Object at ~8 AU, ~53 km/s. 235 days to impact.*
*Earth ↔ Mars: ~0.7 AU, Communications: ~6 min one-way.*

• • •

The call was established through the secure Mars-Earth relay at 09:14 UTC, November 2nd. The channel was encrypted, time-stamped, and recorded — Whitfield had insisted on the recording over the objections of two advisors who preferred deniability. She wanted a record. If this worked, the record would matter. If it didn't, nothing would.

The same room. The same fluorescent light and recycled air. Whitfield at the head, Reeves and Vickers in the second row, the intelligence analyst in his usual seat with his tablet held close. Hamner near the back, where he'd been for every session. The room had the particular atmosphere of a group that had been underground together for too long — coffee cups accumulating, ties loosened or removed, the formality of the first briefing replaced by the blunt fatigue of the third day.

Dren's image appeared on the wallscreen at the far end of the room. It arrived six minutes after the channel opened — six minutes of the room watching a frozen frame while the connection handshake traveled to Mars and back. When the feed resolved, it was steady, composed, shot from the same office where he'd testified before Beckett's committee six weeks earlier. The pressed-regolith wall. The Martian light. The slight, immaculate man at his clean desk, hands resting on the surface just below the camera's frame. Everything was the same. The context had changed entirely.

"Madam President, I'll be direct." His voice was unhurried — the voice of a man who had rehearsed nothing because he had been running these numbers for months. "I've run the same trajectory analysis your team has. I've seen the Cassini data. I assume by now you've confirmed what I confirmed: the object is a cylinder, roughly four and a half kilometers in diameter and thirty-seven kilometers long, on a direct impact trajectory. Nominal strike in the central Pacific. Velocity at intercept approximately sixty-five kilometers per second. We don't know the mass — could be hollow, could be solid, could be anything in between — so I can't give you a number in megatons. What I can tell you is that nothing this size has entered the inner solar system since Theia. The impact that formed the Moon. At sixty-five kilometers per second, the energy is beyond any model we've built. Your existing deflection fleet — ten platforms, five hundred megatons each, standoff detonation — gives you a margin of roughly eight-to-one against a passive target. You need six thousand kilometers for a miss. You have enough. Assuming the target cooperates."

He paused — his own pause, not the delay.

"I have interceptor platforms. More than your intelligence estimates suggest. The Mars production that Senator Beckett asked about — your estimate was three to five platforms. The actual number is thirteen. Completed. Pulsed fusion propulsion. Nuclear-armed."

Another pause.

"The belt production your intelligence community did not detect. Six additional platforms, fabricated at three separate facilities under commercial manifests. Your analysts weren't looking for them because they weren't looking in the belt."

Another pause.

"And the part you're not going to like. I retooled three Earth-side manufacturing facilities under dual-use commercial cover. Components were fabricated on sovereign territory and assembled in Earth orbit. Eight platforms. Nuclear-armed. In orbit around your planet."

Another pause. The last one.

"Total: twenty-seven interceptor platforms. Combined with your ten, the deflection capacity against a passive target is massive overkill. You'll notice that twenty-seven is considerably more than is required against a passive target, even accounting for operational failures. I expect that will be discussed at length. Here is why I built that many."

He leaned forward slightly — the first movement he'd made since the feed began, and in the context of Dren's stillness, it was like watching a wall shift. "The target has corrected its trajectory four times. Each correction larger than the last. The fourth used more fuel than the first three combined. It is being guided. Something that is guided was built. Something that was built for this purpose was designed to succeed. I find it unlikely that something designed to succeed would be sent without the means to resist interference. I engineered for the possibility that it fights back. If I'm wrong, we've wasted hardware. If I'm right and I'd built less, we'd be dead."

His image was replaced by a slide — clean, minimal, the kind of visual a man who built spacecraft would build. Four waves, staggered by launch origin and propulsion type. The belt platforms launched first and arrived first — pulsed fusion, sixty-five days transit, reaching the object at roughly a hundred and seventy-five days before impact. The Mars platforms followed — thirteen of them, seventy-five to eighty days transit. Then Dren's Earth-orbit platforms, a hundred and ten days out. And finally Earth's own fleet

— chemical propulsion, the slowest, arriving last at roughly eighty-seven days before impact.

Dren's voice continued over the slide. "You'll notice that your fleet arrives last. Slowest propulsion, longest transit. If the target is passive, the first three waves do most of the work and your fleet provides margin. If the target is not passive, your fleet arrives into whatever is left. I will wait for your response."

The feed froze on his face — composed, patient, the expression of a man who had said what he came to say and was content to wait twelve minutes for the world to catch up.

The room received it in layers, each one worse. Thirteen on Mars — more than estimated, but at least that production had been disclosed at the Beckett hearing. Six in the belt — invisible, built under commercial cover. Eight in Earth orbit — nuclear weapons above their heads, placed by a private actor, undetected by any government. Twenty-seven platforms. The intelligence community had missed twenty-two.

Whitfield absorbed the number without visible reaction — the same focused stillness she'd held since the briefing began. Around her, the room reacted. The secretary of war leaned forward and placed both hands flat on the table. The national security advisor's expression hardened into something raw — the look of a man recalculating the threat while the threat was recalculating him. The intelligence analyst — the same man who had estimated three to five platforms two days ago — was staring at the screen with the specific expression of a professional who had just been shown the size of his failure.

Vickers sat very still. His reaction was different from the rest of the room's, and Hamner — watching from the back row, watching faces because that was what he'd been doing for three days — noticed the difference without understanding it. The others were shocked by the number. Vickers was shocked by something else — something behind the number, some implication that the rest of the room hadn't reached yet. His jaw tightened. His hand, resting on the table, closed once and opened. Then the expression was gone, replaced by the same measured composure he'd worn since the first briefing, and Hamner couldn't have said what he'd seen or why it mattered. He filed it the way he filed anomalous data — noted, timestamped, unexplained.

The twelve minutes passed. People shifted in their chairs. Someone refilled a coffee cup. The intelligence analyst typed something on his tablet, deleted it, typed it again. Whitfield sat motionless, hands folded, watching Dren's frozen image on the wallscreen with the patience of a woman who had decided what she was going to say and was waiting for the protocol to let her say it.

Finally, she spoke.

"Mr. Dren, I have two questions. First: you said nuclear armed. That's an odd way to put it. Describe what you've built."

Her words left the room at the speed of light and would not reach Dren for six minutes. His answer would not return for six more. Dead air in a room full of people who had just learned that a private citizen had built the largest nuclear arsenal in the solar system.

The twelve minutes were not silent. They were filled with the particular noise of people who couldn't yet argue about the answer because the answer hadn't arrived — low conversations, muttered calculations, the intelligence analyst making calls on a secure phone in the corner. Whitfield let it happen. She didn't try to fill the gap. She sat and waited, and the room took its cue from her, and the noise settled into something that resembled patience.

Dren's answer arrived.

"My platforms carry a different weapon than your fleet. Your warheads are designed for standoff detonation — fly close to the target, detonate within a kilometer of the surface, let the radiation ablate the surface and transfer momentum through plasma expansion. That works against a passive target. Against something with active defenses, your platform has to survive long enough to reach detonation range, which means flying into the kill zone at a hundred and fifty kilometers per second closing velocity."

He paused.

"My warheads don't need to get close. Each platform carries five independently targetable warheads — twenty megatons each, one hundred megatons per platform. Each warhead is a directed nuclear charge. A nuclear device detonates behind a shaped package of uranium pellets. The detonation accelerates the pellets to approximately a hundred kilometers per second in a focused cone toward the target. Think of it as a nuclear uranium shotgun. Five shots per platform, fired from a thousand kilometers out. The pellet cloud reaches the target in about ten seconds, spreading to cover the broadside surface. Thousands of individual impacts, distributed across the center of mass. Lateral momentum transfer with minimal torque."

Another pause.

"The advantage is threefold. First, survivability. My warheads detonate a thousand kilometers from the target. Your warheads must detonate within one kilometer. If the target has defenses — and I believe it does — your platforms have to survive all the way into the kill zone. Mine don't. They fire from a thousand klicks out and the pellet cloud does the rest. Second, redundancy. Your defense has to stop ten warheads on final approach — ten individual targets, each one a single point of failure. Mine puts a cloud of thousands of uranium pellets moving at a hundred kilometers per second into the target's path. You can't intercept a cloud. Third, geometry. Your colonel showed the room a pen — I saw that briefing. He's right. You have to hit the cylinder broadside, dead center, or you waste energy in rotation. A standoff detonation is a point source — miss the center and you get torque instead of deflection. A pellet cloud is distributed across the entire broadside face. Better coupling, less torque, more deflection per megaton."

He let that settle.

"The yield per warhead is twenty megatons. That is not a strategic weapon. It is a shotgun shell designed to push a thirty-seven-kilometer cylinder sideways. The total yield of my entire fleet — twenty-seven platforms, one hundred megatons each — is twenty-seven hundred megatons. Your single fleet carries five thousand. I have less total yield than you do. What I have is a delivery system that works at range, against a target that may not want to be pushed."

His image returned. "Second question, Madam President."

Whitfield studied the screen — the face of a man six light-minutes away who had just described a weapon system that no government on Earth had conceived of, let alone built.

"You built nuclear weapons on sovereign soil — in Earth orbit, in the belt, and on Mars. You did this without authorization, without notification, and without oversight. Why should I believe the number you just gave me is the real number?"

Twelve minutes. The room waited. Whitfield had asked the only question that mattered, and every person in the room knew it. This time the silence was real — no side conversations, no phone calls, no muttered calculations. Just the hum of the ventilation system and the frozen image of Dren on the wallscreen and the awareness that the answer to this question would determine whether a private arsenal became a planetary defense or an international crisis.

Dren's answer arrived.

"You shouldn't. You have no way to verify my inventory independently, and my credibility with your intelligence community is approximately zero — they missed twenty-two of the twenty-seven platforms I just disclosed. I'm aware of what that looks like."

He paused.

"But I'll offer you something your verification protocols can't give you. I will launch every interceptor platform I have. All twenty-seven. On your order, or on mine if you prefer not to give it. Every platform leaves its facility, every warhead is committed to intercept trajectories, and every launch is visible to your tracking networks from ignition to impact. After the gauntlet, my arsenal is expended. Every last platform. There is no post-crisis weapons stockpile because there are no weapons left. You don't have to trust my number. You just have to count the launches."

• • •

The room erupted — not loudly, not theatrically, but in the specific way that rooms full of serious people erupt when the ground shifts under a conversation they thought they were controlling.

The legal questions came first and loudest. MIRVed nuclear warheads — a hundred and thirty-five independently targetable devices across twenty-seven platforms — built without authorization, deployed without oversight, eight of them currently orbiting Earth. The Outer Space Treaty, the Comprehensive Nuclear-Test-Ban Treaty, the Earth-Mars Governance Framework — violated so thoroughly that the lawyers couldn't agree on which violations to prioritize. Dren's legal team would later argue that the Earth-orbit platforms were in transit, not stationed. The distinction was legally meaningless and practically irrelevant.

Then the verification problem. If the intelligence community had missed twenty-two platforms, what confidence did anyone have that twenty-seven was the complete count? Dren's offer to launch everything was operationally elegant — you could count launches, track trajectories, verify detonations. But you couldn't verify that the launches represented the complete inventory. If Dren had built thirty-five and launched twenty-seven, eight remained. There was no way to know, and Dren knew there was no way to know, and his offer was designed to make the question feel answered without actually answering it.

But the issue that generated the most heat was Dren's justification for the overcapacity. **I find it unlikely that something designed to succeed would be sent without the means to resist**

**interference.** It was the first time anyone had explicitly stated the implication: the object might have active defenses. The room split.

A handful of the scientists — Patel among them, and two of the trajectory specialists — heard Dren's logic and recognized it for what it was: a reasonable inference from observed behavior. The object maneuvered. It was engineered. Assuming it was undefended was assuming bad engineering.

Most of the room rejected it. Not with hostility — with the measured, professional skepticism that institutions produce when a conclusion is both logical and unacceptable.

Vickers spoke first. He had recovered his composure fully — whatever Hamner had seen in his face when the number twenty-seven landed was gone, replaced by the deliberate calm of a man who had spent thirty years making arguments in rooms like this one. He leaned forward, hands folded on the table, and when he spoke his voice had the particular weight of someone who was about to reframe the conversation.

"Let's separate the engineering question from the political one," he said. "Dren may be right that the object is defended. He may be wrong. But notice what he's built. A hundred and thirty-five independently targetable nuclear warheads on twenty-seven platforms, with a delivery system that works at a thousand kilometers. He's calling it a shotgun. I'd call it the most sophisticated nuclear arsenal ever constructed by a private citizen. The fact that it happens to be pointed at an interstellar object right now doesn't change what it is."

He looked around the room — not quickly, not nervously, but with the slow sweep of a man making eye contact with every person who mattered. "Course correction and active defense are fundamentally different capabilities. One is propulsion. The other is weapons. He's conflating them to justify an arsenal that happens to give him the largest weapons stockpile in the solar system." He paused. "I understand the impulse to prepare for the worst. But the overcapacity he built tells you more about his ambitions than about 7I."

Several heads nodded. The framing landed the way reasonable framings land in rooms full of serious people — not as a conclusion, but as the most comfortable interpretation of an uncomfortable situation.

The room chose the comfortable conclusion. The overcapacity was about Dren, not about 7I.

Hamner, sitting near the back, watched General Vickers deliver the assessment and watched the room accept it. Every comfortable conclusion the system had offered about 7I had been wrong. Every uncomfortable one had been right. And the room was choosing comfort again.

He also thought about Vickers's face — the moment when the number had landed and something behind the composure had cracked, just for a second, before the mask went back on. Hamner didn't know what it meant. He knew what it looked like: it looked like a man who had heard news that was not just surprising but specifically, personally bad. Not the reaction of someone shocked by a threat. The reaction of someone whose plan had just been complicated.

He filed it. He said nothing. He had learned what speaking accomplished.

Whitfield let the debate run for twenty minutes. She asked questions. She listened to answers. She let the lawyers argue with the military and the military argue with the intelligence community and the intelligence community argue with itself. She gave every voice in the room the opportunity to be heard, because she understood that decisions made without process generated resentment, and resentment generated obstruction, and obstruction was something she could not afford.

Then she ended it.

"People," she said. Not loudly enough.

“People!” she tried again. The arguments continued — a lawyer from State was talking over the NORAD liaison, who was talking over the intelligence analyst, who was on his phone again.

Whitfield picked up the heavy briefing folder open in front of her — two inches of paper, classified annexes, damage projections — and slammed it flat on the table. The sound was like a gunshot in the underground room. Every conversation stopped.

“People,” she said into the silence, her voice dropped into a register she hadn’t used in a briefing room in years — flatter, harder at the edges, the polish gone. “We are not gonna argue ourselves to death while the actual death is on its way. Everybody just settle down.“

She heard it and corrected it. When she continued her command voice had returned.

“Here’s what I know. I know that we have two hundred and thirty-five days. I know that our combined fleet gives us capacity against a passive target. I also know that nobody in this room can guarantee me the target is passive. Mr. Dren’s theory about active defenses may be wrong. It may be self-serving. But I am not willing to bet the species on an assumption.”

She paused.

“The question of whether Mr. Dren has additional platforms that he is not disclosing is a legitimate concern. It is a concern for after the deflection. If there is an after.” She let that settle. “I am ordering the following. Mr. Dren will launch all twenty-seven platforms immediately. Our fleet will launch all ten platforms immediately. Every launch will be tracked. Every trajectory will be monitored. Embedded officers will be stationed at Ares City for operational coordination during the gauntlet. Verification of Dren’s complete inventory is deferred — not abandoned, deferred — until the object is deflected. And let’s all pray to God that it is deflected. Otherwise, we know the date we’ll all meet Him.”

She turned to the screen where Dren’s image waited, six minutes away.

"Mr. Dren. Launch everything. All twenty-seven. Immediately. Our ten will follow within seventy-two hours. I want warheads on intercept trajectories by the end of this week."

Dren's response arrived. "Understood. Belt launches immediately — locked and loaded. Second wave from Mars in forty-eight hours. Earth-orbit platforms within ninety-six. My operations lead is Tomoko Sato. General Okoro is welcome at Ares City to coordinate."

The room exhaled.

• • •

Patel found Hamner during the break that followed. He was standing in the corridor outside the briefing room, leaning against the wall with a paper cup of coffee he hadn't drunk, staring at nothing in particular.

"He built twenty-seven interceptors," she said. "Nuclear. MIRVed. While we were arguing about footnotes."

"He started building when we were at forty percent," Hamner said. "Two events. Two Earthward corrections. He didn't wait for three."

"Nobody waited for three except us."

"The system waited for three. We were part of the system."

"Were," Patel said. She left it there.

• • •

Within hours, the operational reality replaced the political debate.

Okoro departed for Mars on November 5th, three days after the call, aboard a high-priority transport. He was a tall, quiet man — career military, Army Corps of Engineers before transferring to the joint chiefs' strategic planning division, with the particular bearing of someone who had spent decades building things under pressure and had learned that the building mattered more than the talking. He carried three staff officers, a secure communications package, and the awareness that by the time he arrived at Ares City, the Mars platforms might already be outbound. The coordination he had been sent to provide would happen in flight, not in planning sessions. The timeline did not permit planning sessions. The timeline permitted launching and adjusting.

Sato, on Mars, had begun launch preparations before Whitfield's order arrived. She had been preparing since the fourth correction. When Dren forwarded the presidential authorization, she read it, set it aside, and returned to the pre-flight checklist she had started two days earlier.

"She anticipated the order?" Okoro would ask, weeks later, when he arrived and reviewed the logs.

"She anticipated the math," Sato would reply. "The order was a formality."

• • •

Hamner watched the first launches from Paranal.

He was back in Chile, returned from Washington on the same military transport that had brought him. The assessment was over. The decision was made. The launches were happening.

He stood in the control room — the room where he'd found the first anomaly thirteen months ago — and watched the telemetry feeds as the first Mars-based interceptors lit their engines. Thirteen points of light, accelerating outward on trajectories that would carry them to a rendezvous with 7I. Each one engineered to move the Hammer – to move the needle measuring the end of the Earth.

Soares came into the control room and stood beside him. They watched the telemetry together — the thirteen traces climbing away from Mars, each one a fusion engine burning at a thrust that would have been theoretical five years ago.

"I spent thirteen months trying to get someone to listen," he said. "Now everyone's listening. And there's nothing left for me to say."

Soares didn’t answer. She stood beside him and watched the traces climb, and that was enough.

“Thirteen away from Mars,” she said finally. “Belt launches in twenty-four hours. Earth orbit in forty-eight.”

“And Earth’s fleet?”

“Seventy-two hours. They’re loading the warheads now.”

Hamner nodded. Thirty-seven platforms committed. Against a passive target, the math said it was massive overkill. Against whatever 7I actually was  the math was a guess dressed in the language of certainty.

“How long until Wave One reaches it?” he asked.

“Eighty days. Give or take,“ she answered.

He sighed.  “Eighty days until we find out if Dren’s shotgun can move a demon god.”

# CHAPTER 9

## *Satan's Fist*

*January 12th, 2060.*
*Object at ~6 AU, ~55 km/s. 163 days to impact.*
*Wave 1: 6 belt platforms, 48 days in transit, 22 days to intercept.*
*Wave 2: 13 Mars platforms, 43 days in transit, 27 days to intercept.*
*Earth ↔ Mars: ~1.1 AU, Communications: ~9 min one-way.*

• • •

The name started in the Pentagon.

Not in a briefing, classified assessment, formal communication or press release. In the hallway outside the planetary defense coordination office, where staffers who had been staring at trajectory plots and engagement scenarios for weeks gathered around a tablet showing the Kimura reconstruction — the first detailed image of the cylinder, grainy and false-colored but unmistakable — and started doing what staffers do when the formal nomenclature stops fitting the thing on the screen.

The first name that stuck was "Rod from God" — old military slang for a kinetic orbital weapon, a tungsten telephone pole dropped from space. Someone held the Kimura image next to a schematic of the theoretical weapon pulled up on a phone. The shape fit. The intent fit. It was on three status boards within the hour.

It lasted about a day. A staffer in the next meeting killed it. “It’s not from God,” she said. “Whoever sent this isn’t on our side.” Someone else — nobody would later remember who — followed: “And it’s not a rod. Rods are tools. This is a fist. Satan’s Fist.”

By end of day it was on every display in the building, the Rod from God crossed out and replaced. By the following morning it was in the secure chat channels, replacing “the object” and “the cylinder” and “7I” in conversations between people who had been trained to use formal designations and couldn’t bring themselves to anymore. A NORAD analyst used it in a briefing slide. A Pentagon spokesperson used it in a background call with a Reuters correspondent, not for attribution. The correspondent used it anyway.

The Cassini III data had leaked weeks earlier — officially classified, practically everywhere. By late November the elongated shape was on every news feed, every amateur astronomy board, every conspiracy forum. The cylinder was public knowledge. The phrase “planet killer” had entered the vocabulary of people who had never thought about impact physics and now couldn’t stop saying it. What the public didn’t have was a name that felt right. 7I/Hamner was a catalog entry. Hamner’s Hammer had served for the weeks when people still reached for metaphors. Neither fit the thing on the screen — the engineered cylinder with geometric edges and a surface that didn’t vary, aimed at Earth, closing at fifty-five kilometers per second.

Satan’s Fist fit.

From Reuters it crossed to every outlet on three planets in forty-eight hours. The IAU’s working group convened to discuss appropriate nomenclature. The working group’s preference was noted and universally ignored.

A hammer is a tool. You swing it. A fist is a choice. Someone threw it.

By January, the name was everywhere. Stenciled on protest signs. Printed on magazine covers. Spoken by heads of state in addresses that no speechwriter had imagined writing a year ago. It appeared on the hulls of two of Dren's Mars-based platforms — painted by ground crew before launch, unauthorized, uncorrected. It appeared in the graffiti of a hundred cities, sprayed on walls beside countdown numbers that ticked down daily. One hundred and sixty-three days. One hundred and sixty-two. One hundred and sixty-one.

The name carried something the formal designations didn't. It was a statement about the thing's nature — not what it would do, but what it was. A weapon. Aimed. Thrown. By someone who had chosen to throw it. And perhaps more frightening, had the capability to build it.

The public had arrived at the conclusion that the scientific community had spent fourteen months avoiding. It was artificial. It was hostile. It now had a name that said both things in two words.

• • •

The clearer image arrived on January 12th.

It came from Kimura's long-baseline interferometry array — four optical telescopes on separate asteroids in the belt, their baselines measured in millions of kilometers. The array had been tracking Satan's Fist continuously since the observation campaign began. The data was processed autonomously. The results were relayed to every node in the observation network simultaneously.

The image was not a photograph. It was a model reconstruction — a best-fit surface map built from phase and closure-phase data across the four-telescope baseline, constrained by the cylinder geometry that Cassini III had established in November. It was grainy, false-colored, more inference than portrait. But the baseline was enormous, the integration time was long, and it was the most detailed image of the object anyone had produced.

The shape was already known. Every calculation since November had used the cylinder geometry. The targeting packages had been updated. The shape was not a surprise.

What Kimura's image showed was detail. And the detail changed things.

The surface was uniform — not approximately uniform, not statistically consistent, but uniform in a way that no natural process produced at this scale. No craters, ridges, or variations in albedo across the resolved elements. The edges, where the reconstruction had sufficient contrast, were geometric. Not eroded. Not rounded by billions of years of micrometeorite bombardment and thermal cycling. Sharp. Straight. Manufactured.

And there was something else.

Near the trailing end of the cylinder — the end facing away from the direction of travel — the image showed three protrusions. Structures extending from the surface, thin and linear, spaced evenly around the circumference and angled away from the long axis. The resolution was insufficient to determine their exact dimensions, but they were distinct from the cylinder body.

Kimura's accompanying note was three sentences: "Interferometric composite attached. Surface morphology and geometric regularity inconsistent with any known natural body. Note structures at trailing end — morphology suggests antenna or sensor array."

• • •

Hamner was in the unified command center at Paranal when the image arrived.

The command center had been built into the observatory complex in November — a repurposed conference room fitted with secure communications, telemetry displays, and enough screens to track thirty-seven interceptor platforms simultaneously. It smelled like new carpet and paint. Hamner had been spending fourteen-hour days here since the launches, reviewing trajectory data, monitoring the observation feeds, doing the work he'd always done except that now the work mattered to people who had spent a year telling him it didn't.

He was reviewing Wave 1 telemetry — six belt platforms, forty-eight days into their transit, twenty-two days from intercept — when the alert came through on the observation network feed. He opened it expecting another trajectory refinement.

The image filled his screen.

"That's not a rock," Soares said. She was standing behind him — she must have gotten the same alert, must have come in while he was still staring. He hadn't heard her.

"No, it is not," Hamner said.

He put his hand on the screen. He didn't know why. The gesture was absurd — a man touching glass as if the thing behind it could be felt. But his hand stayed there, fingers spread against the false-color surface of something that had been built by hands he would never see, launched from a place he would never know, aimed at the only home his species had ever had. The glass was warm from the display. The thing behind it was four hundred degrees below zero and closing at fifty-five kilometers per second.

"The edges," Soares said quietly. "Look at the edges."

"I see them."

"No weathering. No erosion. Nothing rounded." She leaned closer. "That's a hull."

Hamner pulled his hand back. "You remember the phase curve? The anomaly I raised in the characterization meeting — the brightness that didn't fall off with viewing angle?"

"Mercer said it was surface roughness," she said.

"It wasn't surface roughness. It was a flat face. The circular end of a cylinder, aimed straight at us. Every point on that face had the same angle to the observer. The brightness was uniform because the surface was flat." He looked at her. "We were staring down the barrel of this thing for fourteen months and the photometry was telling us the whole time."

Soares was quiet for a moment. Then she pointed at the trailing end. "What's that?"

"Kimura says antennas or sensor arrays."

She tilted her head, studying the three thin lines. "If it has antennas, it's communicating. Or navigating. Or both.  But with who?"

Hamner didn't answer. They both knew what was twenty-two days away from it.

• • •

The image reached unified command formally — through classified channels, with verification stamps and chain-of-custody headers — four hours after Hamner first saw it on the open network. By then, every astronomer in the observation network had already seen it. The classification was a formality applied to data that was already public.

General Okoro had arrived at Ares City after the Mars launches were complete. He was the operational commander now — the man responsible for coordinating thirty-seven platforms across four waves launched from three locations, all converging on a target that was six AU away and closing at fifty-five kilometers per second. He had set up in the command center with two staff officers and a communications specialist, and he ran the room the way he'd run every operation in his career: quietly, methodically, with an engineer's preference for problems that had numbers attached to them.

He looked at the Kimura image on the main display and asked the operationally relevant question: "What does this change for Wave 1?"

Reeves — the same NORAD colonel who had briefed Whitfield in November, who had demonstrated the cylinder's targeting geometry with a pen, now embedded at Ares for the duration — pulled up the engagement parameters.

“Wave 1 is on an opposing approach — heading outbound, the Fist heading inbound,” Reeves said. “Relative closing velocity approximately a hundred and fifty kilometers per second. The platforms are offset laterally from the Fist’s track — about a thousand kilometers out, running a parallel course. Each platform fires its directed charges as the Fist approaches. The pellet clouds cross the thousand-kilometer gap while the Fist closes the distance. It drives into them. One pass per platform. No second shot. The six belt platforms are staggered along the approach corridor, with the thirteen Mars platforms arriving five days behind.”

He looked at Okoro. “That geometry hasn’t changed. The targeting packages were recomputed after Cassini in November. The antennas don’t affect momentum coupling or dispersion.”

“Then what do the antennas change?” Okoro asked.

Reeves looked at the image. “For the targeting math? Nothing. The antennas are small relative to the cylinder.”

He paused.

“For the threat assessment? Potentially everything. Antennas imply receivers. Receivers imply a system. A system on an object that is already confirmed to be engineered, confirmed to be guided, confirmed to be on an impact trajectory — that is consistent with active sensing capability.”

The room was quiet.

“Consistent with,” Okoro said. “Not confirmed.”

“No, sir. Not confirmed. But consistent with the scenario Mr. Dren described in November.”

The antennas didn’t prove defenses. Antennas could serve navigational purposes. They could be relics of the object’s launch phase, communication links to its origin, sensors for environmental data. There were explanations that didn’t involve weapons.

But the antennas proved systems. It proved that the cylinder was not inert — not a shaped rock flung on a ballistic arc, not a kinetic impactor that did its work through mass and velocity alone. It had components. Subsystems. Hardware that extended from the hull for a purpose its builders had considered necessary.

Something that builds antennas is something that processes information. Something that processes information can respond to its environment. Something that can respond to its environment can respond to a threat.

The logical chain was not proof. But it was the chain Dren had built his twenty-seven platforms against, and the antennas were one more link.

"The targeting packages don't need revision," Okoro said. His voice was the same unhurried tone it always was — the voice of a man who had learned decades ago that urgency in the voice didn't make the work go faster. "The threat posture does. Update the engagement protocols. Assume the possibility of active response. Wave 1 commanders to be briefed on defensive contingencies."

"Sir, Wave 1 is on autonomous approach," Reeves said. "Communication delay is growing — nine minutes and increasing. Any contingency updates we send now arrive with an eighteen-minute round trip. If the object responds during the engagement, the platforms react on their own programming, not on our commands."

"Then make sure the programming is right," Okoro said.

• • •

The Batch G-7 platforms — Dren's eight from Earth orbit, Wave 3 — had been validated against the cylinder targeting geometry in November. The firmware ran on Sato's proprietary Mars-centric coordinate system. The translation layer that converted targeting data to NATO-standard J2000 reference frame had been built under time pressure, validated six hours before deadline, with one integration test skipped.

The antennas changed nothing about the targeting math. But the updated engagement protocols — the defensive contingencies Okoro had ordered — required new response parameters to be loaded into the autonomous engagement software. Parameters that told the platforms what to do if the target did something unexpected during the approach.

The new parameters had to pass through the same translation layer.

Simmons — the lead engineer on the translation layer — pulled up the validation queue and stared at it. The coffee in her hand trembled. Nine hours of sleep in the last seventy-two.

"We skipped integration test four," she said to Chen, who was running the parameter upload. "In November. Before the first load."

"I remember," Chen said. He didn't look up from his console.

"The new parameters go through the same layer. Same code path. Same test we didn't run."

"I know."

"So we run it now."

Chen looked at her. "We have twenty-two days. The upload window for Wave 3 closes in six. If we run the full integration suite, that's three days we don't have."

"If we don't run it and the layer drops a sign or truncates a coordinate, the platforms fire their charges wrong. And we don't get a second shot."

"I know what it means."

"Then we run the test."

Chen was quiet for a moment. "I'll flag it for Okoro."

"I already flagged it in November," Simmons said. "I flagged it in writing. It was acknowledged, noted, and overridden by the timeline." She set her coffee down. Her hand was still shaking. "I kept the email."

Chen looked at her. She looked back. The look said what the words didn't: I am not going to be the person who didn't say it twice.

"Flag it again. Okoro's the boss," he said. "But start the upload. We don't have three days."

• • •

Hamner found a quiet terminal after the briefing broke for operational planning.

Patel found him there. She had been at Paranal since the launches — embedded with the observation team, running trajectory updates and Monte Carlo refinements that nobody asked for anymore because the trajectory was no longer in question. She was a small woman with sharp features and the slightly disheveled look of someone who had stopped caring about appearance roughly around the time the impact probability crossed fifty percent. She leaned against the doorframe the way Soares had leaned against Hamner's doorframe fifteen months ago, when the second event data had come in — the posture of someone bringing news that changed the conversation.

The image was still on his screen. The model reconstruction, false-colored for contrast, the long axis horizontal across his display. Thirty-seven kilometers of engineered structure, aimed at the planet where he'd been born, traveling at a velocity that would convert its mass into an energy release that ended civilization. And at the trailing end, the three thin lines of the antennas.

"Wave 1 is twenty-two days out," Patel said. "Six platforms closing at a hundred and fifty kilometers per second on something that was built. By someone who isn't us. And now we know it has antennas."

Hamner didn't look up. The numbers were on the screen. The shape was on the screen. The antennas were on the screen. Everything he had tracked for fifteen months — the photometry, the phase curve anomalies, the corrections, the density, the absent coma — had been telling the same story. He had heard parts of it. Kimura had just shown him the last page.

"If Dren was right about defenses," Patel said, "we're about to find out."

"If he was wrong, we wasted twenty-seven platforms."

"I can live with that."

"So can everyone else. That's the point."

• • •

Twenty-two days.

Wave 1 — six belt platforms, pulsed fusion, five directed nuclear charges each — was closing on Satan's Fist at a relative velocity of a hundred and fifty kilometers per second. Behind them, thirteen Mars platforms followed, days behind. The platforms could not be recalled. The warheads were armed. The programming that would govern their autonomous engagement had been updated, tested, and transmitted — the last human input they would receive before the closing velocity made communication irrelevant.

The first shotgun would fire against something that was confirmed engineered, confirmed maneuvering, confirmed to have subsystems extending from its hull — and, if the engineering logic held, possibly defended.

Twenty-two days until they found out what the Fist did when you tried to push it.

# CHAPTER 10

## *The Gauntlet*

*February 1st, 2060.*

*Object at ~4.9 AU, ~56 km/s. 143 days to impact.*

*Wave 1: 6 belt platforms, two days to intercept.*

*Earth ↔ Mars: ~1.6 AU, Communications: ~13 min one-way.*

• • •

Whitfield wanted to understand it before it happened.

Not the trajectory plots or the operational summaries. She wanted to know, in concrete terms, what six platforms would do when they met Satan's Fist at a hundred and fifty kilometers per second. She wanted it explained so that when the engagement data arrived — thirteen minutes after the fact, uncorrectable — she would know what she was looking at.

The briefing ran through the Mars relay. Thirteen-minute delay each way. Okoro's staff had prepared a walkthrough, with live follow-up on the twenty-six-minute loop.

Reeves gave the brief.

"Ma'am, the engagement geometry isn't intuitive, so I'm going to walk through it step by step."

He brought up an animation, paused it — two arrows converging from opposite directions, offset by a gap.

"Our platforms are heading outbound. The Fist is heading inbound. The platforms are not alongside the target. They're offset a thousand kilometers laterally, running a parallel course. Two trains on parallel tracks, heading toward each other."

He pointed to the gap. "Each platform carries five directed nuclear charges. Each charge fires a cloud of uranium pellets sideways — perpendicular to the platform's direction of travel — across that thousand-kilometer gap toward the Fist's track."

"Sideways," Whitfield said. "Not forward."

"Sideways. But here's where the math matters. The platform is heading outbound at eighty-five kilometers per second. The Fist is heading inbound at sixty-five. Combined closing speed: a hundred and fifty kilometers per second. When the charges fire, the pellets go sideways at a hundred kilometers per second across the gap. But the pellets don't just go sideways. They were on a platform moving at eighty-five kilometers per second, and that forward velocity doesn't disappear when the charge detonates. The pellets carry it with them. So from the Fist's perspective, the pellets are coming in on a diagonal — a hundred kilometers per second sideways, and a hundred and fifty per second forward, because the Fist is also closing at sixty-five."

He traced the vectors on the screen. "The gap is a thousand kilometers. At a hundred per second sideways, the pellets need ten seconds to cross. In those same ten seconds, the hundred and fifty per second of closing speed eats up fifteen hundred kilometers along the track. So the platform fires when the center of the Fist is fifteen hundred kilometers ahead. Ten seconds later, the pellets have crossed the gap and the Fist's midline has arrived at the same point. Everything converges. The platform is about eighteen hundred kilometers from the Fist when it fires — the diagonal of a thousand sideways and fifteen hundred along-track."

He ran the animation. The pellet cloud crossed the gap on a diagonal. The cylinder drove into it. Thousands of impacts along the broadside.

“That sounds like it requires precise timing,” Whitfield said.

“The Fist is thirty-seven kilometers long. At a hundred and fifty kilometers per second, the entire cylinder passes through the convergence point in about a quarter of a second. Fire a fraction too early, the cloud hits the nose. Too late, it catches the tail. Either way, you lose concentration on the midline and waste energy in torque instead of lateral push. The firing window is roughly a quarter of a second.”

“Mr. Dren described a ten-second advantage over the standoff weapons.”

“He misspoke. Or simplified for the briefing. Ten seconds is the flight time of the pellets — how long they’re crossing the gap. The actual firing precision is comparable to what the standoff warheads require. The advantage isn’t timing. It’s range. The platform fires from eighteen hundred kilometers out. A standoff warhead has to survive all the way to one kilometer from the surface. If the Fist can reach out and kill something at five hundred kilometers — or a thousand — the standoff platform is inside that radius for its entire approach. The shotgun fires and the pellets are away before the platform is ever at risk. That’s the difference. Not the timing window. The distance.”

Whitfield studied the animation. “What does impact look like?”

“Thousands of individual pellet strikes across the broadside surface. Each impact transfers lateral momentum. The cylinder gets pushed sideways. Distributed impacts, minimal torque — it moves without tumbling.”

“How much?”

“If all six fire successfully, our models predict approximately a hundred kilometers of deflection at this time-to-impact. Roughly seventeen per platform. The uncertainty is in the coupling — how efficiently the pellet energy transfers to lateral momentum. Yield isn’t the question. Coupling is. We won’t know the actual number until we see the tracking data.”

“And we need six thousand.”

“Wave 1 is six platforms out of thirty-seven. It’s the first punch. If the weapon works and the geometry holds, the subsequent waves deliver the rest.”

“Two days,” Whitfield said.

“Two days.”

• • •

*February 3rd, 2060.*

*Wave 1. Intercept day.*

The operations center at Ares City was built for this — a curved wall of screens showing telemetry from every platform in the fleet, trajectory overlays, and the tracking data from two planets’ worth of observatories. Dren stood at the back, arms folded, watching the screens with the stillness he brought to everything that mattered. Okoro sat at the main console beside Sato. Reeves was at the communications terminal, relaying updates to Washington on the thirteen-minute loop.

The six platforms were staggered along a fifty-seven-thousand-kilometer corridor, each on its parallel track a thousand kilometers from the Fist’s line of travel. Heading outbound. The Fist heading inbound. Converging at a hundred and fifty kilometers per second.

“Platform 1 is in the engagement window,” Sato said. “Firing.”

The first platform fired. Five directed charges detonated in sequence, two seconds apart. Ten seconds later, the pellet clouds struck the broadside of Satan’s Fist. Thousands of kinetic impacts distributed across the cylinder’s midline.

“Lateral displacement confirmed,” Reeves said, reading the tracking feed. “Platform 1 has passed the engagement point. Outbound, nominal.”

“Platform 2 firing,” Sato said. “Platform 3. Platform 4.”

Each one the same — five charges, pellet clouds away, displacement confirmed. The geometry was working. Dren’s shotgun was pushing the Fist sideways.

“Platform 5 firing,” Sato said. “Tightest offset — eight hundred kilometers.” A pause. “Five charges away. Nominal.”

“Platform 6 is next,” Reeves said. “Far end of the corridor. Thirty seconds.”

Platform 6 did not fire. Seconds before its scheduled sequence, containment failed in its primary warhead housing. Thermal spike, structural alarm, loss of integrity. All five warheads cooked off — a hundred megatons of uncontrolled detonation. Two nearby platforms, already spent, were caught in the blast.

“We just lost three feeds,” Sato said. Her voice was flat — not calm, controlled. “Platform 6. And Platforms 2 and 4 — both spent, caught in the cook-off.”

“Deflection loss?” Okoro asked.

“Platform 6 only. Two and 4 had already fired. Five of six delivered.”

The room exhaled. Five of six. A mechanical failure, not an interception. The telemetry confirmed it — thermal cascade, containment breach, cook-off. That was what hardware failure looked like. The weapon worked. The geometry held. The Fist could be pushed. Someone in the back of the room started clapping. Then someone else. Then the operations center — forty people who had spent months underground running scenarios that ended in extinction — erupted. Sato closed her eyes and pressed both hands flat on the console. Reeves pumped his fist once, hard, then caught himself and went back to the telemetry. Okoro didn’t cheer. He sat very still with his jaw tight and his eyes wet, and when Sato looked at him he gave her one short nod that said everything. Even Dren, at the back of the room, unfolded his arms.

Then, forty-one seconds after Platform 5 passed closest approach — heading away from the Fist, still transmitting at full nominal strength — the feed stopped. Clean. No degradation, no dropout, no corruption. Transmitting, then not.

Sato stared at her screen. “Platform 5 is gone.”

“Define gone,” Okoro said.

"Clean termination. Full signal strength until the instant it stopped. No progressive dropout, no error flags. It was working, and then it wasn't."

"Mechanical?" Okoro asked.

"Platform 6 was mechanical," Reeves said. "We have that signature — thermal cascade, containment failure, cook-off. Platform 5 doesn't look like that."

The room was quiet. Platform 5 had been the closest to the Fist.

• • •

Sato pulled the flyby video onto the main wallscreen. The room went still.

The surface filled the frame. Dark, matte, uniform. No craters, scarring, or variation at all — the same featureless hull across every frame of the flyby. Where the flat end met the curved body, the transition was a line. Not a ridge, not a slope. A machined edge. Someone in the back of the room said something under their breath.

"Freeze that," Okoro said. Sato stopped the playback at the trailing end. Three structures — thin, linear, extending from the hull at different angles.

"Those are the antennas Kimura flagged," Dren said. "Clearly resolved now. Three of them. Different orientations."

"What else?"

Sato scrolled forward to the forward face — the flat circular end aimed at Earth. She zoomed the image. Near the center of the disk, partially resolved at the limit of the camera's capability: a feature. Darker than the surrounding surface. Geometric.

"What is that?" Okoro asked.

"We don't know," Dren said. "The resolution isn't good enough. It could be a marking, a sensor, a structural feature. But it's centered on the face, and it's not random."

"Is it a weapon port?"

"It could be anything. We'd need better resolution to say more." If Dren had any inklings, he kept them to himself.

Okoro stared at the frozen image. Thirty-seven kilometers of hull, engineered to tolerances that nothing in the room could match, aimed at Earth at sixty-five kilometers per second. And on its face, something deliberate that they couldn't quite read.

"Move on," he said. "What happened to Platform 5?"

Sato brought up the telemetry timeline. "Platform 5 fired on schedule. All five charges detonated normally. Pellet clouds launched, confirmed impact on the broadside. The platform continued past the Fist on its outbound trajectory. Forty-one seconds after closest approach, the feed terminated."

"Terminated how?"

"Clean cut. Full nominal signal strength until the instant it stopped. No progressive dropout, no signal degradation, no error flags. It was working, and then it wasn't."

"What it could be and what it is might be two separate things," Dren said, his voice carrying the same flat precision it always did. "It could be some sort of hardware failure, stress from the launches, a loose connection, any one of a number of causes. It could also have been external. We simply do not have evidence to make a determination. We also don't have a weapon signature. We don't have a thermal flash, an impact trace, an electromagnetic pulse — nothing that tells us what any sort of external event could have been."

"So we don't know," Okoro concluded.

"No, we don't. We do know it was the closest platform. We know it happened after the engagement, not during. And we know the termination profile doesn't match anything in our mechanical failure library. That said, correlation does not equal causation. However, given the stakes, caution would seem to be the wiser course."

Okoro sat with that.

"There's one more thing," Sato said. She brought up a secondary telemetry channel. "Platform 1's post-flyby telemetry. After it passed the Fist, its sensors were pointed back along its outbound trajectory — standard post-engagement mode. It recorded an emission from the Fist."

The data appeared on the wallscreen. A single spike in the optical band. Narrowband, highly directional, one point seven seconds duration.

"Where was it aimed?" Okoro asked.

Sato overlaid the emission vector on the navigation plot. The line extended outward — away from Earth, away from Mars, away from the engagement corridor. Back along the Fist's own approach vector. Into deep space.

"Back the way it came," Okoro said.

"Yes."

"What does that mean?"

"It means the Fist transmitted something after the engagement. Whether that's a navigational pulse, a diagnostic burst, or a communication to its point of origin — we can't determine from one sample."

"Log it," Okoro said.

Dren leaned forward — one of his rare movements, and Sato glanced at him because she knew what it meant. "Track that vector. Record everything on that bearing. If there's a second burst during Wave 2, I want the comparison on my screen before the engagement telemetry finishes downloading."

The request was noted.

• • •

The deflection data arrived three hours after the engagement, compiled from tracking stations on two planets. Three hours of the room running on adrenaline and coffee and the memory of what it had felt like to watch the telemetry confirm displacement — three hours of wanting the number and being afraid of the number at the same time.

Sato read it and went still. She checked it against the pre-engagement model, then checked it again. Then she turned to the room and her voice cracked on the first word.

"We predicted eighty-five from five platforms. We got eighty-five. Coupling matched the conservative end of the model."

The sound that went through the room wasn't cheering this time. It was quieter than that — a collective release, shoulders dropping, someone putting their head in their hands, someone else gripping the edge of a console and just breathing. The number was real. The weapon worked. The math was right.

"And it hasn't corrected," Reeves said. His voice was steady but his hand was shaking when he pointed at the tracking display.

"Eighty-five kilometers of displacement and no counter-thrust," Dren said. "If it had fuel, it would correct. The four approach corrections consumed the propellant budget. What we're pushing now is the dry mass — the cylinder without its fuel. It can't push back."

Okoro looked at the tracking data. "Has it corrected? Since the engagement?"

"No thrust events detected. It's maintaining the post-engagement course. Eighty-five kilometers offset."

"So everything from here adds up."

"Based on the data we have so far, yes," Dren concluded.

For the first time in months, the room believed it. Not hoped. Believed. Twenty-seven more platforms were in flight behind the first six, and every one of them carried the same weapon that had just moved an extinction-class impactor eighty-five kilometers sideways. The math said six thousand would be enough. They had the platforms to get there. It was going to work.

• • •

Vickers's assessment arrived from Washington on the next relay cycle.

"Five platforms approached. Five fired. The engagement ran exactly as briefed. The Fist did not interfere with any platform during the approach, did not attempt to stop the pellet clouds, and did not engage any platform during the firing sequence. One spent platform, heading away after the engagement, went silent — the one running the closest offset, the one with the highest exposure to the nuclear and electromagnetic environment. I'd call that a strong result."

He paused. "For Wave 2, I'd recommend reducing the offset. Five hundred kilometers instead of a thousand. We know the Fist didn't engage at a thousand. A tighter offset means better pellet concentration, better coupling, more deflection per platform. We should press the advantage."

There was something in the recommendation that Hamner — watching the relay from Paranal, where he'd been monitoring the engagement data alongside the observation team — couldn't quite place. It was a reasonable argument. Better concentration, more deflection. But it pulled the platforms closer to the thing that had just killed Platform 5, and Vickers was making that case with the confidence of a man who had already decided the kill was mechanical. A man who wanted the room to stop thinking about it.

Dren's response, twenty-six minutes later: "I understand General Vickers's reasoning. Wave 1 delivered eighty-five kilometers from five platforms. The coupling was at the low end of the model, which is exactly why I would not reduce the offset. A tighter approach improves concentration but increases risk. The current geometry is working. My advice is to stick with what works."

Whitfield studied the engagement summary for a long moment. Vickers's argument had logic to it — better concentration, more deflection. Against a passive target, it would be the right call. Five platforms fired. One went silent afterward.

"Wave 2 maintains current parameters," she said. "Thousand-kilometer offset."

Vickers nodded. His expression didn't change, but something shifted behind it — the faintest tightening around the jaw, there and gone. Hamner, watching the relay feed from Paranal, noticed it the way he'd noticed the anomalous reaction in the briefing room when Dren had revealed the twenty-seven platforms. He still didn't know what it meant. But it was the second time he'd seen Vickers react wrong.

• • •

Reeves briefed the remaining plan.

"Wave 2 is thirteen Mars platforms. Same weapon, same geometry. Five days out. If Wave 1 is representative, thirteen platforms at seventeen per gives approximately two hundred and twenty kilometers of additional deflection. Cumulative: just over three hundred."

"Wave 3 is eight Earth-orbit platforms. Same weapon. Approximately four weeks after Wave 2. Expected additional deflection: roughly a hundred and thirty kilometers."

"Wave 4 is the Earth fleet. Ten platforms, five hundred megatons each, standoff detonation. Different weapon — closes to within one kilometer. Against an undefended target at their time-to-impact, the deflection is in the thousands of kilometers."

"Based on what we've seen," Whitfield said, "we're in good shape?"

"Based on what we've seen, yes, ma'am."

• • •

*February 8th, 2060.*

*Wave 2: 13 Mars platforms. Intercept day.*

*139 days to impact.*

The operations center was configured for a longer engagement — thirteen platforms staggered across a wider corridor, the telemetry wall showing every feed simultaneously. Okoro at the main console. Sato beside him, her screens mirrored on the wallscreen. Dren standing at the back, in the same position he'd held for Wave 1, arms folded, watching.

The first three platforms in the corridor fired on schedule. Directed charges detonated, pellet clouds launched. The same geometry that had worked five days ago.

"Platforms 1, 2, and 3 have cleared the engagement window," Sato said. "Outbound, nominal. Displacement confirmed."

Then Platform 4 disappeared.

The telemetry feed — full nominal, no warnings — terminated instantaneously. No thermal cascade, structural failure, or containment alarm. Transmitting, then not. The same clean termination profile as Platform 5 in Wave 1.

Sato's hands stopped moving on her console. "Platform 4 is gone."

Platform 5 disappeared four seconds later. Then 6. Then 7.

"They're not failing," Sato said. She stood up from her console. "They're being killed."

Platform 8 disappeared. Platform 9. Platform 10. Platform 11. Each one the same — nominal signal, then nothing. Marching down the corridor in order. Whatever was killing them was sweeping along the engagement line, taking each platform in turn as it came within range.

Reeves was calling each one from the telemetry feed, his voice level, professional, reading the deaths like a man trained to read them. "Platform 9 — loss of signal. Platform 10 — loss of signal. Platform 11 —"

Platform 12's autonomous software had been watching the platforms ahead of it vanish. It fired early — maximum range, maximum dispersal. Two seconds later, its feed terminated. The charges had detonated. The pellets were in flight.

Platform 13 fired at extreme range. Terminated three seconds after firing.

Sato counted. "Four delivered fire. Three in the opening seconds, two at extreme range. Eight destroyed before they could fire." She paused. "Same termination profile as Platform 5 in Wave 1. Same clean cut. Except now it's eight out of thirteen."

The room was very quiet. Five days ago these people had been cheering. They had believed — not hoped, believed — that the interceptors worked, that the math would hold, that they were going to push this thing aside and live. Now they sat in the wreckage of that belief, and the silence wasn't shock. It was the sound of people who had let themselves feel safe and had just had it taken from them. Sato's face was gray. Okoro's hands were flat on the console, motionless, as if pressing down on something that was trying to come apart underneath.

Sato stood up from the console. She walked to the far wall, put both hands against it, and stood there with her back to the room. Nobody looked at her. They understood. She had built nine of those thirteen platforms. She had run the pre-flight checklists. She had watched the engine burns and confirmed the trajectory locks and cleared each one for autonomous engagement. Eight of them had been killed before they could fire, and she had watched each feed go dark on the console she'd designed. After a minute she came back, sat down, and put her hands on the keys. Her face showed nothing. Her hands were steady. She was ready for the next question.

"What's happening to them?" Okoro asked. "What's the weapon?"

Reeves had been reviewing the video feeds from the platforms that survived long enough to record the others dying. "There's nothing visible. No beam, no flash, no projectile. The platforms ahead just — stop. The sensor data shows a thermal spike at the target platform immediately before signal loss. Massive energy deposition, less than one second. But the energy source isn't visible at any frequency our cameras cover."

"Likely directed energy," Dren said. "A beam weapon operating outside our sensor bandpass. Probably high-frequency — UV or X-ray. Doesn't scatter in vacuum. No visible signature at a distance. You wouldn't see it. You'd just see the result. Our platforms weren't instrumented for those frequencies — those sensors were mass we spent on other systems."

"Can we confirm that?"

"Not from the data we have," Dren said. "But the kill pattern is consistent. Sequential targeting, clean kills, less than one second per platform. And there's a range limit — the first three platforms fired and survived because they were ahead of the engagement envelope. Platforms 12 and 13 survived long enough to fire because they were behind it. Everything in between was inside the kill zone. Before I said correlation does not equal causation; however, now I would have to conclude that it does."

"How far does the kill zone extend?"

Reeves overlaid the engagement geometry on the wallscreen. "Based on where platforms died and where they survived — approximately two thousand kilometers along the approach axis. Platforms 4 through 11 were inside that range when the weapon activated. Platforms 1 through 3 had already passed through. Platforms 12 and 13 were outside it, barely."

Okoro sat with the numbers. "Five days. It had five days between Wave 1 and Wave 2. In Wave 1 it didn't fire a shot during the engagement. Now it's killing platforms at two thousand kilometers."

"A safe assumption is that it learned," Dren said. "Or it was updated. The optical emission during Wave 1 — back along its approach vector. If that was a report, someone received it, analyzed the engagement, and transmitted new targeting parameters. Either way, the result is the same. It knows what the shotguns are. It knows the firing range. And it's engaging them before they reach firing range."

Sato pulled up the emission vector data from Wave 1. "The optical burst was directed back along the approach vector. If that was a report to the origin system — wherever it launched from — the nearest star along that bearing is … there are no stars along that bearing."

"So it learned on its own," Reeves said.

"Or it was updated by something closer," Sato said. "Something inside the solar system. Or just outside it. A relay asset within a few light-days could receive the burst, compute new parameters, and transmit them back within the timeline."

The room processed that. The Fist was not necessarily alone.

"Will it reach further by Wave 3?" Okoro asked.

Dren answered. "The prudent assumption is yes. The limitation at two thousand kilometers is power, not physics. A directed energy weapon in vacuum maintains coherence indefinitely — there's no atmosphere to scatter the beam. Range is limited by output power and beam focus. If the Fist can increase either one — or if it receives an update that optimizes its targeting — the engagement envelope expands. The platforms that survived Wave 2 by firing at extreme range fired from approximately twenty-seven hundred kilometers. That's the current edge of the safe zone. And we must presume that whoever is controlling that system has the same data too, and can reach the same conclusions. The only question is: do they have the capability to alter either of those two parameters, or worse, both."

"Four weeks until Wave 3," Sato said.

"Four weeks," Reeves confirmed.

Tracking stations reported: no thrust events after Wave 2. The Fist was at ninety kilometers offset, maintaining course.

"Deflection?" Okoro asked.

"Five kilometers. The two that fired from extreme range had badly degraded coupling — dispersed clouds, almost no concentration on the midline. The rest never fired."

"Cumulative?"

"Ninety."

• • •

*March 8th, 2060.*

*Wave 3: 8 Earth-orbit platforms. Intercept day.*

*111 days to impact.*

Dren had spent four weeks studying the Wave 2 data. The beam weapon's kill zone had expanded from nothing to two thousand kilometers in five days. The progression wouldn't stop. Standard approach geometry — parallel track, thousand-kilometer offset — would put the Wave 3 platforms well inside the kill zone before they reached firing range. Even the twenty-seven-hundred-kilometer edge where Platforms 12 and 13 had survived couldn't be trusted after four weeks of potential improvement.

He proposed a thirty-five-hundred-kilometer offset — well beyond the known kill zone, with margin for expansion. The dispersal penalty was real. At three and a half times the original gap, the pellet clouds would be wider by the time they crossed, less concentrated on the midline, less efficient coupling. But the platforms would survive long enough to fire. Worse coupling from safe range beat perfect coupling from inside the beam.

Okoro approved it. There was no better option.

The new engagement parameters — the thirty-five-hundred-kilometer offset, the revised convergence angles, the updated pellet dispersion profiles — were loaded through the Batch G-7 translation layer, the firmware bridge that converted Sato's Mars-centric coordinate system to NATO-standard J2000 for the Earth-orbit platforms. Waves 1 and 2 hadn't needed it. The belt and Mars platforms ran natively on Sato's system.

• • •

Reeves was on the relay to Okoro when the first telemetry came in. "Platform 1 is gone. Thirty-one hundred kilometers."

Four weeks ago, thirty-one hundred kilometers had been well outside the engagement envelope.

"Platform 2. Twenty-nine hundred. Platform 3. Twenty-eight hundred."

Sato watched the telemetry feeds wink out in sequence. The same clean termination. The same invisible weapon. But the kill zone had expanded past thirty-one hundred kilometers. The thirty-five-hundred-kilometer offset that Dren had calculated as safe wasn't safe enough.

"It's reaching further," she said. "Higher power. Tighter focus. Or both."

Platforms 4, 5, 6, and 7 disappeared without firing. The corridor was being swept clean.

"Platform 8 is firing," Reeves reported. "Extended range. Dren's geometry."

Platform 8 — the last in the corridor, the farthest out — had watched seven platforms die. Its autonomous software computed the firing solution against the thirty-five-hundred-kilometer geometry, aimed for the midline, and fired all five directed charges. The charges detonated. The pellets were away.

"Platform 8 is gone," Sato said. "One point four seconds after firing."

The pellets were in flight. But something was wrong. The charges had gone off too soon — early in the firing sequence, before the Fist's midline had reached the convergence point. At a hundred and fifty kilometers per second of closing velocity, the timing error translated to hundreds of kilometers of along-track displacement. The pellet clouds arrived forward of the midline, most missing entirely. What struck the cylinder hit the bow off-center — pushing the nose sideways instead of the whole cylinder.

"Deflection?" Okoro asked.

The tracking data took hours to compile. When it arrived, Reeves read it without expression. "Zero useful deflection. But the tracking data shows something else."

"Cumulative?"

"Ninety. Same as before Wave 3." The number sat in the room like a stone. Eight platforms expended for nothing. Something in the firing sequence had gone wrong, and it had cost them their only shot. Sato pulled her tablet toward her and began writing — what, Okoro couldn't tell, but her jaw was set and her pen moved with the controlled fury of someone converting grief into documentation. Somewhere behind the operational discipline, behind the numbers and the protocols, the people in the room were beginning to understand that they might not be able to stop it.

• • •

In the weeks between Wave 3 and Wave 4, the tracking data showed something new. The Fist's radar cross-section was changing — slowly, almost imperceptibly, but consistently. Sato caught it in the daily tracking summaries.

"It's rotating," she said. "The pellets that hit — they struck the bow off-center. Not the midline. The cloud arrived forward of where it should have been. Instead of pushing the cylinder sideways, it applied torque. Tipped the long axis off the flight vector. Very slow — maybe ten to fifteen degrees since Wave 3. And accelerating."

"Is it tumbling?" Okoro asked.

"Not tumbling. Tipping. The long axis is coming off its flight vector. At this rate, by the time it reaches Earth, it won't be arriving nose-first anymore. It'll be presenting a partial broadside."

The consequence was unintended. Dren had aimed for the midline — lateral push, same as every previous engagement. But the cloud had arrived on the bow. Instead of pushing the cylinder sideways, the off-center impact applied torque. The long axis was tipping off the flight vector. At this rate, by the time it reached Earth, the Fist wouldn't arrive end-on. It would present a partial broadside — five times the atmospheric cross-section. Five times the energy deposition. Instead of a needle, a barn door.

Nobody said anything. There was nothing to do about it.

• • •

*April 17th, 2060.*

*Wave 4: 10 Earth fleet platforms. Intercept day.*

*71 days to impact.*

Okoro was in the operations center. Sato beside him. Reeves at the terminal. Dren at the back, standing where he always stood, arms folded, watching the screens with the expression of a man who already knew what he was about to see.

The room was full — every station manned, every screen live. Ten platforms, five hundred megatons each, closing on Satan's Fist. The backbone of Earth's planetary defense architecture. What had been hope in the wake of Wave 1 had turned to something close to resignation for Wave 4.

The first platform was destroyed at six thousand kilometers.

Sato marked the time. The second platform was destroyed four seconds later. Then the third. The fourth. Reeves read each termination from the telemetry as it arrived. His voice was level. Professional. The voice of a man who had been trained to give bad news in sequence.

The fifth. The sixth. The seventh.

"They're not even close," Sato said quietly.

The eighth. The ninth.

The tenth platform died at five thousand eight hundred kilometers from the surface of Satan's Fist. It had never been within five thousand kilometers of firing range. Five hundred megatons, purpose-built, the single most powerful nuclear weapon ever engineered. Destroyed as casually as the first.

Eleven seconds. Ten platforms. Zero detonations.

Dren had been quiet through the entire engagement. Now he spoke. "The range nearly doubled again. Thirty-one hundred in Wave 3 to six thousand now. Forty days apart. The improvement between Wave 1 and Wave 2 was enormous — from nothing to two thousand in five days. Wave 2 to Wave 3 was modest — two thousand to thirty-one hundred in four weeks. And now this. That's not a linear progression. Something changed between Wave 3 and Wave 4."

"An update," Sato said. "A major one. Not incremental optimization. A qualitative upgrade."

"Through the relay," Dren said. "The burst went somewhere. Something answered."

The room was silent. Not the silence of shock — they had watched Waves 2 and 3. They had seen the progression. They had known, mathematically, what would happen. This silence was the sound of confirmation. The sound of a number becoming final.

"That's it," Reeves said. "All four waves expended."

Okoro didn't move for a long time. His hands were still on the console, his eyes on the wallscreen where ten telemetry traces had gone dark in eleven seconds. The operational composure he had carried through four engagements was still there — the posture, the voice, the engineer's habit of reaching for the next problem. But something behind it had broken. Not visibly. Not in any way the room could point to. But the man who asked "What's our total?" was not the same man who had watched Wave 1 succeed and believed, along with everyone else, that this was a problem they could solve.

Okoro took off his glasses, set them on the console, and pressed his fingers against his eyes. He held them there for five seconds. When he put the glasses back on, his hands were shaking — the first time anyone in the room had seen that.

"What's our total?" he asked, though he already knew.

"Ninety kilometers. Eighty-five from Wave 1. Five from Wave 2. Zero from Wave 3. Zero from Wave 4."

"Had we been able to launch simultaneously —" Sato started.

"We couldn't," Okoro said.

"I know. But if we could have. All thirty-seven platforms, arriving at once, from multiple vectors. The beam weapon can engage targets sequentially — one at a time, sweeping the corridor. It can't engage thirty-seven simultaneous threats from thirty-seven directions."

"How much deflection?"

"Six hundred kilometers. Maybe more, depending on how many survived to fire. Double what we needed for a clean miss."

"Enough."

"More than enough." She paused. "But pulsed fusion gets to the intercept point faster than chemical propulsion. Earth orbit is farther from the intercept than the belt. We couldn't synchronize the arrival because the hardware wouldn't let us. The waves were staggered because physics staggered them."

"And it used every day," Okoro said.

"Every day."

He looked at the wallscreen. Ninety kilometers. The Fist on its post-engagement course, coasting without fuel, aimed at the central Pacific. Sixty-five kilometers per second. Thirty-seven kilometers long. And tipping broadside.

"Colonel," Okoro said. "Run the terminal approach geometry. Final trajectory, final deflection, miss distance. Everything."

Reeves was already at the terminal.

Ninety kilometers of deflection, bought with the nuclear arsenal of two worlds. Thirty-seven platforms. A hundred and thirty-five directed charges and ten standoff warheads. Everything humanity had.

Was it enough?

Reeves ran the numbers.

# CHAPTER 11

## *Falling Short*

*April 18th, 2060. Object at ~3.5 AU, ~57 km/s.*
*67 days to flyby.*
*Earth ↔ Mars: ~2.0 AU, Communications: ~17 min one-way.*

• • •

The arsenal was spent. The numbers were in. Ninety kilometers of cumulative deflection. The Fist coasting on a ballistic path, fuel exhausted, slowly tipping off its flight axis from the off-center hit in Wave 3.

What remained was the math — the terminal approach geometry, the atmospheric interaction model, the consequence projections. What ninety kilometers of deflection actually meant for the people on the ground.

Hamner was at the Blanco telescope when the final tracking data stabilized.

Not in the command center at Ares City or the Situation Room in Washington. At his facility in Chile, doing what he'd done since the night he'd found it. Watching. Measuring. Verifying.

The post-engagement trajectory data came in from four independent tracking stations — two on Earth, one on Mars, one in the belt. The AI pipeline ingested the terminal approach parameters, computed the flyby geometry, modeled the atmospheric interaction, and populated the consequence display in eleven seconds.

Hamner didn't look at the result.

He pulled the raw tracking data into his own workspace. The same manual verification he'd done on the night he'd found it — plotting positions, checking the math, making certain the number was right before anyone else saw it. The pipeline processed terabytes through validated models in seconds. Hamner's check was slower and covered less — but it tested the assumptions the pipeline took for granted, the ones that mattered when the stakes were species-level. He knew people were waiting. He did it anyway.

The manual computation took fourteen minutes. He checked it twice. It agreed with the pipeline.

He stared at the number for a long time. Then he transmitted it.

• • •

In Washington, the Situation Room had been running its own consequence models since the end of Wave 4. Three days of computation, refinement, sensitivity analysis. When Hamner's independent confirmation arrived — matching their own numbers to four significant figures — Whitfield asked for the full brief.

The National Security Council's senior analyst gave it. The room was full — Whitfield, Vickers, the Joint Chiefs, NSC staff, FEMA liaison, State Department. The relay to Ares City was live, transmitting everything to Mars with a seventeen-minute delay.

The analyst put up the display.

**CLOSEST APPROACH: ~90 KM ABOVE SURFACE.**

**FLYBY VELOCITY: ~67 KM/S.**

**OBJECT ORIENTATION AT FLYBY: ~25° OFF FLIGHT AXIS.**

**EFFECTIVE ATMOSPHERIC CROSS-SECTION: ~75 KM².**

"Walk me through it," Whitfield said.

"The rotation from the Wave 3 off-center impact has continued," the analyst said. "At current rate, the object will be approximately twenty-five degrees off its flight axis at closest approach. It's no longer arriving end-on. It's presenting a partial broadside to the atmosphere."

"What does that change?"

"Everything about the atmospheric interaction. End-on, the cross-section is about fifteen square kilometers — the circular face. At twenty-five degrees off-axis, we're looking at roughly seventy-five square kilometers pushing through the upper atmosphere. Five times more atmospheric coupling. Five times more energy transfer to the air column. And at ninety kilometers, we're in the lower thermosphere. The atmospheric density is orders of magnitude higher than a grazing pass at two hundred. The broadside orientation is the multiplier, but the altitude is what makes this unsurvivable along the ground track."

"Give me the ground track."

"Southern Pacific, roughly equatorial. Entry over open ocean west of South America. Transit across the central Pacific. Exit roughly at the International Date Line. Total atmospheric transit time: approximately ninety seconds."

"Displacement waves?"

"The atmospheric shockwave couples to the ocean surface along the entire ground track. Pacific island nations — Fiji, Samoa, Tonga, the Marshall Islands, the Marianas, Kiribati — are directly in or adjacent to the ground track. Pacific Rim coastlines — the Philippines, Indonesia, Papua New Guinea, New Zealand, eastern Australia, western South and Central America — all see significant wave events from the ocean displacement. More distant coastlines — Japan, Taiwan, Vietnam, Thailand, Korea — receive attenuated but still dangerous wave arrivals hours later. Wave heights from ten to seventy meters depending on coastal geometry and local bathymetry. The broadside orientation at ninety kilometers makes this catastrophically worse than an end-on pass at any altitude."

"Casualties."

The analyst looked at the number on his screen. "Direct casualties from displacement waves, overpressure, and thermal effects: low end, a hundred and fifty million. High end, four hundred and fifty million or more, depending on warning time and evacuation effectiveness. The Pacific island populations are at extreme risk — low elevation, minimal infrastructure, limited evacuation options."

He paused. "Those are the direct numbers. The downstream effects are harder to model. Dust and debris injected into the upper atmosphere along the transit path will reduce solar transmission for one to three growing seasons — possibly longer. Nitrous oxide production from the shock heating will produce acid deposition across a wide band of the Pacific. Global agricultural output drops. How far, we can't say with confidence. Pacific shipping lanes are disrupted. Coastal infrastructure across more than twenty nations is destroyed or severely damaged. Supply chains that depend on Pacific Rim manufacturing and trade cease to function. The secondary mortality from famine, displacement, economic collapse, and resource disruption could exceed the direct toll, but the models can't project that with any reliability. The honest answer is that we know the direct cost, and we know the downstream effects are large, and we cannot put a credible number on the total."

The number sat in the room.

A hundred and fifty to four hundred and fifty million dead in the first days and weeks. An unknowable number after that. That was the good outcome. That was what ninety kilometers of deflection bought. That was what thirty-seven platforms and the combined nuclear arsenal of two civilizations had achieved. The planet saved, but at a staggering cost.

A staffer behind Whitfield made a sound. An aide was staring at the casualty figure with his mouth slightly open. Someone else in the back of the room was shaking his head slowly, back and forth, as if the motion could make the number change.

“That’s awful,” Vickers said quietly. Barely above a murmur. Grief given voice when the numbers became people.

No one responded. The room held still for a moment. Whitfield’s hands, folded on the table, tightened once — the only time anyone in the room had seen them move involuntarily. Then they relaxed, and her voice came back with the same measured authority it always carried, and whatever had crossed behind her eyes stayed there.

Then Vickers spoke again. “The rotation. That’s from Wave 3. The platform that fired early. If those charges hadn’t gone off when they did, the pellets would never have hit off-center. The object would still be arriving end-on. Fifteen square kilometers instead of seventy-five. The casualty numbers would be a fraction of this.”

Eyes shifted. The analyst pulled up the Wave 3 engagement summary. One platform out of eight had survived long enough to fire. It had fired early — the charges detonating before the Fist’s midline reached the convergence point. Zero kilometers of useful deflection. And a torque that was now slowly turning the Fist broadside to the atmosphere.

“A reckless shot that may have killed more people than it saved,” Vickers said.

Whitfield looked at him, then at the analyst. “Is that accurate?”

The analyst chose his words carefully. “The rotation is attributable to the off-center impact in Wave 3. The platform that survived long enough to fire did so early — we don’t yet have a root cause for the timing error. Wave 3 added zero kilometers of deflection. The closest approach altitude is the same with or without it — ninety kilometers. But the rotation accounts for the entire fivefold increase in cross-section. That’s the primary driver of the casualty numbers.“

The room absorbed that. Zero deflection from Wave 3. A firmware error that tipped the cylinder broadside. A fivefold increase in atmospheric coupling. The math was not ambiguous.

“I want Dren’s response to this,” Whitfield said.

"Seventeen minutes for the transmission to reach Ares City, ma'am. Seventeen for the response. Thirty-four minutes minimum."

"Then we wait."

• • •

On Mars, the briefing arrived in full — the consequence model, the casualty projections, the ground track, and Vickers' accusation. Okoro, Sato, and Dren listened to the playback in the operations center at Ares City. Forty staff around them, most already working evacuation frameworks.

Vickers' voice came through the relay speakers, clear and sharp. "A reckless shot that may have killed more people than it saved."

Dren listened to the full exchange without expression. When it finished, he looked at Okoro.

"Do you want to respond?" Okoro asked.

"Yes."

He keyed the relay.

"The platform had one point four seconds between firing and termination. It fired everything it had at extended range. The alternative was to die without firing." He paused. "The concept was to fire from extended range — outside the kill zone — and hit the midline. Accept the dispersal penalty, get what deflection we could. The beam weapon killed seven of eight platforms before they could fire. The one that fired — the charges detonated too early. We'd updated the targeting parameters through the Batch G-7 translation layer for the new offset. The layer was built under time pressure with one integration test skipped. Something in that chain produced the early firing. The pellets hit the bow instead of the midline. Off-center impact applied torque instead of lateral push. I accept responsibility for the engineering chain that produced that result."

The transmission went out. Seventeen minutes to Washington.

The room was quiet after Dren released the relay key. Sato looked at him but said nothing. There was nothing to say. The math was the math.

Okoro noted it for the log.

• • •

Thirty-four minutes after Whitfield's request, Dren's response reached the Situation Room.

Whitfield listened to it once.

Vickers leaned forward. "He accepts responsibility. For skipping a test on a software update that he loaded under time pressure. For an engineering shortcut that turned a punch into a slash and increased casualties fivefold. What does that mean, exactly? What does accepting responsibility look like when the number is a hundred and fifty million? Does he write a letter? Does he resign? What exactly is his responsibility worth to the dead?"

The room was very still. No one looked at Vickers. No one looked away from him either.

Whitfield let the silence hold for three seconds. Then she spoke.

"We are where we are. The deflection is done. The course is fixed. We have seventy days to save as many lives as we can, and that is the only thing this room is going to work on." She looked at Vickers directly. "There will be time after for consequences. Right now, I need solutions."

Vickers held her gaze for a moment, then sat back.

"Visibility timeline," Whitfield said.

The analyst pulled up the approach geometry. "The object is currently too distant and too dark for naked-eye observation. Low albedo — the surface doesn't reflect much light. It becomes visible to the naked eye at approximately one and a half million kilometers — roughly six hours before closest approach. By three hours out, it's as bright as the North Star. In the final hour, it's the brightest object in the sky after the Moon."

"So for the last six hours, everyone on the night side of Earth can look up and see it coming."

"Yes, ma'am."

"We need to begin consequence planning immediately. Evacuation timelines for the Pacific Rim and all Pacific island nations. Warning systems. Coastal defense posture. I want FEMA, DOW, and State working the domestic response within the hour. International coordination — the Pacific Island Forum nations first, then Australia, Indonesia, the Philippines, Papua New Guinea, New Zealand, Chile, Peru, Mexico, and all Pacific Rim nations. Every nation in the impact corridor gets this data today."

The room pivoted. The engagement was over. The consequence was beginning.

• • •

On Mars, Dren waited until the consequence planning was underway. Half the staff at Ares City were on communication links to Washington, FEMA, the Pacific Rim embassies. Then he spoke.

"There's something in the post-engagement data that needs attention."

Okoro looked at him.

"The second optical burst."

Okoro's focus was on the evacuation framework filling the secondary displays. "Go ahead."

"After Wave 1, Platform 1 recorded a narrowband optical emission from the Fist. Directed back along its approach vector. I asked for the vector to be tracked and turned Platform 1 around."

"Turned it around?"

"It's a spent weapons platform with functioning sensors and maneuvering thrusters. It can't catch the Fist — it doesn't have the delta-v. But it doesn't need to. I put it on a trailing course, sensors pointed at the Fist's stern. A listening post."

"When did you do this?"

"Immediately after Wave 1. The order went through my engineering team."

Okoro looked at him for a moment. "Continue."

"Platform 1 intercepted a second emission during Wave 3. Same characteristics — narrowband, optical frequency, highly directional. Same duration. Same vector — back along the approach trajectory. Back to wherever it came from."

"Two bursts. Same direction."

"Two confirmed. There may have been others during Waves 2 and 4 that Platform 1 wasn't positioned to intercept. But we have two, and they're consistent. The Fist is transmitting after each engagement. Status reports, sent to its point of origin."

"It's reporting to whoever built it," Sato said.

"That's the simplest explanation. And it means whoever sent the Fist knows exactly what happened. They know the engagement results. They know the deflection. They know the final miss distance. They have the same data we do."

Okoro looked at the room. Evacuation timelines on one screen. Casualty projections on another. Seventy days to prepare for hundreds of millions of casualties — and whatever came after.

"Log it," he said. "Maintain Platform 1. But the priority is consequence management."

Dren nodded. "Understood."

He didn't argue. He maintained his listening post. He accepted that the room had made its choice. Hundreds of millions of people to prepare for in seventy days. An optical emission pointed at deep space was not going to move to the front of the queue.

But the data existed. The vector was tracked. Platform 1 was listening.

• • •

Across two worlds, the number landed.

In Washington, Whitfield stood at the window of the Oval Office. The consequence projections were on her desk. She had seventy days to coordinate the largest evacuation in human history across more than twenty nations and two hemispheres. She was about to preside over the deaths of hundreds of millions of people —- and the slow unraveling of hundreds of millions more in the years that followed. The alternative had been worse. That was the math. The sky outside was clear. Late April. Cherry blossoms along the Potomac, past their peak but still holding.

She pressed her thumbs against her fingers, left hand then right. She did it looking at cherry blossoms that would be here next year, and thinking about the people who wouldn't be.

On Mars, Dren sat alone in his office at Ares City. The operations center was full — Okoro and Sato and the colonel and forty staff working the consequence framework. Dren had excused himself. On his personal terminal, he pulled up the Fist's post-engagement trajectory and began running intercept calculations. Rendezvous windows. Delta-v budgets. Transit times to match velocity with an object heading outbound at fifty-seven kilometers per second. He opened a ship design file — one he'd started months ago, before the first wave launched — and began updating the propulsion requirements.

In Chile, Hamner stood outside the dome of the Blanco telescope. The sky was enormous and dark and full of stars. The object he'd found — the anomaly in the survey data, the thing that wasn't where it should be — was seventy days from grazing the atmosphere of the planet he was standing on.

He'd verified the number. He'd transmitted it. He'd done his job.

He looked up. In seventy days, for six hours before the end, it would be visible. A point of light that grew brighter and brighter until it crossed the sky and the atmosphere screamed and the oceans rose. But tonight, it was invisible. Just another dark object in a sky full of them, falling toward the Sun.

Somewhere behind it, a spent weapons platform with no warheads and a patched-together maneuvering system was trailing in its wake, sensors pointed at its stern. Listening.

Hamner went back inside. There was more data to collect.

# CHAPTER 12

## *The Kludge*

*June 15th, 2060.*
*Object at ~1.4 AU, ~63 km/s. 9 days to flyby.*

• • •

Torres had walked to the assembly bay in the dark. Kourou predawn — the equatorial humidity already thick at four-thirty, the air heavy with sea salt and engine exhaust from the test the night before. The facility lights made a white island in the jungle. She'd stopped at the personnel gate and looked up. Orion was setting behind the tree line. She'd learned the southern constellations in her first year on Mars and relearned the equatorial sky since arriving at Kourou, and in eleven days none of them would be visible from this latitude because she'd be outbound and the stars would be the ones nobody navigated by. She went inside.

The fuel feed splitter was leaking.

Not badly. A trace amount, condensing on the feed housing and evaporating before it reached the deck plating. Carla Torres had found it during the morning inspection — a faint sheen on the lower bracket that hadn't been there twelve hours ago. She'd photographed it, measured the accumulation rate, and brought the data to Dren before she'd finished her coffee.

Dren had been at the facility outside Kourou for four days. Before that, six weeks in transit from Mars — riding an early pulsed fusion prototype, the same class of engine that powered the ship sitting in the assembly bay in front of him. He'd spent the transit managing the construction remotely, the communication delay shrinking a little each day as he closed the distance. By the time he'd reached Earth orbit the conversations were real-time and the ship was at ninety-five percent.

The ship — it didn't have a name yet, just an internal designation that nobody used — sat in the center of the bay like something that had been assembled from two different vehicles. Which basically it had.

The primary drive occupied the aft third of the ship. Clean lines, integrated mounting, cabling that ran in engineered channels. Dren's belt transit prototype. Two years of R&D. A pulsed fusion engine that worked the way a mature design worked — not elegantly, but consistently. The engineering team had spent eighteen months getting the pulse cycle reliable before Dren had redirected the program. If you looked at the ship from one angle, it looked like any prototype vehicle, with a few structural elements supporting something on the other side.

Viewed from another angle told a completely different story. The secondary drive was bolted to the ship's lateral axis like an afterthought. Because it was an afterthought. The mounting frame had been fabricated from asteroid mining equipment. The fuel feed split off the primary system through a junction that hadn't existed in any design document until eleven weeks ago. The cabling ran in external conduit because there were no internal channels for it. Torres had tested it four times and it held. But it looked like what it was — a field modification made by people who didn't have enough time.

"The splitter's sweating," Torres said, pulling up the images on her tablet. "Micro-fracture in the housing, probably from the thermal cycling during the last test. I can pull it and replace in six hours."

Dren looked at the images. "Replace it. And pull the secondary feed coupling while you're in there. I want both inspected before we button up."

Torres nodded and headed for the drive bay. She didn't ask about the timeline. She knew the timeline.

Dren followed her. He stood at the edge of the drive bay while she opened the access panel on the splitter housing — working methodically, tools laid out on the magnetic strip beside her, the kind of organized efficiency that came from years of maintaining equipment in places where the nearest spare part was three months away.

"I want to talk about the crew," Dren said.

Torres didn't look up from the coupling. "Chandra's solid. You know that."

"I know that. Tell me about the others."

"Jackson wants to go. The fifth integration burn threw a harmonic in the secondary drive — a resonance coupling between the bracket reinforcement and the fuel feed housing. It only shows under sustained thrust. She shimmed it, damped it, re-torqued the assembly. Sixth burn was clean. But she doesn't trust it to stay clean without her on board."

"The ship has three pods," Dren said. "Three crew, three pods. If Jackson joins, there's no pod for her."

Torres pulled the splitter housing free and set it on the inspection rack. The micro-fracture was visible under the work light — a hairline along the grain, exactly where thermal stress would propagate. "She's right. If the harmonic comes back at two AU, she's the only person who can fix it. And something will go wrong with the integration. Something always goes wrong with the integration." She picked up a loupe and examined the fracture line. "You need us both. I keep the ship running. She keeps the drive running. Those are different jobs."

"And Inoue?"

Torres turned the housing under the light, still examining the fracture line. “Inoue’s the best EVA operator I’ve worked with. Better than Kowalski in non-standard environments. She doesn’t freeze, she doesn’t rush, and she doesn’t need to be told what to look at — she sees it before you point.” She set the housing down. “She also has family in Samoa.”

“I know.”

“That’s not a problem. That’s the opposite of a problem. She’ll work harder than anyone on that hull because she needs to know what it is. You won’t have to motivate her. You’ll have to stop her from doing too much.”

Dren nodded. “Kowalski takes it well?”

“Kowalski takes it professionally. He’s not happy. But he’ll run ground support and he’ll do it right.” She reached for the replacement part from the secondary inventory. “Four people in a crew compartment that’s too loud, with a drive held together by field welds and a fuel system that wasn’t designed to split, heading for an alien weapon at fifty-five kilometers per second. You sure about the number?”

“Which number?” Dren asked.

“Twenty to forty percent.”

“That’s the survival estimate.”

“That’s the optimistic survival estimate. And it assumes the drive performs to spec for the entire return transit,” Torres said.

“Put a fourth pod in the cargo bay,” Torres said, not looking up from the loupe. “It’s not designed for it, but the mounting points are standard. The robot can share the space.”

Torres slotted the replacement housing into position and began tightening the mounting bolts. “Fair enough.” She worked in silence for a moment. “You’re sure about this whole thing?”

“No,” Dren said. “But I’m certain we have to try.”

Torres looked at him — a quick glance, direct, the kind of look a person gives when they want to see if someone means what they just said.

Whatever she was looking for, she found it. Or found enough. His face had the expression she'd seen on engineers who'd run the numbers and accepted them — not certainty or confidence, but the specific stillness of someone who'd stopped calculating because the answer wasn't going to change. He meant it. Whether that was enough was a different question, and Torres filed it the way she filed every uncertainty about hardware: note it, watch it, don't let it stop the work.

Then she went back to the bolts.

Sato's face was on the communications display — eighteen-minute delay from Ares City. Dren had made this trip in part to be here for the final construction, in part to be present for the flyby, and in part for a reason he hadn't stated to anyone. He'd accepted responsibility for an engineering shortcut that was going to kill hundreds of millions of people. Being on Mars when it happened was something he couldn't do.

Sato's latest transmission was still queued. He played it.

"Torres says the environmental seal on the crew compartment is cycling within spec but louder than the design target. She's not concerned about function. She's concerned about crew endurance over a multi-month transit. If the cycling noise is forty decibels continuous, sleep quality degrades significantly."

Dren noted it. Perhaps noise canceling earbuds could compensate. Another item on the list of things that were good enough but not right. The ship was a collection of such items. Each one individually acceptable. The accumulation was what kept him awake.

He pulled up the mission status summary and recorded his response for Sato.

"Fourteen months ago you asked me to model interceptor production. Now you're building a crewed ship to land on the thing we couldn't stop," Sato had said at the end of her transmission, the way she did when she wanted him to stop and think about what he was doing.

Dren smiled slightly. Then he stopped smiling, because she was right, and the distance between where the project had started and where it was now could be measured in the kinds of decisions that didn't have good outcomes.

• • •

*Fourteen months earlier. March 2059. Ares City, Mars.*

7I had just made its second course deviation. The mainstream explanation was outgassing — a natural process, consistent with a cometary body. The numbers were small. The trajectory shift was slight. Hamner's alarm was being treated as an interesting data point, not a crisis.

Dren didn't care about the explanation.

He'd called three people into his office at Ares City. Sato. Roberta — Bobby — Jackson, his chief propulsion engineer. And a mission planner named Reinhardt who had been with Dren's operations since the first Martian mining expansion.

"7I is at roughly seventeen AU," Dren said. "It's maneuvering. I don't care why. Something that crosses interstellar space and then adjusts its trajectory inside our solar system is worth landing on."

Jackson stared at him. "You want to land on it."

"I want to match velocity with it and put people on it. Yes."

"It's doing fifty kilometers per second."

"Which is why we're having this conversation instead of filing a mission proposal." Dren pulled up the belt transit prototype's specifications on the wall display. The pulsed fusion drive. The commercial application — fast transit between Mars and the belt, cutting months off current trajectories. "This engine can produce the delta-v. Not as currently configured. The fuel capacity is designed for a belt round trip — roughly twenty-five kilometers per second of total delta-v. We need more than double that."

"More than double for what, exactly?" Reinhardt asked.

"Outbound velocity matching. 7I passes through the inner solar system and continues on a hyperbolic trajectory. After it passes Earth, it's heading outbound at sixty to sixty-seven kilometers per second. That decelerates under solar gravity, but it never drops below about fifty-three. We need to get out in front of it, match that velocity, rendezvous, and ideally have enough fuel to come back."

Jackson was already running numbers on her tablet. "If we scale the fuel capacity — bigger tanks, same drive — we can get the delta-v. Mass fraction gets ugly. Sixty, seventy percent fuel by mass."

"Can the structure handle it?"

"With reinforcement. The mounting frame wasn't designed for that mass ratio. But it's engineering, not physics. It's solvable."

"Dren. 7I is outgassing. That's the consensus."

"Consensus is not my department. Science isn't up for a vote."

"If it's a comet, you're spending two years of propulsion R&D and hundreds of millions of dollars to land on a snowball."

"If it's a comet, we'll know that well before we land on it." Dren looked at him. "And if it isn't a comet, we'll know that too. Either way, we learn something worth knowing. A fully robotic mission. Besides, what we learn about 7I coupled with what we'll learn pushing the envelope is enough justification."

The room was quiet. Jackson was still running numbers. Reinhardt was studying the trajectory display with the expression of someone whose professional life was about to get more complicated.

"There's a second problem," Dren said. "The departure burn. The primary drive is a pusher plate — fixed thrust axis. It can't slew. Point the ship, fire, and you go that way. No steering during the burn. The departure trajectory requires a large lateral component — roughly thirty kilometers per second perpendicular to the primary's thrust line. A single fixed-axis engine can't do that without shutting down, reorienting the entire ship, burning laterally, then reorienting again and resuming. Sequential burns. It wastes time, wastes fuel, and the thermal cycling on the pusher plate during repeated restart sequences shortens its operational life."

Jackson looked up from her tablet. "That's a separate thrust axis."

"Yes."

"You want a second engine. Perpendicular mount."

"I want you to figure out how," Dren said, no trace of mirth in his voice.

The room went very still.

"You want to bolt a second pulsed fusion drive onto a prototype that doesn't have structural provision for it," Jackson said, almost laughing.

"I want you to figure out how," Dren repeated.

Jackson looked at him for a long time. Then she looked at the belt transit prototype's specifications on the display. The mounting frame. The fuel system. The structural margins. She was quiet in a way that wasn't computation — the numbers were already running, she could feel them assembling behind her eyes. The quiet was the moment before she said yes to something she couldn't take back. A second engine meant a second set of failure modes, a second fuel path, a second thing that could kill them at two AU. It meant she was building the ship that people would have to ride. She felt the responsibility of this answer. She looked at the display a moment longer.

"It's possible," she said. "The lateral loads are manageable if we brace off the primary mounting frame. The fuel feed has to split — one supply system feeding two drives. That's a plumbing problem, not a physics problem." She paused. "It'll be ugly."

"Pretty isn't in the design spec. I need it to work."

"It'll work. But the integration is where you'll lose time. The primary drive has eighteen months of testing behind it. A secondary drive bolted on with a split fuel feed and a fabricated mounting frame has zero. We'd need months of integration testing."

"We have what time 7I gives us. Start designing it."

Jackson nodded. She didn't say what everyone in the room was thinking, which was that they were designing a spacecraft around a mission to an object that the entire scientific establishment said was a comet.

• • •

*October 2059.*

7I made its final course deviation at ten AU. Every instrument that could see it confirmed: the trajectory was now a direct Earth intercept. The outgassing theory died in a single afternoon. 7I was artificial, aimed at Earth, hostile.

Jackson was already on Earth. Dren had sent her to Kourou in June to oversee the secondary drive fabrication — the hardware had to be built and integrated at the Earth-side facility, and Jackson didn't trust anyone else to run the mounting frame construction. She'd been there four months, turning her design into metal.

The meeting was split across a ten-minute delay — Dren and Sato at Ares City, Jackson and Reinhardt at Kourou. What should have been a thirty-minute discussion took ninety. The delay had always annoyed Dren. Today it was intolerable.

"The parameters have changed," Dren said. "This is no longer speculative. 7I is a weapon. Everything about the mission profile tightens."

Sato put up the updated trajectory. "After the deflection attempt — assuming some deflection is achieved — 7I continues on a modified hyperbolic path. The outbound velocity depends on the closest approach distance. At sixty-five kilometers per second at perihelion, it's doing fifty-five to fifty-seven at three to five AU. Still on an escape path. Still reachable."

Jackson's report on the construction timeline came back. The primary drive was ready — testing complete, performance verified. The secondary drive was at seventy percent. Mounting frame fabricated and fitted. Fuel feed splitter designed but not built. Integration testing hadn't started. She needed four months minimum for the integration and testing cycle.

"You have five months. The launch window is late spring — mid-June at the outside."

The prototype was also designed for belt runs of weeks, not months. Reinhardt's written updates covered the growing mass problem — crew compartment, life support, radiation shielding, consumables for a multi-month transit. Significant mass additions that pushed the fuel fraction above sixty-five percent by mass.

"Thin margins are what we have," Dren said. "Build it."

After the channel closed, Sato stayed behind. "You knew," she said. "In March. You didn't know what it was, but you knew it wasn't outgassing."

"I knew it was maneuvering. That was enough."

"You redirected a billion-dollar propulsion program based on a hunch."

"I redirected it based on a course. Hunches don't have delta-v calculations."

Sato looked at him. "And now you're asking people to ride that hunch to an alien weapon at fifty-five kilometers per second."

"Volunteers," Dren said. "We haven't selected them yet."

• • •

*April 2060.*

The engagement was over. Twenty-six platforms destroyed by the beam weapon. The Fist deflected by ninety kilometers — enough to avoid a direct hit, not enough for a clean miss. And tipping broadside from the Wave 3 firing sequence error, turning a flyby into a catastrophe. The consequence projections were cascading through every government on Earth. And the optical bursts had been detected. Two confirmed transmissions from the Fist, directed back along its approach vector. It was reporting to someone.

The mission objectives expanded.

Dren laid them out for the full team — Sato beside him at Ares City, Jackson and Reinhardt at Kourou on a thirteen-minute delay.

"First priority: the communication architecture. The Fist transmitted twice during the engagement. Narrowband optical, highly directional. We need to characterize the antenna system, trace the transmission vector, and determine what it's talking to. Chandra handles this."

"Second: the beam weapon. It destroyed twenty-six platforms across three waves. We need to understand the power source, the targeting system, the engagement envelope. Everything we can document about how it works. If there's a follow-up, we need to know how to defend against it."

"Third: hull material. This object crossed interstellar space and survived nuclear bombardment. The hull is intact. I want samples taken and analyzed in situ. Whatever it's made of, it's beyond anything we have. We bring testing equipment because we may not bring the samples home."

"Fourth: continuous transmission. Everything the crew finds is transmitted to Earth and Mars in real time. Every scan, every sample result, every image. If the crew is lost, the data survives. This is non-negotiable."

"The ship also carries an autonomous surface robot — one of our standard industrial units, repurposed. Inoue controls it. It operates continuously — exterior surveys while the crew rests, hazardous environment work, first-contact risk buffer if we encounter anything unexpected on the surface. The robot goes first. Always."

He paused. "Survival estimate for the crew: twenty to forty percent. The range depends on drive performance, dwell time on the Fist, and whether the return burn to the belt succeeds. Everyone on this channel needs to understand that number before we proceed."

Jackson reported from Kourou. They were at ninety percent. The secondary drive had tested clean. The fuel feed splitter was installed. But the integration testing was incomplete — four full-system burns completed of the eight she wanted, and at best two or three more possible before the June seventeenth launch date.

Dren knew the math. Two more burns gave them six of eight. He also knew that if something broke on burn five, there would be no time to repair and retest. The ship was at ninety percent and the distance between ninety and a hundred was measured in the kinds of failures that killed people.

Someone on the channel — one of Jackson's team at Kourou — raised the question that had been sitting underneath the entire discussion. "What about the weapon? The beam killed twenty-six platforms. What happens when we approach?"

"The Fist's weapon engaged objects on intercept trajectories," Dren said. "Platforms coming at it head-on. Things that matched a threat profile — closing velocity, approach angle, radar cross-section of an inbound weapon. Our ship doesn't match that profile. We launch before the flyby, head outbound along the Fist's trajectory, and the Fist overtakes us from behind. We're a co-moving object it's catching up to. We're not closing on it. We're not on a collision course. We're debris in its wake."

"The weapon still faces us as it approaches," Reinhardt said.

"Yes. The weapon is on the bow and the Fist is coming up behind us bow-first. But every engagement we observed was against objects on intercept trajectories. The targeting system responded to a specific threat profile. We watched it adapt during the gauntlet, and in Wave 1 we fooled it because the hardened platforms didn't match the profile it had calibrated against. Our approach is even further from that profile. We're not inbound. We're not accelerating toward it. We're coasting in the same direction it's traveling."

"That's a lot of trust in assumptions about alien targeting logic."

"It is. But it's not blind trust. It's an inference from observed behavior." Dren paused. "And it's the best option we have. Everything about this mission is risk."

Jackson's voice came back from Kourou, quieter than before. "We're assuming it classifies threats by approach vector and closing rate. If it classifies by emissions, reactor signature, or mass — if it just shoots at anything within a certain radius — we're dead before we know it."

The channel was quiet for a moment.

"If it does that," Dren said, "then we learn it the hard way. But the gauntlet data says otherwise. It had opportunities to fire on Platform 1 after Wave 1 — a spent platform trailing behind it with active sensors. It didn't. That's the best evidence we have."

It wasn't enough. Everyone on the channel knew it wasn't enough. They were going anyway.

Dren caught Okoro. "One thing."

Okoro waited.

"I'm going to Earth before this is over. Kourou, for the final construction. Possibly Washington."

"You'll need security."

"I'll need Brandt."

"You always have Brandt. But Earth isn't Mars. Different threat environment. You're going to be the most polarizing figure in public life. Half the planet will think you saved them. The other half will think you killed hundreds of millions of people with a shortcut."

"I know what they'll think."

"Then you know you need more than one man."

Dren considered. On Mars, Brandt was enough. Brandt and the facility's own systems. Earth was different — open environments, uncontrolled crowds, press access, political actors with reasons to see Dren diminished or dead. And the object had given every fringe group on the planet a cause.

"Tell Brandt to put together a four-man detail for the Earth trip. His pick."

Okoro nodded. "Timeline?"

"He has until we finalize the transit window. Two months, maybe three."

• • •

Brandt came to Dren's office the next day. Cole Brandt had been running Dren's personal security for eleven years — recruited from JSOC's tier-one community, came to Mars when Dren's operations scaled past what contract security could handle. He'd built the security infrastructure at Ares City from nothing. Quiet, methodical, no wasted motion, no wasted words. He and Dren communicated the way people do when they've worked together long enough that most of the conversation is unnecessary.

"So three others besides me," Brandt said. Not a question.

"Your pick. People you trust. People who can operate in an uncontrolled environment with political exposure and media proximity."

Brandt had already made his selections. He put three names on the display.

"Tomas Galvez. Eight years with me on Mars. Before that, twelve years JSOC — we overlapped for the last four. He's the most experienced operator I have outside myself. Physically imposing, which matters for visible deterrence. He has a prior service connection with a General Vickers at the Pentagon — they were in the same unit. That'll surface in any background check. It's not a liability, but it's a data point."

Dren filed that. "Go on."

"Raines. Six years on Mars. I recruited him from Meridian Security Group — they ran belt convoy protection. Clean record. Fast. Very fast. Best reflexes on the team, possibly the best I've worked with. Reads crowds well. He's the one I'd want next to me in an uncontrolled environment."

"And?"

"Dex Okafor. Four years. Youngest on the team, but he runs our technical systems — counter-surveillance, communications security, threat detection equipment. He's the reason our kit is a generation ahead of anything government-side. If we're operating alongside Secret Service, which we will be if you're meeting with Whitfield,

Okafor's gear will be the best hardware in the room. He knows it. He's not obnoxious about it, but he's not modest either."

Dren looked at the three profiles. Clean histories. Mars-adapted. Brandt's recruits, every one of them.

"Approved. Start planning the advance protocol."

• • •

Inoue came to Dren's office at the Earth-side facility two days after the consequence projections were released. She filled the doorway — broad-shouldered, tall, built like the Polynesian stock she came from. The tā moko on her chin and jawline was traditional, not decorative. Inoue was big for an EVA operator — big for the suits, big for the hatches, big for the confined spaces where the work happened. Nobody had ever had the nerve to tell her that, because her skills were unmatched and she had a way of looking at people who raised the subject that ended the conversation before it started. She didn't sit.

"I want the EVA position."

Dren looked at her. He already knew what she was going to say and he already knew the professional argument against it.

"Kowalski has more EVA hours."

"Kowalski has more EVA hours on standard maintenance operations. I have more hours on non-standard surfaces — asteroid survey, irregular structure work, unpressurized repair on moving platforms. The Fist isn't a space station. It's a thirty-seven-kilometer cylinder with unknown surface characteristics. My experience profile is a better match."

She was right, and they both knew it. But that wasn't why she was here.

"My family is in Samoa," she said.

Dren waited.

"The ground track crosses the central Pacific. The projections put wave heights at fifteen to forty meters for the island chains.

Samoa is at sea level. Everyone will be evacuated, but my homeland will be wiped clean. My parents are in their seventies. My sister has three children under ten."

She stopped. She didn't say what the numbers meant for her family. She didn't need to.

"I'm not asking for compassion," she said. "I'm asking because the mission matters more to me than it matters to Kowalski. He's a professional. He'll do the job because it's the job. I'll do it because I need to know what that thing is and who sent it and why it's going to kill the people I love. You want someone who won't quit. That's me."

Dren considered for a long time. Not whether her argument was valid — it was. Not whether her emotional investment was a liability — in anyone else it would be, but Inoue was the most controlled operator he'd ever worked with. What kept her precise under pressure wasn't detachment. It was focus. And now she had more focus than anyone on the crew.

"You're in," he said. "Tell Kowalski."

# CHAPTER 13

*Plans*

*June 16th, 2060.*
*Object at ~1.4 AU, ~63 km/s. 8 days to flyby.*

• • •

The advance team arrived at the White House thirty minutes before Dren's vehicle.

Brandt had flown in from Kourou the day before with Galvez, Raines, and Okafor. They'd scoped the route, the facility, and the meeting location — a smaller conference room in the West Wing, chosen for the conversation rather than the audience. Brandt had requested the room specs, sight lines, and entry points through the White House Military Office. He'd received them, eventually, after bureaucratic friction that told him the request was unusual but not unprecedented.

The Secret Service liaison met them at the West Wing security checkpoint. The vetting had been completed two days earlier — backgrounds, service records, biometrics, the full package. Galvez's prior service connection with Vickers had surfaced, as Brandt had predicted. A note in the file, nothing more. The Service had flagged it, confirmed it was historical, and moved on.

The weapons conversation happened at the checkpoint, and it went exactly the way Brandt had expected.

"Your team will need to check all weapons before entering the secure perimeter," the liaison said.

"No," Brandt said.

The liaison paused. He was a twenty-year veteran of the Presidential Protective Division. He'd heard the word before, but not often in this context.

"Mr. Brandt. No private security detail carries weapons inside the White House security perimeter. That's not discretionary."

"Mr. Dren is the principal. My team maintains proximity coverage at all times. We don't hand off protection to another detail, regardless of whose building we're in."

"This is the White House."

"I understand where we are."

The conversation escalated — not in volume, but in the number of people involved. The liaison called his section chief. Brandt waited, hands at his sides, expression neutral. Galvez stood behind him, large enough that his presence was its own kind of statement. Raines watched the hallway. Okafor had already set up the portable counter-surveillance suite on the security desk, and the Service agent next to it was studying the equipment with the expression of a man who recognized hardware better than his own.

The section chief arrived. The compromise took eight minutes: Brandt would carry. The other three would not. Dren's team would maintain proximity in the corridor outside the meeting room. Secret Service would hold the room itself. If Dren requested his team inside, the Service would accommodate one — Brandt's choice.

"Raines," Brandt said. "He's inside with me."

The section chief studied Raines — lean, still, watching the hallway with an attention that didn't look like vigilance unless you knew what you were seeing.

"Fine. Two of yours, armed — you and him. The others hold the corridor."

Brandt nodded. It was close enough.

Okafor was repacking the counter-surveillance kit when one of the Service agents — a younger man, technical branch — stopped him.

"That's a Meridian-Saab array?"

"Modified," Okafor said. "We replaced the signal processor. Theirs has a twelve-millisecond lag on the frequency scan. Ours does it in three."

The agent looked at the unit, then at Okafor. "We're still running the stock configuration."

Okafor closed the case. "I know."

• • •

Dren's vehicle arrived at the West Wing entrance at 10:28. Brandt and Raines were already inside, positioned in the corridor outside the conference room. Galvez met the vehicle at the door. Okafor was thirty meters back, monitoring the press staging area where credentialed media waited behind the rope line for the departure shot.

The meeting was scheduled for 10:30.

Raines saw the man at 10:29.

He was in the press pool — credentialed, lanyard visible, holding a tablet the way reporters hold tablets when they're pretending to take notes. He was standing at the left edge of the rope line, close to where the corridor turned toward the conference room entrance. Nothing about him was overtly wrong. His credentials were real. His position was normal. His posture was normal.

His eyes were not.

Raines had been reading crowds for fifteen years — convoy routes in the belt, public events on Mars, the controlled chaos of spaceport terminals where everyone had somewhere to be and the person who didn't stood out like a frequency spike on a clean signal. The man's eyes weren't tracking the way a reporter's eyes tracked. A reporter watched the principal. This man was watching the geometry — the distance between himself and the corridor, the position of the Service agents, the gap that would open when Dren's party turned the corner.

Raines moved. Not fast — smooth. He stepped away from his position and walked toward the press area with the unhurried gait of someone checking a sight line. He closed the distance to fifteen feet. Then ten. The man didn't notice him. People who are watching geometry tend to miss the person who's already solved it.

At five feet, Raines stepped in beside him the way you'd step beside a colleague. His left hand found the man's right wrist — not a grab, a placement. Fingers closing around the joint with the kind of mechanical specificity that doesn't allow for options. His right hand went to the man's elbow and applied a controlled downward pressure that turned the man's body forty-five degrees away from the corridor and into Raines's chest.

The man's hand had been moving inside his jacket. It stopped.

"Walk with me," Raines said, quietly, the way you'd say it to someone who'd wandered into the wrong hallway.

The man didn't walk. He tried to jerk his wrist free. Raines adjusted his grip — a quarter-inch shift that moved the hold from uncomfortable to structurally non-negotiable — and the man's knees buckled slightly. Not a takedown. A suggestion.

They walked. Raines guided him out of the press pool with a hand on his arm that looked, to anyone more than ten feet away, like one professional helping another find the right door. The two nearest reporters didn't look up. The Service agent covering the rope line glanced over, saw Raines's credentials, and looked away.

Raines delivered the man to the Secret Service checkpoint at the end of the corridor. He transferred the wrist hold to the agent on the desk and said one word: "Check him."

They found it in the jacket. A single-shot polymer frame. Ceramic projectile. Built to pass a standard magnetometer.

The press pool never noticed. No shot fired, no lockdown, no plaster dust. Just a man who'd been standing at the rope line and then wasn't.

Brandt got the report from the Service section chief sixty seconds later. He keyed his comm to Galvez. "Raines pulled someone from the press pool. Ceramic weapon. Service has him."

"Copy," Galvez said. Then, relaying: "Mr. Dren — Raines identified and removed an armed individual from the press area. Ceramic single-shot. Service has him in custody."

A pause. Dren's voice came back, flat. "Who credentialed him?"

"Unknown. Service is working it."

Another pause. "Clear to proceed?"

Brandt looked at the section chief. The section chief met his eyes and gave a short nod — a different kind of nod than the one he'd given during the weapons negotiation. This one had respect in it.

"Clear."

Dren entered the building flanked by Galvez. He passed the press staging area. The rope line was undisturbed. Reporters were checking their tablets. Nothing had happened, as far as they knew.

Raines was back at his post outside the conference room, hands at his sides, expression unchanged.

Dren looked at him as he passed. He didn't say anything, but he looked — a brief, direct assessment of the kind he made about equipment and people and systems. Raines had read the crowd, identified the threat, and removed it so cleanly that the crowd didn't know it had been there. Not reactive. Predictive. And invisible.

*That one is good*, Dren thought. Something in his chest had gone cold for half a second when Galvez said the word ceramic — the specific, involuntary acknowledgment of a trajectory that had almost intersected his. Then it passed, and he filed it the way he filed everything, and he walked into the meeting.

• • •

The meeting with Whitfield took place in the smaller conference room. Dren in a chair across from the President of the United States.

Vickers was there. So was the National Security Advisor. Brandt stood against the wall by the door. Raines was beside him. No one else.

Dren laid out the mission — the ship, the trajectory, the objectives, the crew, the dwell-time framework, the survival estimates. He did not ask for permission. He informed the President that he intended to launch a crewed mission to the Fist in eighteen days.

Whitfield listened without interrupting. When he finished, she looked at Vickers.

"General."

Vickers had been waiting. "This mission represents an unacceptable additional risk of human life, authorized by the same individual whose engineering shortcut increased projected casualties by a factor of five. The crew members are employees of his organization. Genuine voluntary consent is not possible in that power dynamic. I recommend robotic-only investigation. Send probes. Don't send people."

Whitfield looked back at Dren. "Response."

"The communication delay to the Fist at four AU is over thirty minutes round trip. Real-time judgment on the surface isn't a luxury. It's the mission. The antenna system, the weapon, the hull material — these require adaptive investigation by people who can change approach based on what they find. A robot follows a program. The crew follows the evidence."

He paused. "On the question of consent: General Vickers is right to raise it. I employ these people. I selected them. The power dynamic is real. I cannot certify that their consent is free of that influence."

Whitfield studied him. She'd been reading people across tables like this for twenty years. "Then how do I know they're volunteers?"

"You ask them yourself."

The room was quiet. Vickers glanced at Whitfield. The National Security Advisor said nothing.

"The mission is authorized," Whitfield said. "The ship draws from your resources, not Earth's crisis response. And I cannot justify willful ignorance about what's on that object when we have the means to find out." She paused. "But every crew member will be interviewed by me personally before launch. Not by your people. By me. Individually, without you present. I want to know that each of them understands what they're agreeing to and is choosing it freely. If I'm not satisfied that any crew member is a true volunteer, they don't fly."

Dren nodded.

Vickers started to speak again. Whitfield raised one hand, barely, and he stopped.

"That's all, General."

• • •

The interviews were conducted over two days at the facility near Kourou. Whitfield flew in with a minimal staff. She met each crew member in the same room — a glass-walled office overlooking the assembly bay, the ship visible through the windows behind whoever was sitting across from her.

Torres was first. Practical, direct, slightly impatient with the formality. She understood the risks. She'd computed the fuel margins herself. She knew the ship's tolerances better than anyone except Jackson. When Whitfield asked why she'd volunteered, Torres said, "Because I'm the person most likely to bring that ship home in one piece. And if I can't bring it home, I'm the person most likely to keep it running long enough to finish the job."

Whitfield approved her in under twenty minutes.

Jackson was next. She'd built the secondary drive. She knew where every weld had been inspected and where inspection had been deferred. Whitfield studied her for a moment before speaking.

"Ms. Jackson. I'm told you requested a crew position after the integration testing raised concerns about the secondary drive. That you were originally assigned to ground operations."

"The secondary drive developed a harmonic during sustained thrust testing. I fixed it. But I don't trust the fix to hold without someone who understands the coupling on board. That's me."

"Did he ask you to go, or did you ask him?"

"I asked. He said yes."

Whitfield studied her. "You designed the fix. And now you're telling me you don't trust it to hold without you."

Jackson met her eyes. "I trust the fix. I don't trust the fix in someone else's hands. I built that drive. If it fails at two AU because someone else didn't understand the coupling, I'd have to live with that. I'd rather be there."

Whitfield considered. "The survival estimate is twenty to forty percent."

"That estimate assumes the drive performs to spec. If it doesn't, the estimate is zero. I'm the person who makes sure it performs to spec."

Whitfield approved her. Slower than Torres.

Chandra was measured. Analytical. He'd studied the optical burst data from the gauntlet and had already developed preliminary models for the antenna system based on the emission characteristics. When Whitfield asked if he understood the survival odds, Chandra said, "I understand that the probability of returning is low. I also understand that the data from this mission is the single most important intelligence product in human history. If the choice is between a forty percent chance of dying on the Fist and a hundred percent certainty of never knowing what it was transmitting to, the math is straightforward."

Whitfield approved him.

Inoue was last.

She sat down across from Whitfield with the ship visible through the glass behind her — broad hands resting on the table, the dark lines of the tā moko sharp in the afternoon light. The secondary drive's external conduit caught the same light through the glass.

"Lieutenant Inoue. You're the EVA specialist. You replaced the original candidate for this position."

"Yes, ma'am."

"Why?"

"My experience profile is a better match for non-standard surface operations. I have more hours on irregular structures and unpressurized environments than the previous candidate."

Whitfield waited. Inoue said nothing more.

"Lieutenant. The ground track crosses the central Pacific. The casualty projections for the island nations are among the highest in the model. Do you have family in the impact corridor?"

A pause. Not long. But present.

"My parents and my sister's family are in Samoa."

"And that's not why you're here."

"It's not the reason I gave Dren. It's not the reason I'm giving you. The professional case is sufficient."

"I'm not asking about the professional case." Whitfield's voice was quiet. "I'm asking about you."

Inoue held her gaze. The room was very still. Through the glass, someone was working on the secondary drive's fuel coupling.

"Yes, ma'am. It's why I'm here. The professional case is real and sufficient. But I am here because that thing is going to come very close to my home, and I would like to be the person who finds out what it is."

Whitfield looked at her for a long time. Not deliberating. Recognizing something.

"Approved," she said. "All four crew members are cleared for the mission."

• • •

June 15th. Nine days to flyby. Two days to launch.

Torres had replaced the fuel feed splitter. The micro-fracture was where she'd predicted — a stress line from the thermal cycling, propagating along the grain of the housing. The replacement part came from the secondary inventory. Torres had inspected it, installed it, and run a pressure test. Clean.

The secondary drive had completed its sixth full-system burn that morning. Reinhardt had wanted eight. He got six. He looked at the data, looked at the ship, and signed the flight readiness report. The signature was steady. His hand was not.

• • •

The crew briefing was held in the glass-walled office overlooking the assembly bay — the same room where Whitfield had conducted the interviews, the ship visible through the windows. Torres, Jackson, Chandra, and Inoue sat around the table. Dren stood at the display.

"Launch is June seventeenth," Dren said. "I'm going to walk through the mission sequence so everyone has the same picture."

He brought up the trajectory plot. Two lines — the Fist's outbound hyperbolic arc and the ship's departure vector, diverging from Earth and converging at a point roughly two AU from the Sun.

"Departure is a thirty-two-hour burn. Both drives firing simultaneously — the primary accelerates along the Fist's outbound vector while the secondary handles the lateral component that the primary's fixed thrust axis can't reach. When both drives shut down, we're on the Fist's trajectory, coasting outward. Behind us, Earth continues in its orbit."

He paused. He didn't say what they all knew — that seven days after launch, the Fist would graze Earth's atmosphere, and they would watch it happen in telemetry.

"Twenty-eight days after the flyby, at roughly two AU from the Sun, the Fist catches us." He traced the convergence on the plot. "We're both outbound on near-parallel trajectories — the big velocity is shared. The remaining mismatch is phasing and timing. Roughly twelve kilometers per second of residual. The matching burn takes approximately six hours to bleed that off as the Fist closes from behind."

"And then we're alongside," Torres said.

"Alongside a thirty-seven-kilometer alien weapon, traveling outbound at sixty kilometers per second, heading for the outer solar system. Yes."

"Dwell time?" Jackson asked.

"Days. Maybe two weeks, if the fuel holds and nothing breaks. Enough time to characterize the antennas, document the weapon system, sample the hull, and transmit everything."

"And then?" Inoue asked.

"Then we burn for the belt. Full thrust, both drives — accelerate halfway, flip, decelerate the rest. If the drives hold, we're back at the belt in a few weeks. Pods are on board for contingency, not the plan."

"If the drive doesn't hold?" Jackson asked.

"Then we stay. And we transmit until the consumables run out."

The room was quiet. Through the glass, the ship sat in the assembly bay — two drives, a crew compartment that was too loud, an environmental seal that had been field-fitted, a fuel feed that split where no fuel feed was supposed to split. The LOTUS atmospheric unit. Water recycling. Ration stores. An autonomous surface robot and Jackson's fourth stasis pod sharing the cargo bay.

"The LOTUS gives us about eight months of oxygen recycling at full crew," Torres said. "Water recycling is good for roughly the same. Rations for five months if we stretch."

"So if we can't burn for home, we have four to five months on station," Chandra said. He looked at the trajectory plot, then at the ship through the glass. "Just so everyone's clear — we're riding that thing to a target that killed everything we threw at it, and if the drives break, we sit there until we run out of air." He said it the way he said most things — out loud, because someone had to.

"Transmitting the entire time," Dren said. "Everything you find goes home. That's the floor. The crew comes home if the engineering allows it. The data comes home regardless."

Inoue looked at the trajectory plot. "The Fist overtakes us bow-first. The weapon faces us the entire time it's closing."

"Yes."

"And we're betting it doesn't shoot."

"We're betting it classifies threats by approach vector and closing rate. We're not inbound. We're not accelerating toward it. We're coasting in the same direction. Platform 1 trailed behind it for months with active sensors and it never fired." He paused. "That's the best evidence we have."

"It's not much," Inoue said.

"No. It's not."

She nodded. Not agreement — acknowledgment. The look of someone who had already made the calculation and was past the point where the odds changed anything.

Jackson stood and walked to the window. She put her hand flat against the glass and looked at the ship — the secondary drive she'd designed, the mounting frame she'd built, the external conduit that ran where no conduit was supposed to run.

"Six burns out of eight," she said. "Reinhardt signed off."

"He did," Dren said.

"I would have wanted eight."

"I know."

Jackson looked at the ship a moment longer. Then she turned back to the room. "It'll hold."

• • •

The ship sat in the assembly bay at Kourou. It worked. Torres had tested it and it worked.

In two days, four people would climb into a crew compartment that was too loud and ride two engines — one proven, one bolted on — toward an alien weapon that by then would have killed hundreds of millions of people. They would watch the flyby in telemetry. They would see the data arrive — the thermal pulse, the displacement waves, the casualty reports. They would be unable to help. They would be ten days out, heading in the right direction, committed.

Dren stood in the assembly bay and looked at the ship. The two drives. The kludge. The thing he'd started building fourteen months ago because an interstellar object was maneuvering and nobody else thought that mattered.

Torres came out of the drive bay, wiping her hands. "Splitter's clean. Secondary coupling is clean. LOTUS is green. We're good."

"Environmental seal?"

"Forty-two decibels at peak cycle. Chandra says it sounds like his mother's kitchen. Inoue says she's slept through worse."

"And you?"

Torres looked at the ship. "I'll sleep when the drive does."

Dren almost smiled. Then he went back to the status report, because there were two days left and the list of things that were good enough but not right was still longer than he wanted, and every item on it was a decision about what kind of risk was acceptable when you'd convinced yourself the mission was worth more than the people flying it.

He'd made that calculation before. He'd been wrong about the cost.

He was making it again.

The assembly bay was quiet. The overhead lights hummed at a frequency he'd stopped hearing weeks ago. The ship sat under them, the two drives, the split fuel feed, the crew compartment where four people would sleep and eat and wait. This ship might also be their tomb. There were no guarantees of safe return. And he was sending them. No, he was asking them to go, knowing full well that because he asked they would go.

He put his hand on the airlock frame. The metal was cold. He stood there for a moment, his hand on the frame, and then he let go and walked back to the office, because the list was waiting and the list was the thing he could control.

# CHAPTER 14

## *Helpless*

*June 19th, 2060.*
*Five days to flyby. 29 days to intercept.*
*Remora: ~1.03 AU from Sun, ~55 km/s outbound. Coasting.*
*The Fist: ~1.35 AU, ~63 km/s inbound.*
*Separation: ~48 million km. Closing.*

• • •

Jackson had named it.

Not the official name — that was Remora, which Sato had entered into the mission documentation because it described the mission profile and because nobody had objected. A small fish that attaches to something larger. Rides along. Doesn't trigger the predator's response. That was the plan.

Jackson's name was different. She'd said it during the fourth integration test at Kourou, standing underneath the secondary drive's external conduit with a wiring harness in one hand and a torque wrench in the other, looking up at the fuel feed splitter junction that had been designed in eleven weeks and built in six. "We're really going to ride this kludge to an alien weapon," she'd said, and the word had stuck. Torres used it. Chandra used it. Inoue didn't — she called the ship by its designation, IPV-1, which no one else bothered with. But when Torres referred to the environmental seal's forty-two-decibel cycling as "the Kludge singing," Inoue had almost smiled.

Two days out from Earth now. The thirty-two-hour burn was behind them — both drives firing simultaneously, the ship vibrating at a frequency that Torres said was within design tolerance and Jackson said was within "tolerance for a thing that isn't supposed to exist." The primary drive had pushed them outbound along the Fist's track. The secondary had handled the lateral component that the primary's fixed axis couldn't reach. When the drives shut down and the vibration stopped, the silence had been profound. Torres had checked every system. Jackson had checked the drive. Chandra had checked the communications array. Inoue had checked the robot.

Then they'd floated in the quiet and looked at each other, and the reality of what they'd done settled in. Earth was behind them. The Fist was ahead of them, well, behind them actually — still inbound, still five days from flyby, but closing on Earth while they moved away from it. They were on the right trajectory. They couldn't go back.

The Kludge was small. Crew compartment, drive section, cargo bay. The compartment held four people the way a submarine holds a watch section — close enough to hear each other breathe, far enough apart to maintain the illusion of personal space. This was home for the next four months. If the matching burn failed or the drive gave out or the Fist's weapon didn't care about targeting profiles, it was also their coffin. The environmental seal cycled at forty-two decibels, a low rhythmic pulse that Torres had described as "a heartbeat for a ship that shouldn't have one." They'd been aboard for two days and it was already background noise. It would be background noise for months.

"You know, the ship isn't the only thing that hums," Chandra said to Jackson.

She looked up from her tablet. "What do you mean?"

"You hum."

"I do not hum," she responded emphatically.

"Yes you do. It's OK, I like a girl who hums," he said, winking.

"Did you just call me a girl? And did you just *wink* at me?"

"I mean technically," he added hurriedly.

"Technically?" she asked, her voice rising a bit.

"Yes. No one would think of you as a *girl*," he offered as way of explanation.

"You missed your calling. You should have been a miner. You just keep digging," she replied, the ghost of a smile crossing her lips.

"I'll get back to my numbers now," he said, turning awkwardly back to his screens.

"Yeah, that sounds like a good idea."

A moment later she was humming.

Fifty-five kilometers per second. The fastest living humans in history, riding a prototype that had been flight-tested six times, heading toward an alien weapon that had just destroyed twenty-six nuclear platforms. The fact did not require discussion.

• • •

Torres talked to the ship. The AI had configurable voice and personality profiles — Torres changed them depending on the task and her mood, cycling through a half-dozen presets she'd built over the years. Terse and technical for drive diagnostics. Conversational for long monitoring shifts. Dry and understated when she was worried about something and didn't want to be worried alone. From the outside, it sounded like she was talking to a different person every hour. She'd built a dashboard that displayed everything on a single screen, color-coded: green for nominal, yellow for drifting, red for intervention. On day two, everything was green. Torres didn't trust it.

"Secondary mount thermal is reading flat," she said, not looking up from the raw data behind the indicator. "Too flat. It should have a diurnal cycle from the sun shade rotation."

Jackson glanced over from the drive station. "Sensor or actual?"

“That’s what I’m checking.” Torres pulled the raw telemetry and compared it against the shade rotation log. The temperature was varying — just not enough for the sensor to distinguish from noise. “Sensor resolution. It’s a mining-grade thermocouple, not a lab instrument. It’s seeing the average, not the cycle.”

“Is that a problem?”

“It’s a problem if the mount bracket develops a thermal stress issue and the sensor can’t see the gradient that’s causing it. It’s not a problem today.” She logged it and moved on. Every four hours she checked the raw data behind each indicator, because the dashboard only showed what the sensors reported, and the sensors only measured what they’d been designed to measure, and the ship had components that no sensor had been designed for.

Jackson worked the drive — not maintenance, the drives were off, but preparation. The matching burn was in thirty-three days. She ran restart simulations daily, modeling the thermal cycling predictions for the primary drive’s relight. The primary she trusted. The secondary had six integration burns behind it and she trusted it less.

“If the secondary doesn’t restart for the matching burn,” she said one afternoon, not looking up from her screen, “we can do it on the primary alone. Sequential burns. Roll the ship, fire, roll back, fire again. Ugly. Costs fuel. But possible.”

“How much fuel?” Torres asked.

“Eleven percent margin instead of eighteen.”

“That’s the return budget.”

“I know.” Jackson closed the simulation and opened another. “That’s scenario fourteen.”

She had forty-seven scenarios by day three. Forty-seven workarounds. Eleven of the forty-seven had workarounds that depended on components she couldn’t test until the matching burn. She cataloged them because that was what engineers did when they couldn’t fix problems yet — they mapped the decision space so that when a problem appeared, the response was immediate.

Chandra ran simulations at the communications station, headphones on, muttering at his screen. The optical burst data from the gauntlet — two confirmed narrowband emissions, directed back along the Fist's approach vector. He had the waveform characteristics, the emission duration, the spectral profile. What he didn't have was enough data.

"Two points," he said to no one in particular. "Two data points. I'm building an antenna model from two data points. You can fit any curve through two points."

"Then fit the simplest one," Torres said from across the compartment.

"That's what I'm doing. That's what I've been doing. I have twelve thousand Monte Carlo runs and they all say the same thing — the error bars are larger than the answer." He pulled his headphones down around his neck. "I need to see the antenna. Everything I'm doing right now is preparation for the moment I actually see it. When I see it, I'll know which model is right in about thirty seconds."

"Twenty-seven days," Torres said.

"Twenty-seven days." He put the headphones back on.

Inoue worked the robot. Quietly, methodically, folded into the station closest to the cargo bay hatch — a big woman in a space built for smaller people, making herself compact the way she'd learned to do in every confined workspace she'd ever occupied. Its operating software had been updated with every piece of telemetry they had on the Fist's exterior — the side-on imagery, the radar cross-section data, the thermal profile. She ran simulated surface approaches on a model she'd built from the available data, testing mobility protocols on the cylinder's estimated curvature. The simulations were crude — they were working from a shape and a size, not a detailed surface map. But the robot needed approach algorithms that could adapt to what it found, and Inoue was teaching it to navigate a surface it had never seen.

She did this work with the focus and precision she'd demonstrated in six years of EVA operations. The same control that Dren had recognized when she'd stood in his office and said, "You want someone who won't quit. That's me."

*Five days to flyby. The Fist was inbound at sixty-three kilometers per second.*

*Her family was in Samoa. The evacuation was underway.*

Inoue ran the next surface approach simulation.

• • •

*June 24th, 2060. Flyby day.*

*Remora: ~1.18 AU, ~54 km/s outbound.*

*The Fist: ~1.0 AU, ~67 km/s. Atmospheric transit imminent.*

*Separation: ~27 million km. Fist closing at ~13 km/s.*

*Twenty-eight days to intercept.*

They knew the timeline. Six hours before closest approach, the Fist would become visible to the naked eye — a point of light that brightened steadily, moving against the stars. Three hours out, bright as the North Star. In the final hour, the brightest object in the sky after the Moon.

The crew couldn't see any of it — not really. They were 27 million kilometers ahead, facing outward. Earth was a point of light. The transit would be below any resolution they had. Everything they knew came through the Earth relay network — orbital platform telemetry, ground station data, lunar relay feeds. The Moon's permanent bases were unaffected by the flyby and their relay stations provided a second backbone when Earth's orbital network degraded. Two minutes of light-speed delay. Close enough to watch in near-real-time. Far enough away to be helpless.

Mars command received the same data nineteen minutes later. Sato coordinated from Ares City, but the feeds the crew watched came directly from Earth. What was happening on Earth reached the Remora almost as it happened. Just slightly after it happened.

That made it worse.

Torres was at the systems console. Jackson was at the drive station, running pre-restart diagnostics for the matching burn that was still four weeks away. Chandra was at the communications array, recording everything that came through the relay. Inoue was beside him, watching.

The first indication was the thermal signature.

Orbital platforms detected it before ground stations could — a bloom of infrared along the entry corridor, west of South America. The Fist entering the upper atmosphere at sixty-seven kilometers per second at ninety kilometers altitude. Partial broadside. Seventy-five square kilometers of cross-section pushing through air that was thin but not thin enough.

The data arrived in compressed packets from Earth's orbital relay network, two minutes old. Near-real-time. But the transit itself lasted ninety seconds. By the time the first thermal data reached the Remora, the Fist had already crossed the atmosphere and exited over the western Pacific. They were watching the aftermath, not the event. Everything on the display had already happened. The thermal pulse had already propagated. The atmospheric compression wave had already formed. Whatever was happening to the Pacific Rim was already underway.

The visual feeds came next. Orbital cameras captured the transit — a line of incandescent white carved across the upper atmosphere, horizon to horizon, southwest to northeast. Ninety seconds of atmospheric contact. From the orbital perspective, it looked almost beautiful. A streak of light across the curve of the Earth, like a match head dragged across the sky.

Below that line, the atmosphere was screaming.

The crew watched in silence. The feeds arrived in sequence — orbital thermal, orbital visual, then the ground-based data — but the sequence wasn't clean. Timestamps conflicted. A ground station in Peru transmitted overpressure data with a header dated three minutes before the transit. A partial visual frame repeated twice, then corrected. The relay network was stressed and the data showed it. Two minutes old. Already over.

The atmospheric shockwave data came through first. Overpressure measurements from ground stations along the Pacific ground track. The numbers were large. Then the stations began dropping out. One by one. Ground stations along the transit corridor that had been transmitting data went silent. Each lost signal was a location that had been there and wasn't transmitting anymore. Not destroyed — possibly. Disrupted — certainly. The distinction didn't matter to the data stream. The signal stopped and the display showed a gap.

The displacement wave data arrived from ocean buoys and coastal monitoring stations. Wave heights along the Pacific. Numbers that climbed as the data propagated westward from the ground track — ten meters, twenty, forty. The buoy network degraded as the waves reached it. Coastal stations transmitted for seconds or minutes and then stopped.

Torres watched the systems display. Her hands were still. The ship was fine. Everything was green. The ship was fine and the world behind them was breaking.

She checked the primary drive thermal. She'd checked it eleven minutes ago. She checked it again. Her hands moved across the console with the automatic precision of a thousand hours of system monitoring, and if they pressed the keys harder than necessary, if her fingertips whitened against the display surface, that was between her and the console. The ship was her responsibility. The ship she could do something about.

Jackson stayed at the drive station. She didn't turn around. She was running the thermal cycling model for the primary drive restart and she kept running it, because the matching burn was in twenty-eight days and the drive had to work and she couldn't do anything about the feeds behind her except listen. She heard Torres's breathing change. She heard Chandra stop typing. She kept working.

Behind her, Torres's breathing had gone shallow. Chandra's fingers on the keyboard had stopped and then started again, slower. The environmental seal pulsed. Forty-two decibels. The sound she'd learned to sleep through was now the loudest thing in the compartment because nobody was talking, and in the silence between the pulses she could hear the data feeds updating — small chimes, each one a station reporting or a station going quiet. She kept her eyes on the restart model. The primary drive's thermal profile filled her screen, a problem she could solve, and she solved it again.

Chandra recorded everything. Every packet. Every feed. Every data stream that came through the relay, stored and timestamped and indexed. He did this because it was his job and because the data mattered and because having something to do with his hands was the only thing keeping him in his chair. The optical burst analysis could wait. The antenna models could wait. Right now the relay was delivering the largest single dataset in human history — the real-time destruction of a civilization's Pacific infrastructure — and his job was to capture it.

Inoue watched.

The feeds degraded over the following hours. LEO relay satellites took drag hits from the expanded upper atmosphere — some dropped into safe mode, some lost pointing, some simply went out of coverage. The orbital relay network thinned. Ground stations along the Pacific went silent or fragmented. The lunar relay stations held, but they could only pass along what they received. When the Earth-side sources went dark, the Moon had nothing to relay. The coverage map on the communications display developed holes — regions where data had been flowing and now wasn't. The holes grew.

Not total silence. Feeds continued from stations outside the impact corridor — Europe, North America's east coast, Africa, the Middle East. But the Pacific was going dark in patches. Ground stations in Japan, the Philippines, Indonesia, Peru, Chile, the Pacific islands — some continued, some were silent, some transmitted fragments and stopped.

Three hours after the transit, a consolidated update arrived from Sato at Ares City — routed through Mars command, nineteen minutes old by the time it reached them. Sato's voice, measured and careful. Pacific ground track catastrophic. Pacific Rim coastal impact severe. Extent of inland damage unclear. Casualty estimates: not yet available. The systems that would produce comprehensive estimates were among those damaged.

The update was seven sentences. It covered the deaths of — they didn't know. Nobody knew. The systems that counted were broken.

• • •

The crew did not speak about it. Not then.

Torres checked the ship. Every system. Methodically. Green across the board. She checked them again.

Jackson ran another restart simulation. The numbers were the same as the last run. She ran it again.

Chandra began organizing the data archive. Hundreds of gigabytes of telemetry, recorded in real time, from an event that had lasted ninety seconds and would reshape the world for a generation. He sorted it by source, by timestamp, by data type. He didn't listen to the audio feeds. Not yet.

Inoue opened a display. A single feed — a coastal monitoring station on Upolu. Samoa.

The feed returned nothing. Not static or an error message. Nothing. The station had been transmitting standard environmental data — tide height, wind speed, atmospheric pressure — until six minutes after the transit. Then it stopped.

Six minutes. Long enough for the displacement wave to reach the islands. Long enough for the water to arrive.

Inoue looked at the blank display for a long time. Then she closed it. She pulled up the surface approach simulation she'd been working on that morning. The robot's mobility algorithms. The cylinder's estimated curvature. She made an adjustment to the approach protocol for irregular terrain and saved the file.

The other three saw it. None of them said anything.

Torres had watched her close the Samoa feed and open the simulation. The transition had taken less than two seconds. Inoue's face had not changed. Her hands had not paused. She had moved from the blank display where her family's home had been to the approach algorithm where her work was, and the movement was so controlled and so seamless that it was the most frightening thing Torres had seen since launch. That was not a woman who had set the grief aside. That was a woman who had locked it in a room and would not open the door until the mission let her, and Torres recognized the architecture because she'd built rooms like that herself, and she knew what happened when you opened them.

In the cargo bay, the robot ran an automated recalibration cycle on its external sensor array. It had no opinion about the feeds. It was ready.

• • •

*June 25th, 2060.*

*Remora: ~1.22 AU, ~53 km/s outbound.*

*The Fist: ~1.05 AU, ~67 km/s outbound. Post-flyby.*

*Separation: ~25 million km. Fist closing at ~14 km/s.*

*Twenty-seven days to intercept.*

The Fist was behind them now. Outbound. On their trajectory, heading in the same direction, fourteen kilometers per second faster. Closing.

The flyby was over. Ninety seconds of atmospheric transit, and now the object that had crossed interstellar space, survived nuclear bombardment, and carved a line of fire across the Pacific was continuing on its hyperbolic trajectory as though nothing had happened. It would decelerate under solar gravity as it moved outward, but it would never stop. It would never come back. It would coast into the outer solar system and beyond, carrying whatever it carried, transmitting to whoever it reported to, unless someone went after it.

Four humans and a robot were going after it.

Updates continued over the following day — some direct from Earth's surviving relay network, some coordinated through Mars command. Fragmentary. Incomplete. The picture assembling itself in pieces. Pacific Rim coastal damage severe and extensive. Japan's eastern coast — the feed gaps were the size of cities. Indonesia's coastline had been hit from both directions — the direct atmospheric shockwave and the displacement waves channeled between island chains. The Pacific island nations — the updates were shortest here. Small populations, minimal infrastructure, limited communication redundancy. When the feeds went dark from Fiji or Tonga or the Marshalls, there was no backup source. The silence was the data.

• • •

The lunar observatories delivered the first close-range images twelve hours after the transit. The Moon's telescopes had tracked the Fist through its closest approach — ninety kilometers above the surface, moving at sixty-seven kilometers per second, but from the Moon's vantage point the geometry was clean and the resolution was the best anyone had achieved.

The crew gathered around Chandra's station. Nobody suggested it. They just ended up there.

The atmospheric transit had changed the surface. The dark coating that had made the Fist nearly invisible against deep space was partially ablated along the windward face — the side that had taken the atmospheric heating. Underneath, the hull was lighter. Not reflective, but distinctly different from the original surface. The ablation pattern was uneven — heaviest at the midline where the cross-section was widest, tapering toward the edges where the cylinder's curvature reduced the exposure angle.

"That's our surface map," Torres said. "The ablation tells us which side took the heating. We approach from the windward side."

Inoue was already updating the robot's surface model. Real imagery instead of reconstructions. Actual surface texture instead of estimates. She worked through the images methodically, mapping the ablation boundary, the intact dark coating on the leeward hull, the transition zones.

Jackson studied the forward face — the features that Okoro had asked about months ago. The lunar resolution was better but still insufficient. "I can see structure," she said. "Multiple features on the bow face. Recessed. But I can't resolve the geometry."

Chandra had gone straight to the trailing end. Two antennas. Not three.

"The third antenna is gone," he said. "The one closest to the windward surface. Ablated or sheared off during the transit." He overlaid the Kimura reconstruction — three antennas, evenly spaced — against the lunar image. Two remained, offset from the missing one's position. "The surviving two are on the leeward side. Protected from the atmospheric heating."

He pulled off his headphones and stared at the overlay, recalculating. "That tells me something about the antenna construction. The hull survived ninety kilometers at sixty-seven kilometers per second without visible structural damage. The antenna didn't. Different material, or different construction method, or both. Less robust than the hull. Designed for a purpose that didn't require surviving atmospheric contact."

"Because it was never supposed to have atmospheric contact," Torres said.

"No. It wasn't. Not for more than three seconds, and not like that." Chandra updated his models. Two antennas instead of three. The emission geometry changed — the transmission pattern from two dishes instead of three would be different, the coverage narrower, the redundancy reduced. If the Fist transmitted again, it would do so with a degraded system.

Inoue finished updating the surface model and sent it to the robot. Twenty-seven days of better simulations, built on real data instead of inference.

• • •

The next morning, Torres found the first yellow indicator on her dashboard. A temperature reading on the secondary drive's mounting frame bracket — half a degree above the nominal band.

"Jackson."

Jackson looked up from the fuel margin calculations.

"Bracket thermal on the secondary mount. Half a degree above nominal. Probably sun shade angle — we're getting a sliver of direct exposure on the lower strut."

Jackson pulled up the secondary drive's thermal model on her own screen. She studied it for a moment. "Adjust the shade two degrees counter-rotation. That should put the bracket back in shadow."

Torres made the adjustment. The reading drifted back toward green over the next twenty minutes. Half a degree. Nothing. But they'd both watched it, both tracked it, both confirmed it was resolved. That was how they'd do it — every anomaly, no matter how small, worked by two people when two people were awake. Because the ship had components no sensor had been designed for, and the only redundancy they had was each other. Each time something like this surfaced, Jackson worked with the AI to make sure it could handle the scenario autonomously during stasis — detect the condition, diagnose it, correct it, or wake her if it couldn't. The library of known problems grew with every anomaly they resolved. What kept Jackson awake wasn't the known problems. It was the ones the AI wouldn't recognize as problems — the failure mode that didn't match any sensor profile, the gradual drift that looked nominal until it wasn't. The AI could only wake her for things it understood were wrong.

"Fuel margins," Torres said, while the thermal was still settling. "You tracking the same number I am?"

"Primary reserves at eighty-two percent. Secondary at seventy-nine. Matches my model."

"Matches mine." Torres logged the confirmation. Neither of them mentioned that eighty-two and seventy-nine were the numbers that made the return transit possible. Or that the margin between those numbers and the numbers that stranded them was smaller than most people would accept for a drive across town.

Chandra noted something in the relay data and pulled off his headphones. "Two LEO comm satellites shifted orbit during the transit. Measurable drag from the atmospheric expansion. The air itself got shoved aside."

Torres and Jackson both looked at him.

"The transit physically moved the atmosphere," Chandra said. "Enough to perturb satellite tracks at LEO altitude." He put the headphones back on.

It was a scientific observation. He delivered it as one. But the implication sat in the compartment — a ninety-second event that moved the atmosphere was not something that left the surface underneath it intact.

Inoue ran a full systems check on the robot. Mobility, sensors, sampling tools, communications link. She tested each tool individually, cycling through the diagnostic sequence she'd run twice before launch. The robot responded correctly to every command. Nothing had changed since Kourou.

She didn't open the Samoa feed again. There was nothing to see.

• • •

The Fist was behind them and gaining. Fourteen kilometers closer every second. In twenty-seven days it would catch them, and the matching burn would either work or it wouldn't, and then they would be alongside something that had nearly ended a world and kept going.

Chandra pulled up the optical burst data. Two pulses. Two transmissions directed back along the Fist's approach vector. The Fist had reported to someone twice during the gauntlet. It had probably reported again during the flyby — another pulse, sent back toward whatever was listening in deep space. Here is what happened. Here is what they did. Here is what I did to them. But the Fist had passed Earth now. Its mission was complete. It was coasting outbound through the solar system and into interstellar space, forever drifting, a spent weapon with nothing left to do.

The antennas were on the Fist's stern — the trailing end, the end that faced away from its direction of travel. He pulled up the antenna models — revised for two dishes, the emission geometry recalculated from the lunar imagery. In twenty-seven days, he'd know which model was right.

Four humans, one robot, one prototype. Outbound.

The Kludge held together. The drives were silent. The environmental seal pulsed at forty-two decibels. Behind them, the world they'd left was counting its dead. Also behind them, but closing, the thing that had done it.

They couldn't go back. They couldn't help. They could do what they came to do. And realistically, pragmatically, they might never get back.

Inoue saved the approach file and started a new simulation.

# CHAPTER 15

*The Sky Splits*

*June 24th, 2060. Flyby.*

*The Fist: ~67 km/s.*

*Closest approach: ~90 km altitude.*

*Atmospheric transit: ~90 seconds.*

• • •

**Ashford**

She'd been awake since ten.

Not because she couldn't sleep — she hadn't tried. She'd driven up to the overlook above Pasadena at sunset and stayed. The San Gabriel Mountains, fifteen hundred meters above the basin. Below her, Los Angeles spread to the coast in a grid of light. An evacuated city — three months of organized withdrawal, the freeways running one direction for weeks. Most of the basin was empty. Not all. Holdouts who wouldn't leave, couldn't leave, or didn't believe. And the looters who'd followed the evacuation like scavengers trailing a herd, picking the empty neighborhoods clean before moving to the next. She'd watched it happen with a cop's eye and no authority to stop it. The stores were gutted. The houses broken into. The city had been hollowed out and stripped, but the grid was still running because nobody had issued the order to shut it down. Street lights. Building security systems. Traffic signals cycling for nobody.

She'd moved to Los Angeles four months ago, when the consequence projections made it clear that the Pacific Rim would take the worst of it. Greg hadn't come. Where the damage was worst, the stories were. That was how she'd always worked — go to where it hurts and find out why.

Her phone showed the countdown. She'd memorized the timeline weeks ago — every emergency management briefing, every FEMA projection, every classified estimate she'd accessed through channels that technically she should never have had access to. Transit at 23:58 Pacific. Shockwave arrival at approximately 03:15. Displacement waves at approximately 05:45.

She knew the numbers the way she knew case files. Thoroughly, precisely, and with the understanding that the numbers described something that would not feel like numbers when it arrived.

At 23:57 she got off the hood and stood facing southwest. The Pacific was invisible beyond the coastal range, but she knew where it was. The city lights washed out the stars near the horizon. Above them, the sky was clear and dark and full of the usual constellations.

At 23:58, the southwestern horizon turned white.

Not a flash — a brightening. The sky from the horizon to roughly thirty degrees above it lit from beneath, as though something vast and incandescent had ignited beyond the curve of the Earth. The light was the color of an arc welder, blue-white and too bright to look at directly. Ashford looked anyway. The brightening lasted four or five seconds at peak intensity, long enough for her eyes to water, and then began to fade — white to yellow to orange to a deep sullen red that hung on the horizon like a false sunset in the wrong direction at the wrong hour.

The briefings had told her what it would look like. The Fist entering the atmosphere four thousand kilometers to the southwest, carving a ninety-second line across the upper Pacific. The scattered light from the plasma trail — the upper atmosphere fluorescing across a continent-scale area. She'd read the projections. Seeing it was different.

The glow faded over the next two minutes. The horizon returned to darkness. The city lights below her continued their automated cycling, green to yellow to red, green to yellow to red, for streets that were empty and would remain empty.

Ashford's phone had lost its data connection. The cell network was degrading — not from the flyby directly, but from the cascade of satellite and ground station failures that were propagating across the Pacific. She switched to the emergency broadcast band. Static. She waited. A backup channel activated — a military frequency, clipped and compressed. Pacific transit confirmed. Atmospheric interaction along projected track. Assessment ongoing.

She sat back on the hood. The city glowed below her. The timeline said 03:15 for the shockwave. Three hours and seventeen minutes. She had her watch. She had her phone with its degraded connection. She had the view.

She waited.

• • •

At 03:11, she felt it in her chest before she heard it.

A subsonic pressure, below the threshold of hearing but above the threshold of the body. Her diaphragm tightened. Her ears registered a change in pressure without producing a sound. The car's frame creaked — a single tick of metal flexing against a force that wasn't wind.

Then the sound arrived.

Not thunder. Thunder is a point source — a single crack from a single discharge. This was a line source. The shockwave from six thousand kilometers of atmospheric transit, arriving from every point along the track at slightly different times, overlapping into a sustained roar that built over seconds and didn't stop. It was lower than thunder, deeper, a frequency she felt in her teeth and her sternum and the soles of her feet through the ground. The mountain vibrated. The car vibrated. The air itself felt thick.

The sound lasted four minutes. Four minutes of sustained low-frequency pressure that wasn't painful but was inescapable, a sound that came from everywhere at once because the source was everywhere — a line across the Pacific, each point on the line sending its shockwave outward at the speed of sound, the arrival times overlapping into a wall of noise that had no direction and no edge.

Then the wind. Not a gust — a sustained push of air, the overpressure equalizing across the pressure gradient. Warm air from the southwest. The trees along the ridge bent. Ashford's hair blew across her face. The wind lasted two minutes and died.

Below her, the city lights continued. Traffic signals. Street lights. The grid, still running.

The timeline said 05:45 for the displacement waves. Two and a half hours.

She waited.

• • •

Dawn was starting. The eastern sky had lightened from black to dark blue. The city lights below her were dimming against the growing daylight — but not off. Still cycling. Still glowing in the pre-dawn grey.

Ashford checked her watch. 05:38. She stood up.

She didn't see the waves arrive. What she saw was the lights go out.

The coastal strip went first. A band of darkness that appeared at the western edge of the grid and moved inland. Santa Monica. Venice. Marina del Rey. Playa del Rey. Street lights, building lights, the ambient glow of powered infrastructure — all of it dying in a line that swept east as the water reached each substation, each transformer, each junction box.

The second wave was bigger. The darkness pushed further — through the low ground along the channels and flood plains. LAX went dark. The harbor areas. Long Beach. The water was following the low-lying corridors, the old river channels, the paths of least resistance into the basin.

A third wave. Culver City went dark where the ground dipped. Parts of Inglewood. The low sections of South LA along the drainage channels. But the elevated areas held. Baldwin Hills stayed lit — ninety meters above sea level, an island of light with darkness spreading around it. Ladera Heights held. Palos Verdes glowed in the distance, cut off from the mainland, its three hundred meters of elevation keeping it above the water but the roads to it gone.

The grid was failing beyond the water line now — not just flooding but the system protecting itself, transformers tripping, circuits opening, substations shedding load to prevent cascading damage. Some of the darkness was water. Some of it was the grid sacrificing sections to survive.

Dawn was breaking. The sky was light enough now to see what the lights had been hiding — a coastline that was no longer where it had been. Water in the low streets. Water in the channels. The Pacific had pushed miles inland through every low point in the basin and it wasn't going back.

Ashford stood on the ridge above Pasadena and watched the city she'd moved to four months ago go dark in pieces. Somewhere in a file on her laptop, the Batch G-7 firmware records were still waiting. Vickers's signature on the waiver. The timeline she'd been assembling. It felt like evidence from another century.

The numbers were real now.

Below her, the last section of the grid — the eastern basin, Pasadena, the foothills — flickered and held. Still powered. Still connected. The water hadn't reached the higher ground.

Her phone buzzed. The emergency channel, text only. FEMA REGIONAL AUTHORITY ACTIVATED. PACIFIC COAST CORRIDOR STATUS: NON-FUNCTIONAL. INLAND RESOURCES REDIRECTED.

She read it twice. Then she put the phone away and watched the sun come up over a city that was half underwater and half dark and entirely empty.

• • •

**Whitfield**

The continuity-of-government facility was a hundred and twenty feet underground and seventy miles from Washington. Whitfield had been there for six days. So had Dren. So had Vickers. So had eighty-three other people whose presence was mandated by a continuity protocol that had been written for nuclear war and adapted for this.

The situation display occupied the entire north wall. A map of the Pacific hemisphere with data overlay — ground stations, satellite links, relay nodes, communication status. Green for connected. Yellow for degraded. Red for failed. Grey for no data.

At 03:01 Eastern, the display was almost entirely green.

By 03:04, the western Pacific was turning red.

Whitfield stood in front of the display with her hands clasped behind her back and watched the color change propagate eastward. Not fast — the data took time to update, the relay network took time to register losses, the map took time to repaint. But the pattern was clear. A wave of red expanding outward from the ground track, consuming green nodes, leaving grey gaps where even the failure reports had stopped arriving.

Each grey zone was a place where people had lived. She knew this. She had read the population density maps, the evacuation compliance percentages, the estimated residual populations in every coastal zone. She had read them because reading them was her job, and she had absorbed the numbers because absorbing numbers was how she made decisions, and she had set the numbers aside because setting them aside was how she functioned. The numbers were on the display now. They were turning grey.

Her hands, clasped behind her back, were shaking. Not visibly. Not enough for anyone in the room to see. But she could feel the tremor in her fingers and she pressed them together harder and the tremor didn't stop. It had started at 03:02 and it wasn't going to stop for a while and that was fine because nobody could see it.

Eighty-three people at consoles and displays, doing their jobs with the controlled efficiency of professionals who had trained for catastrophic scenarios and were now living one. Voices low. Keyboards clicking. The hum of environmental systems providing air to a room that was designed to function when the surface didn't.

"Pacific ground stations are failing faster than the relay can track," the communications officer said. "We're losing nodes before we can confirm their status."

Whitfield watched. Japan's eastern coast went from yellow to red to grey in under ten minutes. The Philippine Sea stations followed. Indonesia fragmented — some nodes held, some went red, some went grey. The grey was worse than the red. Red meant failure reported. Grey meant no report at all.

She had authorized this. Not the flyby — nobody had authorized the flyby. But she had authorized the defense that produced this specific outcome. The platform deployments, the autonomous targeting waiver, the operational parameters. Every decision she'd made since the folder had landed on her desk had been aimed at deflection, and the deflection had produced this specific geometry, this specific angle, this specific broadside transit across the Pacific. She had made the best decisions available with the information she had. The display was showing her what the best decisions looked like.

Whitfield didn't look away from the display. "Regional command authority. Effective immediately. Western region to Colorado Springs. Pacific to Elmendorf. Each regional hub operates independently until communications are restored."

"Ma'am, that fragments national command."

"National command requires national communications. That's gone." Her voice had lost a layer — not the authority, just the polish. Her hands were still clasped behind her back. The tremor was still there. "Document it. Executive order, emergency authority. Regional commanders have full civil and military authority within their zones until unified command is re-established."

It was the right call. It was also the acknowledgment that the United States of America, as a unified governed entity, had just become several pieces. The infrastructure that connected the pieces was under water or off the air or degraded beyond function. The regional hubs would govern their areas. Some would do it well. Some would not. The federal government would exist in this room and in whatever the backup channels could reach and nowhere else until the communications were rebuilt.

Whitfield made the call in forty seconds. She'd been thinking about it for months. Thinking about it was different from doing it. Thinking about it was a planning exercise. Doing it meant standing in front of eighty-three people with steady eyes and shaking hands and speaking the words that dissolved the federal structure of the country she'd sworn to preserve.

The room absorbed the order and resumed. Keyboards. Voices. The hum of systems doing what systems did. Whitfield stood in the same position, hands clasped, and listened to the machinery of governance reorganize itself around the hole she'd just cut in it. Nobody looked at her differently. Nobody paused. That was the courtesy of professionals in a crisis — they pretended the decision hadn't cost what it had cost, so the person who made it could keep functioning. The tremor in her fingers was still there. She pressed her hands together and let the room move on without her.

She turned to the intelligence officer. "Casualty estimates."

"Not available, ma'am. The systems that would generate comprehensive estimates are among those affected."

"Best guess. Order of magnitude."

A long pause. "Pacific Rim total, including secondary effects. Hundred million. Plus or minus fifty."

The room was very quiet. Someone at the back console set down a coffee cup and didn't pick it up again.

"That's the low end," Whitfield said. It wasn't a question.

"Yes, ma'am."

She looked at the display. The grey areas were still growing. She kept her hands clasped behind her back.

• • •

**Dren**

Dren watched the display from the second row of consoles, fifteen feet behind Whitfield's position. Close enough to see every node change color. Far enough to be clearly not in command. His hands were flat on the console in front of him. They had been flat since 03:01. He hadn't moved them.

Vickers was ten feet to his left. Had been all night. The general hadn't spoken to Dren in six days — not since Dren had arrived at the facility from Kourou. But Vickers watched him. Every time a node went red on the display, every time a communication officer reported another station lost, every time the grey expanded into another region of the Pacific, Vickers's eyes moved to Dren and stayed there for three or four seconds before returning to the display.

Dren didn't look back. He knew what Vickers was thinking. He was thinking it himself.

The deflection had turned a direct hit into a flyby. It had saved the species. And Wave 3 — his wave, his concept, his firmware — had tipped the Fist broadside and multiplied the casualties by a factor no one had finished calculating. Five times the atmospheric cross-section. Every additional red node on the display, every grey zone that had once been a coastline, was the geometry of his firing sequence error writing itself across the planet.

Without deflection, the Fist would have hit the surface. Extinction-level. Ninety kilometers was the difference between civilization-ending and civilization-damaging. That was the counterargument, and it was correct, and it changed nothing about the display.

Vickers wasn't arguing about the deflection. He was arguing about the tilt — Wave 3's contribution that had added zero kilometers to the miss distance and turned the flyby from end-on to broadside. Seven platforms spent for zero deflection and a fivefold increase in atmospheric coupling. That argument would come later, in investigations, in hearings. For now it was just Vickers's eyes, every few seconds, measuring him.

The display showed the Pacific going dark. A hundred million people, plus or minus fifty. The plus or minus was doing a lot of work.

He knew the coastlines. He'd studied the impact projections when he designed the deflection sequence — every coastal city, every population density gradient, every evacuation corridor. Sendai. Manila. Surabaya. Lima. Names he'd read on planning charts for months, attached to numbers that represented people who would move or wouldn't. The grey zones on the display weren't abstractions to him. They were the specific geographies where his firing sequence error had turned a flyby into a catastrophe, and he could name every one of them.

Whitfield issued the regional command order. Dren listened. The right call — fragmented authority for a fragmented nation. He noted the forty-second decision time. He'd seen her make the platform authorization in similar time. She processed institutional decisions the way he processed engineering decisions: identify the constraint, accept the cost, execute.

His phone — the facility's internal comm system — showed a message from Sato at Ares City. Nineteen minutes old. Mars facilities nominal. Industrial capacity standing by.

Dren looked at the display. Then he composed a response.

"Mars industrial output: redirect to Earth relief and reconstruction. Priority one: communication satellite fabrication and launch. Priority two: orbital relay network reconstruction. Priority three: heavy equipment for coastal infrastructure. Begin immediately. All other programs suspended."

He sent it. Mars was the only fully functional industrial base in the solar system. Earth's Pacific infrastructure was broken. Earth's Atlantic and continental infrastructure was intact but would be consumed by the relief effort for months or years. Mars had manufacturing capacity, launch capability, and orbital access. It was nine months from Mars orbit to Earth orbit for cargo. The first relief wouldn't arrive until 2061. But it would arrive.

Vickers watched him send the message. Dren felt the gaze and continued working.

The display updated. Another grey zone. Another region where the data had stopped.

Dren looked at the Pacific — the real Pacific, the one made of water and coastlines and the cities that used to line them — and thought about ninety kilometers of deflection and a firmware error and what it meant to be right about almost everything and wrong about the one thing that mattered.

He picked up the stylus — his father's — and held it. He didn't write anything. There was nothing to write. He held it the way you hold something solid when the rest of the room has gone abstract, and after a moment he set it down exactly where it had been and went back to the display.

• • •

**Hamner**

The instruments didn't care.

The AI pipeline at Cerro Tololo processed the flyby data with the same mechanical thoroughness it had applied to every observation since October 2058. Thermal signature: detected.

Atmospheric interaction cross-section: computed. Entry corridor: mapped. Exit trajectory: tracked. The algorithms populated his screens with numbers in the same format and color-coding they'd used when the object was a curiosity at seventeen AU.

Hamner sat in front of the screens and watched the numbers arrive. 03:02 local time. Chilean winter. Cold and clear, the seeing conditions excellent — which was irrelevant now, because the instruments weren't using optical tonight. Everything was thermal and radar, tracking the atmospheric interaction.

Satan's Fist. Every feed used the name now. The broadcast networks, the scientific channels, the emergency frequencies. Satan's Fist. Not Hamner's Hammer or 7I or the provisional designation he'd filed on the night he'd found it, sitting in this chair, running the same pipeline.

He was relieved. Somewhere in the part of his brain that should be ashamed of itself, he was relieved that his name was no longer on it. The thing that had just carved a line across the Pacific was Satan's Fist, not Hamner's anything. The catalog designation was his. The name that would appear in history was not.

He noticed the relief and hated himself for it. A hundred million people — or whatever the number turned out to be — and a small, shameful part of him was grateful for a rebranding.

Nineteen months. He had tracked this object for nineteen months. He had flagged the pattern, run the Monte Carlo, written the email that three colleagues ignored and two rejected and one forwarded to Mercer as a problem to manage. He had been right about every single thing he'd said, and the thing he felt — sitting alone in a control room on a Chilean mountain while the Pacific burned — was relief about a name. He pressed his palms against his eyes and held them there until the feeling passed. It didn't pass. He put his hands back on the console and kept working.

The thermal bloom data was still coming in. The atmospheric interaction had deposited enough energy to heat the upper atmosphere across a region the size of South America. His instruments measured the thermal pulse, the spectral signature, the decay curve. Numbers on screens. The same numbers that had tracked the object's course deviations, its artificial course, its targeting. The pipeline didn't distinguish between discovery and catastrophe. It processed data.

At 05:27 local time, the shockwave reached Cerro Tololo.

He felt it before he heard it — a subsonic compression that made the walls of the control room flex slightly and his ears ache. Then the sound — deep, sustained, lower than the thunder that sometimes rolled across the Andes. A rumble that came from the west and didn't stop. His coffee cup — the same one he'd been using for nineteen months, since the night he'd found it — rattled against its saucer on the console. The liquid trembled. The cup walked a centimeter toward the edge. He caught it and held it until the shaking stopped.

The rumble lasted three minutes. Then it faded, leaving a silence that felt wrong — too complete, as though the atmosphere itself had been exhausted by the effort.

The data kept recording.

The post-flyby trajectory populated his screens. The Fist had exited the atmosphere and was continuing outbound. Sixty-seven kilometers per second and falling — solar gravity pulling it back as it climbed away from the Sun. In a month it would be at two AU, doing fifty-eight or fifty-nine. In a year it would be beyond Jupiter. In a decade it would be in the outer solar system, heading for interstellar space.

Unless the four people in the prototype caught it first.

Hamner knew about the intercept mission. He wasn't supposed to — the mission was classified, Dren's operation, not shared with the broader scientific community. But Hamner's pipeline tracked everything along the Fist's approach and departure vector. It was what the pipeline did — monitor that line of sky. A launch signature from Kourou seven days ago had appeared in the tracking data like a new star on the wrong trajectory. He'd computed the orbit and understood immediately what it was. A ship heading outbound on the Fist's track. Someone going after it.

He didn't know who was on board. He didn't know the crew or the ship or the odds. He knew the trajectory, and he knew what it meant: someone had decided that the thing that had just done this was worth chasing.

His instruments tracked the Fist outbound. The intercept vehicle was too small to track from this distance — a prototype, a speck, a mote of human ambition heading in the same direction as the weapon that had just reshaped the Pacific.

The pipeline would continue tracking the Fist for as long as the instruments could see it. Months, probably. Years, if the radar stations stayed funded. Hamner would sit in this chair and watch the numbers change as the object that bore his catalog designation receded into the outer solar system.

He picked up the coffee cup. Set it back on its saucer. Centered it on the console.

The data kept recording.

# CHAPTER 16

## *The New Map*

*July – August 2060.*

*Remora: ~1.5 AU from Sun, ~53 km/s outbound. Coasting.*

*The Fist: ~1.3 AU, ~60 km/s outbound, decelerating.*

*Separation: ~27 million km. Closing.*

• • •

The haze came in layers.

Not fog or cloud cover. A thinning of the sky itself — a reduction in the clarity of sunlight that showed up in agricultural monitoring stations before it showed up in human perception. The instruments measured it first. Solar irradiance down four percent globally, seven percent in the Southern Hemisphere where the atmospheric injection was heaviest. The upper atmospheric debris from the transit — shocked nitrogen compounds, thermally decomposed particulate, ocean surface material lofted by the shockwave — had distributed across the upper atmosphere in the weeks following the flyby and was settling into a persistent haze layer that the models said would take eighteen to thirty-six months to clear.

Four percent didn't sound like much. The agricultural models said otherwise, and so did the energy models — the solar generation capacity that had replaced most fossil infrastructure over the previous two decades was producing measurably less power across every grid that depended on it. The growing season in the Northern Hemisphere — already underway when the flyby occurred — would complete, though yields in the Pacific watershed would be catastrophic for independent reasons. The Southern Hemisphere's planting season, beginning in September, faced a compounding problem: reduced sunlight plus disrupted precipitation patterns plus contaminated coastal aquifers. The models disagreed on how bad it would be. The range was "significant crop failure in affected regions" to "global food insecurity for eighteen months." The difference between the two was whether the haze cleared faster or slower than the median projection.

Nobody trusted the models. The models had been built for volcanic eruptions, asteroid impacts, nuclear winter scenarios. They had not been built for a thirty-seven-kilometer alien cylinder transiting the upper atmosphere broadside at sixty-seven kilometers per second. The input parameters were unprecedented. The outputs were the best available guess applied to a situation that had no precedent.

Whitfield's regional delegation order — issued at 03:15 Eastern on the night of the flyby, forty seconds of decision-making that dissolved the federal structure — had become the governing reality. It had been intended as temporary. Regional commanders with full civil and military authority within their zones, until unified command was re-established. Six weeks later, unified command had not been re-established. The communications infrastructure that connected the regions was being rebuilt, but rebuilding was measured in months and the regional authorities were making decisions in days. Colorado Springs ran the western interior. Elmendorf ran Alaska and the northern Pacific. Jacksonville ran the eastern seaboard and the Gulf. Each hub had adapted its authority to local conditions, and each adaptation created institutional gravity that would resist recentralization.

The regional structure was functional. Supply chains were being redirected. Evacuation populations were being resettled. The Pacific coast corridor — the strip from San Diego to Seattle that had been the economic engine of the western United States — was being reclassified from "non-functional" to "limited recovery zone" as the displacement waves receded and the damage assessments replaced the gray zones on the map with actual numbers. The numbers were bad but they were numbers, and numbers could be worked with.

Mars had become the variable nobody had planned for.

Dren's order — redirect all Mars industrial output to Earth relief — had been issued from the continuity facility on the night of the flyby. By July, the first tangible result was visible: a constellation of twelve communication satellites, manufactured at Ares City, launched from Mars orbit, transiting to Earth on high-energy transfer trajectories. The first four would arrive in February 2061. Eight more would follow by June. They would replace the orbital relay nodes that had failed during the flyby's electromagnetic pulse and restore the satellite communication backbone that connected the regional authorities to each other and to what remained of the federal government.

It was a nine-month supply line. Earth couldn't wait nine months for communication satellites, so the Atlantic infrastructure was being cannibalized — European and African relay capacity redirected to cover North American gaps, at the cost of degraded coverage elsewhere. The temporary fix worked. It also created dependency. The permanent fix was arriving from Mars.

Behind the communication satellites, the next wave was already in production. Habitat modules for coastal resettlement. Prefabricated water treatment systems. Agricultural equipment designed for the reduced-sunlight growing conditions that Earth's manufacturers hadn't started tooling for because Earth's manufacturers were occupied with immediate survival.

The dependency inversion was quiet. Nobody stated it publicly. No analyst wrote the memo that said: the only fully functional industrial base in the solar system is on Mars, and Mars is run by Dren. But the logistics told the story. Earth needed what Mars could build. Mars could build what Earth needed. The balance that had existed before the flyby — Earth as the economic center, Mars as the industrial frontier — had shifted, and the shift would deepen with every cargo shipment that crossed the nine-month gap.

• • •

Sky was on the bed when she got back. He was always on the bed. It was the only surface in the hotel room that was warm enough and wide enough for a cat who had decided, after weeks of homelessness in a flooded city, that comfort was non-negotiable.

She'd found him in early July, three weeks after the flyby. A grey Siamese, soaked and thin, huddled under an overturned dumpster near a relief staging area east of Long Beach. He'd looked at her with the flat, evaluative stare of an animal deciding whether a human was worth the risk. She'd held out her hand. He'd sniffed it, considered, and climbed into her jacket. That had been the entire negotiation.

She'd named him Sky because of his blue eyes. But also, because the sky had been wrong that day — the haze layer turning the afternoon light a color that wasn't quite yellow and wasn't quite grey. The wrong sky. The new sky. The cat didn't care about the name. He cared about the bed and the canned food she brought back from the relief supplies and the fact that she came back every night, which was apparently enough.

"So here's the thing," she said, dropping her bag on the chair and sitting on the edge of the bed. Sky opened one eye. "Five editors. Five variations of 'not now.' All within six weeks. All using the same framing — the formal investigations have it covered, don't step on the process, focus on reconstruction."

Sky closed the eye.

"The phrasing is too consistent. Not identical — nobody's that clumsy. But the framing is the same. 'Duplicative.' 'Premature.' 'Overtaken.' Those aren't words reporters use about stories. Those are words lawyers use about parallel proceedings."

She pulled off her boots. Sky shifted to accommodate the movement without fully waking up. She'd had longer relationships that were less accommodating.

"And here's the other thing." She opened the laptop — the local one, the air-gapped one — and pulled up the reconstruction staffing data she'd been collecting as part of the press pool's infrastructure coverage. Regional authority appointments. The new positions created by Whitfield's delegation order — each hub staffing its own civil administration, its own logistics, its own communications infrastructure. Hundreds of positions filled in weeks, the kind of rapid institutional buildout that happened when there was no time for normal vetting.

She'd been cross-referencing the appointments against her old investigation data — what remained of it — because cross-referencing was what she did. It was reflexive. She cross-referenced restaurant menus against health inspection records. She couldn't help it.

"Fourteen names," she said. Sky's ear rotated toward her voice. "Fourteen people in regional authority positions across three different hubs who show up in the Haldane Institute's public fellowship records. Colorado Springs has five. Jacksonville has four. Elmendorf has three. Two more in the secondary hubs."

She looked at Sky. Sky looked at the wall.

"Fourteen out of how many total appointments? Hundreds. Maybe a thousand. So it's one and a half percent. That's nothing. That's statistical noise. Except that the Haldane Institute's fellowship program graduated maybe two hundred people over its entire existence. Fourteen of them landing in regional authority positions within six weeks of the fragmentation isn't statistical noise. It's placement."

Sky rolled onto his side, exposing his belly. This was not an invitation to touch the belly. Chloe had learned that lesson once.

"The Haldane fellows aren't in the headline positions. They're not the regional commanders — those are military, appointed by Whitfield's order. The fellows are in the second tier. Deputy administrators. Logistics coordinators. Communications directors. The positions that control information flow and resource allocation. The positions that decide what the commanders see."

She typed the fourteen names into the encrypted file, alongside the suppression data. Two patterns now, sitting next to each other. The investigation being steered away from the waiver story. And Haldane-affiliated personnel filling structural positions in the regional authorities that were supposed to be temporary but were becoming permanent.

She didn't draw the line between them. Not yet. She had two patterns and zero proof that they were connected. Correlation was not causation, and fourteen names was a small number in a large system. Every placement had an innocent explanation — the Haldane fellows were well-credentialed policy professionals, exactly the kind of people you'd recruit in an emergency staffing surge. Their presence in the regional authorities could be competence, not conspiracy.

"The thing about talking to you," she said to Sky, "is that it's not actually that different from talking to Greg. Same level of feedback. Same commitment to the conversation." She scratched behind his ear — the one gesture he permitted. "But you don't leave your underwear on the bathroom floor, so on balance, it's an upgrade."

Sky purred. It was the most validation she'd received from a male in months.

She saved the file. Closed the laptop. Turned off the light. Sky settled against her hip, a warm weight in a cold room in a city that was still half underwater.

Tomorrow she'd file the water reclamation story. And she'd keep cross-referencing, because that was what she did, and because fourteen names was enough to keep looking and not enough to stop.

• • •

Three weeks later, the texture changed.

The bureau editor — the one who had been actively encouraging the investigation since January, who had called it "the most important accountability story of the decade" in a conversation she'd logged — reached out. Not to commission the piece. To redirect.

"I've been thinking about your Batch G-7 story," he said. The call was on the reconstruction press pool's shared channel — not a private line, which was unusual for him. "And honestly, Chloe, I think the landscape has shifted. The accountability question is going to be answered by the formal investigations — Congressional, international, the joint commission. Those processes have resources and subpoena power that we don't. A journalistic reconstruction is going to be duplicative at best and premature at worst. I think your reconstruction work is where the real impact is."

It was reasonable. Every word of it was reasonable. Congressional investigations were underway. A joint international commission had been chartered. The formal processes existed and had authority she didn't. The advice to focus on reconstruction work was practical and defensible.

She thanked him and ended the call.

Then, a week later, the press pool colleague — a correspondent named Faisal whom she'd gotten to know over six weeks of shared deadlines and pool-sharing rotations. Competent. Well-connected. He knew which editors were buying what, and his instincts about the news cycle were reliable enough that other reporters used him as a barometer. He'd been helpful — sharing contacts, flagging stories, offering the easy professional camaraderie that made press pools functional.

They were filing from the same site — a water reclamation facility east of Long Beach — when he mentioned it. Casually, the way useful information was always delivered in press pools.

"I've been hearing some pushback on the waiver story," he said. "Not from anyone specific. Just the general temperature. People feel like the formal investigations have it covered, and a parallel journalistic effort might complicate things. Step on the commission's work. The advice I'm hearing is that it's dead weight — not wrong, just overtaken."

He said it the way someone says something they believe is helpful. No edge. No pressure. The professional courtesy of a colleague sharing the room's temperature.

Ashford heard it the way she heard everything: as data.

She'd heard this texture before.

Not the words. The quality. In the months before the flyby, when she'd been tracing the Fresh Start network, she'd encountered the same ambient pressure — not a wall, not a threat, just a persistent gentle steering away from certain questions. Editors suggesting other angles. Sources becoming slightly less available. The story not killed but slowly suffocated by the accumulated weight of reasonable alternatives.

If the investigation truly didn't matter — if the formal processes had it covered, if the story was dead weight, if the accountability question would be answered through proper channels — no one would bother mentioning it. She would simply be ignored. Reporters chasing dead stories were ignored all the time. It was the natural fate of stories that didn't matter.

The attention was the tell. Not Faisal specifically — Faisal was delivering information he'd received, the same way he delivered every piece of professional intelligence. The information had reached him through the channels that information moved through, and it had the shape of advice and the function of direction.

That evening, in her room at the press pool's temporary accommodation — a repurposed hotel east of the damage zone, still running on generator power — she opened a new file. Offline. Encrypted. Stored on local hardware, not synced to any service.

She typed the date. Then she typed the editor's name, the date of his call, the channel it had come through, and the exact language he'd used. Then Faisal's name, the date, the location, and the language. She added the three earlier rejections — dates, outlets, the phrasing of each refusal.

She didn't name the pattern. Naming it would be a conclusion, and she didn't have enough for a conclusion. She had five data points that could be coincidence — an industry overwhelmed by crisis, editors making rational allocation decisions, a colleague sharing the room's temperature. Every point had an innocent explanation, and every innocent explanation was true as far as it went.

She saved the file. She encrypted it. She put it in a directory that wasn't indexed by her system's search function.

Then she went back to the story about the water reclamation facility and filed it by deadline.

• • •

The Remora was sixty-three days outbound and the silence had settled into the walls.

Not literal silence — the ship was loud, the way small ships were always loud. The environmental system cycled with a rhythm that Torres had learned to read like a diagnostic: the compressor's pitch told her the $CO_2$ levels before the sensors did, the fan harmonics shifted when the humidity crept above spec, and the low hum of the LOTUS unit was the baseline note under everything — the sound of the ship breathing. The drive — dormant now, coasting on the trajectory the matching burn had established — still clicked and pinged as thermal gradients moved through the fuel feed lines and the pusher plate's mounting brackets contracted in the cold. The ship talked constantly. After two weeks in stasis on the outbound coast, Torres had spent the first days awake relearning its vocabulary — the stiffness wearing off, her ears recalibrating to what was normal and what wasn't. Now the ship's noise was hers again. The crew had stopped.

"LOTUS sounds different," Jackson said from the drive bay hatch one morning, coffee pouch in hand.

Torres listened. The low hum — the baseline note. She'd been hearing it for hours without flagging it. Jackson had been awake for ten minutes and caught it.

"Bearing wear," Torres said. "The recirculation fan. It's been drifting for about three days — I logged it, it's within spec. But you're hearing the harmonic shift."

"How long before it's not within spec?"

"At current rate, six weeks. I've got a replacement fan in stores. I'll swap it during the next maintenance cycle."

Jackson nodded and drifted toward the galley. She stopped halfway. "Add it to the AI library."

"Already did."

That was most of their conversations now. Short. Technical. The language of two people maintaining a machine that kept them alive. The personal exchanges had tapered after the flyby data arrived. Not hostility — just economy. They talked about the ship. The ship was enough.

Inoue had withdrawn into her work since the flyby data arrived. Not from the crew — she performed her duties, maintained the EVA equipment, ran the daily diagnostic on the autonomous survey robot, responded to questions with precise, adequate answers. She ate with the crew. She took her sleep rotation without variation. She was present in every operational sense and absent in the one that mattered. The displacement wave data from the Tōhoku coast had arrived in a compressed packet from Ares City, relayed through the Mars-Earth link, nineteen days after the flyby. Two days later, a Red

Cross relay message confirmed that her parents and her sister's family had been evacuated to a camp in the Yamagata highlands, sixty kilometers inland. They were alive. All of them.

She had read the message at her station. Her mouth pulled tight at both corners and then released, the way a hand opens after gripping something too hard. Four seconds. Then the equipment check, the diagnostic screen, the hands moving on the keyboard as if nothing had changed. She had not mentioned it. Torres had looked away before Inoue could catch her watching.

Her family was alive. Ishinomaki was not. The city where she'd grown up, the coast where her parents had lived for forty years — the displacement wave data said fifteen-meter surges along the Tōhoku coastline, sustained flooding, infrastructure non-functional. The city was in the grey zone. Her family was in a tent in the highlands. The relief was real. So was everything else.

Chandra was the opposite — not louder, but more focused. The signals analyst had been running burst simulations since the flyby data confirmed that the Fist's optical emissions had continued post-transit. The leeward antenna — the one shielded by the hull during the atmospheric passage — was still transmitting. Short bursts, the same directional pattern as the pre-flyby emissions, aimed back along the approach vector toward nothing that any catalog listed. He had the emission profiles from the four gauntlet waves, the post-flyby sequence, and the models he'd built during the weeks before flyby when the data was still theoretical. Now the data was real and his models needed revision and the revision consumed him.

"The burst structure changed after the flyby," he told Torres one morning, forty-seven days out. They were in the galley — a generous name for the two-meter section of counter between the water recycler and the equipment locker. "Pre-flyby, the pulses were regular. Metronomic. Same duration, same interval, same power profile. Status reports — that was my working model. Automated telemetry. Post-flyby, the interval is variable. The duration varies. The power profile has a modulation pattern I haven't decoded yet."

Torres poured recycled water into a pouch and squeezed it. "Meaning?"

"Meaning the content changed. It's not just reporting status anymore. It's communicating something more complex. Or it's communicating with something that's responding, and the responses are altering the transmission pattern."

Torres looked at him. "The relay."

"Sato's relay asset hypothesis. If there's something along the approach vector — something close enough for meaningful round-trip — the post-flyby transmissions could be a dialogue, not a monologue."

"But what would it be saying? It's past Earth, just coasting away. What's there to say?" Torres asked.

"Could be a complaint," Chandra said lightly. "I doubt they're sending a thank-you note." He looked back at the relay plot. "Or something nobody on this ship wants translated."

Jackson was in the drive bay, where Jackson always was. She'd found a vibration in the secondary mount bracket during the matching burn — a harmonic that shouldn't have been there, detectable only through a contact sensor she'd mounted on the bracket during construction. The vibration had disappeared after the burn ended, which meant it was load-dependent, which meant it would return during the deceleration burn at intercept. She was designing a reinforcement that could be fabricated from ship's stores — a brace that would dampen the harmonic without altering the mount's thermal expansion profile. It was the kind of problem that could consume an engineer for weeks, and Jackson was letting it.

The operational update from Ares City arrived on schedule. Sato's voice, nineteen minutes old.

"Fist tracking at two-point-three AU, fifty-seven kilometers per second, decelerating on solar gravity as predicted. No thrust events detected since the flyby. No trajectory deviations. Rendezvous window confirmed: September 14th plus or minus three days, contingent on your deceleration burn performance. Defense status:

unknown. Approach protocol remains as briefed — passive observation phase first, active investigation contingent on threat assessment at close range. Sato out."

Torres played the message for the crew. They listened. Chandra made a note about the burst timing relative to Sato's tracking data. Inoue acknowledged the message with a nod and returned to her equipment check.

"Defense status unknown," Chandra said, after the silence had settled. "We know more than that."

Torres waited.

"The post-transit imagery is clear. The antenna structure on the windward side is gone. Not damaged. Gone. The atmospheric transit stripped it."

"And the leeward antenna?" Torres asked.

"Still transmitting. The burst data confirms it. Whatever was on the leeward side survived, and it's active." He pulled up the lunar imagery on his tablet — the false-color reconstruction, the windward face scoured and glazed, the trailing end where one antenna had been and wasn't anymore. "So we know the windward face is damaged, possibly stripped of external hardware. We know the leeward side has at least one functional system. If the beam weapon had emitters on both sides, the windward emitters took the same plasma sheath that destroyed the antenna. Five hundred megawatts per square meter for ninety seconds."

"You want to come in on the windward side," Torres said.

"Approach, survey, and set down. The windward stern. If something on that face survived the atmospheric transit, we weren't going to survive it anyway. The leeward side is where the intact systems are."

Torres considered. The beam weapon had killed twenty-six platforms during the gauntlet — range progressing from two thousand to six thousand kilometers. The Remora would be approaching at matching velocity, not opposing. Slow. Close. An easy target if the defenses were active. But the windward face had taken the worst the atmosphere could deliver at sixty-seven kilometers per second.

"And the Fist's threat posture toward us?"

"Dren's position still seems reasonable," Chandra said. "If it were worried about being intercepted from ahead, it would be looking forward. Everything it's done — the beam weapon, the range progression, the course corrections — has been oriented toward threats from behind. From the direction it came from. We're ahead of it. Out in front. That's outside its threat model."

"If it has a threat model," Torres said.

"Everything with a beam weapon has a threat model."

Torres flagged the approach vector to Sato: windward side, initial survey from the damaged face, landing at the windward stern. The nineteen-minute round-trip delay meant Sato's response would arrive tomorrow. Torres didn't expect objection. The logic was clean.

September 14th. Fifty-one days.

The ship talked. The crew worked. The Fist receded ahead of them at fourteen kilometers per second, and every hour the gap closed by another fifty thousand kilometers, and the thing that had carved a line across the Pacific waited at the end of the math.

Torres checked the humidity membrane. It was within spec. She made a note to check it again in twelve hours.

The compressor cycled.

# CHAPTER 17

*Contact*

*July 18th, 2060.*

*Day 24 post-flyby. Rendezvous.*

*Remora and Fist: ~1.9 AU from Sun, ~60 km/s outbound. Matched.*

*Mars–Crew: ~2.3 AU. Communications: ~19 min one-way.*

• • •

The matching burn lasted five hours and forty minutes.

Torres felt every second of it. The ship accelerated at six-tenths of a meter per second squared — a gentle, sustained push that pressed her into the couch like a hand on her chest. Not uncomfortable. Relentless. The secondary drive fired along the lateral axis while the primary held attitude, the dual-engine configuration doing what Jackson had designed it to do: add velocity without reorienting the ship. The fuel feed splitter held. The secondary mount bracket — Jackson's reinforcement fabricated and welded in place over seventy hours of continuous work — held.

The harmonic appeared at hour two.

A low vibration Torres felt through the deck plating, the same frequency Jackson had warned about. It stayed within the predicted range for forty minutes. Then it grew.

"I'm seeing it," Torres said, watching the contact sensor readout climb. "Bracket harmonic is above the predicted band."

"How far above?"

"Twelve percent and rising."

Jackson's voice from the drive bay, flat and controlled: "Throttle back to sixty percent. Now."

Torres pulled the secondary drive to sixty percent thrust. The vibration dropped. The burn profile, which had been calculated for full power, was no longer valid.

"Fuel margin?" Jackson asked.

Torres ran the numbers. "At sixty percent for the remaining burn, we're twenty-three percent over planned consumption. That's the return budget and then some."

"Bring it back to eighty. Slowly."

Torres brought the secondary up in five-percent increments, watching the contact sensor at each step. Seventy — clean. Seventy-five — clean. Eighty — the harmonic returned at a lower amplitude.

"It's back," Torres said. "Lower. Manageable?"

"Manageable if it stays there. If it doesn't, drop to seventy and hold."

It didn't stay. The harmonic crept upward over the next hour, and Torres dropped to seventy, then back to eighty when Jackson recalculated the gimbal correction. Every throttle-back forced a purge cycle on the fuel feed to clear vapor bubbles from the splitter; each restart bled efficiency. The secondary drive wasn't designed for this — it was designed to fire at full power for a computed duration and shut down. Nursing it through a six-hour burn at variable thrust was like driving a race car in first gear. It worked, but at a cost.

"Twenty minutes over the planned duration," Torres reported at hour five. "Fuel consumption is fourteen, fifteen percent above profile."

"I know," Jackson said. "Hold the burn. We're almost there."

The burn ran forty minutes long. When it was over and the velocity differential was zero, Jackson ran the fuel audit and sent the number to Torres without commentary.

Fifteen percent over the planned consumption, and the drives were damaged. Jackson had nursed the secondary through five hours of variable thrust, and she was now in the drive bay running diagnostics on a bracket mount that had shifted under sustained load. The harmonic she'd predicted had done exactly what she'd warned it would do — degraded the coupling between the bracket reinforcement and the fuel feed housing until sustained thrust at rated power was no longer an option. She could fire in short bursts, or she could run continuously at roughly one-eighth rated. The return transit had just gone from weeks to months.

Both objects — the thirty-seven-kilometer alien cylinder and the ship that Jackson had named the Kludge — were outbound at sixty kilometers per second, separated by four hundred kilometers of empty space, and the distance was no longer changing.

Torres ran the post-burn diagnostic. Fuel reserves: below nominal, but sufficient. The return trip was longer now — months instead of weeks with the degraded engines — but the pods would handle it. Four pods, four crew, everyone sleeps. The AI manages the ship. They had time on the Fist, and they had fuel to get home. The harmonic had cost them convenience, not survival.

Eight days. Life support: nominal — LOTUS cycling, atmosphere clean. Drive temperature: elevated but cooling within parameters. She logged the numbers, checked them twice, and reported to Sato.

"Matching burn complete. Velocity differential zero."

The response would arrive in thirty-eight minutes. By then they'd be closer.

Inoue had three gel packets open at her station — the standard protein-carbohydrate ration that passed for meals on a ship this size. She wasn't looking at them. She was looking at her personal display, angled away from the others. Torres could see enough to know what it was — the Samoa feed, the same silent loop Inoue watched every night. Empty streets. Broken buildings. The tide coming in where it shouldn't.

Torres glanced at the packets. Inoue was a big woman on a ship where the ration schedule had been calculated for average metabolic loads. Three wasn't unreasonable for her frame. But Torres had been watching the pattern since the flyby, and it wasn't about the frame. "That's three."

Inoue closed the feed. "I know they taste like paste, but I like paste," she said, and squeezed the third one without looking at Torres.

"Ration schedule exists for a reason."

"It doesn't matter. We're sleeping the whole way back."

She was right. The return transit was months now, not weeks — the degraded engines had seen to that — but four pods meant four sleeping crew. Jackson's pod in the cargo bay wasn't pretty, but it worked the same as the other three. The AI would manage the ship. The gel stores would go untouched. Torres let it go. Everyone coped with something.

• • •

The Fist resolved on the cameras at two hundred kilometers.

Chandra had the optical feed on the main display, and the crew gathered in the compartment to watch it emerge from the dark. The tracking overlay had shown it for weeks — a point of data, a velocity vector, a closing rate. Now it was a shape.

A cylinder. The long axis held precisely perpendicular to its direction of travel. Not tumbling, not drifting, not wobbling. Maintained orientation. Something was still holding it steady — residual attitude control, or gyroscopic stability from its own rotation, though the instruments detected no spin. It simply held its line, the way a rifle bullet holds its axis in flight.

The surface was dark. Low albedo, consistent with what the astronomers had measured from Earth — the spectral data that had fueled two years of debate about organic crusts and irradiated regolith. From this distance, the darkness resolved into texture. The windward face was visibly different from the rest — lighter, scoured, the original surface stripped by the atmospheric transit. The leeward side was darker, untouched.

At fifty kilometers, they could see the damage.

The windward face bore the marks of the flyby. The atmospheric transit had sandblasted the leading surface, ablating whatever coating had originally covered the hull and exposing the structural material beneath. It was lighter in color — metallic grey where the rest of the hull was near-black. The ablation was uneven, deeper at the edges where the plasma sheath had been thickest, shallow at the center where the geometry had offered some aerodynamic shadowing. The windward antenna — the structure the lunar imaging had shown as destroyed — was gone. Not broken. Gone. The mounting point was visible as a raised platform of slightly different geometry, scorched clean.

The weapon system had destroyed every deflection platform before detonation. No impact scars were visible — if anything had struck the Fist during the gauntlet, it hadn't left evidence at this resolution. The only damage was from the atmosphere itself — and the atmosphere had done what twenty-six nuclear weapons had not been given the chance to do.

"It's intact," Jackson said. She meant the hull itself. Thirty-seven kilometers of structural material that had crossed interstellar space, destroyed everything Earth threw at it, transited a planetary atmosphere at sixty-seven kilometers per second, and emerged whole. The surface was damaged. The structure was not.

Torres turned the ship and began the approach.

• • •

The robot went first.

Inoue launched it from the cargo bay at fifteen kilometers, a gentle push that sent it drifting toward the windward hull on its own cold-gas thrusters. The surface robot — an autonomous unit from

Dren's asteroid mining operations, repurposed and updated with every piece of telemetry they had — crossed the distance in forty minutes, decelerating in the final hundred meters, and touched down on the scoured windward surface with a contact velocity of eight centimeters per second.

It stuck. The grippers — designed for irregular asteroid surfaces — found purchase on the hull material. Inoue confirmed contact, confirmed stability, and began the first sequence.

Material sampling. The robot's drill bit — tungsten carbide, rated for basalt and nickel-iron — penetrated three millimeters into the hull surface and stopped. The bit was intact. The hull was harder. Inoue switched to the diamond-coated bit. It reached nine millimeters before the cutting rate dropped to near zero.

"Spectrometer's getting data from the drill tailings," Inoue reported. Her voice had the flat precision of someone reading instruments, not interpreting them. "Tungsten base. Heavy tungsten content. Rhenium, hafnium, traces I'll need to process. Density is… nineteen-point-six grams per cubic centimeter."

"Tungsten-rhenium-hafnium," Jackson said from the drive bay. "High-temperature structural alloy. The rhenium gives it ductility, the hafnium strengthens the grain boundaries. It's what you'd use if you wanted something that could survive reentry heating and deliver kinetic impact without fracturing."

"Grain structure is wrong, though," Inoue added after a pause. "Not cast, forged, or sintered. The crystal lattice is continuous across the sample boundary. Grown at the molecular level. Nothing in the database matches the process."

Chandra was recording everything. Torres was watching the robot's camera feed. The surface, close up, was not featureless. The atmospheric ablation had exposed texture that the original dark coating had hidden — a faint pattern of lines running parallel to the cylinder's long axis, spaced at irregular intervals. And crossing them, at precise right angles, circumferential lines. Seams.

"Assembly joints," Torres said.

The Fist had been built from sections. The seams were almost invisible — sub-millimeter tolerances, the mating surfaces bonded at a level the robot's instruments couldn't fully characterize. But they were there. Longitudinal and circumferential, dividing the hull into panels. The largest panels were roughly four hundred meters by two hundred meters. The smallest, near what appeared to be structural reinforcement ridges, were half that.

"Jackson, are you seeing this?"

"I'm seeing it." Jackson had the robot's feed on her display in the drive bay. "The bond across the joint — the lattice is nearly continuous. That's not welded. That's not brazed. That's cold welding."

"In vacuum," Torres said.

"Clean surfaces, no oxide layer, pressed together with enough precision — the atoms can't tell where one panel ends and the next begins. We spend half our lives preventing this on station hardware. Someone built a construction method out of it."

Chandra cut in. "The panel dimensions — four hundred seventeen point five three by two hundred twenty one point one six meters. Is that significant?"

"That's the unit size," Jackson said. "That's the biggest piece they could fabricate and handle as a single component. You don't accelerate three quadrillion kilograms to interstellar velocity in one go. You can't. You accelerate the pieces separately, match them in speed, and assemble in transit."

"Assemble at sixty kilometers per second," Torres said.

"Assemble at whatever velocity they were doing at the time. Match speed, align to sub-millimeter, press the surfaces together. Vacuum does the rest."

Nobody said anything for a few seconds. The implications of assembly at interstellar velocity were still settling.

"It also means they likely have a wildly different scale of measurement than we do," Torres said.

"How many panels?" Chandra asked.

Torres looked at the seam grid stretching away along the hull. "Thousands."

Torres logged the dimensions and spacing. That data would matter to engineers on Earth and Mars who would spend years trying to understand what they were looking at.

"Hull is clean for landing," Inoue said. "Surface is stable. Grippers hold. Gravity is negligible — I'm reading point-zero-zero-five meters per second squared."

Torres did the math in her head. One two-thousandth of a g. A dropped tool would take half a minute to drift to the surface from waist height. But the escape velocity was less than a brisk walk — push off too hard and no amount of waiting would bring you back. The tether wasn't a safety precaution. It was the only thing between a careless step and a permanent departure. It wasn't gravity in any meaningful sense. It was a suggestion that could be overruled by a firm shove.

Torres told the AI to bring the Kludge in.

• • •

The ship touched the hull with a contact velocity that Torres held below two centimeters per second. At the moment of contact, she felt nothing — the deceleration was too small to register through the structure. The hull sensor array confirmed: contact, stable, no lateral drift. The Kludge sat on the windward surface of Satan's Fist the way a barnacle sits on a whale, and the whale did not notice, or if it did, it didn't react.

Inoue and Torres suited up for the first EVA. Chandra monitored from the ship. Jackson was in the drive bay — her choice, her logic. If something went wrong on the surface, the ship needed to be ready to detach and maneuver, and Jackson was the only one who could restart the secondary drive from a cold state in under ten minutes.

Torres opened the airlock. The surface was two meters below her — the scoured, metallic-grey windward face of an alien weapon, lit by the sun at 1.9 AU. Dimmer than Earth, sharper, no atmosphere to scatter it. The shadows were absolute.

She pushed off the airlock sill and drifted down. Two meters at one two-thousandth of a g would take nearly thirty seconds, a slight push and no need to wait. She watched the hull rise to meet her boots with geological patience, the surface approaching so slowly that she had time to study the grain of the metal, the faint discoloration where the ablation had been deepest, the hairline seam of an assembly joint passing beneath her.

"Contact," Torres said. The gripper pads engaged — the EVA boots were standard asteroid mining hardware, reactive soles that sensed load direction and responded accordingly. Push down or stand still and the grip engaged, micro-structures interlocking with the surface texture. Lift a foot and the grip released cleanly.

She felt the surface through the suit — hard, unyielding, cold. Minus two hundred and thirty degrees Celsius in the shadows, the instruments said. Deep-space cold on a surface that had never been designed for visitors.

"Footing is solid," Torres reported. "Grippers are holding better than the robot's. The ablation texture gives them something to bite."

Inoue followed. Drifting down to slow contact, the grip engaging. Even in the EVA suit — oversized for the standard frame, refitted at Kourou to fit her shoulders — she landed with a precision that made the micro-gravity look easy. She touched down two meters from Torres and immediately looked along the hull — not at the surface beneath her feet but at the horizon line where the windward face curved away toward the leeward side.

"Tether points confirmed," Inoue said, checking the piton anchors the robot had set in a seam joint — the anchors seated in the gap between hull panels, the only points where the drill had been able to penetrate to a useful depth.

Torres took a step. Release the boot grip, push gently forward and down, drift for a few seconds, feel the boots contact and engage. The tether was everything — without it, any step that broke the gripper seal risked sending you off the surface permanently. The tether lines were the real locomotion system — clipped to piton anchors the robot had placed in advance, the lines let the crew pull themselves along the surface in a controlled glide. Every twenty meters, a new anchor point. Every movement deliberate.

"It's like walking on ice," Torres said. "Except the ice is an alien weapon and the gravity forgot to show up."

"Don't push so hard on the third step," Inoue said from behind her. "You're overcorrecting."

Torres adjusted. Inoue had six years of EVA on irregular surfaces — asteroids, station exteriors, moving platforms. She read micro-gravity the way Torres read ship systems. By the fifth anchor point, they'd found a rhythm.

The windward surface told the story of the atmospheric transit. The scoured zone faded as they moved away from the leading edge, the ablation tapering where the plasma sheath had thinned. The original dark coating survived in patches — a material the spectrometer flagged as carbon-based, layered, possibly designed as a thermal ablative. If so, it had worked. The coating had sacrificed itself to protect the hull beneath. On the windward face, it was gone. Everywhere else, it remained.

They reached the cylinder's horizon line — the curve where the windward surface began its transition toward the leeward side. Torres stopped and looked along the hull's length. Thirty-seven kilometers of it, curving away from her in both directions, the surface falling away toward the leeward side that they could not see from here. The sun was behind them. Ahead was the dark.

"Going over," Torres said.

• • •

The leeward side was a different surface.

The dark coating was intact here. The hull was near-black, absorbing the dim sunlight and radiating nothing. The robot had scouted ahead, placing tether anchors along a path that curved up and over the hull — three kilometers of careful traverse to bring them from the windward landing site to the leeward face. It had taken two hours. The robot had done it in forty minutes.

The first features they found were the maneuvering nozzles.

A cluster of four circular ports, each roughly a meter across, recessed into the hull surface within a shallow depression. Opposed by a matching cluster on the other side of the cylinder — Torres could see them on the robot's survey map. The ports were simple geometry: circular throats, converging walls, no moving parts visible inside. Exhaust residue discolored the hull around each port — a faint staining that the spectrometer read as partially ionized reaction mass. Cesium traces. Ion drive exhaust.

"These are what Hamner detected," Chandra said over the comm from the ship. "The non-gravitational accelerations. Course corrections."

Torres logged the nozzle geometry and positions. The clusters were small — trim thrusters, not main propulsion. The Fist had arrived in the solar system with its interstellar velocity already established. These nozzles were for aiming.

They moved forward along the leeward surface toward the bow. The robot's survey map showed features ahead — areas of different surface geometry that the autonomous algorithms had flagged without being able to classify.

At a kilometer forward of the nozzle cluster, they found the first emitter array.

A recessed panel, roughly six meters by four, set into the hull surface below the level of the surrounding material. Within the panel, a dense grid of hexagonal apertures — each aperture approximately fifteen centimeters across, hundreds of them arranged in a precise geometric pattern. The apertures were dark. The panel surface, where it was visible between the hexagons, had a different texture from the main hull — smoother, more reflective, clearly a different material or surface treatment. Conduit channels ran from the edges of the panel back into the hull, disappearing into the structure.

Chandra's voice, very quiet: "That's it."

They found four more arrays within the next two kilometers of forward traverse. Different sizes — the largest nearly ten meters across — but the same geometry. Hexagonal apertures, recessed panels, conduit channels. All on the forward third of the hull. All facing outward from the leeward surface. All dark, all cold, all unpowered.

"Phased emitters," Torres said. She was photographing each array in detail, the suit cameras logging in continuous high-resolution. "Fixed position, beam steering through phase control. No moving parts. Multiple banks for multiple simultaneous engagements."

"Five banks that we can see," Chandra said. "This is just the leeward face. There could be more on the surfaces we can't reach."

The weapon that had killed twenty-six platforms in three waves. Torres stood over one of the arrays and looked down into the hexagonal apertures. Fifteen centimeters across and very deep — her helmet light couldn't find the bottom. The engineering was precise in a way that made the Kludge feel like something built from sticks.

They continued aft.

• • •

The antenna was at the stern.

It sat on a raised platform similar to the destroyed windward mounting point, but intact. A structure roughly twelve meters tall — a tapered column supporting a concave dish, if "dish" was the right word for a geometry that wasn't quite parabolic. The surface of the reflector was segmented, and the segments were individually articulated — visible gimbal points at each segment edge, allowing the entire assembly to physically reorient.

It was pointed. Not at the sun. Not at Earth. Back along the Fist's approach vector — the direction it had come from, out toward interstellar space.

"Consistent with the burst data," Chandra said. "It's been transmitting along the approach vector since we started tracking it. Reporting back along the path it came from."

Torres studied the antenna from the base of the platform. It was a live system — the only thing on the Fist that was demonstrably still functioning. Everything else they'd found was dark and cold. This was active. The robot's thermal sensors confirmed it: the column's base registered eleven degrees warmer than the surrounding hull. Something inside was generating power, and had been for weeks. And she was about to attach hardware to it.

"Chandra, if I put a monitor on the antenna structure, what's the risk? If it detects interference — if something on the Fist classifies that as tampering —"

"We don't know," Chandra said. "We don't know what triggers a response. We don't know if it has that capability in its current power state."

Torres looked at the antenna for a long moment.

"We didn't come here to watch from a safe distance."

Tethered, Torres launched up to the array. Once there she attached a monitor to the base of the column — a passive sensor that would log any electromagnetic activity through the structure, incoming or outgoing. If beams went in either direction, they'd know. And by monitoring the interval between transmission and response, they'd know how far away the other end of the conversation was, more or less.

Nothing happened. The antenna continued its quiet, regular transmissions as if she weren't there.

They reeled Torres back to the hull.

Inoue had the robot running a detailed survey of the antenna structure while Torres documented the mounting platform. The construction was different from the hull — lighter materials, more complex geometry, clearly designed for precision rather than mass. The articulation mechanism at the base allowed the entire column to slew through what Torres estimated as at least a hundred and twenty degrees of arc. It was curious as to why it would need such a degree of rotation. She noted it.

The robot, continuing its autonomous survey spiral, logged a second antenna-like structure two hundred meters aft of the primary. Smaller, different geometry, recessed rather than elevated. Inoue tagged it in the survey data as a secondary feature and continued the primary antenna documentation. There were too many features to examine everything.

Near the base of the primary antenna, Torres found a potential ingress point.

A rectangular section of hull, roughly three meters by two, with a surface texture that differed from the surrounding material. The seam around it was wider than the assembly joints elsewhere — still sub-millimeter, but visible to instruments and, once you knew to look for it, to the eye. The spectrometer read the same tungsten alloy, but the robot's ground-penetrating sonar showed a thinner cross-section. Twelve centimeters where the surrounding hull was twenty-plus.

Not a door. A construction access panel — sealed after the antenna installation, never intended to be reopened. The Fist hadn't been built with visitors in mind.

Torres flagged it to Sato. Thirty-eight minutes later, the response came back.

"Your call. You're there."

"So glad I asked," Torres said.

• • •

They set the charges while the antenna watched.

Jackson designed the extraction from the drive bay, working from the robot's sonar data and the panel's estimated material properties. The panel was thinner than the main hull — twelve centimeters — but twelve centimeters of tungsten-rhenium alloy was not something you cut casually. And they didn't want to blow it inward. Whatever lay behind the panel was unknown, and filling an alien corridor with shrapnel on the first day was not the plan.

The solution was to pull it out.

The robot drilled anchor points around the panel's perimeter — deep holes in the thinner material, spaced every ten centimeters along the seam line. The diamond bit penetrated far enough for the expanding bolt anchors to seat. Thirty-two anchor points in total, tracing the rectangular outline. Through each anchor, Inoue threaded a loop of braided carbon fiber cable — mining tether line, rated for asteroid extraction loads.

The cables attached to eight shaped charges mounted on hull anchors outside the perimeter.

The shaped charges were oriented outward — away from the hull surface. When they fired, the explosive force would push outward into space, and the reactive tension in the cables would transmit that force inward to the anchor points around the panel's edge. Uniform pull, distributed across thirty-two attachment points, concentrated at the seam. The seam was the weak point. The panel would come out like a lid.

In theory.

"The margin is thin," Jackson said over the comm. "If the seam bond is stronger than my estimate, we get a loud noise and a panel that doesn't move. If it's weaker, we get a clean extraction. I don't have a way to test it without doing it."

The crew pulled back to the ship. Inoue recovered the robot to a safe distance. Torres ran the arming sequence from the airlock.

"Charges armed. Firing on my mark."

She waited. The antenna stood twelve meters from the panel, its reflector pointed outward along the approach vector, transmitting to whatever it had been transmitting to for the past twenty-four days. The weapon arrays were two kilometers forward, dark and cold. The maneuvering nozzles were behind them. The Fist drifted outward at sixty kilometers per second, carrying all of them — the alien machinery and the four humans and their small loud ship — toward the outer solar system.

Torres fired the charges.

Eight simultaneous flashes. The shaped charges vented their energy outward — eight brief jets of superheated gas expanding into vacuum and dissipating. The cables snapped taut.

Four of them broke.

The carbon fiber lines on the port side of the panel held. The starboard lines — three of the eight cable runs — snapped at the anchor points, the expanding bolts tearing free of the drill holes as the seam bond resisted the pull. A fourth cable parted at the splice where it attached to the charge mount. The panel shifted — Torres saw it move, a millimeter of displacement along the long edge where the surviving cables had loaded the seam — and then stopped. The unbalanced force had cracked the bond on one side and done nothing on the other.

The panel sat in its frame, visibly loosened on the port edge, still bonded on the starboard side and at both narrow ends. Four cables drifting in the negligible gravity, their broken ends catching the sunlight.

"Partial failure," Jackson said from the drive bay. Her voice was neutral. She'd warned them about the margin. "The seam bond on the starboard side is stronger than my estimate. The anchors on that side pulled out before the bond could fail. We need deeper holes, heavier anchors, and more cables on the starboard run."

Chandra's voice came over the suit comm. He sounded careful. "Torres. The antenna transmitted. Outside the regular interval. Burst transmission, four point two seconds, along the approach vector. It fired thirty seconds after the charges went off. I think it knows we're here."

Torres looked at the cracked panel. They hadn't even gotten inside. They'd hit the hull with shaped charges and something on the Fist had decided that was worth reporting.

"I agree, too much for a coincidence. Did anything else change?" she asked. "Any other system activity?"

"Nothing. The weapon arrays are still cold. Maneuvering nozzles inactive. Just the antenna."

Torres looked at the panel for a long time. One day on the Fist, spent on the exterior survey and a breach that hadn't worked. And now the antenna had told someone they were trying.

"We rerig for tomorrow," she said. "Inoue, get the robot drilling new anchor points on the starboard side. Deeper this time. Jackson, redesign the cable geometry for asymmetric loading — heavier on the starboard, lighter on the port where the bond is already cracked. We go again in the morning."

There was no morning on the Fist. No sunrise, no rotation, no day-night cycle. The ship's clock said 22:14 GMT. They'd been on the hull for fourteen hours. Torres called it.

• • •

*Day two.*

The robot had worked through the night — deeper anchor points on the starboard side, heavier cables, the load path redesigned by Jackson to concentrate force on the surviving bond. Torres and Inoue suited up and went back out. Three hours of EVA work to rig the revised layout. Four additional shaped charges from the ship's demolition stores. Asymmetric loading — heavy on the starboard where the bond had held, light on the port where it was already cracked.

Torres ran the arming sequence from the airlock for the second time.

“Charges armed. Firing on my mark.”

She didn’t wait this time.

Twelve flashes. The asymmetric pull did what Jackson had designed it to do — the heavier starboard load broke the remaining bond, and the already-cracked port side failed a fraction of a second later. The panel tore free with a slow, twisting motion — no sound in vacuum, just the visual of a three-by-two-meter slab of tungsten alloy rotating away from the hull surface, trailing cables from both attempts, drifting outward into the dark.

The rectangular opening gaped in the hull surface, its edges rough where the seam had failed. Beyond the edges was darkness.

Torres moved to the opening and looked in. Her helmet light punched into the interior and found a space larger than the opening suggested — a chamber, or the beginning of a corridor, the walls the same dark material as the exterior hull, extending inward beyond the reach of the light. The air inside — no, there was no air. Vacuum. Whatever atmosphere the interior had once held, if any, had been vacuum for a long time. The temperature reading from the sensors at the edge of the opening was the same as the exterior. Cold. Dead.

Except for the antenna, twelve meters away, still operational.

Torres looked into the interior of Satan’s Fist. Inoue stood beside her, the helmet lights making two cones of white in the dark. Behind them, the stars. Below them, the hull of something that had been sent to destroy their world and had nearly succeeded and was now carrying them away from everything they knew at sixty kilometers per second.

The darkness inside went deeper than the light.

“Chandra,” Torres said. “Tell Sato we’re in business.”

# CHAPTER 18

*Inside*

*July 20–23, 2060.*

*Days 3–6 on the Fist.*

*Remora and Fist: ~2.0 AU from Sun, ~59 km/s outbound.*

• • •

Torres went in first.

The breach opening was three meters by two — the panel they'd pulled on Day 2, the edges still rough where the seam had failed. Her helmet light punched into the space beyond and found a corridor. Not a chamber. A corridor — running perpendicular to the hull surface, angling inward, the walls the same dark tungsten alloy as the exterior. The ceiling was low. Torres's helmet cleared it by less than ten centimeters.

"Corridor," she said. "Perpendicular to the hull. Width approximately one meter. Ceiling clearance ten centimeters above my helmet. Walls are the same alloy. No features visible for the first ten meters."

Inoue followed. They moved in silence — no sound transmitted through vacuum, no sound inside their suits except their own breathing and the faint hiss of the oxygen supply. The corridor was narrow enough that they couldn't walk side by side. Single file.

Torres in front, Inoue behind, both tethered to a line anchored at the breach.

Twenty meters in, the corridor turned. Not a curve — a sharp right angle, the walls meeting in a clean joint.

"Right angle turn at twenty meters," Torres said. "Clean joint. No radius. Putting my light around the corner."

She put her helmet light around the edge. Another corridor, identical in dimension, running parallel to the hull. Doors along the left wall — or openings, at least. Rectangular, dark, spaced at regular intervals. The ceiling height was consistent.

"Parallel corridor," she reported. "Openings on the left wall. Count six in the first fifty meters. Spacing looks regular. Ceiling consistent — one point eight meters."

"One point eight," Inoue repeated from behind her. She'd been ducking since the breach. The implication sat between them for a moment.

"Built for something shorter than us," Torres said.

They moved along the corridor. Torres counted the openings — six in the first fifty meters, each one roughly a meter wide, each leading to a space she couldn't see the back of from the corridor. She didn't enter any of them. Not on the first run. The first run was about the route in and the route out and nothing else.

At eighty meters, a junction. The corridor intersected another running perpendicular, with passages continuing in three directions. The walls at the junction bore markings.

Torres stopped.

"Inoue. Markings."

Inoue moved up beside her — barely room for both of them at the junction. They stood shoulder to shoulder and looked at the wall.

The markings were incised into the wall surface — shallow, precise, the same sub-millimeter relief as the assembly seams on the exterior. Not scratched or painted. Cut into the tungsten alloy with the same molecular-level precision as everything else on the Fist. Characters, or symbols, or whatever they were — angular forms, grouped in clusters, positioned at eye level for someone shorter than Torres. Each of the three corridor entrances at the junction had a different cluster above it.

"Navigational," Inoue said.

Torres agreed. Labeling. Not decoration, not art, not communication intended for visitors. Functional markings for whoever had built this, or maintained it, or moved through it on whatever business had brought thirty-seven kilometers of weapon to another star system. The symbols were at every junction, she was certain of that before they'd seen another one. You don't build a maze this size without way-finding.

They went another forty meters down the center passage before Torres checked her suit oxygen.

Six hours and twelve minutes remaining. They'd been inside for fifty minutes. The walk back to the breach would take another fifty. The walk from the breach to the ship, across the hull in negligible gravity, would take ninety minutes. Every meter deeper into the Fist cost oxygen twice — once going in, once coming out — and the working time at depth shrank with every step.

"Oxygen check," Torres said. "Six twelve remaining. Turning back."

"Confirmed," Inoue said. "Six twenty-eight on mine."

They retraced the route. Tether line, junction, corridor, corner, the rectangle of starlight at the breach growing from a dot to a shape. They climbed out onto the hull surface and began the long, slow traverse back to the Kludge. The stars and the silence were the same. The Fist carried them outward at fifty-nine kilometers per second and the corridors behind them extended into a darkness that their helmet lights had barely scratched.

Back at the ship, Chandra was waiting.

"Comms dropped the moment you went through the breach. The hull blocks everything — radio, optical, everything. Four hours of nothing. I had telemetry from your suits up to the breach threshold and then the signal died."

"The tungsten," Jackson said from the drive bay. "Nineteen-point-six grams per cubic centimeter, minimum twelve centimeters thick. It's a Faraday cage. Nothing reliable gets through that."

Torres pulled off her helmet. The ship's air tasted different after hours of suit supply — warmer, wetter, the faint machine smell of the LOTUS recycler. She breathed it in.

"How deep did you get?" Chandra asked.

"Hundred and twenty meters. One junction. Three corridor branches. The ceilings are under two meters. It was built for someone smaller."

Chandra processed that. "Little green men," he said.

Nobody laughed. But nobody told him he was wrong.

Torres uploaded the suit camera footage and the instrument logs. Chandra began processing. The footage showed what Torres had seen — dark corridors, low ceilings, angular turns, alien markings at a junction — but the camera also caught details her eyes had passed over. Texture variations in the wall surfaces. Faint conduit channels running along the ceiling line. A barely visible seam pattern on the floor that might be drainage, or cable routing, or something with no human analog.

"The markings," Chandra said. "Three different clusters at the junction. Three corridors. If each cluster is a label for the corridor it's above —"

"Then every junction is labeled," Torres said. "And the robot can map the labels while it maps the corridors."

Chandra nodded, but he wasn't looking at the junction data. He was looking at a second display — the antenna monitor feed. He'd been waiting for the robot discussion to finish.

"There's something else," he said. "While you were inside."

He pulled up the antenna monitor timeline. Torres saw it immediately — the steady bearing along the approach vector, unchanged since the burst during the first breach attempt, and then a sharp discontinuity. The gimbals had activated. The dish had slewed to a completely new bearing.

“A signal came in along the approach vector,” Chandra said. “Tight beam, same frequency structure as the burst it sent during the breach attempt, but modulated differently. The antenna received it, and two seconds later it pivoted and retransmitted.”

“Something answered,” Torres said. “From the fleet direction. Thirty-six hours after our first breach attempt. And the Fist relayed it to … who?.“

“No way to know, just that it was in a completely different direction,“ Chandra said. ”The Fist is a relay node. It received from the approach vector and forwarded to someone or something else. Whatever is out there is talking to whatever is in here, and the Fist is the switchboard.“

“How long ago?”

Chandra checked the timestamp. “Forty-one minutes.”

Torres looked at the monitor feed. Forty-one minutes.

“Keep watching,” she said.

Seventeen minutes later, Chandra’s console chimed.

He turned to the display. His face changed.

“Incoming signal! From the same bearing.“ His voice had gone flat. He checked the time. “Fifty-nine minutes after the relay transmission. The antenna is pivoting —“

They watched it happen in real time. The antenna received the new signal, swung back to the approach vector — the gimbals completing the slew in under two seconds — and retransmitted.

Three-node relay. Fist to approach. Fist to other direction. A conversation, conducted through a thirty-seven-kilometer weapon, while four humans sat inside the ship bolted to its hull.

“Twenty-nine and a half minutes one way at lightspeed,“ Chandra said. ”That’s somewhere in the outer belt. Three, maybe three and a half AU.“

Torres was already on her feet. “How many shaped charges do we have left?”

“Eight. After the breach attempts.”

“Suit up. Take what you need. The primary antenna and the secondary the robot logged on the aft survey. Blow them both off the hull.”

“The transmissions have already —”

“It stops the next one. Go.”

Chandra went.

• • •

*Ares City. July 21.*

Dren read the first data packet at 04:00 local time, sitting in the operations center with a coffee that had gone cold an hour earlier. The telemetry had traveled nineteen minutes from the Fist to Earth relay, then been forwarded through the Mars-Earth link. By the time he read it, the data was six hours old. Torres and Inoue had already been inside and come out and filed their report and gone to sleep.

The relay data hit him first. Torres’s report was clinical — timestamps, bearings, signal characteristics — but the implications were not. The Fist’s antenna had received a signal from the approach vector, thirty-six hours after the first breach attempt, and relayed it to a new bearing. Fifty-eight minutes later, something at the other end of that bearing had responded. Three-node relay. The Fist was a switchboard in an active communications network, and one node was approximately three and a half AU from the Fist along a bearing Chandra had logged.

Torres had ordered both antennas destroyed. Dren agreed with the decision. But the data those antennas had generated — the bearings, the timestamps, the signal modulation patterns — was now the most important intelligence product of the mission. He flagged it for immediate distribution to the tracking teams and started composing the tasking order. Find what’s at three and a half AU along that bearing.

He studied the corridor dimensions. One point eight meters. The implications of that number would occupy xenoarchaeologists for decades, if anyone survived long enough to become a xenoarchaeologist. For now it meant the crew's mining robot — the autonomous unit that had surveyed the exterior hull and drilled the anchor points — wouldn't fit. The robot was two meters tall and nearly as wide, designed for asteroid surfaces, not corridors built for beings that apparently stood about a meter and a half.

The mining robot wouldn't fit. Torres would already know that — she'd been standing in the corridor. The operational notes confirmed it: she was configuring the smaller survey unit. Dren went back to the data. Behind the corridor telemetry, buried in the day's operational traffic, was a preliminary note from the firmware audit team. The Wave 3 targeting system review — the one he'd ordered after the gauntlet — had found the race condition they'd expected. But the team lead had flagged an anomaly. A bounds-checking routine that should have been present in the uploaded binary appeared to be missing. They were still verifying. Could be a build-chain artifact. Could be nothing.

Dren read it twice and marked it for follow-up.

• • •

The robot went in on Day 3, late afternoon by the ship's clock.

Chandra had returned an hour earlier. Both antennas destroyed — shaped charges at the base of each structure, the primary shattered at the column joint, the secondary broken free after two charges. Six hours of hull traverse each way, four detonations, and the Fist's only live systems were now debris drifting in its wake. He'd logged the relay bearings and timestamps. Three vectors, three timestamps. Enough to calculate distances.

The Fist wouldn't be talking to anyone ever again.

It was smaller than the mining unit — a humanoid-frame survey platform, chest-high on Torres, articulated for confined spaces. Inoue had configured it with the mapping suite from the larger robot:

LIDAR, thermal, spectrometer, and a high-resolution camera array. She'd also mounted a paint dispenser on its left arm.

"Low-tech navigation backup," she said when Torres raised an eyebrow. "It paints directional arrows on the floor pointing back to the entrance. Every intersection. Every corridor. If the mapping data corrupts, the arrows still work."

Torres looked at the paint dispenser. "What color?"

"Orange. Best contrast against the dark alloy."

"So we're spray-painting the inside of an alien weapon."

"We're marking our way home," Inoue said.

The robot entered the breach and disappeared into the dark. It returned ninety minutes later, docked at the breach threshold, and dumped its data to the ship's systems via hardline. Chandra processed the results.

First run: the robot had mapped four hundred meters of corridor in three branching paths from the entry junction. Fourteen additional junctions, each with the same incised symbol clusters. Forty-seven side chambers of varying size, most empty, a few containing what the robot's instruments flagged as mounting hardware — brackets, rails, contact points with residual electrical signatures. The construction was uniform. The temperature was uniform. The vacuum was uniform.

"It's a grid," Chandra said, studying the emerging map overlay. "Not random. The corridors run in three primary orientations — longitudinal, circumferential, and radial. They follow the hull geometry."

The robot went in again. And again. Each run extended the mapped territory by three hundred to five hundred meters, limited by its battery capacity. Between runs, Inoue swapped battery packs and Chandra processed the data dumps. The AI began correlating the alien symbol clusters with spatial position, looking for patterns.

By the end of Day 3, they had seventeen hundred meters of mapped corridor and the first results from the symbol analysis.

“It’s not random,” Chandra reported. “Certain symbol clusters correlate with direction. There’s a cluster that appears exclusively above bow-ward corridors. A different cluster for stern-ward. A third set for radial passages. It’s not translation — I can’t read it. But I can see the clustering. The symbols are navigational. They’re telling you which way you’re going.”

“Label the junctions,” Torres said. “Robot marks each intersection with our numbering overlaid on the alien markings. Junction one, junction two, junction three. When we go in, we follow the robot’s numbers.”

Chandra didn’t answer immediately. He was still looking at the symbol data on his display — the frequency distributions, the positional correlations, the clustering patterns he’d extracted from the robot’s camera logs. The others saw navigation markers. He saw something else. The clusters weren’t just labels — they had internal structure. Recurring elements in different combinations, modifiers that shifted meaning based on position within the group. Not random. Not simple. A system with rules he could detect and couldn’t decode.

He’d spent his career listening to signals. Radio telescopes, interferometer arrays, deep-space survey data — twenty years of sorting noise from pattern, pulling structure out of chaos. He was good at it. Better than good. And now he was looking at the clearest, most structured signal he’d ever encountered, produced by an intelligence that had crossed interstellar space, and he couldn’t read a single word of it.

He’d stopped scrolling. His hand was on the display and he wasn’t moving it — just resting his fingers against the screen. His lips were moving. Not speaking — subvocalizing, the way he did when he was running frequency counts in his head, except this wasn’t frequency counts. This was something else. Torres had known Chandra for four months of training and two months of transit and she had never seen him look like this. He looked like a man who had opened a door he'd been knocking on for twenty years and found a room he couldn't enter.

"Chandra?" Torres said.

He blinked. Looked at her. For a second his face was open — not the professional mask, not the quiet competence, but something raw and startled, the expression of someone caught in the middle of a feeling they hadn't expected to have.

He didn't answer. His eyes went back to the display — the frequency distributions, the clustering patterns, the structure he could see and couldn't read. Torres waited. She'd seen this look on engineers staring at a failed weld, on pilots watching a landing they couldn't save. She'd never seen it on someone staring at something beautiful.

He turned back to his console. His hand was steady. But Torres noticed that he kept the symbol frequency display open in a corner of his screen, and every few minutes his eyes drifted to it, and every time they did his fingers twitched toward it before he pulled them back.

"Chandra?" Torres said, a little louder.

"Oh, sorry. Labeling the junctions," he said. "On it."

• • •

*Days 4 and 5.*

The robot mapped. The AI's three-dimensional model grew with each data dump, and the pattern that emerged was not a hollow structure but a perforated one — the corridors sat within a deeper load-bearing matrix of solid alloy, threading through mass rather than replacing it. The Fist wasn't a shell. It was thirty-seven kilometers of structural material with passages bored through it like capillaries through bone.

Torres and Inoue went in on Day 4, following the robot's painted arrows and numbered junctions eight hundred meters deep — farther than any previous run. The corridors were the same:

uniform dimensions, alien markings at every junction, the faint conduit channels running along the ceiling line. But at Junction 23, something changed.

Torres saw it on the robot's sonar overlay first — the channels behind the walls, which had been running parallel in ones and twos, were converging.

"Inoue. Look at the sonar."

Inoue pulled up the overlay on her suit display. Three conduit channels from the corridor behind them. Two from a circumferential passage to the left. Another pair from a radial branch ahead. All routing toward a single point.

"They're merging," Inoue said. "Trunk line. Running radially inward."

Torres found the convergence point on the corridor wall. The channels were sealed behind panels, invisible to the eye, but the wall here bore a symbol cluster larger than any they'd seen — three times the size of the junction markers, incised deeper, with a complexity that Chandra's frequency analysis would later place near the top of the hierarchy.

"Something important is further in," Torres said. She pressed her glove against the wall and felt nothing — cold tungsten, the same as everywhere. But behind it, the conduit trunk line ran inward like an artery, and arteries led to hearts.

"How much oxygen?" Inoue asked.

"Four forty-two. We need to turn."

"Mark it. We come back tomorrow."

They turned back at the oxygen margin and reported to Chandra. The AI cross-referenced the convergence with the robot's expanding map and identified two more convergence nodes along different corridor paths. All three pointed inward. All three routed toward the same region — a zone roughly three hundred meters from the breach, at a junction of four major corridor paths, where the robot's sonar had detected a sealed door.

On Day 5, the robot confirmed it. A sealed door at the junction — closed, solid, bearing a prominent symbol cluster that Chandra's analysis placed at the top of the frequency hierarchy. Whatever was behind it, the Fist's builders had considered it important enough to mark distinctly and seal off from the surrounding corridors.

The door material was different from the hull. Torres's spectrometer readings from the previous day, taken at the conduit convergence, had shown a lighter alloy in the sealed panels — still tungsten-based, but with different trace elements and a lower density. Not the twenty-centimeter hull plating. Something thinner, more varied in composition. Cuttable, given time and the right tools.

"How long?" Torres asked.

Jackson ran the numbers from the drive bay, working from the spectrometer data and the robot's sonar. "Diamond blade, powered through an umbilical. Roughly a centimeter per hour in that alloy. The perimeter is about ten meters. Call it eighteen to twenty hours of continuous cutting."

"The sooner we're done, the sooner we leave," Torres said.

Inoue rigged a portable power supply on the hull surface outside the breach, with a cable run down through the breach opening and along the robot's mapped route to the sealed door. Three hundred meters of cable, anchored at intervals, threading through corridors and junctions.

Torres looked at the sealed door for a long time before she gave the order. Everything they'd done so far — the hull traverse, the EVA, the corridor mapping — had been observation. Moving through open spaces that the Fist allowed them to move through. This was different. Someone had sealed this door. Whatever was behind it had been deliberately closed off, and they were about to force it open with a diamond blade and a power cable.

She thought about the antenna — the hesitation she'd felt before attaching the monitor, the question of what triggered a response. About the weapon arrays on the leeward face. About what "defensive response" might mean inside a thirty-seven-kilometer alien weapon.

She looked at the sealed door for another moment. Then she stopped looking.

"Cut it," she told Inoue.

The robot began cutting on Day 5, working along the door's edge seam with a diamond-tipped rotary tool powered through the umbilical.

It would take time, and Chandra used that time.

While the robot cut and the others slept in rotation, he sat at his console with the accumulated symbol data from five days of mapping looking for structure. Except the radio telescope data had always been noise, and this wasn't noise, and the difference was destroying him.

He tried clustering by position. By frequency. By co-occurrence. He built adjacency matrices and ran entropy calculations and mapped the symbol elements against spatial coordinates in the robot's three-dimensional model. He found patterns — too many patterns. The data was so structured that every analytical approach produced results, and none of the results told him what the symbols meant. He could see the system's skeleton. He couldn't find its voice. He bounced question after question against the AI, but nothing made sense.

At 03:00 GMT, Torres came through the compartment on her way to check the drive temperatures. Chandra was still at his console. The display showed a cluster analysis she didn't recognize — colored nodes connected by lines of varying thickness, rotating slowly in three dimensions.

"Have you slept?" she asked.

"I will."

"That wasn't the question."

He turned to her. His eyes were red-rimmed and bright. "There are forty-seven unique base elements. They combine in clusters of three to eleven. The combination rules are consistent — certain elements never appear together, certain pairs always appear in fixed order. It's a writing system, Torres. Not marks. Not labels. A writing system with syntax." He paused. "And I have four days of robot camera footage and no Rosetta Stone and no time."

Torres looked at the display. She didn't understand what the colored nodes meant, but she understood the look on his face. She'd seen it on Jackson when the harmonic appeared — the expression of someone who could see the problem clearly and couldn't solve it in the time they had.

"Get some sleep," she said. "The symbols will still be there tomorrow."

"That's what I'm afraid of," Chandra said. "They'll still be there. And I still won't be able to read them."

• • •

*Day 6. July 23.*

The robot had been cutting for eighteen hours. The door seam was nearly through — the lighter alloy yielding to the diamond-tipped tool at roughly a centimeter per hour, the cut progressing around the perimeter in a slow, patient line. Inoue monitored the robot's progress from the ship through the data dumps, checking the cut depth and tool wear after each retrieval cycle.

Torres and Inoue suited up for the Day 6 interior run at 08:00 GMT. They followed the robot's painted arrows and numbered junctions — Junction 1, turn left, Junction 4, straight, Junction 7, right, Junction 12 — through three hundred meters of corridor to the sealed door. The robot was there, parked beside the cut line, waiting. The last dump showed ninety-two percent of the perimeter cut. The remaining eight percent was the top edge, where the alloy was slightly thicker.

"Finish it," Torres told Inoue.

Inoue checked the robot's power supply — the umbilical cable running back through three hundred meters of corridor to the hull surface — and restarted the cutting tool. The robot resumed its slow traverse along the top seam. Torres stood in the corridor and waited, her helmet light making a cone of white against the dark alloy walls.

While the robot cut, she walked back along the corridor to the previous junction — Junction 11, thirty meters from the door. She'd been here on the Day 5 run but hadn't explored the side passages. One of them, a radial corridor leading deeper into the structure, had markings she hadn't logged. She went twenty meters down the passage, recording with her suit cameras.

The markings here were different. Not the incised navigational clusters she'd seen at every junction. This was a raised element on the wall surface — a relief, not an incision. She stopped and put her helmet light directly on it.

Two concentric triangular forms sharing a common apex, the inner form nested within the outer, both open at the base. Below the triangles, a pair of horizontal trapezoidal elements flanking a small rhombus at center. The relief was shallow — less than a millimeter — but precise, with clean double-bordered edges.

It was not navigational. It was not at a junction. It was on the wall of a side passage near the sealed door, positioned at what would have been eye level for the builders. A symbol, or an emblem, or a designation. Torres had no context for it and no way to classify it. She photographed it from four angles, logged the coordinates relative to Junction 11, and tagged it in the data stream.

One data point among hundreds. She went back to the door.

She'd sent the photographs ahead through the data dump when she returned to the breach threshold for the suit camera download. Chandra had them before she was back at the ship.

When she climbed through the airlock, he was standing at the display with both hands flat on the console, leaning in, his face six inches from the screen.

"This is different," he said without turning around.

"I know. It's not at a junction."

"It's not navigational. The base elements don't match the junction clusters — there's almost no overlap. This is a different register. A different vocabulary." He pulled up the image Torres had taken from directly in front, the two concentric triangles and the flanking trapezoids sharp in the helmet light. "The navigational symbols tell you where you are. This tells you what's here. Or who."

"Who?"

"A designation. A name. An insignia." He traced the outer triangle with his finger, not touching the screen. "If this were a military facility — and it is a military facility, it's a weapon — this is where you'd put the unit crest. Outside the command center. At eye level."

Torres looked at the symbol on the screen. The mark of whoever had built this thing, or commanded it, or sent it across interstellar space to kill a world they'd never seen.

"Can you read it?" she asked.

"No," Chandra said. The word came out flat and final. Then, quieter: "It may not even be words. But I can see it. That's more than anyone's ever been able to say."

The robot had finished the cut. The seam was through — a continuous line around the entire perimeter, the door panel held in place only by its own weight in the negligible gravity. Torres checked the edges. Clean cut, minimal kerf. The panel would need a push.

"Seam is through," Torres said. "Clean all the way around. Ready to push."

Inoue positioned the robot at the door's center and extended its manipulator arm.

"Pushing," Inoue said.

Torres stood to the side, her helmet light aimed at the widening gap as the robot pushed.

The panel moved. Slowly — heavy even in microgravity, dense alloy resisting the robot's hydraulics — but it moved. It separated from the frame with no sound and no resistance beyond its own inertia, tilting inward, the gap widening from a hairline to a centimeter to a hand's width.

"It's moving," Torres said. "No resistance beyond inertia. Gap is widening. I'm getting light in there — stand by."

Her helmet light punched through the gap and found a space beyond. Larger than a corridor. Much larger. The light scattered off surfaces at different distances — walls, but farther apart. A ceiling, but higher. The suit's rangefinder gave her the first measurement.

"Forty meters to the far wall," Torres said. "This is a room. A big one."

The robot pushed the door panel clear. It drifted inward and settled against the far wall with a contact so slow Torres almost didn't see it arrive.

The room opened before them. Torres stepped through.

Her helmet light swept the space. She called it out as she saw it — for Inoue behind her, for the suit cameras, for the record that Chandra would process when they got back.

"Forty meters deep. Twenty meters wide. Ceiling at four meters — double the corridor height. Structures along both walls — recessed panels, contact surfaces, geometric elements. Not consoles or shelving. Nothing I have a word for, but purposeful. Conduit channels visible in the walls and ceiling — multiple directions converging on this room."

She moved further in, her light sweeping from wall to wall.

"Everything the corridor system routes toward — the conduit junctions, the symbol hierarchy, the sealed door — it all leads here. This is the center."

The room was dark. The room was dead, the way everything on the Fist was dead — the antennas destroyed, the weapon arrays cold, thirty-seven kilometers of silence carrying them outward.

But this was where the decisions had been made.

Inoue stepped through behind her. Their helmet lights made two cones in the dark, sweeping the alien geometry, recording everything.

“Chandra doesn’t know we’re in here,” Inoue said. The comms blackout. Four hours of silence at the ship, Chandra watching telemetry that had gone dead at the breach threshold.

“He’ll know when we get back,” Torres said.

They began documenting.

# CHAPTER 19

*The Isomer*

*July 23–27, 2060.*
*Days 6–9 on the Fist.*
*Remora and Fist: ~2.1 AU from Sun, ~58 km/s outbound.*

• • •

The control room gave them the map.

Torres and Inoue spent four hours documenting the space on Day 6 — the large chamber behind the sealed door, forty meters deep, twenty wide, ceiling at four meters. The walls lined with structures that had no human analog: recessed panels, contact surfaces, geometries that suggested interface points for beings shaped differently than the crew. The robot's instruments cataloged everything — thermal profiles, material composition, electromagnetic signatures. All dead. All cold. All vacuum.

But the conduits told the story. They converged on this room from every direction — the trunk lines that the robot had been mapping for three days, routing through the Fist's corridor grid like a nervous system. Some terminated here, at the interface panels on the walls. Others passed through, continuing forward toward the bow.

Chandra, studying the data dump after the crew returned to the ship, overlaid the conduit map on the exterior survey. The lines that passed through the command room ran forward and outward — toward the leeward hull surface. Toward the emitter arrays.

"The cargo bays," he said. "The conduits from the command room route directly to the DEW positions on the hull. Five emitter banks on the leeward face — the conduits branch to all five."

Torres looked at the overlay. The robot had mapped a sealed door along one of those forward conduit paths during its Day 4 survey runs. The door was roughly two hundred meters from the command room, on a radial corridor that ran outward toward the hull. The conduit trunk line passed through the wall beside it.

"That's the back end of the weapons," Torres said.

"One of them," Chandra confirmed. "The closest emitter bank is directly above that door, based on the exterior survey coordinates."

Torres was already reaching for her helmet.

"We're going back in," she told Inoue. "Now."

• • •

They followed the now-familiar route — painted arrows, numbered junctions, the three hundred meters of corridor to the command room — and continued forward along the conduit path to the sealed door the robot had flagged.

The door was lighter construction than the command room seal. Same tungsten-based alloy, but thinner — the robot's sonar read six centimeters, less than half the command room door. Torres didn't hesitate. Inoue connected the umbilical cable and the robot started cutting.

An hour and forty minutes. The thinner alloy yielded faster, the diamond tool biting deeper with each pass. The robot completed the perimeter cut and pushed the panel inward. It drifted into the space beyond and settled against a wall in the negligible gravity.

Torres went through.

The space was different from anything they'd found. Not a corridor, not a chamber, not the command room's broad open floor.

This was a bay — an equipment bay, clearly purpose-built around the hardware it contained. The room was roughly eight meters deep and six meters wide, the ceiling matching the corridor height. And filling most of the volume, mounted on heavy structural rails that ran from the interior wall to the outer hull, was the weapon.

Torres had seen the emitter arrays from the outside — the recessed panels of hexagonal apertures on the leeward hull, dark and cold and precisely engineered. She was now looking at the other side. The back end. The business end faced outward, through the hull, and behind it was the machinery that made it work.

The unit was a single integrated module, roughly two meters long, a meter and a half wide, and a meter deep. The emitter array was the front face — the hexagonal apertures visible through the hull opening, each one a precisely machined channel extending back into the body of the unit. Behind the emitters, a dense geometry of waveguide structures converged on a cylindrical core — the beam generator. And mated directly to the beam generator, occupying the rear third of the module, was a second cylinder. Heavier. Denser. Featureless except for four heavy conduit ports on its outer surface and the mounting lugs that connected it to the structural rails.

The whole assembly sat on its rails the way an engine sits in an engine bay — designed to be installed and removed as a single unit. Most of the module's volume was structure, not mass — the hexagonal channels extending through the emitter face, the waveguide geometry, vacuum cavities between the beam paths. The dense material was concentrated in the rear cylinder. Six tonnes total, most of it in that last third. The mounting lugs were the only connection to the Fist's structure. Four lugs, bolted to the rails, the bolt geometry visible and mechanical. No welding or cold bonding. Modular.

Inoue was already running the spectrometer.

"The rear cylinder," she said. "Same tungsten-rhenium outer casing as the hull. But the interior — the density profile is wrong.

It's reading hafnium. Heavy hafnium. The isotopic signature doesn't match anything in the database."

Torres looked at the cylinder. Dense, dark, featureless. The same alloy as everything else on the Fist, but whatever was inside it was different.

"What kind of hafnium?" Torres asked.

"One-seventy-eight. But the nuclear state is anomalous. It's not ground state. The spectrometer is flagging it as a metastable excited configuration." Inoue paused. "It's a nuclear isomer. The nuclei are in a higher energy state. Stable, but storing energy at the nuclear level."

Torres didn't fully understand the physics. She understood the implication. "How much energy?"

Inoue ran the calculation on her suit display. The number came back and she was quiet for several seconds.

" Per kilogram, roughly 1.3 terajoules. Six orders of magnitude above chemical energy storage — roughly a sixtieth of fission yield per kilogram, but without a chain reaction, without criticality requirements, and without the radiation signature of a nuclear weapon. The energy is stored in individual nuclei." Inoue paused. "The entire cylinder, if the density profile is consistent throughout — it's consistent with the energy budget from the gauntlet telemetry. Whatever their trigger mechanism is, it isn't passive decay. Something in the emitter assembly is driving the release."

Torres looked at the cargo bay. Five emitter banks on the leeward surface. Five integrated units, each with its own isomer power cell. Self-contained. Independent. Kill one and the others keep firing. The command room didn't power the weapons — it aimed them. Each DEW was its own system: emitter, beam generator, power source. Modular. The same design philosophy as the hull panels — independent units, assembled into a larger whole.

She photographed the mounting lugs, the rail geometry, the bolt pattern. Inoue documented the conduit interfaces and the spectrometer readings. They backed out through the door and began the traverse back to the breach.

• • •

At the ship, Torres pulled off her helmet and looked at Jackson on the drive bay monitor.

"How fast can you process a spectrometry dump?"

Jackson had the data thirty seconds after Chandra received it. Torres watched her face on the monitor — the moment Jackson saw the hafnium isotopic reading, the moment she cross-referenced it against the hull alloy spectrometry from Day 1, the moment the connection landed.

"The hull alloy uses hafnium as a grain boundary strengthener," Jackson said slowly. "Standard metallurgy. But this — this is hafnium at the nuclear level. Same element, completely different application. They use it structurally in the hull and as an energy store in the weapons. The hull material is literally the base stock for the isomer."

"Can we take one?" Torres asked.

"One what?"

"One complete unit. Emitter, generator, isomer. The whole module. It's mounted on rails with mechanical bolts. The robot can remove the mounting hardware. We push it out through the hull aperture and pull it clear on the exterior with the mining robot."

"Where do we put it?" Jackson asked.

Torres didn't answer. She didn't need to. There was only one space on the Kludge large enough for a two-meter module.

"My pod is in the cargo bay," Jackson said.

"I know."

"How heavy?" Jackson asked.

"Approximately six tonnes."

Jackson was quiet for a long time. Torres could hear her running the numbers — not in her head, on her tablet, the way she did when she didn't trust mental math with people's lives.

"Six tonnes on degraded engines. More mass, same thrust. The return stretches to about a year."

Jackson stopped, running something through her head. Then she nodded to herself, though she didn't seem happy about what she'd concluded.

"Three pods, four crew. We rotate. Each person takes roughly a three-month shift awake while the other three sleep. Reduced rations for whoever's up — the gel stores don't cover four people eating for a full year, but they cover one person eating light for three months at a time. You lose weight on your shift. You're hungry. But it closes."

Torres heard it. A year. Three-month shifts. Hungry but survivable. She understood why Jackson didn't seem happy about it.

She thought about what was sitting in that cargo bay — an energy storage technology that powered a weapon capable of destroying twenty-six nuclear platforms in three volleys. A technology humans didn't have, couldn't replicate, couldn't even theorize without seeing the physical lattice structure of the trigger mechanism.

She couldn't ask Sato. Thirty-eight-minute round trip, and the answer would be what she already knew.

"We take it," Torres said. "The pod comes out. Jackson, Chandra — start stripping the ship. Everything we don't need for the return transit goes out the airlock. Mining equipment, survey stores, spare cable, tools we won't use again. Every kilogram you dump buys margin. I want the Kludge as light as possible before we load the cargo."

"And the return course?" Jackson asked.

"Calculate it as a moving target. The ship gets lighter as you strip it. I want updated numbers every hour."

• • •

*Washington, D.C. July 24.*

Whitfield hadn't slept in the residence for four weeks. The East Wing had structural damage from the seismic effects — nothing catastrophic, but the engineers had flagged load-bearing concerns and the building had been partially evacuated while assessments continued. She worked from the emergency operations center in the sub-basement, slept on a cot in the medical unit when she slept at all, and held her daily briefings in a conference room that had been a storage facility six months ago.

The morning brief covered three items. Her chief of staff delivered them standing, because there weren't enough chairs for the expanded security detail that now accompanied every briefing.

"Atlantic coastal reconstruction first," he said. "Army Corps timeline has slipped again. Governors of four states have sent a joint letter requesting federal resources."

"Resources we don't control," Whitfield said.

"Resources the regional commanders hold under the delegation order. The governors are asking you to override the regional authority."

Whitfield set the letter aside. The delegation order she'd signed on the night of the flyby — necessary and temporary. Now, four weeks later, neither.

"Second item. Mars. Dren's communication satellite constellation is on schedule — first four birds arriving in February, full coverage by June 2061."

The dependency that nobody stated publicly was becoming structural. The regional commanders were already planning their 2061 infrastructure around Mars-manufactured hardware. The procurement channels bypassed the federal acquisition system entirely — the regional authorities contracted directly with Ares City because the federal system was too slow and Dren's supply chain was the only one that worked.

“Third item.” The chief of staff paused. He set a letter on the table with the care of someone handling something that might detonate. “Beckett.”

Whitfield picked it up.

Senator Beckett had co-signed a letter with three members of the oversight committee requesting a formal inquiry into the deflection tilt. The letter cited the casualty figures — the deaths attributable to the ninety-kilometer deflection shortfall, the coastal communities that would have been outside the damage zone if the tilt had been calculated differently or not attempted at all. The letter named Dren. It framed the tilt as a unilateral decision made by a Mars-based civilian with no elected authority, using military assets, resulting in preventable deaths. It requested that the Department of War preserve all communications and decision logs related to the tilt authorization.

The letter was procedurally correct. The argument was legally sound. The casualties were real.

Whitfield set it down. She knew Beckett. He’d gone after Dren in the committee hearing over the unauthorized interceptor production — measured, precise, the kind of legislator who built cases over months and didn’t overreach. The letter was careful — it requested an inquiry, not a prosecution. But inquiries had momentum, and the direction this one pointed was clear.

The political calculation was ugly in every direction. Dren had made the tilt call. The off-center deflection had torqued the Fist from end-on to partial broadside, multiplying the energy it coupled into the atmosphere across roughly the same ground track. The communities in the impact corridor hadn’t been hit by a wider path — they’d been hit by a path five times more destructive. People had died who would have survived a straight-on transit. Beckett’s letter didn’t need to exaggerate. The physics was the physics.

But Dren was also the only reason Earth had a functioning supply chain. Mars industrial output was keeping the reconstruction alive. Prosecuting the man who ran it — or even subjecting him to a formal inquiry that consumed his time and political capital — carried costs that Beckett's letter didn't address.

"Draft a response," Whitfield told the chief of staff. "Acknowledge receipt. Confirm all relevant records will be preserved. Don't commit to an inquiry timeline. Don't refuse one."

"That buys a week. Maybe two."

"Then it buys a week."

The delegation order. Mars dependency. Beckett. Every problem on her desk was a problem she'd deferred because the immediate crisis was bigger, and every deferral was compounding.

She moved to the next item.

• • •

The extraction began on Day 7.

While Torres and Inoue went back into the Fist, Jackson and Chandra stripped the Kludge. Mining equipment went first — the drill rigs, the sample containers, the geological survey packages that had justified the ship's original mission profile. Then the spare EVA tool kits, the backup cable reels, the hull anchor inventory they'd never use again. Chandra carried loads to the airlock; Jackson calculated mass savings after each dump and updated the trajectory. The equipment piled on the hull surface outside the ship — a growing mound of human hardware abandoned on an alien weapon, drifting outward at fifty-eight kilometers per second.

Inside the Fist, Torres and Inoue reached the cargo bay and the robot went to work on the mounting lugs.

The bolts were alien engineering, but the principle was mechanical — compression fittings seated into the rail channels, each one a heavy alloy cylinder driven into a precision-machined socket. The robot's high-torque manipulator arm could grip and rotate them. The question was whether the fittings would release after unknown years — possibly centuries, possibly longer — of compression in vacuum.

“First lug,” Inoue said. “Robot is engaging. Torque is climbing.”

Torres watched. The robot’s arm gripped the fitting and rotated. The torque readout on Inoue’s display climbed — fifty, a hundred, two hundred Newton-meters. The fitting resisted.

“Three hundred,” Inoue reported. “Three fifty. Still holding.”

“Robot’s rated for five hundred,” Torres said.

“Four hundred. Four twenty — it’s moving.”

The fitting broke free with a sudden rotation that Torres felt through the rail beneath her hand — a sharp jolt transmitted through the mounting hardware, local and immediate. She held still. Inoue held still. The robot held still.

Nothing responded. The Fist remained dead.

“Lug one free,” Inoue said. “Forty minutes for one bolt. Three to go.”

The second and third lugs came faster — twenty minutes each, the robot’s manipulator arm now calibrated to the torque pattern. The fourth lug was on the outboard side of the module, closest to the hull. When it released, the module shifted on its rails — a millimeter of movement toward the hull aperture, the six-tonne mass responding to the slight gravitational gradient.

“It moved,” Torres said.

“The weapon is free,” Inoue confirmed.

Pushing it out through the aperture took the rest of Day 7. The robot braced against the interior wall and drove the module along its rails toward the hull opening. Six tonnes of inertia resisting every Newton the robot could deliver — the hydraulics at maximum pressure, the manipulator arm flexing under the load, the module accelerating in centimeters per second over minutes of sustained push. Torres walked beside it, one hand on the casing, monitoring the rail alignment. If the module jammed or drifted off-axis, they’d have to reposition the robot and start again. There was no way to stop six thousand kilograms by hand. There was no way to redirect it. The rails were the only control they had.

The emitter face emerged through the hull aperture at 21:00 GMT. On the exterior, Inoue had rigged a pulley system through hull-mounted anchor bolts — the same bolt pattern they'd used for the panel extraction — with the mining robot positioned to pull from the far end. Arrest cables ran from separate anchor points to the module's mounting lugs, ready to catch the mass once it cleared the aperture and prevent it from drifting.

The first pull broke an anchor bolt. The module shifted two meters laterally, the asymmetric load swinging it into a slow rotation.

"Stop!" Inoue called. "Bolt failure, port side. Module is rotating."

"How fast?" Torres asked from inside.

"Slow. Maybe a degree per minute. I can damp it with the starboard arrest line, but I need twenty minutes."

Torres waited inside the hull while Inoue worked outside — the heavy rigging suited her build, the physical work of cable and anchor and brake that would have exhausted a smaller operator in half the time. Careful cable tension adjustments, feeding line through the friction brake, letting the module's rotation bleed off against the controlled resistance. Twenty minutes.

"Rotation damped," Inoue reported. "Re-rigging the failed anchor. Doubled cable, heavier bolt. Give me another thirty minutes."

They started again. By midnight they had the module clear of the hull — six tonnes hanging in the cable rigging, motionless, tethered to the Fist's surface. The cargo bay aperture gaped behind it, empty for the first time since the Fist had been assembled.

• • •

Day 8. The hull traverse.

Eight hundred meters of curved hull between the cargo bay and the Kludge. The mining robot would tow. The cables would guide. The problems were mass and geometry.

Every meter of traverse changed the cable angles. The hull curved beneath the module in two axes — circumferentially around the cylinder and longitudinally along its length. Momentum built in one direction became momentum in the wrong direction as the surface curved away. The mining robot pulled, the module moved, and then the module wanted to keep moving along a straight line while the hull curved underneath it.

"It's drifting port," Torres said, watching the cable angles. "Two degrees off line."

"I see it," Inoue said. "Arrest line."

Every correction meant stopping six thousand kilograms — absorbing the momentum through cable tension, reorienting the pull geometry, and starting again.

The first hundred meters took three hours. The module drifted off-line twice, requiring full stops and cable re-rigs each time. On the second drift, the module's casing contacted the hull surface and ground along it for four meters before the arrest cables caught, leaving a bright scar on the dark tungsten alloy.

"We can't keep doing this," Torres said. "Every drift costs us an hour."

Inoue was quiet for a minute, looking at the cable geometry. "Guide cable," she said. "Anchored to the hull at fifty-meter intervals, threaded through loops on the mounting lugs. The module slides along the guide. It can't drift laterally."

"How long to rig?"

"Two hours for the first four hundred meters."

"Do it."

The traverse along the first guide section took ninety minutes. Progress, but slow.

They reached the Kludge on Day 9 after thirty-one hours of hull work spread across two days — pulling, stopping, re-rigging, pulling again. The last two hundred meters were the worst. The hull curvature steepened near the Kludge's landing site, and the module's momentum carried it along trajectories that diverged farther from the intended path with each meter. Inoue ran out of guide cable and had to improvise the final stretch with a direct tow, the mining robot pulling at an angle while Torres managed the arrest lines by hand, feeding cable through friction brakes she'd rigged from spare hardware.

• • •

The cargo bay was tight. Jackson's stasis pod had already been removed — pulled from its mounts and secured on the hull beside the other discarded equipment. The space it left was barely enough.

Torres and Inoue guided the module toward the bay opening. The mining robot pushed from the hull side. Arrest cables controlled the approach — two lines through friction brakes, one on each side, Torres and Inoue each managing a brake. Six tonnes of mass approaching the ship at centimeters per second. The bay opening was four meters wide. The module was a meter and a half. Plenty of clearance. On paper.

The module eased through the opening. Torres watched the clearances — port side, starboard side, the fuel feed housing that ran along the interior wall of the bay.

"Looking good," Inoue said. "Clearance is —"

The starboard arrest cable slipped in its brake. Not much. A centimeter of line through the friction surface, just enough to change the angle.

The module's aft end swung. Not fast — six tonnes didn't swing fast — but six tonnes didn't need to. The trailing edge of the casing, the corner where the isomer cylinder met the mounting frame, contacted the fuel feed housing on the port interior wall.

Jackson saw it before the sound reached them — the pressure telemetry on her drive bay display dropping in a step function, the kind of drop that meant rupture, not leak.

"Cut it! Cut it off NOW!"

Torres grabbed the port arrest line and hauled. Inoue threw herself against the starboard brake. The module stopped, but the damage was done. Torres could see it — a crease in the fuel feed housing where the module's corner had struck, and at the center of the crease, a split. Fuel — hydrazine, liquid in the pressurized line — sprayed into the cargo bay as vapor, the liquid flashing to gas the instant it hit vacuum. A fine mist, catching the work lights, expanding in a slow cloud that filled the bay with glittering crystals.

Jackson was already moving. Torres heard her boots on the deck plating — fast, not running, the controlled urgency of someone who knew exactly where the manual cutoff valve was because she'd memorized every system on the ship. Ten seconds. The spray stopped. Jackson had isolated the line.

The cargo bay was full of crystallized hydrazine, drifting in the negligible gravity like snow in a room with no floor. Torres watched it settle against the module's casing, against the tiedown anchors, against the walls. Their fuel supply, turned to frost.

Nobody spoke for a long time.

"How much did we lose?" Torres asked.

Jackson was quiet for thirty seconds. Torres could hear her checking gauges, running numbers, checking them again. When she came back, her voice was stripped of everything except the numbers.

"Enough. The secondary tank is empty. We have what's left in the primary. Enough delta-v to kill fifty-seven kilometers per second. Barely. Perhaps a little more. That's it. No powered return. At best a push before fall back under solar gravity. One hundred and sixty-three days of braking. Then we coast. Four hundred and seventy odd days of freefall. A tug meets us at the belt." Another pause. "Around twenty-one months, Torres."

She paused. "If we're unlucky, and we don't hit zero ..."

She didn't need to finish that. If not zero, then they continue to drift, with what ever residual speed they had, right on out of the solar system. The Fist's final victims.

Nobody spoke. Inoue was motionless at her station. She was staring at the arrest cable — the starboard line that had slipped in the brake. The one she'd been managing.

"The rotation," Torres said. "Run it."

Jackson already had. Torres could hear it in the silence before she answered. "Three pods, four crew, twenty-one months. Each shift is five and a half months awake. Solo. The gel stores don't cover it — not at any ration level I can make work. At minimum survival intake, the person on shift loses fifteen, twenty percent of their body mass before they go back under. Every rotation."

Torres looked at the crew. Chandra had gone pale. Inoue was staring at the cargo bay indicator — the six-tonne number that had been the most important object in the solar system a minute ago and was now the reason someone might starve.

"We can dump it," Torres said. "Open the bay, push it out, we're back to four pods."

"No," Inoue said. The word came out fast. Too fast. Everyone looked at her.

"That module killed two hundred million people," Inoue said. Her voice was steady but her hands weren't. "The next one kills everyone. If we bring it back, they can build a defense. If we don't, we came here for nothing and everyone who died in the flyby died for nothing." She looked at Torres. "We keep it."

"We all decide this," Torres said. "Chandra?"

Chandra looked at the deck for a long time. "Keep it," he said quietly.

"Jackson?"

"Keep it. But I want the record to show I told you the numbers."

"Noted." Torres turned to Inoue. "You understand what you just voted for. Five and a half months. Alone. On starvation rations."

“I understand,” Inoue said. She was looking at the cargo bay indicator again. Not at the number. Through it. Torres recognized the expression — she’d seen it in the Samoa feed Inoue watched every night. The empty streets. The broken buildings. The tide coming in where it shouldn’t.

Jackson had spent the last hour running the braking calculation. One hundred and sixty-three days of continuous thrust at one-eighth rated power. The drives could sustain it — the harmonic stayed within limits at low thrust. It was the only thing about the return that was going to work as designed.

“The drives will hold at low thrust,” she told Torres. “Hundred and sixty-three days. After that we’re on gravity’s schedule.”

Torres accepted it. There was no alternative. Both robots were powered down on the hull. The Kludge was stripped to the bones — four crew, three stasis pods, the LOTUS unit, the drive, the cargo, and enough gel packets for twenty-one months.

Chandra compiled the final data packages and queued them for burst transmission during the departure burn. Interior maps, spectrometry, camera footage, robot survey logs, the full isomer analysis, the antenna relay bearings and timestamps. If the Kludge didn’t make it back, the data would.

They were ready to leave.

“That monster in the cargo bay better damned well be worth it,” Torres said.

# CHAPTER 20

*The Envelope*

*July 26–27, 2060.*
*Days 9–10 on the Fist.*
*Remora and Fist: ~2.2 AU from Sun, ~57 km/s outbound.*

• • •

*Los Angeles. July 26.*

Chloe was at the kitchen table with her laptop and a cold cup of coffee when the knock came. Three sharp raps on the front door. She checked the time. Just past nine in the evening. Sky lifted his head from the couch cushion, ears forward.

She went to the door and looked through the peephole. The front step was empty. The street beyond was quiet.

She opened the door. No one. Empty in both directions.

On the doormat, a plain manila envelope. No name, no address, no postmark.

She picked it up. Light. Something small and rigid inside. She closed the door, locked it, and carried the envelope back to the kitchen. Sky jumped down from the couch and followed her, threading between her ankles as she walked.

Inside was a data token. Matte black, unmarked, the kind sold in bulk at any electronics shop. No label or note.

Ashford set it on the table and looked at it. Sky jumped onto the table and sniffed it.

"Don't touch that," she said. Sky looked at her with the expression cats reserve for unreasonable instructions.

A data token left on her doorstep by someone who knocked and vanished. It could be what it appeared to be. It could also be a port killer — a device that looked like a storage token but delivered a high-voltage charge through the port, frying whatever it was plugged into. Or it could be something worse — a payload device, firmware-level malware that would own any machine it touched.

She did not plug it into her working laptop. She went to the hall closet and retrieved one of the three burner machines she kept — clean-wiped, no network connection, no personal data, expendable. She powered it on, waited for the boot sequence, and inserted the data token.

The screen didn't die. No surge, no smoke, no voltage spike. The drive mounted normally. Two folders.

She opened the first and stopped breathing.

Her organizational charts. The funding flow analyses. The compiled datasets that had been destroyed when the cloud service lost its Pacific data center. Complete. She opened files at random, cross-referencing against the partial reconstructions on her working machine. The data matched — her research, her compilation structure, her naming conventions. All of it.

But it was more complete than her backups. Whoever had copied these files had accessed the originals before the server went down.

She sat back in the chair. Sky was sitting on the table beside the burner laptop, watching her the way he watched birds through the window — alert, patient, waiting for movement.

"Someone copied my research before the server failed," she said. "Not after. Before. They knew it was going to go down, or they were already inside the system when it did."

Sky's tail twitched.

"Which means the data loss wasn't collateral damage from the flyby. It was targeted. And whoever targeted it kept a copy." She looked at the data token. "And now they're giving it back."

She opened the second folder. A single file — a technical document she'd never seen before. Not her research or naming conventions. Someone else's work.

She read it slowly. Most of it was engineering language she didn't fully follow — firmware revision histories, binary checksums, something called a bounds-checking routine. But the summary section was written for a non-technical reader, and the summary was clear.

The Wave 3 targeting system — the final salvo in the gauntlet — had been uploaded with a software defect. A validation routine that should have been present in the flight binary was missing. The defect had caused the targeting error that produced the off-center deflection. The deflection that had tilted the Fist from end-on to broadside. The tilt that had killed people.

The document didn't say who was responsible. It didn't say whether the defect was accidental or deliberate. It laid out the technical chain — what was supposed to be in the code, what was actually in the code, and what the difference had caused — and stopped.

She closed the laptop and sat very still for a long time. The organizational charts were a gift. This was a weapon.

Then she went to the front door, opened it, stepped out. The street was empty. The parked cars were the same ones that had been there all evening. Whoever had delivered the envelope was gone, and they'd meant to be gone. This wasn't an introduction. It was a dead drop.

She went back inside, locked the door, and sat down at the burner laptop.

"I have an ally," she said to Sky. "I don't know who. And they know more about this than I do."

Sky settled onto the table beside the laptop, paws tucked under his chest, and closed his eyes. The organizational charts were her work, returned. The firmware document was someone else's work, delivered. Two different kinds of information, in two different folders, from a source who had access to both.

She'd figure out who later. Right now she had reading to do.

• • •

The departure burn was loaded and ready. Jackson had the drive spooled and the trajectory sequenced. Torres had run the pre-departure checklist with Chandra. Stasis pods: three functional. LOTUS: cycling. Cargo: secured — six tonnes of alien weapon locked down in the bay where Jackson's pod used to be. Data packages queued for burst transmission during the burn.

They were forty minutes from ignition.

Torres looked at the rear camera feed. The Fist filled the frame — thirty-seven kilometers of alien weapon, scarred by nuclear fire, breached by human hands, stripped of its antennas, still falling outward at fifty-seven kilometers per second. They'd spent ten days on it. They were leaving with a directed energy weapon in the cargo bay, a relay bearing into the solar system, and the knowledge that something was out there, listening.

"Ignition in sixty seconds," Jackson said from the drive bay.

Torres strapped in. Inoue strapped in. Chandra was already at his station.

"If the harmonic is still there, you'll feel it in the first twenty minutes," Jackson said. "I've got the throttle."

Ignition. The drive lit. Torres felt the thrust build as Jackson brought the power up — watching the fuel feed, watching the bracket, feeling for the vibration that had nearly killed the mission on the way in.

One minute. Five minutes. Ten. The thrust was steady. No vibration. No harmonic.

Twenty minutes. Jackson's voice came through the intercom, and Torres heard something she hadn't heard from Jackson in ten days.

Relief.

"The shim is holding. Thrust is nominal. Fuel consumption is on the curve." A pause. "The harmonic is gone."

Jackson let the burn run for another hour, confirming stability across the operating range, before throttling back to the braking profile — one-eighth rated power, continuous, the first of a hundred and sixty-three days of constant thrust. The drives could sustain it. It was the only thing about the return that was going to work as designed.

The Fist shrank on the rear camera. Smaller. Smaller. A shape becoming a line becoming a point. Then gone.

"Fuel state," Torres said.

Jackson ran the numbers. Torres heard her checking, rechecking, the same methodical process she'd used after the rupture.

"Hundred and three percent of what we need to stop," Jackson said. "If nothing else happens."

Torres let the number sit. Three percent margin. Enough to stop, with a little left over. Maybe enough for a push. Maybe.

"Good enough," Torres said. It wasn't. But it was what they had.

Jackson spent the next six hours programming the AI. Every contingency she could think of, every threshold, every decision tree. If the harmonic returns, throttle to sixty percent and hold for twelve hours before attempting to resume. If fuel consumption exceeds the curve by more than two percent, recalculate the braking profile and adjust thrust duration. If a drive temperature sensor fails, use the adjacent sensor as primary and flag for manual review on the next waking shift. If both sensors fail, drop to minimum sustainable thrust and wake someone.

She talked to the AI the way she talked to her engines — precisely, without ambiguity, assuming nothing. The AI didn't need to understand why. It needed to know what, and when, and how much.

"Braking burn terminates when velocity relative to the Sun reaches zero," she said. "Not when the fuel gauge says stop. Not when the clock says stop. When the velocity reads zero. If there's fuel remaining after zero, hold position for two hours, confirm the reading, then execute a single corrective burn sunward — maximum duration sixty seconds at minimum thrust. After that, coast. The tug will find us."

The AI confirmed each instruction. Jackson checked each confirmation. Then she checked them again.

Torres watched from her station. She'd never seen Jackson talk this much. The woman who communicated in numbers and silences was now narrating every scenario she'd spent the last ten days running in her head — every failure mode, every edge case, every way the ship could kill them.

"What if something happens that isn't on your list?" Torres asked.

"Then the AI asks whoever is on shift and they make the call." Jackson paused. "And if they can't handle it, they wake me. I can deal with it, and go back under."

She uploaded the final instruction set, locked it, and backed it up to the secondary system.

"That's everything I know how to plan for," she said. "The rest is luck."

• • •

Torres went first. She climbed into pod one, and Jackson ran the stasis sequence — the gel flooding the cradle, the monitors latching onto her vitals, the sedation cycle beginning. Torres looked at Jackson through the closing visor.

“Wake me when it’s my turn to starve,” she said.

Jackson sealed the pod.

Chandra was next. Pod two. Quiet. Jackson ran the sequence. The gel rose. The visor closed.

Two pods occupied. One empty. Inoue standing beside it.

Jackson finished Chandra’s pod checks and turned to Inoue.

“OK. Your turn.”

Jackson turned back toward the console.

The world went dark.

# CHAPTER 21

*For Now*

*July 28, 2060.*

*Remora: return transit. ~330 million km from the asteroid belt. 57 km/s, decelerating.*

*Ares City, Mars. August 3.*

• • •

Dren sat in his office at 02:00 local time, the door locked, the network isolated. On the screen in front of him was the firmware audit report — the final analysis of the Batch G-7 translation layer that had been uploaded to the Wave 3 platforms.

The audit had confirmed what he already knew. The translation layer had corrupted the platform's position. Platform 8 had believed it was farther from the Fist's track than it actually was — farther out meant more lead, and more lead meant firing earlier. The charges had gone off too soon. The pellets hit the bow instead of the midline. Torque instead of lateral push. The tilt.

His fault. The skipped integration test, the time pressure, his decision to ship without full validation. He'd accepted that weeks ago. He'd said it on the relay to Washington. He'd meant it.

But.

He'd been staring at the position error for three hours, and something about it wouldn't let him go. A rushed build produced garbage — crashes, garbled outputs, obvious failures that announced themselves the first time you ran the code. This error hadn't announced itself. The platform had performed correctly against incorrect data. The position offset was precise — not random noise, not a truncation artifact, not the kind of drift you got from a unit conversion mistake. It was a clean wrong answer that looked right.

That was not what bugs looked like. Bugs were messy. Bugs left fingerprints — stack traces, boundary violations, the diagnostic debris of code that had failed in the way code failed. This error had left nothing. The telemetry had reported nominal. The platform had fired on schedule, at the coordinates it believed were correct. Everything in the log said the system had worked. The system had worked. It had worked against data that someone had made wrong.

Someone. He couldn't prove it. The error was consistent with a build-chain artifact — a coordinate transform that rounded differently under the new geometry, a precision loss in the thirty-five-hundred-kilometer offset that the original thousand-kilometer parameters hadn't triggered. That was the innocent explanation. It was plausible. It was the explanation seven people on his team would give if asked.

Seven people had push credentials to the translation layer repository. Seven people he'd trusted with the code that was supposed to save the planet.

The precision of the error was what kept him in the chair at 02:00. A sloppy mistake produced a sloppy result. This result was exact enough to produce a marginal failure — one that looked like an engineering shortcut, not an attack. One that a post-mortem would attribute to time pressure and a skipped test. One that pointed at Dren.

He picked up his father's stylus. The normal feeling of holding it didn't come.

The tilt was his. Whether the position error was a bug or something worse, the chain of responsibility ran through him — his layer, his team, his decision to ship without full validation. That was real. That was on him. But if the error was deliberate, then someone on his team had understood exactly what the position offset would do and had calibrated it to look like carelessness. And that person was still inside his operation.

He snapped the stylus in two.

And now there was the belt.

Chandra's relay data had arrived three days ago — the antenna bearings, the signal timing, the three-node communication chain. Fleet to Fist to outer belt. Something was out there, past the heliopause, and something else was hiding in the outer belt at roughly three and a half AU from the Fist, and the two had been talking through the Fist as a relay station. Torres's crew had destroyed the antennas, but the assets were still there. The fleet. The belt object. Whatever they were.

Dren stared at the dark screen. Someone on his team had sabotaged the deflection. Someone — or something — was hiding in the outer belt along a bearing his mining ships crossed every week. He couldn't prove the two were connected. He couldn't prove they weren't. But the sabotage was too precise, too well-hidden, too perfectly timed to be the work of a disgruntled engineer or a random actor. Whoever had done this understood what the deflection was for and wanted it to fail. Not completely — ninety-one percent wasn't zero. The platforms had fired. The deflection had partially worked. The sabotage had been calibrated to look like an engineering shortfall, not an attack.

That was the signature of someone who didn't want the mission to fail entirely. They wanted it to fail just enough.

He couldn't investigate openly. If the saboteur knew Dren had found the discrepancy, they'd cover their tracks — or worse. And he couldn't go to Whitfield or Beckett, because the moment this became public, the political machinery would consume it. The inquiry would become a prosecution. The prosecution would become a spectacle. And the saboteur would disappear into the noise.

Dren saved the comparison to an encrypted partition and deleted the working files. Seven people. One of them was the enemy. And now there was something in the outer belt, and he didn't know if the enemy on his team and the thing in the belt were part of the same problem.

He sent a message to Sato. "Get me an inventory of everything in that sector of the outer belt. The Fist was talking to somebody, and I mean to know who that somebody is."

Sato's reply came nineteen minutes later. "Already running. I started the sweep two days ago. Every rock in that bearing corridor, out to the signal range. If there's something there that isn't on the mining registry, we'll find it."

Dren read it twice. Sato had been ahead of him. That was either very good or one more thing to worry about. He wasn't going to go there. For now.

• • •

*Washington, D.C. August 5.*

The joint letter arrived with fourteen signatures. Beckett and thirteen co-signers — a bipartisan coalition that had coalesced over the past two weeks around a single proposition: the deflection tilt required a formal accounting.

Whitfield read it in the operations center with her chief of staff and the acting attorney general. The language had sharpened since Beckett's first letter. This was no longer a request for an inquiry. It was a demand for a special counsel, with subpoena authority, empowered to investigate the chain of command that led to the deflection decision and the resulting casualties.

The political math had shifted. Two weeks ago, Beckett had three co-signers. Now he had thirteen. The tilt deaths had become a rallying point — not because the public demanded accountability, but because the regional commanders did. The same commanders who held their authority under Whitfield's delegation order. The same commanders who were building their reconstruction plans around Mars-manufactured hardware. They wanted Dren held accountable because Dren's authority threatened theirs. The tilt inquiry wasn't about justice. It was about power.

But the dead were still dead. And the argument was still sound. Dren had made a unilateral call that changed who lived and who died. The fact that his motives were good and his logistics were essential didn't erase the bodies.

And now there was the belt.

The relay data from the Remora had arrived through Sato's relay — the antenna bearings, the signal chain, the confirmation that an alien asset was communicating with something in the outer belt. Whitfield had read the briefing twice. The Fist wasn't a lone attacker. It was a node in a network. Something was beyond the heliopause — a fleet, a staging area, something — and something else was already inside the solar system, sitting in the outer belt, undetected, while humanity rebuilt from the flyby.

She added it to the stack. The delegation order that was becoming permanent. Mars dependency deepening. Beckett's coalition growing. Regional commanders consolidating power. And now an alien communications network with an asset embedded in the outer belt, and a crew of four on starvation rations trying to bring back the evidence.

"Options," Whitfield said.

The acting attorney general laid them out. "Appoint the special counsel. Legally defensible, politically neutral. But Dren gets subpoenaed. His time and attention get consumed. Mars supply lines suffer. Reconstruction slows."

"Or?" Whitfield said.

"Refuse. The coalition frames it as a cover-up. The regional commanders use it as leverage. You spend your remaining political capital defending a man who isn't even on your continent."

"Middle path?"

"Acknowledge the request. Form a preliminary review committee with a six-month reporting timeline. Hope that reconstruction progress makes the inquiry less viable by the time the committee reports."

"That solves nothing."

"It buys time."

Whitfield looked at the letter. Fourteen signatures. "What else do I have?"

Silence from both sides of the table.

She signed the order establishing the preliminary review committee and set the reporting deadline for February 2061. By then, either the reconstruction would be far enough along that Dren's role was less critical, or it wouldn't, and the committee's findings would be irrelevant against the necessity of the Mars supply chain.

Either way, she was deferring. Again. Every problem on her desk was a problem she'd deferred, and every deferral was compounding into something she couldn't control.

That took care of the Dren question. For now.

• • •

*Remora. Return transit. Day 1.*

The ship was quiet.

Inoue sat at the console in the dim light of the status displays. Three pods behind her — Torres in one, Chandra in two, Jackson in three. All vitals steady. All stasis cycles running. The gel cradling three sleeping bodies, the monitors tracking heartbeats and respiration and neural activity, the thermal systems holding each pod at the precise temperature that kept the body alive and the mind absent.

Jackson would be angry when she woke. Torres would be furious. Inoue had considered this. She'd considered it for hours while the others argued about the tag-team rotation, while Jackson laid out the shift schedule, while Torres reluctantly agreed. She'd nodded at the right moments. She'd said nothing that contradicted the plan.

Then she'd struck Jackson in the back of the head with the emergency medical kit — the heaviest object within reach — caught her as she fell, and put her in pod three.

Three people. Three pods. The math was different now.

Jackson's plan had been built around four people and three pods. Rotating starvation shifts, each person awake for five months on six hundred calories, losing twenty-five to thirty kilograms per shift, hoping that the accumulated damage didn't kill anyone before they reached the belt. It was brutal. It was the only option that closed the mass budget.

Except it didn't close. Jackson had said it herself: they were six person-days short. A hundred and eighty-six remaining against a hundred and ninety-two needed. The gap was small — thirty-six hundred calories, less than two days of full eating. But it was there, and every calculation Jackson ran came back the same way.

Inoue knew where the six days had gone. She could count. Forty-one days outbound, and she'd eaten roughly a quarter more than her share. Not dramatically or recklessly. Her frame demanded more than the ration schedule allowed — it always had — but the excess wasn't metabolic need. She'd eaten because she was afraid—afraid for her parents, afraid for her sister's children, afraid of the silent feed from Samoa that she watched every night before her shift and that never showed her anything except empty streets and fallen buildings and the patient tide moving through the wreckage. She ate because the fear lived in her stomach and the gel packets were the only thing that quieted it.

Nobody had said anything. Torres had noticed. Jackson had definitely noticed — Jackson noticed everything that affected the mass budget. They hadn't confronted her because there was nothing to gain from it. The food was eaten. The calories were consumed. The margin was gone.

And she had eaten it.

Three people and three pods changed everything. The others didn't need to do starvation shifts. They didn't need to rotate. They could sleep the entire transit — all 640 days — in stasis, burning almost nothing, arriving at the belt with their body mass intact. The pod systems would sustain them. The pre-programmed timers would wake them at the belt approach, or earlier if something went wrong. She'd checked the automation three times. It would work without her.

The food — all 186 person-days of it — could sit untouched in the ration store. A full contingency reserve. If a pod failed and someone woke early, there was food. If all three had to be awake for the belt approach, there was food. If something happened that nobody had planned for, there was food. As long as Inoue didn't eat it.

She pulled a single gel packet from the ration store and placed it on the console in front of her.

Six hundred calories. One third of a day's survival. The first decision of her shift, and the one that everything else depended on.

She opened a channel to the ship's AI.

"Run a scenario for me," she said. "Three crew in stasis for the full transit. No tag-team rotation. All food reserves held in contingency. One crew member awake, zero caloric intake, water only. How long is that crew member functional?"

The AI processed for less than a second. "Estimated functional duration at zero caloric intake, assuming adequate hydration and a starting body mass within normal parameters: thirty-five to fifty-five days. Cognitive impairment begins at approximately day twenty. Motor function degradation significant by day thirty-five. Risk of cardiac arrhythmia increases sharply after day forty. These estimates carry substantial uncertainty due to individual variation in fat reserves, metabolic rate, and stress response."

Fifty-five days at the outside. Forty was more realistic. After that she'd be making mistakes — misreading displays, missing alerts, drifting in and out of focus. The kind of errors that killed people on ships.

"Same scenario. Two hundred calories per day."

"Estimated functional duration extends to seventy-five to one hundred days. Cognitive impairment onset delayed to approximately day forty-five. Motor function remains adequate for light monitoring tasks through day seventy. Cardiac risk remains elevated after day sixty."

A hundred days. Maybe. If she was lucky, if her body cooperated, if she could hold to two hundred calories and not more.

"Same scenario. Six hundred calories per day."

"Functional duration extends to the full transit if caloric intake is sustained. The crew member will experience significant muscle wasting, fatigue, cognitive slowing, and immunosuppression. Expected body mass loss of approximately twenty-five to thirty kilograms over a five-month period. Medical risk is substantial but survivable for a healthy adult."

She stared at the gel packet.

Six hundred calories a day. A hundred and eighty-six person-days of food at 0.3 rations stretched to 620 days. The transit was 640. She'd run out twenty days short. Twenty days with nothing — no calories, no reserves, just water and whatever was left of her body. The AI's estimate for zero intake after prolonged starvation was clear: cardiac failure within two weeks.

Six hundred calories didn't mean she lived. It meant she died slower.

And that assumed she held to six hundred. That she didn't crack on day thirty, or day sixty, or day a hundred and twenty when her body was screaming and the packets were right there and nobody was watching. That last part was the real danger: nobody was watching.

She knew herself. She had forty-one days of data on what she did with food when she was frightened. She'd sat in front of the Samoa feed every night, watching the empty streets, and she'd eaten.

Not because she was hungry. Because she was afraid. And she hadn't been able to stop.

Zamperini, she thought. The story she'd read in school. Three men on a life raft in the Pacific, and one of them ate the entire emergency ration the first night. Not because he was evil. Because his hands moved faster than his judgment. Because panic converted directly into consumption, bypassing every rational thought between the fear and the chewing.

She was alone with all the food. For six hundred and forty days.

Two hundred calories a day. That was the compromise. She could monitor the ship for three months — maybe longer — while consuming almost nothing. Enough to keep her brain functioning, enough to catch problems, not enough to drain the reserve. When she couldn't function anymore, she'd stop eating entirely and let the timers handle the rest. The food she hadn't consumed would still be there for contingency.

And if she couldn't hold to two hundred — if she started eating more, if the fear came back, if her discipline failed the way it had failed on the outbound leg — then she'd know. She'd feel it happening. And she could make the other choice before it was too late.

She picked up the gel packet. Held it. Set it back down.

Not yet.

The cargo bay indicator glowed on the status panel. Six tonnes. The DEW module — emitter array, beam generator, isomer power cell. The technology that could change everything, if it got home. The relay bearings were in the navigation computer — the vector into the belt where something was hiding, and the vector out past the heliopause where something was waiting. Chandra had transmitted the coordinates to Mars before they left. The data was already traveling. Even if the Kludge didn't make it, the bearings would.

But the physical evidence had to get back. The isomer. The trigger mechanism. The proof that a directed energy weapon existed, that an alien intelligence had built it, that the intelligence was communicating with assets already inside the solar system.

Inoue looked at the stars through the forward viewport. The belt was out there — twenty-one months away, a thin band of rock and ice and human infrastructure, and somewhere in it, something that had been listening to the Fist's transmissions and answering.

She dimmed the console lights to save power. She knew she should sleep. Rest as much as possible. Conserve her energy. It was OK now, but soon it wouldn't be. And then the test would begin for real.

Not the hunger. Not the loneliness. Not the six hundred and forty days.

Whether she could trust herself with the food.

She closed her eyes. The gel packet sat on the console in front of her, unopened. For now.

# EPILOGUE

*Los Angeles. September 2060.*

• • •

Chloe put aside her latest story on the recovery efforts. It was important, but it just couldn't quite compare with the package she'd obtained two days ago.

She spread the files across the burner laptop's display, tiling them so she could see them all at once. Sky watched from his spot on the chair beside her, one paw draped over the armrest. The Fist material had come through three separate channels — a partial data release from the Department of War, a leaked spectrometry report that had surfaced on a technical forum before being taken down, and a set of interior photographs that someone had forwarded to her encrypted address without explanation. She didn't know if the photographs were from the same source as the data token. She had no one to ask.

She went through the material methodically, the way she went through everything. The metallurgy reports first — hafnium-tungsten alloy compositions, structural analysis of the hull panels, grain boundary data. Then the DEW documentation — what little had been released, heavily redacted, but enough to confirm the existence of a directed energy system with an unidentified power source. Then the interior survey photographs.

There were hundreds. Corridor walls. Junction markers. Sealed doors with cutting marks around the perimeters. The command room — a broad, low-ceilinged space with recessed panels and contact surfaces designed for beings shaped differently than humans. And on the walls, markings. Raised geometric forms pressed into the alloy surface at regular intervals — direction indicators, the accompanying notes suggested. Navigation markers for the interior layout.

She studied them with professional interest and no particular recognition. Alien symbols on an alien ship.

She set the Fist material aside and went back to her FEMA story. The regional funding discrepancies were more immediately actionable, and her editor wanted the draft by Friday. She opened her working files and started cross-referencing the latest disbursement figures against the reconstruction contracts.

A minute later, she stopped typing.

Something had clicked. Not a thought — a connection that shouldn't be. Something that her conscious mind had passed over but her pattern-matching hadn't.

"It can't be," she said.

Sky's head came up.

She pushed back from the table and went to the hall closet. The burner laptop. The data token files — her recovered research, the organizational charts, the funding flow analyses. And the other folder. The one she hadn't fully cataloged yet. She started paging through it.

She stopped. Stared. "My God," she said. "It IS the same."

# About the Author

Mark Kennedy got his start writing video games for the Intellivision at Mattel Electronics, and has spent the last thirty-five years as a cybersecurity engineer at Symantec/Broadcom, where he is a Distinguished Engineer. His career has taught him this lesson: every system has rules, every rule has a cost, and somebody is always looking for the exploit.

His research in Victorian-era criminal history has produced published work challenging established theories on the Jack the Ripper case, and his fiction draws on the same instinct — following evidence wherever it leads, even when the answer is uncomfortable.

He lives in Las Vegas with his wife Chloe and a household of cats and dogs.

Other titles: Satan's Hand, the second book in Operation Clean Slate, and The Devil's Own Luck (his debut novel) Available on Amazon.

He is currently at work on Satan's Consequence, the third book in Operation Clean Slate, a hard science fiction series.

www.ingramcontent.com/pod-product-compliance
Lightning Source LLC
LaVergne TN
LVHW100513110826
845146LV00002B/615